DERMOT BOLGER was born in Finglas, north Dublin, in 1959. One of Ireland's best known authors, his eight novels include *The Journey Home* – one of the most controversial Irish novels of the 1990s; *Father's Music* and *Temptation*, both of which are available from Flamingo; and *The Woman's Daughter*, which will be reissued by Flamingo in the autumn of 2002. His eight plays, including *The Lament for Arthur Cleary*, *The Passion of Jerome* and *April Bright*, have received several awards including the Samuel Beckett Prize, and have been staged in many countries. *Plays: 1*, the first volume of his *Selected Plays*, was recently published by Methuen.

A former factory hand and library assistant, he founded the Raven Arts Press while still in his teens. In addition to being a poet and editor, he was the instigator of the collaborative novels, *Finbar's Hotel* and *Ladies' Night at Finbar's Hotel* (which have appeared in twelve countries) and editor of *The Picador Book of Contemporary Irish Fiction*. He lives and works in Dublin.

From the reviews for *The Valparaiso Voyage*:

'A highly original and often brilliant novel. Bolger knows his landscapes, local political intrigue, north Dublin gangsterism and provincial pride, and brings the reader at pace through a complicated storyline. He might even have invented a genre.'   *In Dublin*

'This is a gripping expression of family warfare and of rural, small-town Irishness. From the first to the final page, you read and read.'   *Scotsman*

'The brooding ambience captures the underlying darkness of modern Ireland and the characterisation is excellent. Bolger sustains our sympathy for his flawed, fragile hero having to dig deep into his emotional reserves.'   *Sunday Telegraph*

'A tale of Irish fatherhood in its various avatars: stern, combative, sentimental, guilt-wracked… The rhythms and energy are irrepressible and hoist us towards an unexpected final poignancy.'   *TLS*

Dermot Bolger

The Valparaiso Voyage

Flamingo
An Imprint of HarperCollins*Publishers*

Flamingo
An imprint of HarperCollins*Publishers*
77–85 Fulham Palace Road,
Hammersmith, London W6 8JB

Flamingo is a registered trade mark of HarperCollins*Publishers* Limited

www.**fire**and**water**.com

Published by Flamingo 2002
9 8 7 6 5 4 3 2 1

First published in Great Britain by Flamingo 2001

The Author and Publisher are grateful to Mrs Maire Mhac an Tsaoi for
permission to reproduce two verses, in Irish, from the poem 'An Long'
by Padraig de Brun. Thanks also go to Theo Dorgan for permission to
reproduce his English translation of those same two verses.

This novel is entirely a work of fiction. With the exception of one or
two public figures whose real names have been used, the names,
characters and incidents portrayed in it are the work of the author's
imagination. Any resemblance to actual persons, living or dead, events
or localities is entirely coincidental. At the time of writing, two
tribunals investigating payments to politicians are still sitting in Dublin
Castle, but have not, to the author's knowledge, investigated politicians
or planning decisions from the county of Meath.

ISBN 0 00 655237 4

Set in Bembo

Printed and bound in Great Britain by Clays Ltd, St Ives plc

Bernadette

Tháinig long ó Valparaiso,
Scaoileadh téad a seol sa chuan;
Chuir a hainm dom i gcuimhne
Ríocht na greine, tír na mbua

'Gluais,' ar sí, 'ar thuras fada
Liom ó scamall is ó cheo;
Tá fé shleasaibh gorm-Andes
Cathair scáfar, glé mar sheod . . .'

A ship came in from Valparaiso,
Let go her anchor in the bay,
Her name flashed bright, it brought to mind
A land of plenty, of sun and fame.

'Come,' she said, 'on a long journey
Away from this land of cloud and mist;
Under the Andes' blue-grey slopes
There's a jewel city, by the sun kissed . . .'

From **An Long** *(The Ship) by Pádraig de Brún, 1899–1960,*
translated from the Irish by Theo Dorgan.

*W*hat was the Scottish train driver thinking about at that moment? Or the first-class passengers who glanced up from laptops and papers to see the gathering mesh of rail tracks converging at that junction on the outskirts of Glasgow? A labyrinth of points, signals and sidings, graffiti disfiguring the crumbling railway sheds and steep oil-stained concrete walls. Indistinguishable birds circling in the high grey light of the sky.

As a child, watching the Christmas toy display in Alcock's shop window off Market Square in Navan, I used to imagine that trains drove themselves. A perfect clockwork world of engines bobbing beneath bridges and emerging from hillside tunnels where plastic sheep grazed placidly.

Occasionally something might go amiss but all you had to do was bang on the window until a shop assistant picked up the engine whose wheels kept whirling uselessly around. Set back on the track, it glided past again, while toy workmen looked impassively on, as if nothing could ever disturb their pristine universe.

Within seconds of that head-on collision between the 7 a.m. train from Perth and a local commuter service, the top carriages of each train had become a fireball, six times hotter than the furnaces used for cremation. Back along the track voices sang out from a concertina of derailed carriages. 'Help me!' 'Save me!' 'Sweet Jesus!' Shards of broken glass everywhere, even littering the upturned windows that refused to break. Passengers hammering on them with their shoes and briefcases and fists. Doors opening upward to the sky, as people reached down to pull other survivors out.

A man, who nobody knew was alive or dead, lay beside his severed leg. *A young woman in a white skirt clutched one shoe as she sat on the embankment shivering. A helicopter's drone blended with a growing symphony of sirens. A child's watch stopped dead at seven-fifty-four. Stubble further darkened a thickset chin, which an undertaker would have to shave twice. A mother held her nine-year-old son who cried because his homework was destroyed.*

Early shift workers from local factories swarmed towards the rear of the train, desperate to help, prising open doors to scramble into carriages and search under rubble. Others simply stood beside the red signal, which the express driver had missed in slanting winter sunlight, staring at the spot where the two engines met. Inside that inferno the bodies of both drivers, plus a lottery of first-class passengers, were being consumed by such scorching sheets of flame that not even blackened sets of teeth would survive among the ashes to testify to their number.

The frosty air was heavy with smoke, billowing upwards and out, like the sail of a tall ship that had left a West of Ireland quayside and steered out into the wind, setting forth across the ocean for the dreaming white streets of Valparaiso.

I

———•—•—•———

SATURDAY

Navan, Co. Meath. Thriving hometown of carpets and wooden furniture. Warehouses and showrooms, neat factories dotting its outskirts. Strong farmers' wives who would arrive in during my childhood to search for bargains, while their husbands belched and, with top buttons undone, slept off enormous lunches in broad armchairs in the hotel lounge.

Navan. With narrow streets as tight as a nun's arse, falling downwards to where the Boyne and Blackwater meet. The fulcrum of Market Square where a kindly barber had clipped hair for half a century, discussing painting and amateur drama, rarely mentioning his nights on the run in an Old IRA flying column. An unlovely trinity of streets spreading out from it: Ludlow, Watergate and Trimgate.

Their medieval gates are long felled, their town walls disappeared. An ugly motorway scars the landscape now, necklaced by new estates with Mickey Mouse names. Dublin commuters forced into exile here by rising house prices, resenting their daily drive thirty miles back into the capital and suspicious of locals who are more suspicious of them. Outsiders and blow-ins circling each other around the closed fist of my native town.

'Navan itself has little to detain you,' *The Rough Guide to Ireland* says. A pity that one unfortunate black sailor at the start of the nineteenth century didn't heed this advice. Hiring a rig of horses when his ship docked in Dublin after a voyage from some exotic foreign port, he took off through the morning rain to explore this land. It was noon when his black horses trotted into Market Square in Navan. He climbed down, his black boots and cloak startling the gaping locals. He found the local tavern and ordered. The innkeeper served him with true Irish hospitality, then withdrew to join the throng on the street, none of whom had ever seen a black man before.

They decided that there was only one person he could be. Old Nick, Lucifer himself come to tempt them. A rope was fetched, a horse chestnut tree selected in the field where my street was later built. It was the final lynching in the Royal County of Meath. This story doesn't make *The Rough Guide*, nor any of the historical brochures welcoming visitors in the tourist office on Railway Street. Perhaps it was just a myth invented by Pete Clancy to frighten me as a boy. It certainly succeeded, hearing the creak of a tree at night beyond the outhouse where I slept, expecting to see a dark body still twitching in mid-air if I peeped out through the chicken wire.

Who ordains which stories are remembered and what tales discreetly forgotten in any town? Were there many in Navan who recalled mine, with my family gone? Few would wish to be reminded, in this new traffic-choked prosperity they live in. Yet nobody can control the ghosts that haunt these streets. Lost foreign sailors; starved serving girls who shivered, waiting for their muscles to be felt at hiring fairs; barefoot messenger boys who contracted gangrene by running with open sores through worm-infested horse dung on the cobbles; our local poet, Ledwidge, killed by a stray shell at Ypres and appearing to a friend that same night outside the *Meath Chronicle* printing works. I just knew that such ghosts existed, because, walking up Flower Hill, I was taking my first step amongst them.

━━━┥■┝━━━

Opening her garden gate everything looked the same, even the way the estate agent watched me from the doorway. Lisa Hanlon's father had stood in that spot once, an old man who avoided my eye, wary of finally admitting me onto the premises.

I took the estate agent's brochure and gave a false name and phone number. Not that anyone was likely to recognize me, but I still felt nervous pushing open the sitting-room door. The electric heater set into the old fireplace remained in place, as did the nest of small tables, the thickset re-upholstered armchairs and the long sofa with its lace frills. This room was always too choked with reminders of Lisa's childhood and mine.

It had felt strange making love to her here, when we were both twenty-two, while her younger self looked down from a gold-framed communion photo. That mouth, which looked so devout after receiving its first wafer of Christ, surprising me by its sudden wantonness.

But at twenty-two I wasn't that interested in Lisa, to be honest; the attraction behind our brief affair was more about gaining access to this sitting-room. Listening to her parents ascending the staircase, enjoying the sense of danger that they might come back down. I remember Lisa's astonishment at my ability to grow erect again so quickly after I came. She was quiet and plain. Possibly no man had ever been this passionate in her presence before. But I couldn't explain how it wasn't her tiny breasts, still pert as a schoolgirl's, which excited me. It was being able to fondle the furniture – the uncomfortable cushions on the sofa, the patterned carpet faintly reeking of mothballs, the never-to-be-touched china plates in the sideboard, the ornaments from the parish's first Diocesan Pilgrimage to Lourdes. The cloying scent of small-town respectability that I was always excluded from.

If Lisa had left me alone on those nights I might have simply carried on making love to the furniture. Here on the lit side of Hanlon's sitting-room window at last. Not crouched outside in the cold, like on the evenings when I had risked climbing from our outhouse roof down into Casey's garden next door. Creeping from there into Hanlon's garden to peep through apple branches at Lisa's mother drying her only daughter's hair, reading her bedtime stories, bringing in hot milk and biscuits while they watched television together in winter.

She would switch the light off so that the sitting-room was lit by a glowing coal fire, with images from the unseen television literally transposed across their faces. At least that was how I saw it from outside, at the age of ten and eleven, living out those television programmes at second hand by mimicking the expressions on their faces. I laughed when they laughed and ducked down if they glanced towards the window, even though I knew they could not see me crouched against the hedge.

I could always tap against Casey's kitchen window and Mr Casey would chance taking me in for an hour to get warm. Some nights I was hungry enough to swallow my pride and risk doing that, though twice I was discovered and beaten for it, with my father shouting at our next-door neighbour across the hedge to mind his own business. But the fact that sanctuary was obtainable in his kitchen made me view Mr Casey as inferior. Hanlon's house was impenetrable, with its warmth as unimaginable as sex. Hunger didn't lure me to spy on Lisa's window. It was to live out a fantasy where I imagined myself allowed to add coal to the fire with the brass tongs and have someone brush my hair instead of yanking at it with a steel comb.

The estate agent coughed in the doorway behind me now. I had forgotten about his presence. Other viewers moved noisily around upstairs, testing the floorboards, checking walls for dry rot, envisaging attic conversions and PVC windows.

'Why is it for auction?' I asked.

'An executor's sale. The old woman who lived here died. Her daughter lives in England.'

'Is she home now?'

'Why do you ask?' The estate agent was careful of his profit margin. Too many tales of under-the-table bribes to owners, desperate illegal bids from desperate people trapped by the housing shortage in this new booming economy.

'I'd just feel self-conscious looking around a house if I felt the owner could be watching.'

'We encourage people to stay away while their homes are being shown,' the man replied. 'It's better for everyone. She's coming home on Thursday morning for the auction in the Ard Boyne Hotel that afternoon.' He scrutinized me carefully. 'At three thirty. You're leaving it late if you want to bid. Most people have already had it surveyed and are just taking a last look.'

'I've been abroad. I only saw it in the paper today.'

They were the first true words I had spoken. The ad was in the property section of a discarded *Irish Independent*, which I pocketed at Dublin airport this morning when passing through the first-class section of an Aer Lingus flight from Lisbon. Maybe it was cold feet at actually being back in Dublin, but after the airport coach reached Busaris I'd sat on a bench, too terrified to venture out. When a bus to Navan was announced I had left my bags in a locker and boarded it, thinking that Navan seemed as good a place as any to start my homecoming.

The estate agent walked back out into the hallway to hand a brochure to a young couple, launching into his patter about the south-facing garden and how, with the motorway, it was less than an hour's drive from Dublin.

Why had I asked him about Lisa? The dead cannot intrude on the living, even to apologize. She was one of the few people to have ever loved me. In return I had abandoned her, lacking the self-confidence to believe that anyone could truly care for me. Before meeting Miriam I had been afraid to let people get close, feeling they would only be disgusted when they uncovered the lice-ridden Hen Boy beneath the thin veneer of normality I'd gained in Dublin. At twenty-two I had been acting out a role every Thursday evening for seven weeks when I had washed and shaved and took the provincial bus back out here from the capital to visit Lisa. One of many roles I'd taught myself to hide behind, whereas Lisa was simply always just herself. Would she have understood if I had broken down and tried to explain the insidious stench of dirt and disgrace I carried inside? How could I, when I didn't fully understand it myself back then? Instead – after enduring two hours of Country'n'Irish music down the town while we waited for Lisa's parents to retire to bed – I would make love to her in this sitting-room, never slackening off in my terror that some tenderness might develop if we lay motionless for too long.

Now I pulled out the electric fire to examine the grate behind it. On the first night she brought me home I had been intensely disappointed to discover this two-bar monstrosity blocking the fireplace where flames used to light her face. We'd only met by fluke when snow prevented racing at Newton Abbot and I was forced to return to Navan dog track for the first time in a decade because it was the only place where I could place a bet on a freezing January evening.

'This heats the room in no time,' Lisa had said, plugging in the fire, tipsy from the champagne I'd splashed out on after sharing the tote jackpot with six other punters. 'Don't worry, I've warned my parents never to come down here when I'm with someone.'

But the fire's dry heat didn't feel right that night, nor her white skin or deep French kisses. Being real and available, they could never hope to match my gnawing hunger, any more than the gesture of buying champagne could change who I knew I was inside.

'I used to wonder about you,' Lisa had whispered afterwards. 'The way people avoided mentioning you. What did you do to deserve all that?'

As a child I didn't exactly know what I had done, just that I deserved such punishment and more. Wicked, dirty and dumb. 'The Hen Boy,' as Barney Clancy's son, Pete, christened me at primary school. 'Chuck, chuck, chuck, chuck – here comes the Hen Boy. Get up the yard and lay an egg, Hen Boy, there's a smell of shite off you here!' His taunting voice, two years older, four inches taller, and a dozen social castes above me. The son of my father's Lord and Master. Children don't talk in whispers. They understand small-town distinctions and lack adult inhibition about openly shouting them out.

The estate agent returned to hover behind me, concerned lest I damage the electric fire. He probably had a sixth sense to distinguish between potential bidders and nuisance viewers.

'The house needs work, of course,' he said, steering me from the sitting-room. 'But just think what you could do with a little imagination.'

I had no interest in seeing the other rooms, but felt that it would look suspicious to depart. Old people leave something behind them in a house. Not a physical smell or even miasma, but the aftertaste of lonely hours spent waiting for a phone to ring. Everything about the kitchen looked sad – a yellowing calendar from the Holy Ghost Fathers, an ancient kettle, a Formica table that belonged in some museum. Its creeping shabbiness stung me, like a tainting of paradise. One should never go back, especially to Navan – a town so inward-looking it spelt its own name backwards.

Wallpaper had started to droop on the landing, with faint specks of mildew caused by a lack of heat in winter. Finally I was going to see upstairs. Lisa's voice returned from nineteen years before: 'Wait till they go on the pilgrimage to Fatima this summer. You can stay over, sleep in my bed. We can really do fun things then.'

A Dublin family clogged the stairwell as I squeezed past, sandwich-board people togged out in an array of expensive logos, trailing an aura of casual affluence behind them. Lisa's room was empty. I knew it was her room. I had watched her here often enough as a child when she seemed unaware that if she closed the blinds by slanting them down instead of up her outline remained visible. Lisa who spent ten minutes each night brushing her long straight hair; who often stared into space, half-undressed, like her mind was switched off. Lisa aged eleven, twelve and thirteen, when her breasts made that single surge outward so that her body had looked the same silhouetted in this window as when I first saw her properly naked. Some nights she had remained at the window for so long that I feared she suspected me of spying on her. Eventually I had realized that she, in turn, was peeping through her blinds at the outhouse where she presumed that I was sleeping. Perhaps she had been as fascinated by my life back then as I was by hers.

I switched off the bedroom light which the estate agent had left on and raised the blind fully. Hanlon's garden was now a wilderness with one apple tree cut down and the other besieged by sour cooking apples rotting in the unkempt grass. There was no way that I was going back out there. I had never quite banished their sour taste and the nausea that replaced my night-time hunger if I stole them.

Whoever now owned Casey's house had built on a Victorian-style conservatory and a patio. A barbecue unit stood against the pebble-dashed wall replacing the hedge which once screened off my old garden next door. My father's crude outhouse had been knocked down. A pristine building stood in its place, with a slated roof and arched windows strategically angled for light. A trail of granite stepping-stones twisted through a sea of white pebbles up to the newly extended kitchen. A Zen-like calmness pervaded the whole garden. I found my fingernails scraping against the glass.

Two elderly women entered the bedroom behind me, their Meath accents achingly familiar. I knew their names but didn't turn around in case they recognized something about my face. As a weekend pastime, house viewing seemed like solitary sex – it was cheap and you didn't need to dress up for it. With no intention of bidding, they gossiped about how much Hanlon's house would fetch and what their own modernized homes were worth in comparison – immeasurable fortunes, leaving them weak-kneed at the very thought of auctions. I could imagine Cormac mimicking their accents: *'I don't know how you held out until it reached the reserve, Mrs Mulready, I'd already had my first orgasm just after the guiding price.'*

'God help any young couple starting out,' one of them remarked, moving to stand beside me at the window. 'Didn't that American computer programmer make a lovely office for himself out in the Brogans' garden?'

'Poor Mr Brogan.' Her companion blessed herself. 'There was a lovely crowd at his funeral. A terrible way to meet your death. The guttersnipes they have in Dublin now, out of their heads on drugs!'

'Maybe with all these scandals it's just as well that he's gone,' the first woman said. 'Mr Brogan was from the old school, not some *"me féiner"*.'

Her companion tut-tutted dismissively. 'Sure the Dublin papers would make a scandal out of a paper bag these days. You get sick of reading them. They can say what they like about Barney Clancy now that he's dead, but they've never proved a single thing. That man did a lot for Navan and the more they snipe at his memory the more people here will vote for his son.'

'Don't I know it.' The first woman turned to go, sneaking a quick glance in my direction before dismissing me as another Dublin blow-in. 'Still you'd feel sorry for Mrs Brogan, no matter what two ends of a stuck-up Jackeen bitch she could be in her day. The papers say she's not long for this world with cancer.'

They moved on to the front bedroom, talking over my head like I didn't exist.

I was almost fourteen when I left Navan. By seventeen I'd cultivated a poor excuse for a beard to conceal the onslaught of acne. It was never shaved off until the age of thirty-one. Clean-shaven and bespectacled now (even if the frames only contained plain glass), my dyed hair had receded so much that my forehead resembled my father's. But I found that I had still sweated in their presence – perhaps half-hoping to be recognized. I touched Lisa's single bed, kept made up for her during all the years she was away in England. I had never lain between its sheets, as she wanted. Nineteen years ago, on the final night when we returned here from the pub, her mother intruded upon the spell, overcome by curiosity or guilt as she blundered into the sitting-room with a tray of tea and biscuits that I knew Lisa didn't want.

'How are you keeping since the family moved to Dublin, Brendan?'

'I'm keeping well, Mrs Hanlon.'

Her pause, then in a quiet voice: 'I knew your mother. We went to Lourdes together. The first ever pilgrimage from this parish.'

Mrs Hanlon didn't say any more. She didn't need to, the pity in her eyes destroying everything. Their sly plea for forgiveness at having never lifted a finger to help. Suddenly I had ceased to belong in that room. I was an object of sympathy dragged in from outside; the boy raised by his stepmother in an outhouse. Indifference would have made me her equal. Hatred or distrust might have given me strength to screw her precious daughter so hard that Lisa's cries would summon her mother back down to gape at us among the communion photographs and smashed china and knick-knacks from Lourdes. But her pity had rendered me impotent. Lisa's parents might have been horrified by what my father did, but – like the rest of this town – they never stood out against him. Only Mr Casey ever did, and he got no thanks from anyone back then in their turn-a-blind-eye world.

After her mother left the room, I knew that Lisa was too nervous to make love. I hadn't wanted to either. I'd simply longed to vanish back to the anonymity of flatland Dublin where no one knew or cared about me, except that I was Cormac's slow-witted gambler of a brother, always in the bookies. It hurt me now to recall Lisa's face as I left that night, aware that something beyond her comprehension was wrong as she urged me to phone and probably continued waving even when I was out of sight. And how I walked out along the blackness of the Dublin road after missing the last bus, although I knew how hard it was to hitch a lift after leaving the streetlights behind.

But I had needed to escape from Navan that night, just like I had to flee from Lisa's house now. I descended the stairs, left the estate agent's brochure in the hall, closed the gate and refused to glance towards the house, two doors down, into which my parents had once driven me home with such pride from the Maternity Hospital in Drogheda.

———◆———

Athlumney graveyard on the Duleek Road out of Navan. Twice a year my father came here – on Christmas Eve and 12 November, my mother's anniversary. He always arranged for 7 a.m. mass to be said for her on that day, calling me from sleep in the outhouse with an awkwardness that verged on being tender. He'd have rashers and sausages cooked for us to share in silence before anyone else was awake, watching the clock to ensure that we still managed to fast for an hour before communion. We drove, in our private club of two, to the freezing cathedral where the scattering of old women who knelt there glanced up at us. Afterwards in the doorway people might whisper to him, with supplications for Barney Clancy, our local minister in Government, to be passed on through his trusted lieutenant. An old woman sometimes touched my arm in a muted token of sympathy, as I shivered in the uneasy role of being a rightful son again. On our return from visiting the grave, my stepmother Phyllis would be up with the radio on and the spell dissipated for another year.

Standing now beside the ruined castle in this closed graveside I wondered what had possessed him to be buried with his first wife? Was it an act of atonement or another example of miserliness? My father, careful with his pence, even in death. In recent days the doctored version of his life had been freshly carved in gold letters on the polished black marble: *Also, her loving husband, Eamonn, died in Dublin . . .*

The wreaths from his funeral were not long withered, the earth still subsiding slightly so that the marble surround had yet to be put back in place. I hadn't anticipated his body being laid here, where only the old Navan families retained rights, nor that I would feel a surge of anger at him for seizing the last possession that my mother owned.

I should remember something about her, a blur of skirts or just a memory of being hugged. It's not that I haven't tried to recall her, but I was either too young or have blocked them out. My first memory is here in Athlumney. Her coffin must have been carried three times around the outer boundaries, as was the tradition then, before being lowered into the earth. But all I recall is adult feet shuffling back from the graveside as someone let go my hand. I stand alone, a giddy sensation. A green awning covers the opened grave but through a gap I can see down – shiny wood and a brass plaque. When I scuff the earth with my shoe, pebbles shower down. I do this repeatedly until a neighbour touches my shoulder. I am three years and eight months of age.

It is night-time in the memory which occurs next. I wake up crying, with the street quiet outside and my room in darkness. Yellow light spills onto a wallpaper pattern of roses as my door opens. My father enters and bends over my bed, wrenched away perhaps from his own grief. He climbs in, rough stubble against my neck as his arms soothe me. How secure it feels as we lie together. I want to stay awake. A truck's headlights start to slide across the ceiling, with cattle being ferried out along the Nobber Road. I love having this strong man beside me in the dark. I don't remember waking to find if he was still there in the morning.

The polished floorboards in the outhouse come to mind next. I am playing with discarded sheets of transparent paper, crammed with lines and angular patterns which he allows me to colour in with crayons. Lying on my tummy to breathe in the scent of Player's and Major cigarettes. His only visitors are men with yellow-stained fingers who laugh knowingly and wink at me as they talk. The extension bell on his phone frightens me, ringing so loudly down in the shed that it can be heard by half the street who are waiting the seven or eight years of wrangling, lobbying and political pull that it takes to have a phone line installed back then.

This was before my father was headhunted by Meath County Council as a planning official. He was simply a quantity surveyor, running his own business from a converted shed, which had been constructed in our garden by a previous owner as a hen-house. Here he received courtiers in a black leather swivel chair, men who tossed my hair, slipped me coins and excitedly discussed rumours of a seam of mineable zinc being located outside the town.

Some had business there, like Slab McGuirk and Mossy Egan – apprentice builders knocking up lean-to extensions and milking parlours for the bogmen of Athboy and Ballivor. Others, like old Joey Kerwin, with a hundred and forty acres under pasture near Tara, simply sauntered up the lane in search of an audience for their stories, like the mock announcement of a neighbour's death to the handful of men present. 'All his life JohnJo wanted an outdoor toilet, but sure wasn't he too fecking lazy to dig it himself. He waited till the mining engineers sunk a borehole on his land, then built a bloody hut over it, with a big plank inside and a hole cut into it to fit the queer shape of his arse. The poor fecker would be alive still if he hadn't got into the habit of holding his breath until he heard the fecking plop!'

I remember still the roars of male laughter that I didn't understand. New York might have Wall Street but Navan had my father's doorway, with men leaning against it to spit into their palms as they shook hands on deals. Occasionally raised voices were heard as Slab McGuirk and Mossy Egan squabbled about one undercutting the other. It took Barney Clancy to bang their heads together, creating an uneasy shotgun marriage where they submitted joint tenders for local jobs that the big Dublin firms normally had sewn up.

My first memories of Clancy are in that outhouse: the squeak of patent leather shoes that set him apart, the distinctive stench of cigar smoke, deeper and richer like his voice could be. The way the other men's voices were lowered when he arrived and how his own accent could change after they left and himself and my father were alone. Often, after Clancy in turn departed, my father's sudden good humour could be infectious. I would laugh along with him, wanting to feel in on his private joke, while he let me sit on his swivel chair. With my knees tucked in, the makeshift office spun around in a blur of wallcharts, site maps, year-planners and calendars from auctioneers; all the paraphernalia of that adult world of cigarettes and rolled banknotes, winks and knowing grins.

But I remember sudden intense anger from my father there too, how I grew to dread his raised voice. Just turned eight, how could I know which architectural plans were important and which were discarded drafts? A gust of wind must have blown through the opened door that day when my father saw Slab McGuirk out. Half-costed plans slid from his desk onto the floor. I still remember unfathomable shapes on the wafer-thin sheet as I began to colour them in, absorbed in my fantasy world. That was the only time he ever struck me until Phyllis entered our lives. Curses poured forth, like a boil of frustration bursting open. Curled up on the floor, I understood suddenly that everything was my fault. I was the nuisance son he was stranded with, perpetually holding him back.

Then his voice changed, calling me to him. Tentatively I dared to glance up at this man who was my entire world. His arms were held out. Old familiar Dada, beckoning and forgiving. Then the black phone rang. He picked it up. From his tone I knew that it was Barney Clancy. I might not have been there. His swivel chair was empty. I sat in it, with my ear throbbing. But I didn't cry. Instead I spun myself round until the whole world was flying except for me, safe on my magic carpet.

The revolving slows to a halt in my mind. A bell rings, a crowd rising. Zigzagging on a metal track with its fake tail bobbing, I fret for the mechanical hare. The steel traps open, greyhounds pound past. Floodlights make the grass greener, the packed sand on the track sandier, the sky bluer above the immaculate bowl of light that was Navan dog track.

Men jostled around gesticulating bookmakers with their leather bags of cash. A young blonde woman laughed, teasing my father. I couldn't stop staring at her, like somebody who seemed to have stepped through the television screen from an American programme into our humdrum world, except that her Dublin accent was wrong. The woman teased him again for not risking a small bet on each race, as she laughed off her loss of a few bob each time the bell went. But my father would have regarded the reverse forecasts on the tote as a mug's game, when an average dog could be body-checked by some mongrel on the first bend. He would have been holding off to place one large bet on a sure tip handed to him on the back of a Player's cigarette packet.

I was an eight-year-old chaperone on that night of endless crisps and lemonade when I first saw Phyllis. Hair so blonde that I wanted to touch it, her fingers stroked the curved stem of a gin and tonic glass. She didn't smoke back then, her palms were marble-white. Her long red nails gripped my father's arm when one of her dogs finally won, leaving an imprint on his wrist as we sat in silence while she collected her winnings.

I had four winners that night. If a dog broke cleanly from trap six with sufficient speed to avoid the scrum on the first bend it invariably featured in the shake-up at the end. Dogs in trap five generally faded, but trap four always seemed to get pulled along and challenged late if they had closing strength. The knowledge and thrill were instinctive within me, my heart quickening at the bell, my breath held for twenty-nine point five seconds, my ears pounding as time moved differently along the closing straight. Except that all my winners were in my head – they never asked if I wished to place a bet. Indeed, all night I had a sense of being airbrushed out as they spoke in whispers. They didn't even spot my tears as I jigged on a plastic chair after soiling myself. It was my fault. I should have touched his arm to ask him could I go to the toilet on time, but was afraid to intrude on their private world until the stench alerted Phyllis.

I remember the cubicle door slamming and the marble pattern on the stone floor as shiny toilet paper chaffed my soiled legs. My father hissed in frustration while I gagged on the reek of ammonia cubes from the flooded urinals. Most of all I remember my shame as men turned their heads when he led me from the cubicle. Outside the final race was being run, with discarded betting slips blown about on the concrete and whining coming from dog boxes. Phyllis waited, shivering in a knee-length coat.

'How is *he* now?' Her voice was disconcerting as she glanced at me, then looked away. On the few occasions during the evening when I had caught her watching me I'd felt under inspection, but the brittle uncertainty in her tone made her sound like a child herself.

They walked together without touching, edging ever more fractionally apart as they passed through the gates. Lines of parked cars, the greasy aroma of a van selling burgers. I kept well back, suffocating in the stench of self-disgrace. They whispered together but never kissed. Then she was gone, turning men's heads as she ran out between parked cars to flag down the late bus to Dublin. I didn't know whether to wave because she never looked back.

It was Josie who cleaned me up properly before school next morning, standing me in the bath to scrub my flesh pink with thick bristles digging into me like a penance. My father didn't have to warn me not to mention the blonde woman. Of late Josie was paid to walk me to school each morning and wait for me among the mothers at the gate. My afternoons were increasingly spent in her damp terraced cottage in a lane behind Emma Terrace, playing house with her seven-year-old granddaughter or being held captive by pirates and escaping in time to eat soda bread and watch *F-Troop* on the black-and-white television.

Cigarette smoke rarely filled the outhouse now, with the telephone jangling unanswered. The first mineshaft was being dug on the Kells side of town, the streets awash with gigantic machines, unknown faces and rumours of inside-track fortunes being made on lands that had changed hands. My father was away every second night, working in Dublin, while I slept beneath the sloping ceiling of Josie's cottage. Her granddaughter shared her teddies, snuggling half of them down at the end of my bed after she swore never to tell my father or any boy from my school that I played with them.

It was Josie who found the first letter in the hall, opening up the house to light a fire for his return. She tut-tutted at the sender's insensitivity in addressing it to 'Mr and Mrs Brogan'. It was an invite for a reception in Dublin to announce details of the next phase of the mine. Some weeks later a second envelope arrived, this time simply addressed to 'Mrs Phyllis Brogan'. Josie stopped in mid-tut, her tone scaring me. 'But your mother's name wasn't *Phyllis?*'

It was Renee to her neighbours, but spelt 'Irene' on this gravestone in the quietude of Athlumney cemetery. Below my father's recently carved name space existed for one more, but surely Phyllis could not intend to join them?

I knelt to read through the withered wreaths left there three weeks ago. 'Deepest sympathy from Peter Clancy, TD and Minister for State'. 'With sympathy from his former colleagues in Meath County Council'. A tacky arrangement of flowers contorted to form the word DAD could only have come from my half-sister Sarah-Jane. It resembled something out of a gangland funeral. Rain had made the ink run on the card attached to a bunch of faded lilies beside it, but I could discern the blurred words, 'with love from Miriam and Conor'. I fingered their names over and over like an explorer finding the map of a vanished continent. Next to it lay a cheap bouquet, 'In sympathy, Simon McGuirk'. It took a moment for the Christian name to register. Then the distant memory returned of a teacher in the yard labelling McGuirk as 'Simple Simon'. Pete Clancy had battered the first boy who repeated that name as he offered McGuirk the protection of his gang and rechristened him 'Slick'. It was only the thuggish simpleton himself who did not grasp that his nickname was coined in mockery.

Meanness and premature baldness were passed on like heirlooms in the McGuirk family. Slab's son resorting to such extravagance perturbed me, but not as much as the small wooden cross placed like a stake through the heart of the grave. I only spotted it as I rearranged the wreaths. My father must have placed it here some time in the past decade. The unexpected gesture shocked me. I knelt to read the inscription: *Pray also for her son, Brendan, killed, aged thirty-one, in a train crash in Scotland.*

———————

Market Square. The old barbershop was gone; its proprietor one of the few kindly faces I remember. A boiled sweet slipped into my palm on those rare occasions when I was allowed to accompany Cormac there. Mostly my father cut my hair himself, shearing along the rim of an upturned bowl. A video outlet stood in its place, between a mobile phone store and a discreet lingerie window display in a UK High Street chainstore. Shiny new toys for the Celtic Tiger. McCall's wooden-floored emporium had disappeared, with its display of rosary beads threaded by starved Irish orphans with bleeding fingers who were beaten by nuns. Instead, music blared from a sports store displaying cheap footballs handsewn by starved children with bleeding fingers in safely anonymous countries.

The Dublin buses still stopped outside McAndrew's pub, where an 'advice clinic' caravan was double-parked, belonging to Pete Clancy. No election had yet been called, but with the delicately balanced coalition only hanging by a thread, more experienced politicians were getting their retaliation in early. Pete Clancy's face stared from a poster, like a touched-up death mask of his father. I recognised the two men dispensing news-letters outside the caravan, though their faces had aged since their days as young Turks laughing in my father's outhouse. They were mere footsoldiers now, ignored by the younger men in suits talking on mobile phones in the caravan doorway.

Jimmy Mahon was the older of the two. A teetotaller barman, he had been nicknamed 'the donkey' by Barney Clancy who got my father to dole out the most remote hamlets for him to canvass. Mahon was known to work all night on the eve of an election, leaflet-bombing letterboxes. He would have happily died for Barney Clancy and reappeared as a ghost to cast a final vote for him. At one time there were dozens like him in Navan, but now he cut a lonely figure as he approached the bus queue, impassive to the cynicism and indifference of Saturday afternoon shoppers. He reached me and held out a leaflet.

I stared back, almost willing him to recognize me without the beard. Three weeks ago he had probably followed the cortège here from Dublin at my father's funeral and perhaps knelt unwittingly in the same pew as the man who killed him. He glanced at me with no recognition in his eyes, then passed on. The four-page leaflet contained eleven pictures of Pete Clancy, claiming personal credit for every new traffic light, road widening, tree planting, speed ramp, public phone or streetlight installed in Meath over the past six months. As old Joey Kerwin used to joke, the Clancys only just stopped short of claiming credit for every child conceived in the constituency. *Help me to help you*, a headline proclaimed on the last page. *Contact me at any time at my home phone number or by e-mail.* I almost discarded the leaflet like most of the bus queue, but then pocketed it, deciding that the e-mail address would be useful.

The first bus to arrive was a private coach from Shercock. I boarded it, wondering if anyone in that small town still remembered Peter Mathews, a petty thief who limped into town on a crutch and got caught withdrawing money from a stolen post office book, which he hid before the guards came. He found himself stripped and bent over a chair in the police station. He found himself dead from a heart attack with his pancreas bleeding from a blow to the stomach. Guards who'd had better ways to spend their Saturday afternoon contradicted each other in court. Swearing in the jury, the judge asked anyone if they had to declare an interest in the case. One juryman had spoken up. 'I have no interest in the case, Your Honour, I'm not interested in it at all.' He might have been a spokesman for my father's generation. 'I have no interest in seeing what's in front of my eyes, no interest in things I don't want to know about. If people didn't turn a blind eye, Your Honour, we'd all be fucked.'

Half the bus would be fucked tonight if they got the chance, I suspected as I looked around it. Thick-calved Cavan girls wearing skirts the size of a mouse's parachute and platform heels that needed health warnings for acrophobia. They shared lipstick and gossip in a suffocating reek of perfume. A radio almost drowned out the lads behind me discussing the new satellite channel a local consortium had set up to beam video highlights of junior local hurling matches into selected pubs until 10 p.m., when the frequency was taken over by a porn channel from Prague.

We crossed the Boyne near the turn for Johnstown. To the left a line of mature trees blocked out any view of the Clancy family residence, a Palladian mansion with an additional wing built on by Slab McGuirk and Mossy Egan the year my father left private employment. County Council workers had extended a six-foot stone boundary wall for free when the road was being widened. Beyond it the road grew lonely, broken by the lights of isolated homesteads and live-stock huddled in the corners of fields. I stared out into the dusk as we reached the first turn for Tara, the dung-splattered seat of the ancient High Kings.

'Let's stop at Tara, I've never seen it,' Phyllis had pleaded as we passed here on the second occasion I met her, six months after our night at the dog track. By then, the secret was all over Navan about my father having remarried. Nobody seemed sure about how long he had been living a double life in Dublin or why he told none of his old friends. But people were impressed by stories of Barney Clancy being best man at the wedding and treating them to dinner in the Shelbourne Hotel. Brian Lenihan and two other Government ministers were rumoured to have joined in their celebrations, which became a near riot when Donough O'Malley arrived and my father reluctantly allowed his wedding night to be hi-jacked, flattered by the attention of such great men.

My father ignored Phyllis's request to stop at Tara in the car that day. Her interest in seeing it would have been negligible. But her apprehension and self-doubt about having to confront her new neighbours was evident, even to me, two months past my ninth birthday. Even the way she spoke was different from how I remembered her Dublin accent at the dog track, so that she seemed like a child unsuccessfully trying to sound posh.

My father, on the other hand, wanted the business finished, with his new bride installed and the whispers of neighbours faced down. He had accepted the job of heading a special development task-force within the planning department of Meath County Council and needed to live in Meath full-time. A more than respectable period of mourning had passed since my mother was knocked down by a truck on Ludlow Street, and it was several years since Phyllis's first husband, a Mr Morgan, passed away in his native Glasgow, leaving her with one son, Cormac, a year younger than me.

Neither Cormac nor I spoke to each other on that first journey into Navan. Cormac looked soft enough to crush, pointing out cattle to his teddy bear through the window and keeping up an incessant, lisping commentary. We shared the same freckles and teeth but his hair was a gingery red. Even though I was preoccupied in struggling against back-seat nausea, I could see the effect that his whispered babbling and the unmanly teddy bear were having on my father.

'Does this mean we'll be going to see the dogs again?' I asked.

'You never saw your mother at the dog track. She was never there. Do you understand?'

My father didn't turn as he spoke, but his eyes found mine in the rear-view mirror. *Mother.* Was that what I was meant to call her? Half the town probably saw them at the dog track, but to my father power was about controlling perceptions and this was to be his wife's stage-managed arrival into Navan.

Some time during their first night in the house I cried out. Perhaps my tears were caused by a sense of everything changing or maybe the inaudible shriek of a ghost being banished woke me, with no untouched corner left for my mother to hide in. All evening the house – already immaculately cleaned by Josie, whose services were now dispensed with – had been scrubbed by Phyllis. Neat cupboards were pulled apart like an exorcism, old curtains torn down before her new Venetian blinds had even arrived, and alien sounds filled up the house.

I just know that I cried out again, waiting for the creak of his bed in response and for yellow light to spill across the pattern of roses. Cormac's eyes watched like a cat in the dark from the new camp-bed set up across the room. But it was Phyllis who entered to hover over my bed. My crying stopped. How often have I relived that moment, asking myself who Phyllis was and just how insecure she must have felt? A young twenty-five years of age to his settled, confident thirty-eight. Had they been making love, or did I startle her from sleep to find this house – twice the size of the artisan's cottage she was reared in – closing in around her like a mausoleum to the goodness conferred by death onto another woman, knowing she would have to constantly walk in that other woman's foot-steps, an inappropriately dressed outsider perpetually scruti-nized and compared.

Her hand reached out tentatively towards my wet cheeks, her white knuckle showing off a thickset ring. I flinched and drew back, startling Phyllis who was possibly more scared than me. Eyeball to eyeball with a new life, sudden responsibilities and guilts. We were like two explorers wary of each other, as she stretched out her fingers a second time, hesitantly, as if waiting for me to duck away.

'Why were you crying?' Her voice, kept low as if afraid of wakening my father, didn't sound like a grown woman's. I didn't know what to say. 'Were you scared?'

'Yes.'

It wasn't me who replied; it was Cormac, his tears deliber-ately staking his claim to her. Phyllis turned from my bed, crooning as she hugged her son, her only constant in this unfamiliar world of Meath men.

I never knew proper hatred before Cormac's arrival. Josie's granddaughter and I had played as equals, conquering foes in the imaginary continent of her back garden. But soon Cormac and I were fighting for real territory, possession of the hearth-rug or ownership of Dinky cars and torn comics. He watched me constantly in those first weeks, imitating my every action and discovering my favourite places to play in, then getting there before me. 'It's mine, mine, mine!' Our chorus would bring Phyllis screeching from the kitchen.

It was the same in the schoolyard, where he shadowed me from a distance. Phyllis watched from the gate, making sure I held his hand until the last minute. But once she was gone I let him stew in the stigma of his different accent, refusing to stand up for him when boys asked if he was my new brother. The funny thing was that I had always wanted a brother, but I could only see Cormac as a threat, walking into my life, being made a fuss of by people who should have been making a fuss of me. Previously my father had been away in Dublin a lot, but I'd always had him to myself when he got home. Now Phyllis was there every evening in the hallway before me, perpetually in my way like a puppy dog needing attention. I was put to bed early just so they could be alone and even then I had to share my room with a usurper.

It was more than cowardice therefore that stopped me intervening when Pete Clancy's gang started picking on Cormac. They were doing my work for me. I would slip away into a corner of the yard and experience a guilty thrill at hearing the distant sounds of him being shoved and kicked. Only when a teacher's whistle blew would I charge into their midst, always arriving too late to help.

That ruse didn't stop me being blamed to my face by Phyllis and blamed to my father when he came home from his new offices in Trim, which seemed to have been deliberately set apart from the main Navan Council headquarters. The out-house lay idle, with his private practice gone. The box-room had been filled with my father's old records and papers, ever since the morning, some months previously, when Josie and I found the outhouse door forced and the place ransacked. My father had dismissed it as a prank by flyboys from down the town, refusing to phone the police. But that night after Josie was gone Barney Clancy and he had spent hours down there clearing boxes out.

Any extra paperwork at home was done from a new office in the box-room now, though generally he preferred to work late in Trim where he had a small staff under him. News of an outsider being parachuted into this new position – created in a snap vote by councillors at a sparsely attended meeting – had surpassed even his second bride in making him the talk of Navan. Some claimed that the two in-house rivals for the new post had built up such mini-empires of internal support that a schism would have occurred within the planning office had either of them got the job. An honest broker was required, without baggage or ties, to focus on new developments. But others muttered begrudgingly about clout, political connections and jobs being created to undermine the structures already in place.

These whispers went over my head. I just knew that he came home later, seemed more tired and was more prone to snap. Joey Kerwin stopped one Saturday to watch Phyllis's hips sway into the house ahead of us as though wading through water. 'You know what they say about marriage, Eamonn?' he gibed. 'It's the only feast where they serve the dessert first!' My father ushered us in, ignoring the old farmer's laugh. But sometimes I now woke to hear voices raised downstairs and muffled references to Cormac's name and mine. Once there was a screaming match halted by a loud slap. One set of footsteps rushed up the stairs, followed some time after by a heavier tread. Then I heard bedsprings and a different sort of cry.

But I experienced no violence, at least not at first. Perhaps the unseen eyes of my mother's ghost still haunted him from the brighter squares of wallpaper where old photos had been taken down. Once I woke to find him on the edge of my bed watching me. This isn't easy, you've got to help me, son. I didn't want to help. I wanted Cormac beaten up so badly by Pete Clancy that Phyllis would pack and leave. I wanted my father to myself, like in the old days when we'd walk out along the Boyne or I'd stand beside him as he swapped jokes in shop doorways in the glamorous male world of cigarettes and betting tips. But Cormac merely dug in deeper, accepting Clancy's assaults with a mute, disarming bewilderment that was painful to watch and was countered by an increasingly strident assertiveness at home. Why can't I drink from the blue cup? Why does Brendan say it belongs to him? I thought you owned everything now, Mammy? Why can't I sleep in the proper bed?

Why couldn't he? The question began to fixate Phyllis. If her own son wasn't good enough for the best, then, by reflection, neither was she. Why didn't her new husband take her side? Was it because he did not respect her as much as his first wife who had been the nuns' pet, educated with the big shopkeepers' daughters in the local Loreto convent? I can only imagine what accusations she threw at him at night, the ways she found to needle him with her insecurities, the sexual favours she may have withheld – favours not taught in home economics by the Loreto nuns.

I woke one Monday to find two bags packed in the hallway and raised voices downstairs. I pushed the kitchen door open. Startled, my father turned and slapped me. 'Get out, you!' I stood in the hallway and stuck my tongue out at Cormac who was spying through the banisters.

My father silently walked me to school that day while Cormac stayed at home. It was the last year before they stopped having the weekly fair in the square, with fattened-up cattle herded in from the big farms at 6 a.m. and already sold and dispatched for slaughter by the time school began. I remember the fire brigade hosing down the square that morning, forcing a sea of cow-shite towards the flooded drains, and how the shite itself was green as if the terrified cattle had already known their fate.

I was happy when nobody came to collect me after school. I walked alone through the square, which shone by now although the stink still lingered from the drains. I didn't know if anyone would be at home. On my third knock Phyllis opened the door. Her bags were gone from the hall. Cormac was watching television with an empty lemonade bottle beside him. Upstairs, his coloured quilt lay on my bed, his teddies peering through the brass bars at the end. My pillow rested on the smaller camp-bed in the corner. Two empty fertilizer bags lay beside the door, filled to the brim with shredded wallpaper. Scraps of yellowing roses, stems and thorns. On the bare plaster faded adult writing in black ink that I couldn't read had been uncovered. I changed the beds back to the way they should have been. Then I locked the bedroom door, determined to keep it shut until my father returned home to this sacrilege.

I don't know how long it took Phyllis to notice that I had not come down for my dinner. Furtively I played with Cormac's teddies, then stood by the window, watching children outside playing hopscotch and skipping. I didn't hear her footsteps, just a sudden twist of the handle. She pushed against the door with all her weight. There was the briefest pause before her first tentative knock. Almost immediately a furious banging commenced.

'Open this door at once! Open this door!'

The children on the street could hear. The skipping ropes and chanting stopped as every eye turned. I put my hand on each pane of glass in succession, trying to stop my legs shaking. Cormac's voice came from the landing, crying for some teddy on the bed. Phyllis hissed at him to go downstairs. A man with a greyhound pup looked up as he knocked on Casey's door. Phyllis was screaming now. Mr Casey came out, glanced up and then winked at me. He turned back to the man who held the puppy tight between his legs while Mr Casey leaned over with a sharp iron instrument to snip off his tail. The greyhound howled, drowning out Phyllis's voice and distracting the children who gathered around to enjoy his distress, asking could they keep his tail to play with.

I desperately needed to use the toilet. I wanted my father to come home. I wanted Phyllis gone and her red-haired brat with her. Lisa Hanlon came out of her driveway, nine years of age with ringlets, white socks and a patterned dress. Watching her, I felt something I could not understand or had never experienced before. It was in the way she stared up, still as a china doll while her mother glanced disapprovingly at Mr Casey and the greyhound and then briskly took her hand. I wanted Lisa as my prisoner, to make her take off that patterned dress and step outside her perfect world.

Then Lisa was gone, along with the man and his whimpering pup. Mr Casey glanced up once more, then went indoors. I had to wee or it would run down my leg. There was a teacup on the chest of drawers, with a cigarette butt smeared with lipstick stubbed out on the saucer. Smoking was the first habit Phyllis had taken up after arriving in Navan, her fingers starting to blend in with the local colour. But I couldn't stop weeing, even when the teacup and saucer overflowed so that drops spilled out onto the lino.

Phyllis's screams had ceased. Loud footsteps descended the stairs. I wanted to unlock the door and empty the cup and saucer down the toilet before I was caught, but I couldn't be sure that she hadn't crept back upstairs to lie in wait for me. I was too ashamed to empty them out of the window where the children might see. Ten minutes passed, twenty – I don't know how long. My hand gripped the lock, praying for my father's return. I had already risked opening the bedroom door when I heard her footsteps ascend the stairs. I locked it again and sank onto the floor, putting the cup and saucer down beside me.

'Brendan. Open this door, please, pet. You must be starving.' This was the soft voice she used when addressing Cormac, her Dublin accent more pronounced than when speaking to strangers. 'Let's forget this ever happened, eh? It can be our secret. Your dinner is waiting downstairs. Don't be afraid, I promise not to harm you.'

Sometimes in dreams I still hear her words and watch myself slowly rise as if hypnotized. I try to warn myself but each time the hope persists that she means what she says. Her voice was coaxing, like a snake charmer's. I turned the key with the softest click. Everything was still as I twisted the black door-knob, which suddenly dug into my chest as she pushed forward, throwing me back against the bed. I tried to crawl under it, but was too slow. She grabbed my hair, dragging me across the lino.

Her shoe had come off. She used the sole to beat me across my bare legs. I thought of Lisa Hanlon and her doll-like body. I thought of Cormac, sitting on the stairs, listening. My foot made contact with her knee as I thrashed out. Phyllis screamed and raised her shoe again, its heel striking my forehead above the eye. I bit her hand and she fell back, knocking over the cup and saucer. From under the bed where I had crawled, I watched a lake of urine slowly spread across the lino to soak into her dress. Even in my terror, something about how she lay with her dress up above her thighs and her breasts heaving excited me. Suddenly I wanted to be held by her, I wanted to be safe. Phyllis slowly drew herself up so I could only see her hands and knees. Cormac's feet appeared, his thick shoes stopping just short of the puddle.

'I'll not mind you!' she screamed down. 'You're worse than an animal. I was free once. I won't stay in this stinking, stuck-up, dead-end, boghole of a town, not for him or any of yous!'

She was crying. I felt ashamed for her, knowing that the children on the street could hear. Cormac stood uselessly beside her. 'Can I get my teddy now, Mammy?'

I closed my eyes, dreading my father's return home. The lake of urine had almost reached me. I could smell it, as I pressed myself tight against the wall, but soon it began to seep into my jumper. My temple ached from the impact of her shoe. My legs stung where she had beaten them. When I opened my eyes Phyllis and Cormac were gone.

———❙❙———

Dublin – the most ungainly of capital cities, forever spreading like chicken pox. A rash of slate roofs protruded from unlikely gaps along the motorway. Cul-de-sacs crammed into every niche, with curved roads and *Mind Our Children* signs. Watching from the bus it was hard to know where Meath ended and the Dublin county border began. Or at least it would have been for somebody whose father hadn't virtually ruled a small but influential sub-section of the planning department within Meath County Council.

Dunshaughlin, Black Bush, Dunboyne, Clonee. Every field and ditch in every townland seemed to be memorized in my father's head. Each illegally sited septic tank, every dirt road on which some tiny estate appeared as if dropped from the sky, with startled city children peering into fields that bordered their rubble-strewn back gardens. He knew every stream piped underground and the ditches where they resurfaced as if by magic. Within a couple of years he had become Mr Mastermind, able to track in his head the labyrinth of shell companies that builders operated behind, and willing, if necessary, to pass on their home phone numbers to residents' groups wondering whatever happened to the landscaping that had looked so inviting in the artist's impression in their advance brochures.

Fifteen years ago these townlands had seemed like a half-finished quilt that only he understood the pattern for. But by the time he retired surely not even my father could have kept track of the chaotic development that made these satellite towns resemble a box of Lego carelessly spilled by a child. Builders from Dublin, Meath, Kildare, Northern Ireland and the West vying with each other for the smallest plot of land. Men who once spat into palms in my father's outhouse to seal deals to build lean-tos and cowsheds, were now rich beyond their imagination. The sands of their retirements would be golden were it not for the tribunals into corruption currently sitting in Dublin Castle to investigate hundreds of frenzied re-zoning motions by councillors against County Development Plans around Leinster.

The new motorway petered out at the Half Way House pub, beside the old Phoenix Park racecourse which had mysteriously burnt down. I was back among familiar Dublin streets, with chock-a-block traffic being funnelled down past my old flat in Phibsborough. The bus crawled past an ugly triumphalist church, then onto the North Circular Road, before turning down Eccles Street. The driver stopped to drop off a girl with two bags and I slipped away too.

It was 7 p.m. Visiting time at the Mater Private Hospital across the road. A discreet trickle passed through the smoked-glass doors into a lobby that looked like a hotel, with plush sofas and soft piped music. I could never pass such buildings without remembering how we tried to nurse Miriam's dying mother in her rented house at the Broadstone.

An elderly man in a black leather jacket leaned on a crutch beside the railings, so circumspect that from a distance you wouldn't know he was begging. He had my father's eyes. The older I got the more I found that old beggars always had, staring up slyly as if only they could recognize me. I slipped a coin into his hand and walked past, up the street to where people streamed towards the huge public hospital, with cars and taxis competing for space outside. The open glass doors drew me towards them. I scanned the lists of wards with saints' names and quickly wagered on Saint Brigid's, then leaned over the porter's desk before I lost my nerve.

'Brogan?' I asked. 'Have you a Mrs Phyllis Brogan here?'

He checked his list, then scrutinized me. 'You're not a journalist?'

'No.'

'Family?'

'An old acquaintance.'

'Second floor, Saint Martha's ward.'

I cursed myself, having wanted to change my bet to Saint Martha's, but the first rule in any gambling system was never to switch once a choice was made. A familiar stab of self-disgust swamped me, though it was only a wager in my mind. For two years I had managed to avoid placing a bet, except for the dozens of imaginary ones that I tortured myself with daily.

'Do you get many journalists?' I enquired.

'Just one from a tabloid and some bogman who became aggressive. Her daughter-in-law asked us to keep a check. It's distressing, in the woman's condition.'

I noted how Miriam had made the arrangements and not Sarah-Jane. The porter was directing me towards the lift.

'I'm just waiting for my brother,' I lied. 'He's getting flowers. We said we'd go up together.'

It was the first excuse to enter my head. He nodded towards the sofas. It felt strange to be under the same roof as Phyllis, but I needed to ensure that she was out of the way and hadn't moved back home. I picked up an *Evening Herald* somebody had left on the sofa. *Romanian Choir Hoax*, the headline read. *Organizers of a choral festival in Westport were left red-faced today after the thirty-five-strong Romanian choir they invited into Ireland* turned out to be bogus. *While a two-hundred-strong audience waited in Westport church, the alleged singers took taxis from the airport to join the queue of illegal immigrants seeking asylum outside the Department of Foreign Affairs.* I pretended to read on, awaiting a chance to slip away when the porter left his desk.

It was a more comfortable wait than others I had known involving Phyllis. The eternity of that evening I spent as a child soaked in urine beneath my bed came back to me. Afraid to venture out, even after Phyllis went sobbing downstairs, with Cormac like a dog behind her. Teatime came and the playing children were called in, their skipping ropes stilled and the silence unbroken by the thud of a ball. Afterwards nobody ran back out as usual, still clutching their bread and jam. It felt like the whole street was awaiting the judgement of my father's car.

Finally he arrived home. The car engine was turned off and the front door opened. I expected screaming from Phyllis, but it was so quiet that I prayed she had left. Then my father ascended the stairs, his polished shoes stopping short of the pool of urine. He sat on the camp-bed so that all I could see were his suit trousers.

'Come out.'

'I'm scared.'

'I'm not going to hit you.'

I clambered stiffly out, my clothes and hair stinking of piss. 'I want my wallpaper back,' I said. 'I've always had it.'

'You'll speak when I tell you to. Your mother says you threw wee over her.'

'She's not my mother.'

The slap came from nowhere. I didn't cry out or even lift a hand to my cheek.

'If she doesn't become your mother then it will be your choice. This isn't easy for any of us. Since she arrived you've done nothing but cause trouble. I'll not come home to shouting matches. This is my wife you're insulting. She doesn't have to keep you. Did you think of that? When I was growing up I never saw my older half-sister. She was farmed out back to her mother's people up the Ox Mountains when Daddy's first wife died. That was the way back then. My own mother had enough to be doing looking after her own children without raising somebody else's leavings. Few women would take on the task of raising a brat like you. Because that's what you've become. You understand? If you don't want a mother then try a few nights without one. Go on, take those fecking blankets off the precious bed that you're so fond of. This is a family house again and you can roost in the outhouse until you decide to become one of us.'

Even when he repeated the instructions they still didn't register. My father had to bundle the blankets up into my arms before I started moving. I could hardly see where I was going. The stairs seemed endlessly steep in my terror of tripping. The hallway was empty. In the kitchen Cormac sat quietly. There was no sign of Phyllis. Eighteen steps brought me to the door of the outhouse. My father walked behind me, then suddenly his footsteps weren't there. I undid the bolt, then looked back. He had retreated to watch from the kitchen doorway, framed by the light. I couldn't comprehend his expression. A blur of blue cloth appeared behind him. Phyllis hung back, observing us. He closed the door, leaving me in the gloom.

I turned the light on in the outhouse and looked around. Anything of value had been removed to the box-room after the break-in some months before. The place had become a repository for obsolete items like the two rusty filing cabinets – one still locked and the other containing scraps of old building plans, a buckled ruler and a compass. Among the old copies of the *Meath Chronicle* in the bottom drawer I found a memorial card for my mother, her face cut from a photo on

Laytown beach. One pane of glass in the wall was cracked. The other had been broken in the break-in and was replaced by chicken wire to keep cats out. The darkness frightened me, yet I turned the light out again, wanting nobody on the street to know I was there.

Casey's kitchen window looked bright and inviting. The back of our own house was in darkness, but I knew *The Fugitive* was on television in the front-room, with Richard Kimble chasing the one-armed man. Cormac would be lying there on the hearthrug, savouring every moment of my favourite programme.

I listened to the beat of a tack hammer from the lean-to with a corrugated roof, built against the back wall of Casey's house. It was answered by other tappings from other back gardens, like a secret code. The official knock-off time marked the start of real work for most of our neighbours who worked in the town's furniture factories. They rushed their dinners so they could spend each evening working on nixers, producing chairs and coffee tables, bookcases or hybrid furniture invented by themselves. Sawdust forever blew across the gardens, with their tapping eventually dying out until only one distant hammer would be left like a ghost in the dark.

Hanlon's cat arched her back as she jumped onto our wall, then sprang down. I miaowed softly but she stalked past. A late bird called somewhere and another answered. The back door opened. My father appeared with a tray. I hunched against the wall. He entered and stood in the dark, not wanting to put the light on either.

'Bread and cheese,' he said. 'And you're lucky to get it.'

'When can I come in?'

'Not tonight.'

'Has *he* got my bed?'

'*He* has a name. My wife decides who sleeps where from

now on.' He put down the tray and stood over me. 'Don't make me have to choose, Brendan. If you do you'll lose.'

'I hate her. I want them to go.'

'She's going nowhere, Brendan. I'll make this family work if it kills me. A man needs a wife. I can't mind you alone. You understand?'

I didn't reply and he didn't expect me to. He sat on the edge of his old desk for what seemed an eternity. Perhaps he was the most lost of us all that night, torn between desire and guilt, remembering simpler times when he was fully in control, the monarch of this makeshift office. I just know that I never felt so close to him again as during that half-hour when he sat as if turned to stone, until Phyllis's voice finally called from the kitchen.

'Make yourself a bed,' he said. 'Let's have no fuss.'

As he stood up his hands fiddled with something in the dark. When he opened the door I saw in the half-light how he had removed his belt and held it folded in half. I watched through the chicken wire as he walked up the path, elaborately running the leather belt back through his trouser loops and fixing the buckle as she watched. He nodded to her. They went in and I heard the heavy bolt on the kitchen door.

———◆———

The glass doors opened in the hospital foyer. An ambulance, with its siren turned off and blue light flashing, had pulled up outside. The porter disappeared through a doorway while staff bustled about, allowing me to slip away unnoticed. The beggar was gone. I crossed Dorset Street – a blocked artery of Dublin which had always refused to become civilized. Shuttered charity shops and gaudy take-aways. Pubs on every corner, alleys leading down to ugly blocks of flats. People walked quickly here, trying to look like they knew where they're going.

Where was I heading, with just two bags waiting for me in a luggage locker at the bus station? But what other sort of homecoming had I any right to expect? I was putting more than just myself at risk by being here, but even without my father's murder I always knew that one day I would push the self-destruct button by turning up again.

I crossed into Hardwick Street and passed an old Protestant church that seemed to have become a dance club. Across the road a tall black girl stood at a phone box, smoking as she spoke into the receiver. I don't think she saw the two Dublin girls emerge through an archway from the flats, with a stunted hybrid of a fighting dog straining on his lead. At first I thought they were asking her for a light, until I saw the black girl's hair being jerked back. She screamed. I stopped. There was nobody else on the wide bend of footpath. Music blared from a pub on the corner. Two lads came out from the flats as well, as the black girl tried to run. The Dublin girls held her by the hair as the youths strolled up.

'Nigger! Why don't you fuck off back home, you sponging nigger!'

There were four of them, with the dog terrifying their victim even further. One youth grabbed her purse, scattering its contents onto the ground – keys, some sort of card, scraps of paper and a few loose coins which they ignored. They weren't even interested in robbing her. I knew the rules of city life and how to melt away. But something – perhaps the look in the black girl's eyes, which brought back another woman's terror on a distant night in this city – made me snap. I found myself running without any plan about what to do next, shouldering into the first youth to knock him off balance.

I grabbed the second youth around the neck in a headlock,

twisting his arm behind his back. The girls let go their victim in surprise, while the dog circled and barked, too inbred and stupid to know who to bite. The black girl leaned down, trying to collect her belongings from the ground.

'Don't be stupid, just run, for God's sake, run!'

'Don't call me stupid!' she screamed at me, like I was her attacker. One girl swung a hand at her, nails outspread as if to claw at her eyes. The black girl caught the arm in mid-flight, sinking her teeth into the wrist. The first youth had risen to leap onto my back, raining blows at my face as I fell forward, crushing the youth I was still holding. I heard his arm snap as he toppled to the ground. He screamed as the first youth cursed.

'You nigger-loving bastard! You cunt!'

My forehead was grazed where it hit the pavement, with my glasses sliding off. Their aggression was purely focused on me now, although the second youth was in too much pain to do much. I heard running footsteps and knew that I was for it. But when the thud of a boot came it landed inches above my head. The youth on top of me groaned and rolled off. I heard him pick himself up and run away. The other youth broke free, limping off with the shrieking girls following.

Only now did the dog realize that he was meant to attack us. I sensed him come for me and raised my arms over my face. His teeth had brushed my jacket when I heard a thump of a steel pole against his flank. He turned to snarl at his attacker as somebody pulled me up. It was a tall black man, around thirty years of age. The black girl knelt beside us, crying, cramming items into her purse. A smaller, stockier black man banged a steel pole along the concrete, holding the dog off. The black girl turned to me.

'Don't you call me stupid! Don't you ever!'

'Stop it, Ebun,' the man holding me said. He looked into my face. '*E ma bínú*. Can you walk?'

'Just give me a second.'

'We haven't got a second. More of your sort will be back.'

'They're not my sort.'

'They're hardly mine.' He bent down to retrieve my glasses from the ground. 'You should get out of here. Have you a car?'

'No.'

'Where do you live?'

'Abroad.'

'Where are you staying then?'

'I don't know yet. Somewhere.'

The girl, Ebun, looked over her shoulder towards the windows of the flats. 'He's the one who's stupid,' she said. 'He jumped right in.'

With a final snarl the dog loped off back towards the entrance. There was a shout from a stairwell. I knew they wanted to get away from there.

'He'd better come with us,' the man told Ebun.

She answered in a language I couldn't understand. My courage had vanished now that the fight was over, I was unsure if my legs would support me.

'I know,' the man replied. 'But we can't leave him here.'

The stockier man put the steel pole back inside his coat. Arguing in their own language, they half-led and half-carried me back onto Dorset Street, past a row of rundown shops and around the corner into Gardner Street. Their flat was at the top of a narrow Georgian house, with wooden steps crumbling away and rickety woodwormed banisters. I had once haunted the warrens of bedsits around here, knowing every card school in the anonymity of flatland where one could sit up all night to play poker and smoke dope.

But the journey up the stairs now had a dream-like quality.

Every face that appeared on each landing was black or Eastern European. I had spent a decade abroad, but somehow in my mind Ireland had never changed. Maybe they didn't hang black people in Navan for being the Devil any more, but before I left the occasional black visitor was still a novelty, a chance to show our patronizing tolerance which distinguished us from racist Britain. We had always been an exporter of people, our politicians pleading the special case of illegal Irish immigrants living out subterranean existences in Boston and New York. So, with our new-found prosperity, why did I not expect the boot to be on the other foot? Ebun unlocked a door and they helped me onto a chair in their one-room flat. She put some ice from the tiny fridge into a plastic supermarket bag. Kneeling beside the chair she held it against my forehead.

'To keep the swelling down,' she said. 'You were crazy brave. I should not have shouted at you.'

'I didn't mean to call you names. I just wanted to make you run.'

'I don't run,' she said. 'No more running. I see too much to run any more.'

The men talked in low voices in their own language. Another man joined them, staring at me with open curiosity. I tried to stand up, wanting to escape back down onto the street. These damp walls reminded me too much of things I had spent a lifetime fleeing. I wondered at what time the bus station closed.

'Where are you going?' Ebun pushed me back. 'You have been hit. You must rest.' She adjusted the ice-pack slightly.

'He saw everything,' the stocky man said. 'I know those kids. This time we have a witness. I say we call the police.'

'No,' I said quickly. 'I can't.'

'Can't what? Go against your own kind?'

'It's not that.'

'Leave him alone,' Ebun said. 'What's the use of a court case in six months' time? By then we could have all been put on a plane back to Nigeria. Besides, a policeman anywhere is still a policeman. We should never trust them.'

'We thank you for your help,' the man who had picked me up said. 'This should not have happened. I tell my sister not to go out alone, but do you think she listens? Have you eaten?'

'No.'

'We have something. It is hot.'

I had smelt the spices when I entered the flat. The stocky man went to the cooker and ladled something into a soup dish. '*E gbä*,' he said, handing me what looked like a sort of oily soup. 'It is called *egusi*. My name is Niyi.' He smiled but I knew he was uneasy with my presence. Ebun removed the ice-pack and they talked among themselves as I ate. Finally her brother approached.

'Tonight you have nowhere to stay?'

'Nowhere arranged as yet.'

'Then we have a mattress. You are welcome.'

I had enough money for a hotel. I was about to say this when I looked at Ebun's face and the still half-antagonistic Niyi. Strangers adrift in a strange land, refugees who had left everything behind, who lived by queuing, never knowing when news would come of their asylum application being turned down. This flat was all they possessed.

'I would be grateful,' I replied.

'*Lekan ni oruko mi*. My name is Lekan.' He held his hand out. I shook it.

'My name is Cormac,' I lied, with the ease of ten years' practice.

Lekan led me across the landing to a small bathroom. The seat was broken on the toilet, which had an ancient cistern and long chain. I washed my face, gazing in the mirror at my slightly grazed forehead. Then I peered out of the small window: rooftops with broken slates, blocks of flats in the distance, old church spires dwarfed by an army of building cranes, the achingly familiar sounds of this hurtful city.

A few streets away the woman I had been taught to call 'Mother' lay dying in hospital. Out in the suburbs beyond these old streets the woman I had once called 'wife' lived with the boy who once called me 'Father'. Conor's seventeenth birthday was in two months' time, yet he lived on in my mind the way he had looked when he was seven.

On the landing the Nigerians were bargaining in a language I could not understand and then in English as they borrowed blankets to make up a spare bed. My forehead hurt. Everywhere my eyes strayed across the rooftops brought memories of pain, so why was my body swamped by the bittersweet elation of having come home?

II

SUNDAY

A sofa with scratched wooden arms that probably even looked cheap when purchased in the 1970s; a purple flower-patterned carpet; one battered armchair; a Formica table that belonged in some 1960s fish and chip shop; an ancient windowpane with its paint and putty almost fully peeled away. I woke up on Sunday morning in Ebun's flat and felt more at home than I had done for years.

A solitary shaft of dusty light squeezed between a gap in the two blankets tacked across the window as makeshift curtains. It fell on Niyi's bare feet as he sat on the floor against the far wall watching me. He nodded, his gaze not unfriendly but territorial in the way of a male wary of predators in the presence of his woman.

I looked around. One sleeping-bag was already rolled up against the wall. Ebun occupied the double bed, her hair spilling out from the blankets as she slept on, curled in a ball. Niyi followed my gaze. Maybe he had just left the double bed or perhaps the empty sleeping-bag was his. I'd no idea of where anyone had slept. All three Nigerians had still been talking softly when I fell asleep last night.

'Lekan?' I enquired in a whisper.

'Gone. To help man prepare for his appeal interview, then to queue.'

'What queue?'

'Refugee Application Centre. He needs our rent form signed.'

'But it's Sunday?'

'On Friday staff refuse to open doors. They say they frightened by too many of us outside. Scared of diseases I never hear of. By Monday morning queue will be too long. Best to start queue on Sunday afternoon, and hope that when your night-clubs finish there is less trouble with drunks. Lekan does not like trouble.'

'How will he eat?'

Niyi shrugged. 'We bring him food. Lekan is good queuer. I only get angry. Too cold. Already I am sick of your country.'

He pulled a blanket tighter around him. We had been whispering so as not to wake the girl. It was seven-twenty on my watch. There would be nowhere open at this time in Dublin, not even a café for breakfast. I turned over. My pillow was comfortable, the rough blanket warm. My limbs were only slightly stiff from the thin mattress. I could go back asleep if I wished to. From an early age I had trained myself to fall asleep anywhere.

Not that this ability was easily learned. I spent five years sleeping in the outhouse as a child, yet the first few nights, when I barely slept at all, remain most vivid in my mind. My terror at being alone and the growing sensation of how worthless and dirty I was. Throughout the first night I was too afraid to sleep. I knelt up on the desk to watch lights go out in every back bedroom along the street. My father's light was among the first. Yet several times during the night I thought I glimpsed a blurred outline against the hammered glass of the bathroom window. I didn't know whether it was my father or a ghost. But someone seemed to flit about, watching over me or watching that I didn't escape.

I'd never known how loud the darkness could be. Apple trees creaking in Hanlon's garden, a rustling among Casey's gooseberry bushes. Paws suddenly landing on the outhouse roof. Footsteps – real or imagined – stopping halfway down the lane. Every ghost story I had ever heard became real in that darkness. Dawn eventually lit the sky like a fantastically slow firework, and, secure in its light, I must have blacked into sleep because I woke suddenly, huddled on the floor with my neck stiff. My father filled the doorway.

'School starts soon. You'd better come in and wash.'

He didn't have to tell me not to mention my night in the outhouse at school. Instinctively I understood shame. Cormac sat at the kitchen table. He didn't seem pleased at his victory, he looked scared. Phyllis refused to glance at me. She placed a bowl of porridge on the table, which I ate greedily, barely caring if it scalded my throat.

'Comb his hair,' my father instructed her. 'He can't go looking like he slept in a haystack.'

But the tufts would not sit down, no matter how hard Phyllis yanked at them. Finally she pushed my head under the tap, then combed the drenched hair back into shape. Her fingers trembled, her eyes avoiding mine. She snapped at Cormac to hurry up, pushing us both out the door. We were late, trotting in silence at her heels. Lisa Hanlon stared at me as she passed with her mother. Phyllis took my hand, squeezing my fingers so tightly that they hurt. Every passer-by seemed to be gazing at me and whispering.

'You mind your brother this time.' Her hiss was sharp as she joined our hands together, pushing us through the gate. We walked awkwardly towards the lines of boys starting to be marched in.

I glanced at Cormac whose eyes were round with tears. 'If you slept in my bed I'll kill you, you little gick,' I whispered. He released his hand from mine once Phyllis was out of sight.

It was hard to stay awake. My eyes hurt when I rubbed them. I avoided Cormac at small break, while a boy jeered at me in the long concrete shelter: 'What was your mother screaming about yesterday?'

'She's not my mother.'

Cormac moved alone through the hordes of boys, being pushed by some who stumbled into his path. But he seemed content and almost oblivious to them, absorbed in some imaginary world. I watched him walk, his red hair, his skin so white. He was the only boy I knew who washed his hands at the leaky tap after pissing in the shed which served as a school toilet. At that moment I wanted him as my prisoner too, himself and Lisa Hanlon with tied hands forced to do my bidding on some secret island on a lake in the Boyne. I don't know what I really wanted or felt, just that the thought provided a thrill of power, allowing me to escape in my mind from my growing sense of worthlessness.

When lunchtime came I knew Cormac was about to get hurt. Bombs were exploding in the North of Ireland, with internment and riots and barbed wire across roads. I didn't understand the news footage that my father was watching so intently at night. But Pete Clancy's gang had started to jeer at Cormac, chanting 'Look out, here comes a Brit' and talking as though the British army was a private militia for which he was personally responsible.

Yet I had never heard him mention his father or living in Scotland. It was like he had no previous existence before gatecrashing my life in Navan. He spoke with a softer version of his mother's inner-city Dublin accent, but this made no difference to Pete Clancy, who detested Dubliners anyway. Cormac was the nearest available scapegoat and therefore had to suffer the consequences.

I watched from the shed as a circle of older boys closed in on him, while younger lads ran to warn me that he was in trouble. The prospect of violence spread like an electric current through the yard. I wanted Cormac hurt, yet something about his lost manner made me snap. The huddle of boys seemed impenetrable as they scrambled for a look. They let me through as if sensing I meant business. But even if I could have helped him I had left it too late. Cormac's shirt was torn, his nose a mass of blood. Pete Clancy stopped, knowing he had gone too far. Behind him Slick McGuirk and P. J. Egan stood like shadows, suddenly scared. Slick was trembling, unable to take his eyes off Cormac, maybe because when they had nobody else to torment the two companions always tormented him. Pete Clancy let go of Cormac's hair and all three stepped back, leaving him kneeling there.

The circle was dispersing, voices suddenly quiet. I knew Mr Kenny was standing behind me, the tongue of a brass bell held in his left fist and his right hand clenching a leather strap with coins stitched into it. He looked directly at Pete Clancy. 'What's been going on here?'

'Two brothers, *a Mháistir*, they were fighting.'

Clancy's eyes warned me about what could happen afterwards if I contradicted him. McGuirk and Egan took his lead, staring intimidatingly at me.

'Did you try to stop them, Clancy?'

'I tried, *a Mháistir*.'

The Low Babies and High Babies were sharing a single classroom that year, while the leaky prefab, which previously housed two classrooms, was being demolished to make room for a new extension. Every boy knew that the school would never have leapfrogged the queue for grant aid if Barney Clancy hadn't pulled serious strings within the Department of Education. My father might be respected but my word held no currency against a TD's son. I looked at Pete Clancy's closed fist which still held a thread of Cormac's hair.

'Is this true, Brogan?' Mr Kenny asked me.

'No, sir. He's not my brother.'

Someone sniggered, then went silent at the thud of Mr Kenny's leather against my thigh. The stitched coins left a series of impressions along my reddened flesh.

'Don't come the comedian with me, Brogan!'

It was hard to believe that two hundred boys could be this quiet, their breath held as they anticipated violence being done to somebody else. Pete Clancy eyed me coldly.

'Did you strike this boy?' Mr Kenny asked me again.

Cormac looked up from where he knelt, trying to wipe blood from his nose. 'No, he didn't.'

'I did so!' I contradicted him, not knowing if I was trying to save Cormac or myself or us both. Clancy's henchmen haunted every lane in Navan, whereas with Kenny it would simply be one beating. 'He's a little Brit,' I said, parroting Clancy's phrases. 'They're only scum over there in Scumland.'

'Brendan didn't touch me, sir,' Cormac protested. 'Please leave him alone.'

'Stand up,' Kenny told him. Cormac rose. I knew he was crazy, only making things worse. But Clancy and the others stepped back, suddenly anxious. Cormac's honesty was illogical. There was no place for it in that schoolyard and they were suddenly scared of him as if confronted by somebody deformed or spastic.

'You needn't be afraid of what he'll do to you at home. I'll make sure your mother knows about this,' Mr Kenny said, beckoning us to follow him.

A large wooden crucifix dominated the corridor outside the head brother's office, framed by a proclamation of the Republic and a photo of a visiting bishop at confirmation time. I stood outside the office while Slick McGuirk and P. J. Egan pressed their faces against the window on their way home, muttering, 'You're dead, fecking dead!'

Their threats weren't directed at Cormac sitting on a chair near the statue of Saint Martin de Pours, but at me. They ignored the child who had defied them, but, in acquiescing, I had become their new bait.

Phyllis didn't even glance at me when she emerged from the head brother's office. Her silence lasted all the way home as she gripped Cormac's hand and I fell back, one step, two step, three steps behind them. Conscious of watching eyes and sniggers. Aware of hunger and of how my palms stung so badly that I could hardly unclench my knuckles after my caning by the head brother. Cormac didn't speak either. Perhaps he realized that the truth was of no use or maybe he was exacting revenge for every sly pinch I'd ever given him.

The grass needed a final autumn cut in the back garden. I remember that leaves had blown in from the lane to cover the small lawn with a riot of colour. They looked like the sails of boats on a crowded river. I wanted nothing more than to block the real world out by kneeling to open my bruised hands and play with them.

'*Tháinig long ó Valparaiso, Scaoileadh téad a seol sa chuan . . .*'

I remembered Brother Ambrose's voice in class a few weeks before, losing its usual gruffness and becoming surprisingly soft as he seduced us with a poem in Irish about a local man who sees a ship from Valparaiso letting down its anchor in a Galway bay and longs in vain to leave his ordinary life behind by sailing away on it to the distant port it had come from.

Phyllis had left us alone in the garden. I knelt to gather up a crinkled fleet of russet and brown leaves and cast them adrift. Cormac watched behind me, then knelt to help by sorting out more leaves and pushing them into my hands.

'What are they?' he asked.

'A fleet of ships. Sailing across the world to Valparaiso.'

'Where's that?'

'Somewhere that's not here.'

He nodded companionably as if the confrontation in the schoolyard had finally given us something in common. It was the first time we became absorbed in playing together, our hands sorting out the leaves excitedly.

'The purple ones can be pirates,' he suggested, 'slaughtering the goody-goody ones that are brown.'

'Did you come from Scotland on a ship?'

'I don't know.'

'What was it like, Scotland?'

'I don't know.'

Footsteps made us turn. Phyllis was struggling with a spare mattress she had taken down from the attic, trying to force it out the kitchen door. Mutely we watched her haul it down the path. My blankets were already in the outhouse from last night. I have a memory of Cormac and I holding hands as we stood together. But this couldn't be possible, because when she ordered me into the outhouse I was still clutching a pile of leaves tightly in both fists.

'Put those down before you litter the place,' she said. 'Make a bed for yourself. I'll not have a thug under the same roof as my son.'

Her make-up was streaked from tears. I didn't want to simply drop the leaves. Cormac opened his hands and I passed them to him so that he could continue the game. He was still holding them, solemn-faced, when Phyllis slammed the door.

I don't know at what hour my father came home, but it was long after the chorus of wood saws and the tic-tic-tic of upholstery tacks had died out in the garden sheds. He brought down a tray with water and a bowl of lukewarm stew. I told him the truth about Pete Clancy, crying my eyes out, desperate for someone to believe me. The terrible thing is that I think he did believe me, but just couldn't afford to admit it to me or to himself.

Barney Clancy had dominated that outhouse on every occasion he stood there. His rich cigar smoke, the shiny braces, the shirts he was rumoured to have specially made in Paris. After years of hard times Clancy was putting Navan on the map. Without him there would be no Tara mines or queue-skipping for telephones or factories set up to keep the 1950s IRA men out of mischief. The new wing for Our Lady's Hospital would not have been built, nor the Classical School resurrected from the slum of Saint Finian's, and the promise of a municipal swimming pool would have remained just a promise.

Dynasties like the Fitzsimons, Wallaces and Hillards were among the decent honest politicians who would be easily elected for generations to come, but Barney Clancy was different from them and dangerous and special. People talked as if the River Blackwater would stop flowing into the Boyne below the town if he was not there like some Colossus to watch over us. Things were happening to Navan that the aborigines of Kells or Trim could only have wet dreams about. And my father played his part too, not just helping out with constituency matters but increasingly looking after domestic finance and bills and other mundane matters that Clancy no longer had time for. He was respected in the town as a lieutenant to the whirlwind whose audacity was making us the envy of Ireland.

'I want no more trouble,' my father said quietly when I finished crying. 'If and when your mother forgives you you will come back in and stop behaving like a brat.'

He slipped me an old comic from his pocket as he left. It was crumpled and I'd read it a dozen times before. But I studied every word repeatedly to keep the darkness away. Dennis the Menace and the Bash Street Kids. I spoke their lines aloud, imagining myself at one with them for whole moments inside each story, caught up within their anarchic freedom. Then I'd reach the final page and sounds from the street intruded into my loneliness. Toilets flushing, canned laughter from television sets, a woman throwing tea leaves out the back door and banging the empty pot three times like a code.

After undressing I lay in the dark. I thought of Cormac's white skin snuggled against mine as sleep overcame us on our ship with billowing sails of autumn leaves, which we had steered out along the Boyne to the open sea to sail towards Valparaiso.

———————

Time is not a concept any child can properly understand. One night can last an eternity while several years fuse into a blur. Did my father and Phyllis decide on that first night to permanently exile me, or did my punishment simply become a habit, a decision they never got around to reversing? Maybe they rowed for months over it or perhaps my father simply let Phyllis get on with running the house. He was too swamped by internal County Council sniping with the main planning department and his recently acquired voluntary week-end role of trying to balance the household books of Barney Clancy so as to leave the great man free to focus on politics.

I once overheard my father tell Phyllis about Barney Clancy's advice to a businessman moving to Athlone. 'Make them sit up and quake in their boots at the sight of you. Look down your nose on every last Westmeath bog-warrior. Fear is the only way to get Athlone people to respect you.' Respect. The word rankled with Phyllis, gnawing at her dreams like a cancer. She craved respect in the same way as women in

Navan had started yearning to entertain at home with steak fondue evenings or to take foreign holidays that didn't involve pilgrimages or fasting.

But the hardchaw Dublin workmen erecting a new fluorescent sign over O'Kelly's butcher's in Trimgate Street instinctively recognized one of their own as they wolfwhistled after her every morning, and other mothers at the school gate kept a clannish distance. Phyllis mimicked their accents, despising what she regarded as their bog fashions, headscarves and plump safely-married figures that were 'beef to the heel like a herd of Meath heifers'. Yet she clung to any casual remark addressed to her, desperate for some sign of acceptance.

Back then neighbours counted how many tacks a man used to upholster an armchair, knew if the postman delivered a brown Jiffy bag from England or whose wife was spied visiting a chemist shop in an outlying town. It must have been obvious, even to Phyllis, that people knew and disapproved of my growing ostracism at home. Children from first marriages were sometimes treated as second-class citizens within Irish families, but never to this extreme. Furthermore, for all her airs, I was still a local and they regarded Phyllis as just a blow-in, tarting herself up like a woman on the chase for a husband instead of one securely married.

But the more they ignored her the more I bore the brunt of her frustration. Each day I came home from school, ate dinner at the same table as Cormac and was banished to the shed before she produced ice-cream for his dessert from the new refrigerator which gave itself up to convoluted multiple orgasms every few hours. When my father eventually arrived home he was sent down to harangue me over my latest alleged insult to his wife – Phyllis having abandoned the pretence of me calling her mother.

Some nights he lashed out at me with a fury that – even

at the age of ten and eleven – I knew had little to do with my 'offence' or even the inconvenience of my existence. At such moments he became like a savage, needing to dominate me because I was the last thing he could control with life starting to spin beyond him. I'd seen him taunted on the street as 'Clancy's lap-dog in the Council' and heard Pete Clancy's joke about his father taking my father and Jimmy Mahon for a slap-up meal where he ordered steak and onions and when the waiter enquired, 'What about the vegetables, sir?' Clancy replied, 'They can order for themselves.'

The only place where he still felt in command was the outhouse, in which he began to lock papers away in the filing cabinet again, warning me never to mention them to Phyllis. This made me suspect that they were related to my mother, photographs or other souvenirs of her unmentionable absence. Feeling that I was in the same room as them gave me a certain comfort at night.

Mostly, however, he didn't hit me. After some half-hearted shouting he simply smoked in silence or questioned me about school, joking about the soft time pupils had now compared to his youth. 'You're happier down here with your bit of space,' he observed once, more to himself than me. 'Few boys your age have so much freedom.'

Often it felt like he was putting off his return back up to the rigid game of happy families being orchestrated in that house. Mama Bear, Dada Bear and room for only one Baby Bear. 'She's a good woman,' he remarked after a long silence one night. 'It's not easy for her in this town.' He looked at me as if wanting a reply, like he ached for reassurance or justification. Yet I knew he was so wound up that if I opened my mouth his fists would fly.

Some evenings I peered through the chicken wire to watch them play their roles in the sitting-room window. Except that nobody seemed to have told Cormac the plot. He had sole possession of the hearthrug and bedroom, but increasingly he wore the distant look I had first seen in the schoolyard. Self-absorbed, no longer clinging to his mother but largely ignoring them by escaping into his own inner world. He seemed the only one of us not to be bent and twisted like a divining rod by unseen tensions.

With the mines creating an influx of jobs, boom times were hitting Navan. Building sites sprang up. Anxious developers, farmers with land to sell and total strangers would call to the house at all hours, hoping in vain for a quiet word with my father after having no joy with the main planning department. Phyllis had instructions to run people like Slab McGuirk from the door, savouring her status at being able to exclude prominent citizens which made her feel as omnipotent as a doctor's wife or priest's housekeeper. Very occasionally she attended sod-turnings and ribbon cuttings with my father if there was a slap-up meal later in the Ard Boyne Hotel or Conyngham Arms in Slane. A girl was paid to babysit Cormac on those occasions, while I was allowed up into the house, for the sake of appearances.

But the outings were rarely a success. The tension was so electric on their return that the babysitter was barely gone before the rows started. 'What are you sulking about now?' she would nag in a tipsy voice. 'How I held my wineglass or laughed too loud or upstaged Clancy's pig of a wife – the only woman in Navan who doesn't know about his mistress in Dublin?' Phyllis's voice followed me, spoiling for a fight, as I was dispatched to the shed: 'Come on! Tell me to start behaving like a grown woman. But you like me as a girl when it suits you, don't you eh, Mr Respectable?'

I was eleven on the night when they grew so caught up in their row – which now seemed almost like a ritualized game leading to subsequent peace-offerings – that they forgot to properly close the bedroom curtains. The gap was small where they shifted in and out of the light. My father was naked, with black hair down his chest and his belly swelling slightly outwards. I didn't know what an erection was, just that Phyllis knelt, wearing just a white bra, to cure it in the way that you sucked poison from a wasp sting. I should have been disturbed, but everything about the scene – the way they were framed by the slat of light, his stillness with his hands holding her hair and his face turned away – made it seem like a ceremony from some distant world that I would always be forced to witness from outside.

But I was outside everything now. The whole of Navan – and even the Nobber bogmen arriving in bangers with shiny suits crusted in dandruff – knew it. Pete Clancy perpetually devised new means of public ridicule. His fawning cronies brought in soiled straw to fling at me and shout that I had left my bedding behind. They held their noses when I passed, making chucking noises and perching like roosting hens on the bench in the concrete shelter.

The funny thing was that – although Navan would never accept a blow-in like Phyllis – Cormac had blended in, accepted and even slyly admired for his oddity. From the day that he contradicted Pete Clancy any bullying of him had switched to me instead, although I noticed that in the yard Slick rarely took his eyes off Cormac. He even made a few friends, boys who similarly seemed to inhabit their own imaginations out on the fringe of things. But for every friend Cormac made a dozen of mine melted away, aware that even association with me could put them at risk of being bullied too.

The town whispered about what was happening to me at home, with neighbours always on the verge of doing something. Teachers after I fell asleep in class, my mother's only brother who arrived home from England and threatened to call to the barracks. A policeman spent twenty minutes in the front-room waiting to speak to my father, with not even Phyllis daring to send him packing. On another night a young priest came, very new to the parish, after spotting me at school. There was a brief and strained conversation before he left and never came back. Old Joey Kerwin probably called upon the curate with a bottle of whiskey and the advice that he would earn more respect in Navan for not stirring up unnecessary trouble and maybe leaving his guitar in the presbytery instead of flashing it around the altar.

Had my father been unemployed or a mere labourer I would have been taken away to be placed in the chronic brutality which passed for childcare. I would have shared a dormitory with forty other starving boys; been hired out as slave labour to local farmers; taught some rudimentary trade and lain awake, if lucky, listening as naked boys were flogged on the stone stairs while two Christian Brothers stood on their outstretched hands to prevent them moving. After the state subsidy for my upkeep dried up on my sixteenth birthday, the Brothers would have shown me the door, ordering me to fend for myself and keep my mouth shut.

When boys disappeared into those schools they never reappeared as the same people. Something died inside them, caused by more than just beatings and starvation. But that system was designed to keep the lower orders in check and provide the Christian Brothers with an income. For the son of a senior County Council official to be sent to an industrial school was as unthinkable as for a priest to bugger a Loreto convent girl. The middle classes managed our own affairs, with minor convictions squashed by quiet words in politicians' ears and noses kept out of other people's business. No action was ever taken about my confinement, my occasional bruises or burst lip, or the fact that neighbours must have sometimes heard me crying. My father just got busier at work and – corralled in the home – Phyllis grew ever more paranoid about 'the interfering bitches of the town'.

'What were you saying to that Josie woman from the terrace?' she would demand if I was a minute late home from school. 'Don't think I didn't see you gabbing to her when I picked up Cormac in the car. Does she think we're so poor she needs to give you food from her scabby cottage that should have been bulldozed long ago? You get home here on time tomorrow.'

Shortly before my eleventh birthday Mr Casey had begun to interfere. Trenchantly at first, after a long period of simmering observation, and then in subtle ways which made us both conspirators. His garden was an ordered world of potato beds, gooseberry bushes and cabbage plants. A compost heap stood in the far corner, away from the lean-to where he made furniture most evenings. Close to the wall of my father's outhouse he'd erected a small circle of cement blocks, used to burn withered stalks and half his household rubbish. Before Phyllis's arrival I remember accompanying my father and Mr Casey on occasional outings to his brother's farm near Trim on a Saturday morning, returning with a trailer full of logs. Long into the evening his electric saw would be at work, with sparks dancing like fireflies, logs thrown over the hedge into our garden and the softest pile of sawdust for me to play with.

Their joint ventures stopped however after Phyllis perceived some real or imagined slight in Mrs Casey's tone towards her. Afterwards both men kept each other at bay behind a façade of hearty greetings shouted over the hedge. But they hadn't properly spoken for two years before the winter evening when Mr Casey heard me crying through the outhouse wall. I recall the sudden thump of his hand against the corrugated iron and my shock, after being so self-absorbed in my shell, that an outsider could overhear me.

'Is that you, Brendan? Surely to God he hasn't still got you out there on a bitter night like this?'

His voice made me hold my breath, afraid to reply. I knew I had let my father down and done wrong by allowing Mr Casey to hear me, I wanted him to go away but he kept asking if I was all right. Was I thirsty, scared, had they given me anything to eat? 'I know you're in there,' he shouted. 'Will you for God's sake say something, child.'

Possibly my inability to reply finally made him snap. But there was nothing I could say that wouldn't make matters worse. I huddled against the corrugated iron, hearing the dying crackle of his bonfire and longing for him to go indoors so that I could creep out and sit near it for a time until the embers died. Injun Brendan who roamed the gardens at night, forever on the trail with no time for tepees or squaws.

When Mr Casey's voice eventually died away I stopped shaking. Too scared to leave the outhouse, I closed my eyes, imagining that my fist – pressed for comfort between my tightly clenched legs – was the feel of a horse beneath me. I rocked back and forth, forcing the warmth of the fantasy to claim me. Injun Brendan, always moving along to stay free. The bruises on my legs were no longer caused by Pete Clancy's gang lashing out at me as I raced past to get home from school in time. Instead they were rope burns after escaping from cattle rustlers. I fled bareback along trails known only to myself, seeking out the recently constructed makeshift wigwam of corrugated iron sheets which Clancy's gang met in by the river so that I could tear it to the ground. I had seen it one night among bushes by the Boyne but even in the dark I hadn't dared approach it. Now the fantasy of destroying it filled the ache in my stomach, blocking reality out until the sound of raised adult voices intruded.

'Don't you tell me how I can or cannot punish my own son!'

'Punish him for what? He's been two years down in that blasted shed. If his poor mother was alive . . .'

The voices were so loud I thought they were in the garden. But when I checked through the chicken wire I could see Mr Casey in the dining-room window, with my father looking like he was only moments away from coming to blows with him.

'It's no concern of yours, Seamus.'

'It's a scandal to the whole bloody town.'

'There's never been cause of scandal in this house.' Phyllis's voice entered the fray, suddenly enraged. 'Just work for idle tongues in this God-forsaken town.'

The more they argued, the more frightened of retribution I became. I looked up to see that their voices had woken Cormac. He entered the back bedroom and sleepily looked out of the window. By this time I didn't begrudge him owning my old bedroom. He looked perfect in that light, gazing down towards the shed, with his patterned pyjamas and combed hair. I was sure he couldn't see me in the dark but he began to wave and kept waving. We never really spoke now. Phyllis discouraged contact at home and at school we had nothing left to say to each other. The adult voices threw accusations at each other. Cormac stayed at the window until I forced my hand through a gap in the chicken wire, scraping my flesh as I managed to wave back to him. Then he smiled and was gone. When the voices stopped I lay awake for hours, with the memory of Cormac's body framed in the window keeping me warm as I waited for vengeful footsteps that never came.

———◼———

It was half-nine before Ebun stirred. Niyi had made coffee and quietly left a mug on the floor beside me, before relaxing his vigilance long enough to disappear down the corridor to the bathroom. That was when I became aware of Ebun languidly watching me slip into my jeans. I hurriedly did up the zip.

'You slept well,' I remarked.

Ebun curled her body back up into a ball, lifting her head slightly off the pillow. 'Where do you go now, Irishman?'

'I have business in Dublin.'

'Have you?' It was hard to tell how serious her expression was, but I found myself loving the way her eyes watched me. 'I think you are a criminal, a crook.'

'Crooks generally find better accommodation than this.'

'Do they? Are you married?'

'Are you?'

She turned her head as Niyi returned. 'I think he is a gangster, like the men who smuggled us onto their truck in Spain. He has their look. I think we are lucky not to be killed in our beds.'

The man admonished her in their own language, glancing uneasily across, but Ebun simply laughed and turned back to me. 'I don't really think you are much of a crook, Irishman. I should know, after the people we have had to deal with.'

'This is stupid talk,' Niyi butted in.

'I enjoy a joke,' I told him.

Ebun stopped smiling and regarded me caustically. 'I wish to dress. It is time you left.'

I stood up to pull on my shirt, thrown by her curt tone. When I arrived in Ireland yesterday I had been nobody, a ghost, ready to do what had to be done and disappear again without trace. The last thing I needed was attachments, but I found myself lingering in the doorway, not wanting to leave just yet. 'Thanks for taking me in.'

'Forgive us for not being used to your customs,' she replied. 'We didn't make you queue.'

Niyi muttered something sharply, caught between embarrassment and relief that I was going.

'She means no harm,' he said in English. 'But in Nigeria I did not live this way. I had a good job in my village, yet here I must queue with gypsies.'

'They have the same rights as us Yorubas,' Ebun contradicted him from the bed. 'None.'

Niyi accompanied me out onto the landing and had already started down the stairs when I glanced back. Ebun's expression was different in his absence as she quietly called out, '*E sheé*. Thank you for last night. Call again, Irishman.'

Her words caught me off guard. I was unable to disguise my look of pleasure from Niyi who escorted me down to the front door.

'Thank you again. *Ó dábò.*' He shook my hand formally, as if entreating me to ignore Ebun's invitation and regard our encounter as finished. He watched from the doorway until I reached the corner into Dorset Street.

There were more cars heading into town at this early hour than I remembered. Walton's music shop still stood on North Frederick Street, but the shabby café on the corner was gone, with workmen even on a Sunday morning swarming over steel girders to erect new apartments there. The bustle of O'Connell Street felt disturbing for 10 a.m. Tourists moved about even in late autumn and there was a striking preponderance of black faces compared to ten years ago, although one could still spot the standard fleet of Sunday fathers queuing at bus stops. I would probably be among them if I had stayed, although, approaching seventeen, Conor would be too old for weekly treats now, more concerned about having his weekends to himself.

Those separated fathers on route to exercise their visiting rights were a standard feature of the streetscape in every city I had lived in over the past decade. Too neatly dressed for a casual Sunday morning as they felt themselves to be on weekly inspection. Their limbo in Ireland would have been especially grim, with divorce only just now coming into law. Existing in bedsits on the edge of town with most of their wages still paying the mortgage of the family home, arriving there each weekend at the appointed hour to walk a tightrope between being accused of spoiling the children or neglecting them. Living out fraught hours in the bright desolation of McDonald's or pacing the zoo while the clock ticked away their allotted time.

I knew that I could never have coped with such rationed-out fatherhood. It was all or nothing for me and the only gifts that my gambling could have brought Conor were disgrace, eviction and penury. My feelings for the boy had grown more intense as my love affair with Miriam died. Died isn't the right word. Our marriage suffocated instead inside successive rings of guilt and failure, disappointments and petty recrimination. The pale sprig of first love remained buried at the gnarled core of that tree, but it was only after the axe struck it that I glimpsed the delicate lush bud again when it was too late. One final gamble, a lunatic moment of temptation had cast me adrift from them like a sepal.

Ten years ago when I flew out to visit Cormac in Scotland there was graffiti scrawled in the toilet in Dublin airport: *Would the last person emigrating please turn out all the lights.* Half the passengers on that flight were emigrants, fleeing from a clapped-out economy. I had been on protective notice for two months already at that stage, knowing that soon I would receive the minimum statutory redundancy from the Japanese company I worked for in Tallaght who insisted on blaring their bizarre company anthem every morning. *Together our workers lighten up the world* . . .

The world needed serious lightening up back then, with life conspiring to make us bitter before our time. Mortgage rates spiralled out of control and the Government cutbacks were so severe that Miriam's mother died in lingering agony on a trolley in a hospital corridor with barely enough nurses, never mind the miracle of a bed. Miriam didn't know that it was only a matter of time before we would be forced to sell our house or see it repossessed because of my gambling. There were many things Miriam didn't know back then, so much she should not have trusted me to do.

At seven Conor knew more than her, or at least saw more of my other world. The places where us men went, places men didn't mention to Mammy, even if she dealt with them in her work. Our male secret. Bribed with crisps to sit still while I screamed inwardly as my hopes faded yet again in the four-forty race at Doncaster, Warwick or Kempton. 'What's wrong, Daddy? Why is your face like that?' 'Eat your crisps, son, there's nothing wrong.' Nothing's wrong except that half of my wages had just followed the other half down a black hole. Nothing's wrong except that I kept chasing a mirage where more banknotes than I could ever count were pushed through a grille at me, where Conor had every toy he ever wanted, Miriam would smile again and the shabby punters in the pox-ridden betting shop would finally look at me with the respect that I craved from them.

No seven-year-old should have to carry secrets, be made to wait outside doorways when a bookie enforced the no-children rule, see his Daddy bang his fists against the window of a television shop while his horse lost on eleven different screens inside. I lacked the vocabulary to be a good father, gave too little or too much of myself. I simply wanted to make people happy and be respected. I hoarded gadgets, any possession that might confer status. I loved Miriam because she could simply be herself and I wanted Conor to be every single thing that I could never be.

Possibly Miriam and I could have turned our marriage around if I had been honest to her about my addiction. Perhaps we would now radiate the same self-satisfied affluence as that Dublin family yesterday on the stairwell of Lisa Hanlon's house. I might even have been around to disturb the intruders at my father's house, with him still alive and all of us reconciled. Father, son and grandson. The pair of us taking Conor fishing on the Boyne, watching him walk ahead with the rods while my father put a hand on my shoulder. 'You know I'm sorry for everything I did, son.' 'That's in the past, Dad, let's enjoy our time now.'

How often in dreams had I heard those words spoken, savouring the relief on his lined face, our silence as we walked companionably on? The sense of healing was invariably replaced by anger when I woke. The only skills my father taught me were how to keep secrets and abandon a son. There was never a moment of apology or acknowledgement of having done wrong. Nothing to release that burden of anger as I paced the streets of those foreign towns where I found work as a barman or a teacher of English, an object of mistrust like all solitary men.

In the early years I sometimes convinced myself that a passing child was Conor, even though I knew he was older by then. The pain of separation and guilt never eased, drinking beer beside the river in Antwerp or climbing the steep hill at

Bom Jesus in Braga to stare down over that Portuguese town. It was always on Sundays that my resolve broke and several times I had phoned our old number in Ireland, hoping that just for once Conor, and not his mother, would puzzle at the silence on the line. But on the fifth such call a recorded message informed me that the number was no longer in service. I had panicked upon hearing the message, smashing the receiver against the callbox wall and feeling that the final, slender umbilical cord was snapped. I didn't sleep for days, unsure if Miriam and Conor had moved house with my insurance payout or if there had been an accident. Miriam could have been dead or remarried or they might have moved abroad. Yet deep down I knew she had simply grown tired of mysterious six-monthly calls. She was not a woman for secrets or intrigues, which was why she should never have married me.

I crossed the Liffey by a new bridge now and found myself wandering through Temple Bar, a mishmash of designer buildings that looked like King Kong had wrenched them up from different cities and randomly plonked them down among the maze of narrow streets there. I bought an Irish Sunday paper and sat among the tourists on the steps of a desolate new square. The inside pages were filled with rumours of the Government being about to topple because of revelations at the planning and payments to politicians tribunals, along with reports of split communities and resistance committees being formed in isolated villages that found themselves earmarked to cater for refugees.

I stared at the small farmers and shopkeepers in one photograph, picketing the sole hotel in their village which had been block-booked by the Government who planned to squeeze thirty-nine asylum-seekers from Somalia, Latvia, Poland and Slovakia into its eleven bedrooms. *Racists*, the headline by some Dublin journalist screamed, but their faces might have belonged to my old neighbours in Navan, bewildered and scared by the speed at which the outside world had finally caught up with them. The village had a population of two hundred and forty, with no playground or amenities and a bus into the nearest town just once a day. A report of the public meeting was stormy, with many welcoming voices being shouted down by fearful ones. 'You'll kill this village,' one protester had shouted. 'What do we have except tourism and without a hotel what American tour coach will ever stop here again?'

This confused reaction was exemplified in the picture of a second picket further down the page. This showed local people in Tramore protesting against attempts to deport a refugee and her children who had actually spent the past year in their midst.

There were no naked quotes from the South Dublin Middle Classes. A discreet paragraph outlined their method of dealing with the situation. There were no pickets here, just a High Court injunction by residents against a refugee reception centre being located in their area, with their spokesman dismissing any notion that racism was involved in what he claimed was purely a planning-permission matter.

Two Eastern European women in head-dresses sat on the step beside me, dividing out a meagre meal between their children. I closed the paper and, leaving it behind me, located a cyber café down a cobbled sidestreet which was empty at that hour.

My new Hotmail account had no messages, but there again whenever I left a city I was careful to leave no trace behind. I got Pete Clancy's e-mail address from the leaflet in my pocket, sipped my coffee and began to type:

Dear Mr Clancy,

'Help me to help you', you say. Maybe we can help each other. Your problem in the next election could be how to know you have reached the quota if you're not sure that you have all the magic numbers. Your father once joked that death should not get in the way of people voting. It need not get in the way of the recently deceased talking either.

Fond memories,
Shyroyal@hotmail.com

I stared at the message for twenty minutes before clicking 'send'. It was a hook but also a gamble, pretending to know more than I did. What would Clancy make of it – a local crank, a probing journalist shooting in the dark, a canvasser for another party trying to snare him? Some party hack might check on the messages for him, scratch his head and just delete it. But I figured that the odds were two-to-one on Clancy himself reading it and five-to-two that the word 'Shyroyal' might capture his attention.

I had only heard it once in childhood, when Barney Clancy turned up in a gleaming suit, slapped his braces and joked to my father: 'This is my Shyroyal outfit. Sure isn't Meath the Royal County and don't I look shy and retiring?' Something about his laugh made me glance at him as I came up the path, after running a message for Phyllis, and something in my father's eyes made me look away, knowing it had a buried meaning not meant for the likes of me.

By the age of twelve I had learnt to pick the lock on the filing cabinet, opening the drawers gingerly at night, uncertain of what I hoped to find there. Secrets that would make me feel special, photos of my mother or some other token to break the loneliness. The letterheads were torn off the sheaf of paper in the top drawer but, even at that age, I recognized them as bank statements for something called Shyroyal Holdings Ltd, with an address on an island I had never heard of. The rows of figures meant nothing to me, but I could read the scrap of writing on the cigarette packet stapled to them: *Keep safe until I ask for them.* It was unsigned, but I would have recognized Barney Clancy's handwriting anywhere.

Not that I had considered the statements as suspicious back then. Funds were constantly being raised for the party on the chicken-and-chips circuit or by good men like Jimmy Mahon at church-gate collections. This seemed just another component of the adult world where important people were making things happen for the town. If I hadn't previously overheard Barney Clancy's joke to my father the Shyroyal name would not even have registered. Indeed, at the time I just felt disappointment that nothing belonging to my mother was actually concealed in the drawers.

Even today I couldn't be certain if my suspicions were correct or the product of a need for revenge. I could barely even recognize the country outside the cyber café window and felt doubly a foreigner for half-knowing everything. I found myself thinking of Ebun again, how she had looked calling out from her bed this morning and how Niyi too had looked, staring back at us both.

The café was starting to fill up. I finished my coffee, collected my bags from the bus station, found a hardware shop open on a Sunday where I could purchase a crowbar and booked myself into an anonymous new hotel on the edge of Temple Bar. It was important that I shaved at least once a day to ensure that black stubble didn't clash with my hair. Lying on the bed afterwards, I repeated the name Brendan out loud, as if trying to step back inside it. I remembered how Miriam and Cormac used to say it, the way Phyllis had twisted the vowels, and tried to imagine Ebun pronouncing it. But each time it sounded like a phrase from a dead tongue last spoken on some island where the only sound left was rain beating on bare rafters and collapsed gable ends.

———————— ■ ————————

During the first fortnight after the train crash a sensation of invisibility swamped me. All bets were suddenly off, because not even bookies could collect debts from a dead man. Our endowment policy ensured that once my death was confirmed, the house belonged to Miriam with the outstanding balance of the mortgage written off. A company scheme in work meant that, because I died while still employed by them, my Japanese masters would have to grudgingly cough up a small fortune. That was before taking my own life assurance policy into account, not to mention the discussion in the newspapers that I carefully read every day about a compensation fund for victims. My name was there among the list of the missing. There was even security footage of me splashing out on a first-class ticket at the booth ten minutes before the train left Perth. Death had finally given Brendan Brogan some cherished status. He was virtually a celebrity, but he wasn't me any more.

I was free of all responsibilities, shunting quietly across borders on another man's passport. Not that my initial decision was clear-cut. In the hours after the crash I wasn't sure what I had wanted, except perhaps to make Miriam suffer a foretaste of what it might be like to lose me. Little enough beyond recriminations still held us together. But I knew that her anxiety would be intense as she listened to reports of the crash and prayed for the phone to ring, aware I was supposed to be on the train.

Rarely had I experienced such a sense of power. For months I had helplessly waited on word of the factory closing. At night I had kept dreaming of horses that I knew had no chance of winning, but next day I would back them in suicidal doubles and trebles, waiting for that one magic bet to come up that might buy me space to breathe. By night I woke in a sweat, thinking that I'd heard the doorbell ring with a debt-collector outside. By day I hovered inside the doorway of betting shops in case some neighbour passed who might mention seeing me to Miriam. On buses I found myself incessantly saying to Conor, 'I bet you the next car is black,' 'I bet you we make the lights before they turn red,' 'I bet you . . . I bet you . . . I bet you . . .'

Brendan Brogan was a man who couldn't stop betting. But wandering through Perth on the morning of the crash I had the bizarre sense of having stepped outside myself. I wasn't that pathetic gambler any more. Suddenly I was the man in control who could choose when to release Miriam from her anxiety by phoning home. I imagined the relief in her voice and, with it, an echo of her earlier love. Yet once I made that call my new-found power would be gone. I would have to explain my getting off the train before it started, how I had chickened out of meeting Phyllis in Glasgow. I would return to Ireland to face the hire-purchase men and money-lenders, the pawnbroker who held all of Miriam's mother's jewellery which she believed I had put in the bank for safe keeping, and my seven-year-old son baffled by the civil war fought out in the silences around him.

I knew that my not phoning her was cruel and petty, but it was also a confused attempt to reach Miriam by letting her understand powerlessness. It was not that I hadn't wanted to tell her about my childhood, but I had never found the words that wouldn't make me feel dirty by discussing it. Her mind was too practical to understand why people had done nothing. But the hang-ups were totally on my part. I could never cope with her lack of guile and she had felt hurt by how I clammed up on nights when the memories turned my knuckles white.

Before Conor was born I genuinely believed I had outgrown that hurt. But the older he got the more I found myself forced to relive my childhood, imagining if Conor ever had to endure the same. Surely at some stage my father must have felt this same love for me as I felt for Conor, an overwhelming desire to protect him at any cost, to kill for him if necessary. Yet every time Conor laughed I remembered nights when I cried, with every meal he refused to eat I recalled ravenous hunger. Carrying a glass of milk up the stairs for him in bed I remembered creeping from the outhouse to cup my hands under the waste pipe from the kitchen sink. What father simply abandons his first child? On some nights Miriam would find me cradling Conor in bed, his sleeping cheeks smudged by my unexplained tears. I would want to go to Cremore where my father now lived and punch his face, screaming, 'Why, you bastard, why?'

I did actually mean to phone Miriam from Perth after I had scored my point. But somewhere along the line I left it too late. By 9.15 the phones would already be buzzing, with Phyllis calling my father from Glasgow airport and him contacting Miriam. By half-ten I knew her anxiety would be tinged with anger. If I phoned now she would know that I had deliberately been playing games.

And it was a game until then. Partly I was in shock from the realization of how close I had come to still being onboard the train when it left Perth. But my mind was also in turmoil from trying to comprehend the events that had occurred since my arrival in Scotland two days before.

Eleven a.m. had found me outside a TV shop in Perth,

watching live pictures of firemen frantically working. Reports were booming from the radio in the pound shop next door, with talk of signal failure and dazed survivors found wandering half a mile from the track. I had more cash on me than I had ever handled before, money nobody else knew about. Enough for a man to live on for a year, but not enough to do more than temporarily bandage over the cracks at home, even if I didn't blow it in the first betting shop in Dublin. I had needed time alone to mourn and come to terms with Cormac's last words to me that called for some new start, some resolution. I had also needed time to deal with Cormac's revelations about my father. The facts should have been self-evident had I wished to see them, but in my ambiguity of both hating him and craving his respect, I had always shied away from over-scrutinizing my father's relationship with Barney Clancy.

I had bought shaving foam in a mini-market, sharp scissors and a disposable razor. Nobody came into the gents' toilets in the small hotel beside the bus station while I was removing my beard there. I cleaned the sink afterwards until it shone, putting the scraggly hair and foam and used razor in a plastic bag. The air felt freezing against my cheeks as I dumped them in a waste bin.

People stood around the station in numbed silence as I caught a coach at half-eleven, barely aware of my destination until I saw 'Aberdeen' printed on the ticket. Cormac's voice seemed to be in my ear, giving me strength. *Go for it, brother, take them all for the big one.* Twenty-four hours before I had cradled his body in his flat, trying to hold him up even though I knew from the way he hung on the rope that his neck was broken. But suddenly it felt like we were together in this, thick as thieves, the inseparable duo that strangers thought we were when we first moved into a flat together in Dublin. I had felt as if I was outside my body when the bus pulled away from the station. I was Agatha Christie faking amnesia to scare her husband. I fingered the first-class train ticket that was still in my pocket. After all the useless bookies' slips cradled in my palm there, this was the magic card which I had acquired without even knowing. With it I could fill a royal flush, turn over the card that made twenty-one, see the most impossible treble come up. Cormac's ghost and I were hatching the biggest scam in the history of Navan, laying down the ultimate bet and the ultimate revenge on my father too. This buzz was more electric than seeing any horse win. I didn't crave respect from the other passengers, it was already there because I was someone else now, free in a way that I thought only people like Cormac could ever know.

When we had reached Aberdeen my nerve almost failed. I spent twenty minutes in a phone box, constantly dialling Miriam's number, then stopping at the last digit, biting my knuckles and starting all over again. Cormac's ghost didn't seem inside me any more. I was my old insecure self, about to muddle my way through some excuse, when I glimpsed a hoarding advertising a ferry about to leave to the Orkney Islands from Victoria Quay. *Go for it, go for it.* Cormac's tone of voice was the same as when he had dared me to do things in the outhouse.

An hour into the voyage it started to rain and the wind was bitter, but I stayed up on deck on the ferry, all the way past the Moray Firth and beyond John O'Groats. Eventually in the darkness Stromness port came into view on the island called Mainland. From there I had taken a taxi to a hotel in Kirkwall, where I sat alone in the bar to watch an extended late-night news bulletin about charred bodies still being located among the train wreckage and the death count rising.

Even then it wasn't too late to change my mind. Miriam would be frantic, with Conor crying as he sensed her anxiety.

But life without me was going to occur for them soon enough anyway. The Japanese factory would be the fifth major closure in Dublin since the start of that summer. Every day I had endured the torture of other workers looking for the return of borrowed money. Even if I used the cash in my pocket to clear every debt, how long would it take me to return to the equilibrium of being in the gutter again? It was the one place I felt safe in, where I had nothing more to lose. Winning always unhinged me. Even amidst the euphoria at seeing my horse cross the line I had always been panicked by the money being counted into my hands, knowing that life was toying with me, tauntingly postponing the inevitability of being broke again.

Fragments of my last conversation with Cormac had entered my head:

Maybe you just think you'd blow it because you've never felt the power of fifteen thousand pounds cash in your hands ... Make something of yourself. Ask yourself who you want to be. Suddenly I didn't have to be a loser whose son would learn to cross the street with his mates to avoid me. I could become someone else in his eyes, revered like my mother in a society where goodness was instantly conferred by early death.

I realize now that I wasn't thinking straight back then, still in shock from Cormac's suicide. But as I sat in that hotel bar and listened to the experts being interviewed, it seemed that my getting off the train had been a miracle of Cormac's doing. There had been no cameras that I was aware of on the platform or at the station's side entrance. I could never explain to Miriam where the fifteen thousand pounds had come from, nestling in the envelope between the two passports in my jacket pocket. She would think I had been gambling again and I was. I was taking the biggest gamble of my life to provide every penny they would need for years to come.

Another pundit was talking on television as I left the hotel bar long after midnight. He repeated the only fact that the experts seemed able to agree on. The heat inside the first-class carriages had been so intense that investigators would never establish just how many bodies were reduced to ash inside them.

The old sandstone buildings beside the quay at Kirkwall had an almost Dutch feel in the dark as I walked along the pier. An elderly man and his dog reached the end and turned to walk slowly back. Normally I didn't smoke but I had purchased a packet of the tipped cigars which Cormac liked. I would need to buy red dye for my hair tomorrow and glasses like Cormac wore in his photo, but already with the beard gone a vague resemblance was there. I was an inch taller, but did officials really check such details? I hadn't known where this voyage would take me, but surely far enough away from my old life that if I had to end it nobody could trace me back.

The paper inside my own passport was thick. At first the cigar merely singed it, making the edge of the pages curl up. Then suddenly a flame took hold. I glanced behind. The old man was out of sight, the tied-up fishing boats were deserted. Gulls scavenged under the harbour lights for whatever entrails of mackerel and cod had not been washed away. The flames licked around my photograph, consuming my hair, then my forehead, eyes and mouth. The cover was getting too hot to hold, my date of birth burnt away, my height, colour of eyes. I had flung my old self out into the North Sea and saw the passport's charred remains bob on the waves before slowly sinking from sight.

———◦———

At half-two I got dressed again, ripped the lining inside my jacket so that the crowbar fitted into it without attracting attention, and left the hotel to stroll up towards Phibsborough. That familiar Sunday-afternoon malaise lingered around the backstreets here, but new apartments crammed into every gap along Phibsborough Road itself, standing out like gold fillings in a row of bad teeth.

The tiny grocer's opposite my old flat had been replaced by a discreet one-stop-shop for transvestites. A single-storey country dairy still stood beside it, from which an old man used to emerge each morning on a horse-and-cart. But it looked long closed down, a quaint anomaly which – by fluke or quirk of messy will – the developers had overlooked in their frenzy.

A new stand had been built in Dalymount Park, but little else appeared to have changed to suggest that the ground wouldn't pass for a provincial Albanian stadium. Bohemians were playing Cork City at home. I paid in at the Connacht Street entrance and, once inside, paused to lean against the wall of the ugly concrete passageway beneath the terraces which was empty except for a late straggle of die-hard fans.

Nostalgia brought you to the funniest places. The game had already started but I had no interest in climbing up to the terraces. I wanted to forget the bitter finale of my love affair with Miriam and recall the magic of its origins. Everything about the Ireland I had left seemed summed up in the haphazard disorganization of that February night of mayhem and terror in 1983, when Italy arrived as reigning World Champions to play a friendly international. Rossi was playing that night as well as Conti and Altobelli who scored their second goal. Yet nobody in authority bothered to print tickets for the match. The crowd simply drank in the pubs around

Phibsborough until shortly before kick-off, then spilled out, fumbling for change as we formed the sort of scrum which passed for an Irish queue.

As a nation we knew we were down and out – with Barney Clancy, by then a senior cabinet minister, hectoring us about living beyond our means. The World Bank hovered in the wings, itching to take over the running of the country. But there seemed a sense of anarchic freedom about those years as well. Half an hour before kick-off I was still drinking in the Hut pub with Cormac and his friends; some of them urging us to finish up while others clamoured for a final round.

The crowd was already huge as we approached the stadium, clogging up the alleyway which led to the ground. Yet it might have been okay had an ambulance not passed down Connacht Street with its siren blaring. We squeezed even further up the alleyway to let it pass, but more latecomers surged into the cleared space in its wake, causing a swollen crush. People responded with good-humoured jokes at first, shouts of 'Shift your hand' and 'Mind that chiseller!' But soon it became difficult to breathe.

The tall girl with permed hair was the first person I saw who panicked. But she was not even going to the game; I'd seen her emerge from a nearby house and she was unable to prevent herself getting caught in the crowd. A roar erupted inside the ground as the whistle blew for kick-off. I had ten pounds on Italy to win two–nil, with Rossi to score the opener. The crowd pushed harder, anxious to miss nothing. One minute Cormac was by my side, the next we were separated in the turmoil. But my only interest was in rescuing that brown-haired girl. I couldn't explain the attraction, I just knew I had to reach her.

She turned around, trying to plead with people to let her out. But another surge pushed everyone forward, knocking her off-balance. Her hands flailed out helplessly. She was ten feet away and suddenly I hadn't cared who I hurt in attempting to reach her. Not that etiquette mattered any more. Her panic infected the crowd who realized they were likely to be crushed against the walls long before reaching the turnstiles. There was no way out. Fathers held their children tight, using elbows and fists to try and generate more space.

We were twenty feet from the stadium, nearing the zenith of the crush, when I lost sight of her. Her mouth opened as if to scream, her head went down and never reappeared. I took a blow to my skull as I clawed my way through. Then I was lifted up, my feet no longer touching the ground. People trapped against the wall screamed in terror. I saw her blue coat through a mass of legs. She seemed to be lying on something. My feet trod on somebody, then briefly touched the ground before I was pushed forward, landing on top of her. Her head turned. She looked at me, wild-eyed, terror-stricken.

'It's okay,' I wheezed, 'I've come to help.'

I don't know if she heard or understood. I was just another man crushing her. I couldn't save her or myself or anyone. When I tried to shield her head she pushed me off like an attacker. I wanted to explain, but the breath was knocked from my body.

Then my legs found space in the current of people. I felt myself being lifted off her. The police had managed to open the exit gates and bodies were suddenly sluiced into the ground. I put my arms around her, half-lifting and half-dragging her. She had been lying on a collapsed crowd barrier, in which her shoe was entangled. The wire cut into her trapped foot. I pushed against the crowd, making enough space to free her foot, then tried to help her up but she seemed unable to walk. We were carried inside the ground by the crowd's momentum, before people broke away, rushing in different directions. I found a wall and helped her hunch down against it, trying to offer comfort with my arm around her as she cried. She looked up suddenly, pushing me off.

'Just leave me alone! Leave me!'

She almost spat out the words. I had backed away, finding that my own legs could barely support me. I sat against the opposite wall, watching her cry. The passageway was quiet except for more latecomers wandering in, delighted they didn't have to pay. Parents were leaving, holding sobbing children. Policemen argued with officials. I walked out into the alleyway, wondering how many would have died if the gates hadn't been opened in time. Few clues were left to suggest that panic, except for some lost scarves and, here and there, the odd shoe. I found hers beside the barrier, with its heel broken, carried it back inside and waited until she looked up before offering it to her. She wiped her eyes with a sleeve and tried to smile.

'Stupid bloody match. Who's playing anyway?'

'Italy. The World Champions. Your heel is broken.'

'Only for you my neck would be too. Thanks.'

'That's all right.'

And everything was, too that night, like magic. Rossi scored first with Italy winning two-nil, a fourteen-to-one double off a ten-pound bet. We laughed all the way down Phibsborough Road to the Broadstone. At twenty Miriam Darcy was two years younger than me, just finishing her training as a social worker and ready to change the whole world. She leaned on my shoulder, limping slightly and carrying both shoes in her hand. Double-deckers pulled into the bus depot, with its statue of the Virgin high up on the wall. The King's Inn rose to our left and blocks of Corporation flats to our right. Glass was smashed on the corner where winos had occupied a bench. I gave Miriam a piggyback over it, laughing as she slapped me like a horse when I stalled and threatened to throw her off.

We reached Great Western Way, with its boxing club and row of ancient trees, then the Black Church, around which Miriam's mother was afraid as a child to run three times in case the devil appeared. Every step had seemed magical as I bore her into the old L-shaped street where she lived with her mother.

The barely averted catastrophe outside Dalymount had become an adventure by the time I set her down on the steps to her house. Through the railings below Mrs Darcy appeared from the basement kitchen to ask what all the commotion was about. She was a small, rather hoarse woman with a cackling laugh to whom Miriam introduced me as her rescuer. Three hours later both were still teasing me, coining outlandish descriptions of my forcing a white steed down Connacht Street to sweep Miriam to safety. Their shrieks of laughter increased when Mrs Darcy had finally noticed Miriam's underwear drying on a clotheshorse in the corner. She claimed that it was her own, purchased by one of her many toyboys who serenaded the house at night and with whom she would elope if she hadn't the noose of a spinster daughter around her neck.

I had felt at ease with myself that night, which is to say that I felt myself become somebody different from anyone I'd ever been before. No longer simply Cormac's brother in Dublin or the Hen Boy in Navan. It was only six weeks since I had walked out into the blackness of the Dublin Road, fleeing the contaminating guilt in Lisa Hanlon's mother's eyes. But in Miriam's kitchen the past couldn't touch me. The way we met was so sudden, so out of character that I had slipped free, laughing as a mortified Miriam gathered up her knickers and bras while Mrs Darcy harangued her for not having brought home some handsome Italian footballer with hand-made shoes and a fat leather wallet.

'Still, it could be worse,' Mrs Darcy joked. 'You could be

like the poor Dublin girl who handed in a five-thousand-lire note at the bank, received back seventy-five pence in exchange and moaned, "I wouldn't mind, only I gave him breakfast as well".'

Miriam had walked me to the corner where there was a burnt-out pub with its roof caved in, beside a shuttered garage and a lock-up for sale. Across the road stood a line of Victorian tenements. A taxi pulled out from the all-night petrol station on Constitution Hill. A pub clock was stopped at twenty-to-six. There is no detail I cannot recall from that first night.

'Your father, is he dead?' I asked.

'He got an Irish divorce – went out for a pint of milk four years ago and never came back. He's living in Galway with some girl half his age and quarter his intelligence. They met at Knock shrine, he spent half his life praying at Knock. We'd to leave Stillorgan because he wasn't the best at remembering to send money for the mortgage. I like it better renting here than the Southside. Bus drivers halt between stops for you and nobody would dream of paying the right fare. Mum's back where she belongs and we're happy.'

'I'm sorry.'

'Don't be. At least I'll know what to expect. Men always walk away when there's trouble.'

Miriam's body leaned into me, forcing me back against the spiked railings. Her face was so close, eyes mischievous and then serious.

'Are you always this slow?'

Her mouth opened, the freshness of her tongue. Putting her arms around me, drawing me closer into the possibility of being a new person in a new world. Every sensation was filled with newness. My new girlfriend, my soon-to-be wife, my future widow, the woman to whom I wanted to give so much. The woman I had so abysmally failed.

The memories were becoming too painful now as I stood in that deserted passageway in Dalymount. They were also confused because it wasn't Miriam's features I saw when I closed my eyes. The skin was black and foreign, but the same sense of anticipation filled me as Ebun's almost mocking tone returned. *Call again, Irishman.* The last thing I needed was complications. I had to stay focused and forget Ebun and Miriam and every memory tormenting me. The meagre crowd roared as Bohs forced a corner. I took my place on the terrace to watch the fullback prepare to take it. The crowbar felt heavy inside my jacket. Four o'clock. I had another two hours to kill before burgling my father's house in Cremore. The fullback swung the corner in. Five million wouldn't buy him and I was one of them.

———■■———

Cremore. There had always seemed to be something tranquil and cool even about the name. A tiny nest of 1930s houses dropped onto the slope of a Dublin hillside from an old English chocolate box. Sturdy trees lining grass verges, casting a soft mesh of shadows at night. The city might have sprawled out to encircle this enclave but Cremore maintained its poise and the sense of an ordered world.

At least, that was how it seemed to me just before my fourteenth birthday when my father quickly moved us here from Navan. A fresh start where old wounds and scores were meant to remain, if not forgotten, then at least unspoken. On the day we arrived I had stared out into the garden, confused by the absence of a shed to sleep in, until he beckoned me upstairs and silently pointed to the box-room. It took months to acclimatize to the feel of a house, to footsteps on the stairs and being able to use a toilet at will. Even the air seemed different, fresher than in Navan. My father had told people that he moved to give Phyllis extra space for Sarah-Jane. But it was more complex than just the baby. Because of the bush-fire of rumours circulating around Navan about Cormac and Pete Clancy, Barney Clancy had bluntly advised my father to move if he wished not only to retain their suddenly strained friendship but also his job.

I now realize that in Cremore my father would have felt detached from the pressures of his work. He could attend the feeding frenzy of County Council meetings where his task-force's plan for controlled development was so perpetually hacked away by private members' section four re-zoning motions – slipped in under the pre-emptive heading of 'Matters arising' – that the councillors rarely reached the official opening item on their agenda. Afterwards he could simply close his folder of unsought advice and return to Dublin where neighbours didn't know his business or call at the house so-liciting favours.

Studying for my Leaving Cert. in the box-room I would hear the putt-putt of his clapped-out Fiat and watch him emerge from the car, holding an emptied flask of tea in one hand and a newspaper that some councillor had discarded in the other. There was always a streak of meanness within him, but by the time we reached Cremore it had become a disease.

It was quarter-past-six now as I stood under the old trees to gaze up at a light behind the drawn curtains in the box-room window. It was possible that the house had been rented out since the robbery. But I suspected that Sarah-Jane had left the light on during one of her random visits, unaware that it would become more of an invitation to intruders than a deterrent.

My father's house was flanked by two other slightly larger detached homes, set back from the rest of the street and back-ing onto a new sliproad built two years after we moved from

Navan, when half his garden was seized by compulsory purchase order. He had taken it as the ultimate two-finger salute from the planning department in Dublin – perhaps egged on by their counterparts in the main Meath office who resented his section's autonomy – their joke at the hard-talking culchie's expense. 'You'll never guess where Brogan has moved to. Let's stick a sliproad right up his arse.'

With the money from the compulsory purchase he had installed aluminium single-glazed windows in the front but retained the original wooden frames at the back. His meanness finally caught up with him three weeks ago, but even had the windows not been half-rotten the intruder would have found some other way in. The *Irish Times* website report of the break-in stated that he had just returned by bus from the three warrens of bedsits that Pete Clancy inherited from his father – also inheriting my father's services as poorly paid *gauleiter* and rent collector in the process. The thief, if he was one, had him well sussed – the grey-haired pensioner with rent stuffed into his darned socks. But he could have mugged him at the bus stop or in the driveway. Nothing about his house suggested there was wealth worth bothering about inside.

I stepped back beneath the trees until a car passed, then slipped into the driveway. Teatime on Sunday was still a mournful hour when nobody seemed to move about in Dublin. The adjacent houses had been done up in recent years, but my father's home looked unchanged. Potatoes grew wild – sheltered by a tall hedge in the front garden – with no one left to harvest them. His unused banger seemed part of the vegetation too, with Russian vine tangling itself across the bonnet. I heard a front door open nearby and pressed myself into the tangle of vines. Unfamiliar voices passed down the adjoining driveway on the far side of the wall. Car doors slammed, an engine started and they were gone.

I rang the bell twice, stepping back each time to hide. Nobody answered and not even a curtain twitched, confirming my suspicions about the box-room light. The previous owner had erected a garage door purely for show, with no actual structure behind the gable. I climbed onto the car roof to scale the façade and dropped down into an overgrown side passage littered with planks and cement blocks. My father, the make-shift plumber and electrician, hoarding anything that might one day be useful. This corner of the garden was always his treasure chest, a scene of endless searches to avoid the expense of a visit to the local hardware shop.

The rest of the back garden was laid out in vegetable plots, broken by two plum trees and bordered by a scraggle of rhubarb plants. A hedge grew against the back wall to obscure the sliproad. A crude swing had been constructed from an old tyre attached to a branch. The rear of the house was in dark-ness, but crowbar marks were still visible where the first intruder had forced the downstairs window. Somebody had tried to patch up the scarred wood, then simply nailed the frame back into place. The second intruders, on the day of his funeral, had simply smashed the glass in the front door and reached in to turn the snib.

From beyond the wall a squeal of brakes came as traffic lights changed. A motorbike halted, its rider revving impatiently as he waited for the green light. I waited too, then – under cover of the noise of cars pulling away – used the crowbar from my pocket to smash the small pane of glass in the back door. Years ago my father had got me to place a discreet hook directly beneath the windowsill to hold a Chubb key. Amazingly it still hung there, though I cut my palm on the broken glass while groping around for it. I unlocked the back door, drip-ping blood on the step. The cut wasn't deep, but bled heavily until I tied a dishcloth around my palm to stem it.

I entered the hallway, then stopped. I had never believed in ghosts, but seeing the back of his armchair through the open sitting-room doorway startled me. With every step towards the chair I gripped the crowbar tighter. It was so high that from behind you could never tell if anyone was sitting there. Resting my hands on the clammy leather, I swung it round to confront emptiness. I felt foolish and disappointed as if half-wanting his ghost to be waiting for our showdown now when it was too late.

The dining-room carpet was scorched where the second intruder or intruders had tried to light a fire, but the bookcases had been fixed back. The wall was lined with framed photos. Caddying for Barney Clancy at a pro-am in Portmarnock with Sevvy Ballesteros before the Irish Open. Meeting four different Taoiseigh at sod-turnings and ribbon-cuttings in Meath. The most recent photo looked bizarre. Cut out from the *Meath Chronicle*, it captured him among a crowd of onlookers as Pete Clancy showed Prince Charles around the Newgrange Neolithic burial chamber during a state visit. The Clancy political dynasty had been founded upon the legendary ruthlessness of Pete's grandfather as one of Michael Collins' most trusted assassins of British spies and sundry collaborators during the War of Independence. My father always toed the official Republican line, but had harboured a secret, irrational fetish for the British royal family. He even took a day off work in 1974 so that Phyllis and he could watch Princess Anne's wedding on television, spending the previous evening perched on the roof trying to adjust the aerial for better reception.

The way my father stood outside the tomb at Newgrange angered me. Relegated to wait among the spear-carriers and footsoldiers in a vain hope that Pete Clancy might steer the prince towards him for a handshake. But Clancy would have had bigger fish to fry than his father's retired bagman whose silence could always be relied upon. After the incident with Cormac their relationship was always strained anyway, even if neither would have ever mentioned the rumours about why we had to leave Navan.

I took the photo off the wall, feeling ashamed for him. In his heyday he would have never stood in line like a dog. Barney Clancy would not have allowed him to either, although, there again, it was impossible to imagine Barney having the political dexterity or will to parade an English prince around Meath.

I went upstairs, remembering the light in the box-room. What if someone was there, having ignored the bell and then, after hearing glass being smashed, had already phoned the police? The creak on the stairwell had never been fixed. I listened outside my old bedroom, then – half-expecting the room to look the same – gripped the handle and pushed the door open, ready to flee if someone shouted.

The bedroom was empty. Posters of boy bands and cartoon characters from *South Park* lined the walls. The single bed was made-up, beside a small desk littered with schoolbooks and CDs. Sarah-Jane's tempestuous relationship with a bass guitarist eighteen years too old for her was already on the rocks before I vanished. At sixteen she had shacked up with him so as to be on hand to cater to his most wanton male needs – which, according to Miriam, probably consisted of rubbing *Grecian 2000* hair-dye into the greying locks encircling his bald patch. The last time I saw her was at a strained party to celebrate both her eighteenth birthday and her baby's christening, when Phyllis had fumed over her asking me, instead of Cormac, to act as godfather. There again Sarah-Jane was such a mirror image of Phyllis that mother and daughter had been screaming at each other since she could walk. It must have taken my father's death to persuade her to move back home, safe in the knowledge that Phyllis was unlikely ever to sleep under this roof again. Perhaps I was being unfair. Phyllis and her might have patched their differences up years ago. She had been no dream daughter in her youth, but at least Sarah-Jane never ran away. I just knew that the house was now occupied and I had to be quick.

The pole for pulling down the Stira attic stairs was missing. I found it in the master bedroom where Phyllis and my father had slept. The old dressing table that had belonged to my mother in Navan still stood in the bay window. I glanced into the back bedroom where my sister's clothes hung in the opened wardrobe and were haphazardly draped over a chair. Her taste in fashion had improved, though probably not her taste in men.

The folding stairs descended with a tug of the pole, allowing me to peer up into the dark attic. Had it been worth risking everything over a hunch? I still didn't know if I had returned out of vengeance or love. Without the Internet I would have lost touch. For years I'd avoided thinking about Ireland but over the previous six months had found myself obsessively clicking onto websites for Irish newspapers, hoping maybe for a fluke picture of Conor among a group of secondary-student debaters or at the Young Scientist Awards. One visit to a website was enough to reveal how the façade of my father's generation had fallen asunder – politicians, planners and bankers disgraced. Not just one gilded circle of high-up 'untouchables' exposed, but multiplying ripples spreading out from the top to expose how a whole nation had been on the fiddle. Villages where everyone knew each other, yet the local bank had more bogus non-resident accounts under fake names to avoid tax than ordinary accounts.

I had been initiated into the nudge and wink language of that shadow world while playing on the floor of my father's outhouse, listening to men swap scams in the doorway. But it didn't seem like cheating back then. It was part of a male world of cigarettes and quiet words in ears, a game of hide-and-seek against anonymous officialdom. It had seemed a litmus test of manhood, like evading Garda checkpoints when driving home after-hours from the pub after having consumed eight or nine pints.

Every night when I had logged on, after finishing work in the bar in Oporto, the names of disgraced businessmen tumbled off the website, from the former Taoiseach down. I kept searching for Barney Clancy, wanting to see him shamed in his grave. But in death, as in life, he seemed the ultimate Teflon man. Then three weeks ago the name Eamonn Brogan caught my eye among the small headlines on *The Irish Times* site.

Although post-mortem results are still awaited, Mr Brogan, a retired planning officer with Meath County Council, is reported to have suffered a heart attack, while tied up with his wife, Phyllis, by a raider who spent several hours ransacking their home in Cremore, off the Old Finglas Road in North Dublin. Mrs Brogan, who had just been discharged from hospital where she underwent an intensive course of chemotherapy, is said to be in a deeply distressed condition and this morning was back in hospital being treated for shock. Mr Brogan was due to be called before the planning Tribunal later this month in connection with decisions made by Meath politicians. He is survived by a daughter, Sarah-Jane, and several grandchildren . . .

I had sat up in Oporto until dawn, logging onto any other Irish site that might carry details, while in the background the television screened episode after episode of late-night Brazilian soap operas. The *Irish Independent* report added: *According to police Mrs Brogan said that the raider remained silent until her husband's seizure. He went to Mr Brogan's assistance but took fright and fled after Mr Brogan cried 'quick' when he experienced difficulties in untying the knots. Mrs Brogan managed to untie herself several hours later but her husband was pronounced dead at the scene.*

Reading the reports I had experienced a cocktail of emotions. Firstly a giddy sense of release that it was finally over, the father I had loved and hated in equal measure was dead. Then shame at feeling such relief. This was replaced by guilt for having not been here for him or Miriam or Conor. Then, perhaps because I couldn't handle such guilt, I was overcome with fury at the man who killed the father whose shoulder I had once slept on in a bedroom of rose-patterned wallpaper. The father whom Cormac and I had betrayed and the only person who may have guessed — but would have still kept — my secret.

I ascended into the attic now where it was safe to switch on a light. The raider had been unusually methodical in even looting up here, instead of employing the usual smash-and-grab techniques of petty thieves out for quick cash or jewellery. The rusty filing cabinets from Navan had been forced open and cardboard suitcases smashed apart — although somebody had recently tidied away mounds of yellowing paper into plastic sacks in a half-hearted attempt to restore some order.

It was the website account of the second raid on the day of his funeral that had finally convinced me to come home. This was more a short colour piece than a news report, noting that it was the eighth occasion in as many months when a house was robbed in Dublin while someone was being buried. Relatives were increasingly circumspect about the location of a deceased person's home when placing death notices in the papers. *The Brogan family can be seen as a tragic microcosm of Dublin's growing violence*; the article concluded, *having endured this latest robbery during the funeral, the initial break-in that led to Mr Brogan's death and a recent assault on his teenage grandson,*

Conor, who – some weeks ago – became another statistic in the ever increasing random street attacks on young Dublin males.

Perhaps my suspicions were paranoia. The second break-in might be the work of ordinary robbers attracted by the lack of obvious security in the house. The attack on Conor, which made my blood turn cold, might be as random as the paper suggested. But something inside me refused to believe that these events were unrelated. Perhaps I was inventing the connection, seeking a justification to come home. But I was the only family member who knew something of my father's dealings and I could not take the risk of my family being in danger. With the ongoing tribunals several businessmen once close to Barney Clancy might want documents they suspected could be here – destroyed. It was impossible to know if the raider had found the papers he sought among the jumble of Council minutes and planning applications.

Possibly the only way to truly neutralize the past would have been to torch the whole house, which is what the fire in the dining-room on the day of the funeral seemed intended to do. But it never spread, as if the intruder who started it – or a companion who disagreed with his course of action – had stamped it out. This suggested that he wasn't seeking to destroy evidence but to find something he felt was his by right. Had my father ever thrown anything out, I wondered. There were documents here going back thirty years, memos that Barney Clancy would surely have wished destroyed. But Clancy had died as suddenly – if more pleasurably – as my father, suffering a heart attack in the bath while on a Spanish junket, with stringently denied rumours that an escort agency had supplied a lady to help create a foam from his bubble-bath.

I knelt down to examine the paper value of a life. Bizarrely some of my school copybooks were among the stack of papers. I had never kept them, but it made no sense that he had.

There was a photograph of me with him, aged five, in luridly over-exposed colour. I should have felt touched that he had stored up such mementos but I felt angry. Why did he always keep every emotion hidden? How could a man with mastery of the most complex terminology for drainage schemes and housing densities lack the simplest vocabulary for dealing with his son?

Despite his dexterity with plans, my father always stood out in Navan for lacking even elementary woodwork skills. By the age of nine I knew more about timber than he ever would, simply by flitting between neighbours' sheds until such freedom was curtailed.

Two years after we moved to Cremore my father had summoned me to the attic, grudgingly admitting defeat in his attempts to construct a concealed keep-safe – allegedly for Phyllis's jewellery – inside one of the rafters. Deliberately ignoring his botched attempt I had hollowed out a new section of rafter, planing the wood until it was wafer-thin, then hinged it back so delicately that nobody could ever guess at the large cavity behind it. I had taken my time, never consulting him as I buried tiny screws in the wood, using my limited skill as a weapon of contempt.

The rafters were cobwebbed now, encrusted with fine woodwormy dust. I tapped repeatedly until a hollow sound betrayed where the hinge was. Two memorial cards fluttered down as I opened it, one for Cormac and one for myself. I picked them up to study the photographs of two strangers, two ghosts, two selves.

There was no money or jewellery inside, but Joey Kerwin's 1950s IRA revolver was suspended from two bent nails along with some bullets in an old sock. My final memory of my father at work in the outhouse was of a drunken Joey Kerwin arriving and, with great ceremony, presenting my father with a box for Barney Clancy to pass on to 'the brave lads up the North'. The Arms Trial would have just ended with Charles Haughey and a second Government minister cleared of supplying guns to nationalists under siege in Northern Ireland. I remembered being sent out to play when Barney Clancy arrived and his guffaws through the locked door as he said, 'Jesus, let's give the gun to the Brits – it will blow the hand off whatever poor bastard first uses it. You never showed me this, Eamonn, you understand. I rely on you never to show me things that it's not in my interest to see. Get rid of it.'

Being a hoarder even then my father obviously never did. But otherwise he was a man to follow instructions. I wondered if he ever properly discussed bills with Barney Clancy or where he solicited the donations from to pay them. Not that Clancy wasn't aware of who contributed what, down to the final penny, but if it came to the blame game his hands would have been untainted. Surely it was a form of sadomasochism for a miser to wade through the wastage in those receipts for unfinished bottles of champagne, rounds of rare brandies costing more than the meal, the endless unPalladianization of Clancy's Palladian-style mansion on the Dublin Road. Perhaps my father – to whom extravagance was a twice-yearly holiday to the same cheap hotel on Jersey with Phyllis – found a fetishistic thrill in handling Clancy's bills, his alter ego savouring the flamboyance of dispensing money like a Monopoly player. My father the patsy, who had turned us all into patsies too.

I pocketed the revolver and bullets, then picked up the envelope that had tumbled down with the masscards. There were three pages inside it – the first torn from a child's copybook. It contained a succession of sixteen-digit codes with dates and initials in brackets. Some had Ltd after them, like SR for Shyroyal, suggesting more than one offshore company.

Some bore my initials and others Sarah-Jane's. The only numbers not crossed off were the last two in Cormac's initials, though even these initials had been crossed off and then rewritten, as if my father was utterly unsure of what to do. The ink changed from blue to black halfway down and his writing changed too, growing more cramped and spidery in the years that separated the first and last entry.

Of the four account numbers with Cormac's initials, the first two were underlined, with huge, almost frantic, question marks beside them. Our revenge and perhaps our signing of his eventual death warrant. Cormac had emptied the first account the week before he committed suicide. 'It was simple,' Cormac had told me. 'I walked in, showed my new passport. The cashier was cute, with lovely hands. I was just amazed the poor boy didn't get wanker's cramp having to count out fifteen thousand pounds in cash.'

Perhaps my father could have explained the loss of that account to Clancy, who knew of Cormac's ways. But the closure of the second one, six weeks after my presumed death, must have haunted him. How could he have asked the police to investigate the robbery of money that didn't legally exist and had been surreptitiously held in the names of family members who didn't even know the bank accounts existed? Possibly he had covered up the loss from Clancy's slush fund for years, with Barney Clancy content – once the bills were being paid – not to ask too many questions that might incriminate him. But if my suspicions were correct then the day of reckoning had finally arrived three weeks ago, with tribunals closing in and Pete Clancy desperate to destroy any evidence that could be used against his family.

Our pilfering of that money perhaps explained the cautionary presence of two forms stapled to the list of accounts. The address on the notepaper was for the same bank I had visited in Jersey. Headed *Instructions Mandate* and each bearing one of the remaining account numbers, they declared that '*transactions may be only enacted by the account holder or the other named nominee entitled to draw on the account, Mr Eamonn Brogan, in person and when bearing possession of this mandate*'.

A second envelope was Sellotaped to the top of the keep-safe. I opened it. It contained the thirty-year-old articles and memorandum of association of Shyroyal Ltd, with a registered address on the Cayman Islands and the names of four solicitors listed as proxy shareholders. The only name I recognized was my father as company secretary.

The front door must have been opened so quietly below me that the landing light was switched on and footsteps had come halfway up the stairs before I realized it. A male voice called as the footsteps reached the stairwell and whoever it was descended again. There was no way to escape from the attic in time. Two voices talked in the hall downstairs. If they saw the broken kitchen window I was done for. I flicked the attic light off and pulled the Stira folding stairs up towards me, leaving the trapdoor slightly ajar. It certainly wasn't Sarah-Jane's voice that I was hearing and it wasn't her daughter's either.

I felt trapped as I heard footsteps ascend the stairs again, two male voices kept low like they were intruders themselves. Clancy had come looking for these papers twice already, so why not a third time? The first teenager had blonde hair with a dyed white streak. He wore white jeans with spotless white sneakers and carried several CDs under his arm. The second youth was taller and slightly older-looking, with close-cropped hair and an attempt at a goatee beard that was still a year away from being anything other than downy stubble. The nervous way they stood on the landing made me suspicious. Maybe my e-mail had panicked Pete Clancy into torching the house properly this time. I took a step back so that if they looked up they would see nothing through the gap in the trapdoor.

'Check the front bedroom, just in case.'

I couldn't see which of them spoke, just heard the creak of a bedroom door opening. Another light was switched on then quickly turned off again.

'I told you, Charles, she'd be visiting the hospital.'

Suddenly the landing light was extinguished. There was total darkness until the blonde lad pushed open the box-room door and came into view, framed by the light coming from inside. He stood facing his older companion, watching him approach. They stood in silence, face to face, inches apart. I couldn't see the taller boy's face, but the blonde lad stared into his eyes almost apprehensively. Then he let the CDs slip with a soft clatter and their arms were around each other, the taller boy tugging roughly at the buttons on the white jeans. He had his hand inside the younger boy's briefs now, pushing them both towards the bed. He seemed fully in command, allowing the blonde youth to fall back onto the quilt as he tugged the white jeans down to where they became trapped around the boy's ankles. They had almost disappeared from the tiny slat of light through which I was watching.

'When the cat's away the mouse will play, Conor, eh?' The older youth who spoke glanced around. 'God, the space. Makes a change from the lane behind the Oliver Twist.'

'Who says we won't be slumming it again there tomorrow night,' Conor replied as his companion laughed and kicked the door shut. There was a creak of bedsprings, a muffled name I could not hear, then sounds that were no longer mere words.

I was shaking so much I had to kneel down, not caring what noise I made. There was a slight silence below as if they had heard a sound. Then rock music from my son's bedroom drowned out everything else. What sort of father didn't recognise his own son, even with dyed hair and after the space of a decade? Conor, whom I had carried on my shoulders across the dunes at Bull Island. Conor, who had been obsessed by the Wombles, who used to stagger into the bed, still half-asleep, looking for a cuddle if he woke from bad dreams. My son, who at least had no scars from his recent attack but was now being sucked off or fucked or God knows what else by God knows who in my old bedroom beneath my feet. The boy called Charles was definitely older, a corrupting bastard taking advantage of him.

I was on the verge of lowering the Stira stairs to kick open the box-room door when I stopped. I was dead, or at least had been to Conor, for more than half his life. I had long relinquished the right to lecture him or anyone. The first song ended on the CD. In the brief silence I heard him moan in pleasure. There was excitement in his voice, a zest at being alive. I sat back against an old filing cabinet, unable to stop trembling, recalling all my fantasies about how I might one day meet Conor again. Those clothes in the back bedroom belonged to Miriam and not Sarah-Jane. But what was my family doing living here, in danger from something they knew nothing about?

Conor laughed below me, begging the youth not to tickle. Childish giggles rose and the sound of a mock tussle, with not even the music drowning out their pleasure. Had they the slightest clue about risks and precautions? I couldn't bear to listen to this, yet seemed unable to move. So close at last to my own flesh and blood. Conor's laughter stopped, replaced by a new sound, an intake of breath like somebody who wasn't quite sure if they liked or were ready for what was now happening. Then I could only hear music again, drowning out his pleasure or pain or protests at what might be going on.

I lowered the ladder and stood outside the box-room door, trying to fathom what was happening in there. There seemed an element of nightmare here, of role reversal, with my father's ghost staring out through my eyes. My hand paused, inches from the door. What would I see if I opened it? Would I handle the situation better than my father had once done, or despite the distance that I'd tried to put between Navan and myself would I be equally out of my depth? Would Conor even recognize me, with receding dyed hair and lacking the thick black beard that was so distinctive in the masscard?

I kicked the door suddenly, with such force that the hinges shook. The music stopped inside. There was silence, then a petrified voice – Charles's – tentatively called, 'Hello?' I could visualize them sitting bolt upright on the bed, as terrified to open the door as I was terrified that they would do so. But I had simply wanted to make them stop and ensure that Conor wasn't hurt.

Charles's voice came again, slightly bolder now. I turned to run down the stairs, knowing I had left the folding stairs there and that my fleeing footsteps would give them the courage to emerge. They had not been inside the kitchen, the back door was still unlocked. I raced across the garden and lunged at the wall, scratching my hands on the hedge as I struggled over. Cars were stopped at the traffic lights. Faces turned as I landed on the grass verge. I thought the drivers might get out and surround me until the police came. Instead the lights turned green and they drove quickly on.

Conor and his friend would not venture past the open back door, too scared that they had been tumbled. The list of account numbers and the Shyroyal documents were in my pocket, but the two masscards still lay on the attic floor.

If Conor had cleaned the place up he would know they had not been there before. I could imagine him climbing the Stira stairs with Charles behind him, finding the hinge hanging open in the rafter and turning over the masscards in his hand like pieces of a puzzle he could not even begin to fathom.

———◆———

Everything changed in Navan on the night Phyllis miscarried. Not that I understood what was happening, but the screams from her bedroom woke me. I was eleven years of age, watching through the chicken wire as lights came on in the house and then in neighbouring homes when her cries continued. Back doors opened and people quietly talked in gardens. More lights were turned on downstairs, then went out as her sobs subsided and my father's car started before fading from earshot.

A vindictive pleasure initially outweighed my fear. There was nobody I hated more than Phyllis, nobody I wished to hear suffer as much. But this new silence was more frightening than her crying itself as one by one lights were extinguished along the terrace of houses. I had no idea where the car had gone. My father could be dead or enacting an elaborate trick to punish me. I just knew that I was too scared to venture alone up to that forbidden house. I no longer thought of it as home. The child who once slept there wasn't me. He had been somebody quite different, not branded with my unspecified sin. The previous couple of years had conditioned me to life in the outhouse, making me uneasy in company other than my own. Its walls felt womb-like as I lay on the mattress at night, listening to cats on the roof and watching moonlight filter through the chicken wire that my father blocked up for warmth in winter. Although still allowed to eat my dinner in the kitchen, I rarely saw into other rooms in the house. But often in dreams I found myself trapped upstairs, knowing I no longer belonged there and that my father would punish me if he found out.

Therefore when the back door opened slowly by itself, half an hour after my father's car had gone, I stepped back from the chicken wire, terrified of what might emerge. The house remained in darkness. I could barely distinguish the small shape that seemed to hover on the step. Only when he moved into the moonlight did I recognize Cormac in his pyjamas. He halted at the outhouse, not bothering to knock like he knew that I had been watching all along. When I opened the door we stared at each other. It felt strange to be together without lads jostling around us in the schoolyard or Phyllis hovering to make sure we never spoke.

'There was blood everywhere,' Cormac stated, matter-of-factly. 'Mammy kept crying, "My baby". I think she's lost it.'

I knew that Phyllis was pregnant and the baby lived inside her, but I didn't know what he meant or how Cormac understood it.

'Where are they gone?'

'The hospital in Drogheda. They told me to go into Hanlons but I told Mrs Hanlon I wanted to be down here with you.'

Cormac walked into the outhouse. He had come down here on previous occasions to summon me. But this felt different, like he was an inscrutable visitor and I was his host. He examined the mattress, the makeshift locker where I kept my clothes, the meagre pile of torn comics that my father sometimes rescued from the bin for me.

'Are you ever afraid on your own out here?'

'Would you be?'

'I'm afraid of nothing,' Cormac retorted.

'Except Mr Kenny. Everybody's afraid of him.'

'I'm the one who broke his canes.'

My whole class was still discussing how some boy had slipped back into school one lunchtime to leave two of Mr Kenny's canes smashed on his desk.

'You did not,' I jeered. 'I bet that was some boy from sixth class.'

'A big boy would be seen.' Cormac quietly sat on the mattress. 'Nobody sees me.'

He reached into his pyjama pocket to take out a coin. I watched him roll it in and out between his fingers so that it kept disappearing from view. He closed his fingers tight over the coin and when he opened his palm out again the coin had vanished and a tiny lead weight lay in its place. He flicked it across for me to catch. The centre was hollowed out so that Mr Kenny could screw it onto the tip of his cane and create deeper welts when he savagely beat pupils. The lead weight felt like it was going to burn my palm. I tossed it back, scared and awed.

'Your da got frightened when Mammy kept screaming. He was crying his eyes out too when Mrs Hanlon came in.'

'I was scared too,' I said. 'I hated the screaming.'

'Do you hate them?'

I didn't answer.

'It's okay, I won't squeal,' he said.

'I won't squeal on you at school either.'

'Nobody would believe you. That's why I can do anything to anyone who hurts you.'

Various school incidents came back to me, for which boys claimed to be incorrectly beaten. A fountain pen stolen from the staff room and located in Slick McGuirk's pocket. It took all of Barney Clancy's influence to prevent his expulsion. P. J. Egan squealing like a slaughterhouse pig when beaten after the stink in his classroom was traced to a ham sandwich in his bag with human excrement inside it. Only now did I realize that the scandals always involved boys who had bullied me.

Cormac lay back on the mattress. 'I made your father get me a magic set for my birthday,' he said. 'If you like I'll show you some tricks. Lie down beside me.'

The last person I had snuggled into was my father a lifetime before. Cormac's skin felt warm and comforting through his pyjamas; he kept doing tricks with his hands, and I felt the excitement of knowing that nobody could catch us laughing together. I don't remember falling asleep, just waking to find my father watching from the doorway. Cormac woke, looking far younger than during the night. He seemed lost and bewildered.

'Brendan minded me,' he whimpered. 'I got lonely in Hanlon's house. Where's Mammy, Daddy?'

———⊶⊷———

How did Cormac know more about everything than me? Nothing in his demeanour – as he wandered vacantly through school or studiously sat over homework in the kitchen – hinted at how his antennae were picking up every nuance and coded whisper in adult speech. Nothing betrayed the gift for perfect mimicry either, which he revealed on secret night-time visits to the outhouse over the months following my twelfth birthday. I never knew when he would come or often if I wished him to. He was still the interloper who stole my life but I couldn't hate him. Although I had no reason to do so, I trusted him like nobody else – even Mr Casey, whose propensity to rock the boat frightened me.

Cormac, on the other hand, understood the rules. In

Phyllis's company we stuck to our castes. Even in school we ignored each other. Then twice a week I'd watch him climb out the bathroom window, frightened that he might not have the agility to overcome the obstacle course of flitting from the windowsill onto a waste pipe and leaping fleet-footed onto Casey's kitchen roof before shinning to the ground.

He brought me sweets stolen from shops and my favourite comics if feeling especially daring or generous. Not that I kept anything in the outhouse, in case my father found them and accused me of theft. My stash was hidden in a hollow treetrunk in the lane, along with photos that were starting to attract and disturb me in ways I didn't understand. A girls' sports day in Dunboyne or an ad for bath-soap with a pencil sketch of a woman cloaked in bubbles. A treasure chest I never told Cormac about, consisting of pages from newspapers that I scoured bins for at night, sneaking through gardens, alert to every noise and footfall.

I was terrified my father would find us together, although Phyllis and he had become withdrawn inside their private grief. Neighbours were softer to her now as she lost the brittleness which had made her react to every casual remark like it was an accusation. Since the miscarriage her clothes and make-up had begun to blend with the conformity of other mothers. A vagueness pervaded the house, with only the quantity of fag ends in the ashtray hinting at how long she had been sitting in the one chair before my father came home some evenings to find no dinner on.

Her manner towards me had changed in so far that her previous frequent aggression was gone. Now I seemed little more than a shadow, an unobtrusive lodger to be briefly endured when necessary. But this would change if I was found contaminating Cormac in the outhouse. That was how I felt about myself, like I was a virus that could endanger him. Yet

I lived for the thrill of his visits, longing for his bare feet to leave a trail of dew across the outhouse floor that would have dried by the time he crept back up to his room.

'Lisa Hanlon fancies you,' he whispered one night, as we lay curled into each other for warmth. 'She wouldn't be long whipping her knickers off.'

Older boys in school sometimes talked like that, trying to make their voices sound tough. But Cormac's whisper was matter-of-fact, filled with certainty. It excited my body in the new troubling way that I tried to hide from him.

'I bet you'd like her to kiss you,' he added.

'Stop it, Cormac.'

'Girls don't have willies, you know. They have slots which you put your willie in, and if you're not good enough there's a bone inside they can bring down like a guillotine to chop it off.'

'They have not.'

'They do. That's where sausages come from.'

'Fibber.'

'Not. How come yours was a cocktail and now it's a hotdog?'

'Don't touch it, Cormac. It's wrong.'

'Why is it wrong? If it's nice it can't be wrong.'

'It just is,' I hissed. 'You're too young to understand. Now leave me alone.'

But I didn't want him to leave me alone and Cormac knew that like he knew everything. He giggled in my ear, singing 'You ain't nothing but a hotdog' in a mock Elvis voice. 'Do you know what happens after you put it in them?'

'What?'

'Talcum powder comes out, and your legs go all queer.'

'How do you know?'

'I just do,' he whispered. 'When you get Lisa Hanlon alone make her rub it like this for you.'

Something was moving in the lane, a cat or a marauding fox. Or perhaps it was a plastic bag blown about, brushing against the wall, upsetting loose twigs. A bird whose name I didn't know called twice in the night air. A distant truck changed gear on the bend of Flower Hill. I thought of the time I glimpsed my father through the curtains. I wanted to tell Cormac how you could kneel down too and lick it. Being older I should have been able to tell him something. But I never spoke and neither did he. His hot hand worked deftly as he hummed in my ear, with every outside sound and sensation magnified – the risk of someone finding us, the trouble that we would be in. I thought of Lisa Hanlon's fingers doing this for me, in her sitting-room with its blazing fire and cool milk at bedtime. How warm it would be in there and how white her skin would be. Something was stirring deep within me, in some port I had never even known was there, a voyaging ship with huge white sails. My legs twitched like a rabbit in a trap. My tightly closed eyes could see only whiteness, the white houses of an approaching white city, with my ship sailing ever closer, the sails bursting, surging towards Valparaiso.

—————◄█►—————

I didn't return to my hotel after fleeing Cremore. I had to keep walking, trying to control my thumping heart. Memories of Cormac and Conor jostled in my head. I felt cheated, like Cormac had robbed me of my son. Certainly Conor looked more like him at seventeen than he looked like me. I fingered the papers I had travelled halfway across Europe to retrieve, wondering if Conor knew anything of the danger he and his mother could be in.

I wondered how much money still gathered interest in

those last two accounts in Cormac's name. Until Cormac's revelations about my father I had never wanted to consider properly my father's relationship with Clancy. But during the week I spent in hiding on the Orkney Islands after the train crash I finally had to confront the reality of how his job with Meath County Council fitted into the dynamics of Clancy's operations.

After the controversy over the re-zoning of Josie's old terrace as the site for a shopping centre in the 1970s, Barney Clancy had been careful to place a visible distance between himself and all planning affairs in Meath. He no longer even sat on the County Council, declining to stand for re-election so he could focus on national politics. But this didn't mean that he could not control the bloc votes of a small but vital clique of councillors, who straddled party lines in a model of ecumenism.

I didn't know if my father was a stooge or a willing accomplice, but his role was vital. By drawing up a diligent, responsible plan to preclude residential or business development on certain areas earmarked for agricultural use, my father's taskforce kept down the price of those lands. But when eventually sold by the original owners at farmland prices their value could quadruple overnight if a private member's motion re-zoned them for development. Clancy was in the clear – taking no visible part in the re-zoning and indeed with the planning official known to be his right-hand man vehemently advising against it. This clique could even be reshuffled when residents passionately objected to a re-zoning, so that local councillors sided with their constituents while sufficient councillors from remote outlying realms of Meath – where they still dyed grass blue to hide the congestion of their private parts – were drafted in to steer the re-zoning through.

According to Cormac the not ungenerous developers who

acquired sudden fortunes always acted in a more gentlemanly fashion in Meath than at Dublin County Council meetings, where they were frequently known to lean over the public balcony to tick off lists of councillors whose pockets they had lined as they voted. Perhaps it was easier in Meath where – having drawn a blank in pursuit of other high-profile persuaders – most had simply learnt to deal with one senior figure.

Yet I never understood how my father squared this in his head as I often saw him working late into the night in Cremore to craft the most scrupulously comprehensive development plans which he must have known would be repeatedly sabotaged by Clancy's clique until rendered meaningless. He had always seemed conscientious in his job, hounding any builder who left work unfinished. But perhaps on the day when he let Clancy parachute him in on top of a reluctant County Council he had signed a mental indenture that Clancy made sure was never paid off. Finding the hidden list of account numbers in Cremore had strengthened my instincts that Pete Clancy was involved in my father's death. But it was still a long way short of proof that would stand up in a court of law. Not that going to the police was an option available to me.

I could anonymously mail everything I had found to Dublin Castle. Tribunal lawyers might not be able to prove where the money in the accounts came from, but – using a court order – they could trace to whom it was paid out. But I would hardly avenge my father's death by dragging his name through the courts as an accomplice. I could even panic other developers into suspecting that Miriam had leaked the information and might still hold more incriminating material.

I didn't want Conor to start his adult life under the shadow of having had a grandfather who defrauded the state. There again, as I walked towards town, I didn't know what I wanted.

Brendan Brogan would settle for a trade-off with Pete Clancy. Half the money from those remaining accounts to be somehow paid over to Conor in return for my silence. Plus the provision of a new passport which I desperately needed with only six weeks left before Cormac's old one went out of date. But there again Brendan Brogan was a cur, grateful for scraps and uneasy when dealing with his betters. Cormac would not have been so easily appeased, refusing to slink about in corners. For years I had longed for revenge upon Pete Clancy. An eye for an eye and a life for a life. I fingered the old revolver in my pocket. There might be only one way to ensure that Pete Clancy never sent thugs to trouble my family again. A perfect murder where the killer had ceased to exist years before.

I didn't know what Conor would want, because in truth, there was little I knew about him any more. The altered streetscapes around Baggot Street mocked me. I had once queued outside a kebab shop here with a hundred other hopefuls when two job vacancies were announced on the radio. The denim jackets and dressed-down casualness of those days had been replaced by a flaunting, yobbish affluence. The kerbside was choked with new cars. From a theme bar a chiming of mobile phones broke the once-hick sound of Andy Williams crooning *Moon River*.

What did I expect? Life to stand still because I had chosen to step outside it? I had cursed the semi-derelict streets here, back when half the city looked like it had endured an air bombardment during some forgotten war. Did I really want to return to the stink of flooded pub toilets in cellars that even rats had forsaken, with a ragged towel on a nail changed twice a year? Ireland had grown up and my son with it. I had no claim over either any more. An English stag party approached, blocking the footpath with fake wigs and plastic boobs tied to their chests. Their boorish voices rankled and made me stand my ground. One shouted as they broke ranks but the others pulled him on. Two Dublin girls sneaked a hostile glance at me, like I had deliberately provoked trouble. I walked on, feeling more alone than in any foreign city over the past decade.

The Georgian skyline of Mount Street looked the same at least. An event was on at the old Peppercanister church. Children milled about the steps, with a small crowd gathering around a police motorcyclist who examined the smashed window of a parked car. A waif-like girl climbed onto the railings behind the church, straining for a better view. From a distance she looked twelve years of age. Only when I reached the corner did I realize that she was a teenage prostitute with the dead eyes of a junkie.

I walked past her companions on the canal, feeling that my head would burst if I didn't speak to someone. I kept imagining Conor in some lane behind a pub called the Oliver Twist. The indifferent eyes of the girls scrutinized me, keepers and forgetters of secrets. I moved on, flinging the crowbar from my pocket into the canal. I knew where I was heading and how out of place I would look. But it was the only spot in Dublin where somebody had a name for me – even if a bogus one.

I had already passed Lekan, among the huddled bodies in makeshift sleeping-bags outside the Refugee Application Centre, when he called out. 'Cormac, my man? What you doing here?' He hunched up stiffly on the tarmac, watching me.

'I thought you'd appreciate some company.'

Lekan glanced along the queue as if company was the last thing he needed, then drew his feet up and made space for me to hunch down. Some asylum-seekers were sleeping and more talked in a babble of tongues, with some voices loud

enough to disturb others who called for quiet. Tension pervaded the gathering. Passers-by might see them as a single
entity, but many seemed to have little in common beyond
being washed up in Dublin.

'Is it always like this?' I asked.

'Normally we do not need to queue at night. But people
worry because the office refused to open on Friday. Officials
say they frightened by too many of us. They want more space.
They say they want to help, so they lock us out.' Lekan rubbed
his hands together for warmth. 'You found somewhere to
stay?'

'A hotel.' It was hard to get comfortable on the ground. I
glanced around. 'Do you feel you'll ever go back?'

'It may not be for me to choose. I could be put on a plane
to Nigeria any time.'

'Even if you can stay here, would you wish to go back one
day?'

Lekan shrugged his shoulders thoughtfully. 'In my heart,
yes, but in my mind I know it would be too dangerous. People
don't forgive. It's cold, Cormac, go to your hotel. You don't
belong here.'

'I don't belong out there either.' I glanced at the late-night
traffic on the street. 'Maybe I don't belong anywhere.'

'Neither do half these people,' Lekan replied. 'Why do you
think they want new lives?'

'What happens when your old life catches up with you?'

Lekan was silent for a moment. 'In Lagos I opened a shop
for furniture, tables, chairs. Not on Lagos Island, but on the
mainland near Shomolu, a district which two gangs controlled.
I stood up to them, myself and three others, patrolling our
street with sticks, refusing to pay bribes to them or the police.
Other traders, they saw what we could do. They say they will
join with us. One evening we meet in my shop, talk and talk.

The gangs do not come near us. I think they are afraid until I go home. Blood on the floor and the wall. My wife violated and dead, my child dead after watching. A warning to others. It catches up with me every day, what I saw and did.'

'What did you do?'

'What did you do?' he threw the question back, wary now and annoyed at having spoken.

A voice called his name. It was Niyi with Ebun lagging behind. They stopped, surprised to see me, though Ebun fought to disguise a smile. '*Shé alaáfià ni?*' she asked him.

'*Adúpé,*' he replied.

Niyi muttered something that I could not catch.

'Share it,' Lekan replied in English. 'Maybe Cormac is hungry.'

I found myself ravenous once I began to eat the bread and cheese. Niyi was perturbed at my presence, causing Lekan and Ebun to exchange an amused glance.

'My sister wonders which of us you come to see?' Lekan asked.

'You,' I said.

'She thinks you are a poor liar.'

Ebun angrily hissed something and Lekan threw his head back to laugh, even coaxing a reluctant smile from Niyi. I knew who I had come to see. But now that she was here, among this queue of unsettling faces, the force of my attraction frightened me. A passing cluster of Irish girls shouted at us, their abuse indecipherable but its meaning clear.

Navan had been no insular place during my childhood. Conversations were littered with placenames: The Bronx, Yonkers, Des Moines, Milwaukee, Staten Island – places to export our young. Uganda, Peru, Mozambique, Rwanda – places to send money for our foreign missionaries. Iraq, Jordan and Kuwait were places for nurses to amass fortunes in by the time I left, while my father's generation had already discovered the charms of Liechtenstein, Jersey and the Cayman Islands. The outside world was always part of our lives, but it had remained someplace else, somewhere to escape to or exploit or explore. The tables were being turned in this queue, with distant placenames becoming blood and flesh. I hated the stab of hypocritical prejudice I was discovering inside me, but somehow it felt as if this queue was robbing me of my home-coming.

'I should go,' I said. 'Thanks for the food.'

'Stay if you wish.' Lekan made space for Ebun to sit between us. 'We have all night.'

The tarmac was cramped, with people around us reluctant to surrender space to our swollen number. I felt the warmth of Ebun's leg pressed against mine and became intensely aware of her body. The curve of her neck when she lifted her head back, the upturn of her breasts and how they shook slightly when she laughed at something Lekan said. I also sensed her awareness of my presence, but I could not be certain if her interest was genuine or a means of tormenting Niyi. There seemed little I could genuinely tell about her.

I just knew that I loved the illicit warmth of her leg and that she could never guess at the childhood memories it brought back. Nights when Cormac and I had huddled together for warmth, when he ignored my protestations and we touched each other's bodies in new ways. Explorers with-out maps, stumbling into sensations as we pretended we needed to practise the things that we would do when we had girlfriends. As the elder I knew it was wrong, but Cormac kept driving us forward, like he could never have enough of each new sensation. Side by side, our bodies could not have been more different. My skin was sallow, but his seemed alabaster in the light of the candles he robbed from Saint

Joseph's shrine in the cathedral. I remember how their light flickered across the walls, casting a glimmer over the chicken wire at the window. Just bright enough to puzzle my father when he woke one night and slipped quietly from bed, knowing that Phyllis would need her sleep to cope with her latest bout of morning sickness in a few hours' time. Her sleeping hands wrapped protectively around the tiny bump beneath her nightdress, the fresh start – eight months after her miscarriage – that would become my half-sister.

How long did he stand at the unlocked bathroom window, perplexed by that flickering light, with the world he had painstakingly put back together about to fall apart? I heard the kitchen door open and his steps on the path. Cormac heard them too, but refused to scramble up. His lethargy seemed to paralyse me. Everything felt dream-like, with my worst nightmare becoming true. I lowered my hands to cover my erection as he lifted the latch.

My father stood in the doorway, staring at Cormac who gazed serenely back. At last I knew how he had felt, the same shock as I had experienced in his attic tonight. If I had been alone in that candlelight he would have removed his belt. But Cormac's impassivity altered the balance, like he was already far more a man of the world than my father would ever be. Momentarily my father seemed defeated, confronted by something outside his experience that he could not control.

'Get up to the house.' His voice was barely a whisper.

'Which of us?' It was Cormac who replied. I wanted to pull the blanket over me but was too scared to move.

'Don't you be cheeky, sir. Get up to that house now!'

'Why can't Brendan come? We slept in the same room once.'

'You won't bloody well do so again!' My father was losing his self-control, teetering towards violence. 'Your mother in

her condition . . . after what she's been through . . . if she
knew about this, boy, it would . . .'

'And will you tell her or I?'

My father looked at me directly for the first time, man to
man, almost imploringly like he needed confirmation of what
he had just heard. It was hard to tell which of us was more
shocked by the threat buried inside Cormac's effrontery.

'I want Brendan back in the house,' Cormac demanded,
releasing my father from shock.

'You want locking up! Both of you. Especially you,
Brendan, at your age. Get up!' My father pulled Cormac to
his feet, grabbed his pyjamas and pushed them into his arms.
'Get dressed, damn you, Cormac Brogan! Now I don't even
want to know what's been going on out here.'

'You never did anyway, once the neighbours heard nothing. And my name isn't Brogan! I don't care if you legally
adopted me, I'm no son of yours and never will be.' Cormac
turned to me. 'I'm glad my father is dead, having seen how
your father treats you!'

The slap caught Cormac so hard that the boy was knocked
face-down onto the mattress beside me. I put my arms around
his shoulders to protect him.

'You think you're a know-all, don't you? This has all been
for you . . . you illegitimate little bastard . . .' My father
stopped, shocked by his own words, then stared at the candles.
'Brendan, did you rob these from the cathedral?'

'No. Canon Bourke gave them to me.' Cormac turned his
head to stare defiantly at my father, wiggling his backside
slightly. 'He said I was to stick them up my step-father's tight
arse and light a fire there for Christ.'

There was utter silence. Even Cormac must have been
momentarily terrified behind his defiance because I felt a
tremble pass through his naked body. Then – I couldn't help

myself because the image conjured up was just so funny – I started to laugh, my shoulders shaking as I struggled to disguise it. Cormac joined in, both of us near hysterics and beyond control, tears in our eyes as we pictured my father kneeling with a holy candle burning from his bum. Stepping back into the garden, at a loss about how to deal with us, he sat down on a wheelbarrow, his head in his hands.

Eventually Cormac stopped laughing. He patted my shoulder, then slipped into his pyjamas and walked out past my father. Neither spoke, with my father watching him walk back up to the house. I was in for a hiding now, I thought, with his pent-up fury about to be spent on me. But he just stood up after a few moments and walked away, not even looking back like he didn't know what to say but wanted the unspoken rules understood. None of this had ever happened, he had never seen us and we were never to mention it again. I had pulled the blanket tightly around myself and watched him enter the kitchen, noticing for the first time how he had become a slightly stooped man.

A sudden shouting match occurred in the queue behind us, a flashpoint of near violence between two Eastern Europeans. Wary voices were raised around them, with nobody risking getting involved. One man shook a fist, then spat at his opponent's feet. He stalked off, making it clear that he was postponing unfinished business. Niyi watched him depart.

'Gypsies,' he remarked bitterly. 'Every trick they know.'

'Stop it,' Ebun told him.

'I will not stop. I see every trick,' he retorted fiercely. 'We are not the same as thieves or beggars. I do not forget I am Yoruba.'

'You are nobody now,' Lekan interjected quietly, then glanced at me. 'You ask what I did back then, òré mi. The police were no help, they were with the gangs. I locked up my shop, then I ran away.'

'So did I,' I replied. 'The problem is that I've no more places to run to.'

Ebun's fingers suddenly brushed against my arm. 'Then walk,' she said. 'Even Niyi will think me safe if you walk back with me.'

She rose, catching Niyi by surprise.

'You going home?' he asked.

'I would not call it that.' She beckoned for me to follow, picking her way through the bodies on the ground, never looking back to see if I was behind her. When she reached the corner she stopped to wait for me. My body ached with sudden tiredness. I wanted rid of every memory conjured during that day. But something about how Ebun stood brought back that street corner in Broadstone with its spiked railings and how Miriam had first turned to face me, the sudden promise of her lips and body offering the possibility of a different life. That sensation was here again, different yet offering the same sense of balm.

Ebun watched me as if trying to read my thoughts and having as little success as I had with hers. Then she smiled and shyly held out one hand.

III

MONDAY

My euphoria didn't last long – just the two hundred yards that it took for Ebun and me to self-consciously let go of each other's hand. Every glance from a passer-by killed something of the brief ease between us. We walked in silence along St Stephen's Green, where a car alarm blared through the night air, down Grafton Street with its torrent of young voices and figures, and onto College Green where a huge queue for taxis waited opposite the closed gates of Trinity College. The glances had switched from curiosity to open hostility by the time we reached Westmoreland Street, where the atmosphere held the same edge of menace that I remembered from my teenage years. Youths spilled out from kebab shops in cheap fluorescent tracksuits and runners. Two teenage girls in tiny skirts shivered as they boarded a night bus to Clondalkin, eyes hardening as they watched Ebun pass.

When I offered to wave down a passing taxi she turned the suggestion against me, wanting to know whether I was scared or ashamed to be seen walking with her. I was neither. It was just that since returning home I had felt anonymous but the constant glances made me uncomfortable now as we crossed the Liffey. O'Connell Street was always dangerous at this hour, but Ebun strode up it so resolutely with her chin thrown back that I began to wonder if she wanted my company at all.

A gang of youths passed. One of them shouted something,

then footsteps doubled back. I sensed Ebun tremble slightly before his footsteps stopped, the youth picking up a jacket that had fallen from around his waist. I took her hand in mine.

'I can mind myself,' she insisted, but didn't take her hand away.

We turned onto Parnell Street, past a shop with boarded-up windows. She stopped to look at the shabby pub across the road.

'This was our shop,' she said. 'Nigerian. They came out from the pub three nights ago, flinging stones and bottles across. A battle on the street.'

I knew the pub but had never dared to drink inside it. A criminal was shot dead there the year before I disappeared.

'Most local white people do not like the men from the pub, but they do nothing to help. They just watch from windows. Niyi was here. He and others started throwing the rocks back. The drunkards were shocked, like they expected us to lie down. We are tired of lying down. From now we fight our own battles.' She stopped at the corner of North Great George's Street, where the derelict sites once used as unofficial carparks had been replaced by crude replicas of the original streetscape. The flats where she had been attacked on Saturday were just beyond it. 'I know my way from here. Go back to your hotel if you like.'

'And if I don't like . . . ?'

She scrutinized me. 'What do you want, Irishman?'

'Just to talk to someone.'

'Talk is cheap. That's why we do it all day. You may walk me to my flat. Nothing more.'

I wasn't ready for anything more or at least not like she meant. The image of Conor in my old bedroom still haunted me. I wanted to lie down and yet knew that I wouldn't sleep. Maybe I simply wanted to rest my head on Ebun's breast and forget everything for a time. We walked past Hardwick Street flats, both of us aware of the danger if we were seen by the same youths, and turned onto Dorset Street.

Two Romanians sat on the bottom step outside her house, lowering their voices as we approached. She stopped a few feet from them. 'We are here,' she said. 'These men will think something is going on if I ask you in.'

'Do you care what they think?'

'You are not forced to live among them.' She watched me unsmilingly. 'I care what you might think.'

'Let me come up,' I said. 'I'll leave as soon as you ask.'

'I won't need to ask,' she replied. 'Do you think Niyi will leave us for long?'

Ebun walked past the men whose glances intimated that I was now the outsider. I followed her up the wooden staircase to the flat on the top floor. The window had been left open, making the room cold. It seemed even smaller than when I had left. It was hard to believe that three people could share such a spartan place. I walked to the window, looking out at the blocks of Corporation flats which bordered the tangled back gardens of these old houses.

'Where do you dream about at night?' I asked. 'I mean in what country do you find yourself?'

'I don't dream about countries.' Ebun put some water to boil on the two-ring cooker and checked how much coffee was left in the small jar. 'I dream about people I left behind. Sit. You look like you have walked all evening. Your family, they make you no welcome?'

'Anyone who knows me here thinks that I have been dead for years.'

Ebun turned, having carefully measured out coffee into two chipped mugs. 'Why?' she asked.

'People disappear for all kinds of reasons.'

'I know that. I mean why come back?'

'I have a son.'

Ebun hunched down to examine my face. 'The bruising over your eye is small now. I am glad I put ice on it.' She sat back on the bed. 'Where have you been?'

'Different places, never stopping long, playing out roles. Do you know Halloween?'

'I have never met her.' Ebun's expression remained serious for a second, before she laughed at my ignorance. 'I am from Africa, not Mars. Of course I know Halloween.'

'It was one of the few days as a child when I was allowed to do things with my brother. Both of us racing around wearing cheap masks. I loved looking through the eye sockets and feeling I was somebody else. These ten years have been like wearing an ever-changing Halloween mask, free to be anyone but myself.'

'And now?'

'I can hardly feel my own face any more. I don't know what's skin and what's rubber.'

'Maybe you're just not who you were back then.'

The water was starting to boil. Ebun rose to pour it into the two mugs and brought the coffee over. It tasted good as we sipped in silence. Eight months had passed since I had last touched a woman, three months since even speaking properly to one.

It had been late at night in a bar in Lisbon after chancing a visit to the Irish embassy to inquire about renewing Cormac's passport. I had promised to return the next day with a completed form, but knew from my carefully phrased questions that a computer check would show that Cormac was deceased. I was drinking alone when I met a woman with whom I could have gone home. For the next three hours we shared the unspoken presumption that I would. But at 3 a.m., as we emerged onto the sometimes dangerous labyrinthine streets around Alfama, I found that we had talked too much and too openly for me to carry through the polite deceptions of a one-night stand. I don't think she realized that I wasn't coming until she hailed a taxi to her apartment in Campo de Ourique. But I had hinted about secrets kept hidden from the three women who had shared my life in different countries over the past decade and suddenly I'd grown scared of what I might let slip in bed. That was always the danger about letting anyone get too close. After her taxi departed I had walked all the way back to my *pensao* off the R Portas de Santo Antao, knowing that mentally the fortifications created around my identity were starting to crumble at last.

Lowering the chipped coffee mug, I fought against the urge but found that I couldn't stop myself from doing something with Ebun which I had done with no other woman – strip myself naked by saying my name. I wanted to touch her, yet wanted to run away. I don't know if I feared Niyi or the police pounding through the door, but I didn't care about the risk any more.

'My real name is Brendan Brogan. I faked my own death because I wanted to start again, properly this time. I had a class of half-brother who stole my home once, my status in the world. In exchange I stole his life.'

'Why tell me this?' Ebun asked.

'For years I've wanted to tell someone.'

'But I'm not someone,' she replied quietly. 'Not like your countrymen on the street with passports and rights. You pick me because I do not count.'

'You do.'

'Your name means nothing to me. Who can I inform?'

'You count to me,' I said. 'I didn't stop that attack on Saturday for no reason. I needed to help you so I could feel

I had done one worthwhile thing. You looked . . . you are . . . special.'

'*E jòó*. Don't do this,' Ebun warned, almost scared.

'Do what?'

'Make this play. You don't know me, what things happened, things I saw. I am together now, I need to stay this way. I have a new life to find. I have no time for . . .'

She stopped and picked up the coffee cups, walking to the sink.

'For what?'

'What I might feel.'

'What do you feel?'

'Leave now like you said you would.' She washed the cups loudly, angry with herself or me. 'Niyi will be back soon. He will think we are . . .'

'Who is Niyi to you?' I walked towards her. 'He cannot be your lover. I see how you treat him.'

'Niyi was the cousin of the man I married.'

'Is the cousin,' I corrected.

Ebun turned to face me. 'I do not wish for a grammar lesson. You are not the only one whose life is complex. I am gone from his family. He fled them too, but is still one of them.'

'Your husband?'

'I will have no talk of him.'

'Is he dead?'

'Yes.'

There was a noise in the doorway. We both turned. Ebun seemed afraid. It was Niyi. He said something in their language.

'I am okay,' she replied in English. 'Cormac is leaving. I will walk him down.'

'Only to the door,' Niyi cautioned. 'Remember what happened last time you went outside alone.'

'I will not be caged. I am a free woman.'

Niyi shrugged and reached for the coffee jar that I realized was now empty. Ebun followed me down the stairs, her hand touching my shoulder to warn me where a step had crumbled. I opened the front door. The East Europeans were gone, but two passing Irishmen glanced up. One murmured something to his companion who grinned. There was a creak on the stairs. I sensed Niyi behind us, listening. Ebun glanced back, almost defiantly, then walked me down onto the street.

'Call to see me,' she whispered.

'When?'

'*Meje* . . . seven o'clock. There is a march in O'Connell Street. It will do no good – here or at home people will never accept strangers, they are too scared of what they might lose. But Niyi and Lekan like to think they are doing something. There they will meet other Nigerians and talk, talk, talk. I hate their endless talk. I hate this forever waiting.'

Maybe Ebun heard Niyi move down the wooden staircase, because she indicated for me to walk on. I had only gone a few yards however when I heard her footsteps briefly follow.

'My husband,' Ebun whispered, touching her breast, 'he is dead. But dead and cold only here in my heart.' She leaned forward, then stopped, her hand having brushed against my jacket pocket where Joey Kerwin's old revolver nestled. 'What's that?' she whispered sharply.

'Nothing.'

'I know the feel of that nothing. All you men are the same.' Her eyes were cold, suspicious. Niyi's voice called from the doorway and she turned to go in, without looking back.

Two weeks after my father found Cormac and myself together I got to handle serious money for the first time. The time came for my class to make our confirmation and not even Phyllis could stop my involvement. A suit was purchased – my first one ever and with long trousers too – and a white shirt that almost choked me at the neck. Likewise my shoes were too tight – carefully chosen so that I could just about get away with wearing them once before being put away for Cormac to grow into.

The clothes felt so new that they could not belong to me. I walked to the cathedral, terrified I would stain them. Even the coins I received caused me anxiety in case I was blamed if their weight pulled the lining of the pockets out of shape. I balanced them carefully, noticing how the crinkled texture of Mr Casey's pound note felt different from ordinary paper. When the bishop questioned me at the altar, I did not faint. As I walked back to my seat with a white rosette on my lapel, the suit's prospective owner – Cormac – looked up devoutly from kneeling beside Phyllis, then threw his eyes towards Lisa Hanlon in the girls' pews and winked.

Outside the church a handful of neighbours and some parents of other boys pressed more coins in my hand while Phyllis hovered tight-lipped, waiting to sweep me home. The hot day was upsetting her, and the way other women eyed her stomach. But she was on her best behaviour, not even interfering when Josie pressed a pound note into my fist. The tears in the old woman's eyes made me uncomfortable as she hugged me. I was as relieved as Phyllis to escape back to the house where even local builders knew not to call any more.

To Phyllis's credit, she had a slap-up meal for us afterwards, a Sunday dinner on a Saturday with orange squash and ice-cream and jelly. She laughed and even patted my hair that she had spent half the morning yanking into shape. After the suit was put away, Cormac and I were allowed to play together in the back garden. It seemed as good as the treat of lunch in the Ard Boyne Hotel that other boys had talked about. My father even brought down crisps and chocolate to the outhouse that evening.

He didn't mention the events of a fortnight before, any more than I mentioned how Phyllis had not actually let me keep any of my confirmation money. I knew things to be tight financially. She had the cost of raising her own son, the worry of another forthcoming mouth to feed, plus the expense of keeping me. I cost her a fortune. She was never done telling me this and saying how lucky I was that free second-level education had come in – thanks to the mad generosity of a Government minister whose behaviour had been disgraceful when Barney Clancy allowed him to gatecrash their wedding dinner in the Shelbourne Hotel.

I didn't mind losing my confirmation money, which at least made me feel that I was contributing to the house. It was losing my nocturnal freedom which bothered me. My father had asked Mr Hanlon to put a new Chubb lock on the outhouse, after temporarily removing my mattress so that I could be safely airbrushed from their neighbourly conversation as it was being fitted. This seemed his only method of keeping us apart. It would be impossible to lock Cormac's bedroom without having to explain to Phyllis about us 'queering each other up' – a phrase I overheard older boys use about an FCA instructor but had never previously understood.

Now at eight-thirty each evening I was locked into the outhouse until dawn. I could live without Mr Casey's illicit soup, but the curtailment of my prowling tormented me. I was missing Lisa Hanlon undressing at her bedroom window; her mother finishing the *Woman's Own* crossword by the fire;

my twice-weekly vigil from the roof of Hanlon's shed to spy on Foxy O'Rourke's girlfriend doing to him in the lane what Cormac had taught me to do. I missed her teasing laugh afterwards, wiping her hand on a tissue while he gasped against the shed door as though shot. Most of all I was missing the lights of Navan dog track and my being able to glimpse, through a chink in the corrugated iron boundary fence, the last bend and most of the straight up to the finish. I used to have to try and guess which dog won by the shouts from the crowd on the evenings when I managed to get there in time to spy on the final two races. More than anything in life I longed to stand among that crowd, lay big bets with the bookies and show no emotion as my dog romped home, the boy admired for his acumen. Stories of the man who broke the bank at Monte Carlo would pale beside the legend of the Navan boy who sent the Dublin bookies home with empty bags and tails between their legs.

I missed Cormac's visits too, though I knew that what we had done was wrong. But life felt empty after briefly having known somebody who cared. It was hard not to dwell on memories of him lightly biting my nipple and how his warmth always remained after he was gone. Some evenings he appeared in their bedroom window, when he knew Phyllis and my father were watching Charles Mitchell read the nine o'clock news. Creeping like a cat so they wouldn't hear his footsteps, he stood on the bed so I could see his body framed by light. Often he merely waved but once he stripped off his pyjamas to press against the glass with hands outstretched. I never knew if it was a deliberate mimicry of the crucifixion or just seemed that way.

If I was unsure of how Cormac's mind worked, then my father seemed utterly perplexed. Ever since he had found us I'd started to see him in a different light, no longer king of anything. Bricks and mortar were what he understood, things that followed a logical pattern. Perhaps my mother might have fitted into such a world, trained by the Loreto nuns to be content with her allotted role and to cajole him emotionally to play out his part too. But it wasn't just her death which drove my father to seek Phyllis. All his life he had been a secret misfit. I knew that from the night when I found a notebook of hand-written verses locked in the filing cabinet. They had shocked me more deeply than if he was a Martian or a Protestant. Such softness did not belong in his circle and would have been used to mock and bait him.

Looking back, it revealed how he always needed something more, a glimpse into fantasy worlds that men only laughed about in barbershops in Navan. He had needed to possess a trophy when the term still only existed in the pages of smuggled copies of *Playboy*. He had needed to experience sensations that Loreto girls knew they didn't have to provide to trap a husband. Yet, after my mother, the rough and tumble of some slovenly shop girl from the bog would have been beneath him.

Phyllis didn't look like a Loreto girl. From the start there was something disconcerting about her appearance, like she belonged in *Green Acres* or some other American television programme. From the day he revealed his second marriage my father became almost as big a joke in the town as Slab McGuirk who, when his wife went on pilgrimage to Lough Derg, spent an evening projecting pornographic films onto the closed Venetian blinds in his living-room window, unaware that the images came clearly through on the street outside.

Navan men kept their desires secret, maybe even from themselves, whereas my father had allowed his to become flesh and be scrutinized by everyone. His showgirl, his Princess Grace, his soft-breasted baby doll. Unlike other men's fantasies, she was still there in the morning among the real world of cattle marts, cow shite and oil shortages. She was sensitive to every petty slight, possessed by growing demands and anxieties to which he slowly became ensnared. Now her son had stepped forth from his previous unobtrusiveness to taunt him in ways that my father had no idea how to deal with.

'Isn't bastard a bad word, Daddy?' Cormac had asked in an innocent voice, breaking the terse silence at breakfast on the morning after my father discovered us. Phyllis was struggling to keep down a slice of dry toast beside him. 'I heard Pete Clancy use it about a boy in school. I had to ask the teacher what it means but even he didn't know, Daddy.'

There could be nothing worse for a grown man used to exercising power than to be wound up by an eleven-year-old boy. Another child might be crushed by the revelation my father had let slip, but Cormac seemed quietly pleased with his new status. If he was illegitimate then the whole notion of her having previously been married was just a sham invented for the neighbours. The shame of her son knowing this would have been too much for Phyllis, who was convinced she was about to lose this baby as well at any minute. One day as a treat in school we were shown a Tom and Jerry cartoon, with the mouse perpetually threatening to wake a huge dog while the terrified cat tried to pacify him on tiptoes. It reminded me of Cormac toying with my father, though in the weeks after my confirmation Phyllis grew so withdrawn in self-absorption about her pregnancy that I became both the sole audience for Cormac's games and the object of desire behind them.

Even as he stripped away my fear of my father, I resisted, finding the vacuum that replaced it too painful. I needed to respect my father. His omnipotence made sense of my child-hood. I felt I had been banished to the outhouse for a clear purpose, the penance for an unspecified but definite sin. It was part of my father's God-given plan. But the more Cormac baited him the more I was forced to admit the possibility that only his weakness and inability to stand up to Phyllis kept me there. He was as unable to intervene in a woman's right to run the house as he was incapable of boiling an egg. He had allowed her bastard to sleep in my bed, her bastard to steal my life. Yet her bastard was my only friend. Just saying the word 'bastard' aloud excited me at night. What man had Phyllis once allowed to ride the arse off her? A visiting American perhaps, straight from *Hawaii Five-O* or *Mission Impossible*, attracted by her dyed blonde hair, which of late occasionally betrayed its red roots. Such thoughts made the lure of Cormac more exotic as he displayed himself in their bedroom window. I carried the burden of my mother's respectability, even if I lowered it into the muck. But Cormac's illegitimacy was a clean sheet, giving him the freedom to break any rule.

I woke one Saturday night, knowing something was wrong. There was a scraping noise, like chalk on a blackboard or ghostly fingernails clawing at the door. Slowly it opened to reveal a patch of empty moonlight. Something flew in, striking me on the chest. I put my hand down to pick up two keys on a ring. A Chubb and one that looked like it would fit the new lock my father had also asked Mr Hanlon to fit on the top drawer of his old desk.

'Scared you.' Cormac appeared in his pyjamas in the doorway.

'Where did you get them?'

'Himself and Phyllis must have been going at it backwards like dogs upstairs this afternoon. He sent me for sweets to be out of their way, told me to walk as far as Trimgate Street. I stole the keys from his jacket pocket and got copies made in the locksmith's.'

'Wasn't the locksmith suspicious?'

'Not at all.' Cormac flicked a packet of Silk Cut across to me. 'Sure didn't I forge a note in his handwriting asking for spare keys.'

The image that Cormac conjured up of my father and Phyllis doing it, even when she was pregnant, excited me more than the keys in my hand or the stolen cigarettes. He lit one for us both and I tried to inhale without coughing too much while he took the keys back from me.

'Let's see what he keeps in that drawer. I bet it's dirty magazines.'

I never told Cormac about my ability to pick the filing cabinet lock. I had already tried the same trick with this locked drawer but failed. Now I was torn between wanting to stop Cormac opening it and longing to know what was inside. I dreaded it being more poems – I could cope with my father being cruel but couldn't bear for him to be exposed as an idiot. The key turned with the faintest click. Cormac stepped back, wanting to implicate me.

'You open it.'

I couldn't chicken out. The wooden drawer was stiff and awkward. I stepped back when it was open a few inches as though I had received an electric shock. It was the first time I ever saw Cormac stunned. A severed human hand or Polaroid shots of Phyllis naked would not have left us more dumbstruck. Cormac dropped his cigarette on the floor and reached his fingers out. I stopped him in fear. Then we looked at each other and I let go his hand, helping him to take out and count the fabulous fortune. Five-pound notes, ten-pound notes, the colours of the new twenties. I had never even known that fifty-pound notes existed. We sorted them by colour, our fingers trembling. It reminded me of the day of my banishment, four years before, when we knelt together to sort autumn leaves into ships. This time there was no Phyllis to break us up. We counted the money over and over, laughing like we were drunk. Cormac spread it out on the mattress and we removed our pyjamas, rolling around on top of it, giggling when banknotes stuck to our flesh with sweat.

Cormac made me kneel so he could pretend to wipe my backside with a fifty-pound note. His hand lingered, probing and teasing as he rustled the note around my testicles. I was breathing heavier now, legs trembling as I stared down at riches beyond comprehension, a fantasy fortune that could not belong to my father. Things were tight at home, with my own confirmation money needed by Phyllis. This had to be County Council wages for next week or party money Barney Clancy had asked him to mind. I was getting cold and scared, wishing that Cormac's hand would stop yet wanting him to go on forever.

It took us an hour afterwards to replace the money, arguing about how exactly it had been arranged and then about where we should hide the spare keys so that I could open the door in future. It was typical of Cormac not to mention the ten-pound note he had stolen. There was always one part of the picture I was excluded from.

The following Monday I came home from school to find the outhouse turned upside-down. My mattress lay in the garden, with my clothes scattered on the grass. My father was frantic, not caring how much he upset Phyllis who sat in the kitchen with her hands around her stomach, crying as though he had gone mad. He never told us what he was looking for and never found the keys either, hidden under a loose stone in the corner. But that night when I checked the drawer it was empty and it remained empty ever after, except for occasionally containing a list of hand-written sixteen-digit numbers. I would never handle such sums of cash again until the morning I waited for the paramedics to come and cut Cormac's body down from the ceiling of his apartment in Perth and lay him out naked on a mortuary slab.

———|■|———

Eleven fifty-five a.m. – not quite high noon in Temple Bar as I laid Joey Kerwin's revolver on the bed in my hotel room. I emptied out the ancient-looking rusty bullets, with no way of telling if they still worked or if the gun was as self-destructive as Barney Clancy had once jokingly claimed. What had it been used for, if anything? The 1950s IRA Border Campaign had been a brief idealistic splutter compared to what came after. By the time I grew up all that generally marked out those once youthful volunteers was their later conservatism, success in business and membership of the Tidy Towns Committee.

Joey Kerwin had been far older than most. Could I imagine him killing somebody with this gun? Could I imagine myself pulling the trigger with Pete Clancy's matted hair and skull splattered onto a wall? It was a fantasy I'd played out a thousand times, remembering the stink of ammonia cubes in the flooded concrete shed that passed as a school toilet. The terror that I would choke as they flushed the cistern again and again. My head pressed right down into the bowl, his hands gripping my neck as he laughed: 'Chuck, chuck, chuck the Hen Boy!'

I put the gun down and shaved at the mirror, checked to see if I needed to put more red dye into my hair. Opening my bag I counted out whatever money I had left. There was enough to live on for a month if I was careful. I had little to return to in Oporto, where for the previous two years I had worked in a bar owned by a Greek businessman. As in every other city I had departed silently, giving notice to nobody but with my rent paid up and every bill settled. Nobody was ever inconvenienced by my continual vanishing off the face of the earth, except for those puzzled few hurt for having briefly regarded me as a friend or lover.

For years if I awoke beside some girl in Belgium or Portugal I would watch her sleep, wondering if she might still have come to lie there had I introduced myself as Brendan Brogan? Simply saying Cormac's name gave me confidence. Reaching out in the dark to fondle soft breasts, I could almost feel Cormac inside me, urging me on, his hand buried within my hand as it ran along a girl's back, his breath coming quicker in my mouth. I knew I would never have the self-confidence to make these conquests on my own.

But in the long hours awake while some girl slept I always became myself again, with guilt making me imagine Miriam at dawn in our bed. The young widow burdened with a son, subject to unwelcome offers in her implied loneliness from men who made their services sound like a favour or from the hardchaws queuing for free legal aid in the Citizens Advice Centre if she still worked there. For years she haunted my dreams. Often in them she was fleeing with me from our former selves. 'Will Brendan and Miriam ever find us?' she would ask, staring out through the eyes of some Scandinavian girl whose skin she had borrowed.

Ebun was the first woman I had been attracted to who did not physically resemble Miriam in some way. The irony was not lost on me of having found her in a city where every street conjured memories of my wife. Ebun's husband was dead but only in her mind. Miriam and Conor were alive in mine and even my father was there, tearing at my conscience. I had business to finish, impossible amends to make, futile supplications I could never deliver. It was vital to focus on what had to be done and get cleanly away without implicating anyone. By getting involved with Ebun I was putting my own plans at risk. I could not believe that I had betrayed my name to her. She might have gone to the police already. But I couldn't stop thinking about the possibility that in seven hours time I might see her again, though after discovering the gun I didn't know if she would let me in.

I replaced the gun and money carefully in my bag and lay back to read the morning paper. There was something uncanny about the pages devoted to the ongoing tribunals. Apart from the young solicitors representing them, I remembered every face in the photographs. Yet they had all aged so much they seemed like stooped, bewildered old men. My father's contemporaries, facing a wall of cameras as they walked to give evidence, with their razor-sharp memories suddenly as forgetful about every aspect of their business dealings as my father's mind might have become had he been allowed to live.

One former Dublin planning official had told the judge on Friday that he was now too destitute to buy himself lunch in town. They were just finished hearing evidence of how he had previously needed over thirty bank accounts to cope with apparently unsolicited 'consultancy fees' from builders and developers and would often have to leave notes to remind himself of the location of cash stored in his house. The papers seemed outraged by his selective amnesia and reluctance to incriminate himself.

A Donegal-based builder whose company records were destroyed by fire when stored in a caravan on a building site had followed him into the witness box. This was the third such fire, along with two cases of flooding, the tribunal had encountered in recent months. The elderly builder seemed baffled by large movements of cash from his bank account into offshore companies that he claimed never to have heard of.

On every page not dealing with the Northern impasse, reports of more refugees disembarking from container lorries or the church apologizing for elderly priests up on child-abuse charges, the former practices of the banks, the medical profession, the judiciary and the blood transfusion service were being investigated. Now that the Promised Land of prosperity had finally arrived, Ireland seemed determined to tear itself apart. Letter-writers hectored with a self-righteousness born from having to confront what they always knew about how Ireland worked but previously preferred only to whisper about in half-admiration. Apart from the succession of children crippled in territorial punishment beatings that people were eager to overlook for fear of rocking the boat, the cease-fires held in the North. But here in the South politics seemed to have dissolved into tit-for-tat character assassinations to compensate for the lack of real power now that most important economic decisions were being taken elsewhere in Europe.

The indefinite postponement of the trial of former Taoiseach, Charles Haughey, on charges of obstructing a tribunal investigating his hidden wealth, was relegated to a few paragraphs, with his legal team successfully arguing that it would be impossible to select twelve jurors who were not prejudiced against him.

On the night when I finally ran out of excuses for not bringing her to Cremore to meet him for the first time, Miriam had argued with my father about Haughey. But not argued seriously, they merely took up the stances common at the time. There was no middle ground back then, you were utterly for or against Haughey. Those who queried the source of his mansion, his island retreat or private yacht were West Brit

Blueshirts, unable to stomach the sight of an Irishman living as well as our former masters.

'So what if he has made a few bob for himself,' my father had testily admitted towards the end of an uneasy meal – social workers being people he regarded with suspicion. 'If he can't look after himself then surely to God what chance has he of looking after the rest of us? Where would the old age pensioners be without him, with free phones and travel? Hasn't he paid the rent arrears for every second family in Donnycarney? You ask the people going into your clinic. The poor will always love Charlie because poor times need a strong man, strong enough to lift himself up and drag the rest of us along with him.'

These days, by the look of the letters page, the rest of Ireland didn't seem overly keen to be associated with Haughey any more or reminded of their former adoration of him. I remembered bonfires blazing outside Clancy's house on the night Haughey first visited Navan after his election as party leader. Market Square crammed with red-faced men in white shirts with straining buttons, screaming more shrilly than pigs at the slaughterhouse. Women's faces that night wore a flushed look, like they had drenched their knickers at the fleeting touch of his hand in the throng. It wasn't just the tribunal witnesses who were suffering from selective amnesia now. Bold after the event, the letter-writers were like those Italians who kicked and hacked at Mussolini – when his dead body was safely hung from a lamppost.

Apart from a terror of being contaminated by any association with his reign, there seemed little in the paper to separate the political parties. Even the small left-wing factions had merged into one party that toed much the same line as the others. They seemed happiest bickering over incidentals, with the bitter intensity of rival football supporters in a provincial town.

Maybe this was how it had always been. Real politics was never about important issues when I was a child. The Americans or Russians could bomb wherever they wished, once it wasn't Kingscourt or Dunshaughlin. We were happy to send peacekeeping forces afterwards, but only so that people in obscure countries could discover our likeability. Our soldiers in the Lebanon worked hard to protect the locals, were never corrupt and, while often under fire, generally only ever shot each other and then by accident. Real politics was about drainage grants and septic tanks. It was so intimate that my father, when acting as tallyman at an election count, could lean over to inspect a ballot paper from Rathmolyon or Kilmessan and, by glancing through the preferences, name the family it came from.

Perhaps there was no real difference between the parties because in the main they comprised a succession of hard-won fiefdoms. Forty years ago Barney Clancy's father had decided to retire at the same time as another War of Independence veteran who also held a safe Meath seat from a Navan powerbase. But a gerrymandering of the constituency boundaries meant that it was only considered possible for the party to hold one seat locally. Splitting the vote in Navan could let Labour into Meath. No convention was held to decide whose son would stand as the single agreed candidate. Instead the two octogenarians were found collapsed, faces covered in blood, after privately settling the question in a bare-knuckle contest in which Barney Clancy's father had broken some of his former comrade's ribs.

A nation-wide survey of marginal seats in the paper now suggested that the Clancy family dynasty could finally be under threat in a snap election. This explained his caution in the second reply I had downloaded at the cyber café this morning. The first, sent at seven-fifteen last night, read like an automatic response:

Dear Mr Shyroyal,
Thank you for your e-mail received this evening. I will give it
my urgent attention as soon as possible.
Yours truly,
Peter Clancy,
Junior Minister

The second one had been sent just before midnight from a
different e-mail address:

Dear Shyroyal,
I am at a loss to understand your message or know how it
is that I can help you. If you need assistance with
something please give me more details? Communication is
more immediate at this private e-mail address.
Sincerely
Peter Clancy,
Junior Minister

It was a clever reply: seemingly bland, courteous and circumspect, yet opening the door a fraction. If the name Shyroyal
had not hooked him he would have ignored my e-mail. I had
spent an hour drafting my reply before being satisfied with it.
Headed 'Strictly Private' it had read:

Dear Junior Minister,
I need help in returning something into the right hands.
Indeed I almost feel mandated to do so. Something left
uncollected abroad when somebody died. It doesn't grow on
trees unless under apple boughs protected by bees. Is
Maguire's hill field still there? No back seats this time. One
a.m. was once your favourite time, why break the habit.
Let's meet tonight alone.
Shyroyal, The Jersey Rose

Clancy would be suspicious of the e-mail and yet scared. I could be a journalist but the bees incident was so obscure and went so far back that I couldn't even be sure if he would get the reference.

When I was ten Barney Clancy had installed a beehive in the orchard garden of his house. One night my father inadvertently woke me by entering the outhouse with his face covered in bee stings, unaware that he was being observed as he locked something away in the filing cabinet. It was during the brief flurry of a reluctant, embarrassed police enquiry into Clancy's alleged involvement with a parcel of farmland – adjacent to Josie's terrace of cottages – re-zoned for housing shortly after being bought by an Isle of Man company and then resold for several times the price.

The investigation was seen locally as a dirty tricks salvo by the new Government to oust him from his seat at the next election. It backfired to the extent that, after his exoneration, Barney Clancy was able to bring a running mate into the Dail with him when the party swept back to power. The bees didn't last long, but the image of my father's blotched face had haunted me for years. All his life he had a phobia about bees, so how could he have allowed himself to get so badly stung that night? Years later in Portugal I had examined a beehive and realized how much documentation could be concealed beneath one, once some unfortunate lackey was on hand to retrieve it when required.

Despite the collapse of the police investigation at that time rumours had lingered around Navan. Not just about the farmland (which suddenly benefited from having sewerage and other services laid across it), but about the unknown directors of another Isle of Man shell company who flattened Josie's terrace and then got permission to build Navan's first shopping centre in its place on the nod from my father's development task-force.

This begrudgery was put down to sour grapes on the part of local shopkeepers who felt threatened by the development. Most people were excited by the prospect of different shops and being able to use terms like 'supermarket'. On Sundays families would motor in from as far as Castlejordan and Old-castle to marvel at the scale of the building site, for which Slab McGuirk and Mossy Egan won the joint contract. Its almost inaccessible location behind Emma Terrace caused incessant traffic jams. But I had always blamed Phyllis for its whereabouts, imagining that she had pressured my father into siting it there so as to shift Josie into an old folks' chalet on the edge of town.

The birth of Sarah-Jane changed Phyllis, making her at least in part a Navan mother. Not that people hadn't come to regard Cormac as being as much a local as any blow-in could become. But here was a child who truly belonged to the town, one that neighbours could coo over and ask about.

Phyllis was as nervous as a bride-to-be on the morning of Sarah-Jane's christening – rushing back and forth to the mirror; getting Cormac to light her cigarette, terrified she would smudge her lipstick as she fretted at the front door. I was pressganged back into my now-too-small communion suit, with Cormac gleaming after the bath which she had got him to share with me – to my father's silent apoplexy when he came in. We walked like a proper family to the cathedral, getting there just before twelve o'clock mass started. My father had asked Barney Clancy to be godfather, which accounted for the larger than usual crowd that remained behind after the mass. Neighbours came up to touch the baby and spoke warmly to Phyllis who seemed close to tears. For once she and my father actually looked like a couple. She could almost have passed for a Loreto ex-pupil. There were sandwiches in the house afterwards, with people who had never been inside

the front door admiring her scrubbed kitchen and how the
bread was cut in triangles with the crusts removed. Phyllis
kept the back door locked as though for the first time ashamed
of the outhouse instead of being ashamed of me.

This was meant to be the day of the thaw, when Navan
decided to reach out to her or maybe when Phyllis finally
allowed herself to relax enough to feel accepted. Her anguish
after the miscarriage (and the loss of some of her looks) had
softened attitudes, as had my father's increasing status within
the County Council. Sarah-Jane was passed from arm to arm
in the smoky living-room, as neighbours swapped stories of
other christenings, filling out the interwoven patchwork quilt
of Navan families. I moved around with plates of sandwiches
as people avoided my eye or gave quick sympathetic glances.
I was desperate to hear my mother's name mentioned, but in
every quilt certain patches simply get sewn over.

Josie should never have turned up there, having not been
invited. I didn't hear a knock at the front door which some
neighbour must have opened, but I sensed a sudden tension
and turned to see Josie holding a neatly wrapped Babygro.

'I just wanted to give you this and wish the baby a long
life.' Josie pointedly addressed my father, ignoring Phyllis who
stood beside her. I don't think it would have made much
difference if Josie had been friendly. The great and good of
Navan were initiating Phyllis into their chosen ranks. This
was no place for some old cleaning woman with a cheap print
scarf on her head.

'That's kind of you,' my father replied, embarrassed. 'If
you'll just give it to my wife.'

'I'll give it to you, Eamonn. I remember tasting sherry for
the first time the day you were christened in the town and
making sandwiches on the day poor Brendan was baptized.
My good wishes are for you and the child alone.'

I didn't want my name mentioned. I simply wanted to exist on the edge of things, not belonging there but at least not banished to the outhouse. Phyllis gingerly prised the package from her hands.

'It stinks of those filthy cottages,' she snapped. 'Eamonn should knock them down for the sake of the town. They're only disease traps. Do you honestly think I'd put the likes of this on a child of mine?'

'That will do now, Phyllis,' my father said, aware of everyone present. He had always retained a soft spot for Josie. The room was silence, with the day ruined. I knew people were now just waiting to leave.

'God knows what you'd put on,' Josie said. 'My eyesight may be failing but I still recognize a tramp if nobody else can. At least this poor baby here will know who her father is.'

Phyllis leaned forward. Somehow she found the restraint not to grab the old woman's hair. 'My first husband died in Scotland when Cormac was young,' she whispered, near tears.

'Is that why you married Eamonn in a registry office?' Josie retorted. 'I had my niece check the records. They have you down as a spinster, not a widow. You never saw outside a Dublin slum till Eamon Brogan let his prick override his senses. If these baby clothes smell different to you, it's because you never knew any that didn't have a dozen shitty arses already put through them.' She pointed towards me. 'Brendan's mother's ghost is watching over him, which is more than you do for that bastard son of yours.'

'What do you mean by that?' My father shouted now, furious.

'I'm not the only one to first taste sherry at a christening.' Josie looked at Phyllis and almost spat. 'Should you decide to try your hand at mothering, you'll find him in the lane getting sick, as stocious as the knacker who banged you up with a bastard son after paying for a knee-trembler down some stink-ing Dublin lane.'

Next morning – after Phyllis had cleaned Cormac up, put him to bed and decided, with an Irish mother's logic, that Josie had lured him into unwittingly drinking the sherry – Cormac chanced his most innocent voice over breakfast again: 'What's a knee-trembler, Daddy?'

The slap across the table left a red mark on Cormac's cheek. Phyllis's protestations were silenced by my father's look. Cormac didn't seem to mind as he glanced up and winked at me. Seeing somebody else being hit made us almost seem like a normal Irish family.

———◦■◦———

Already I was accepted as a regular in the cyber café where I spent the late afternoon, even recognizing some of the cus-tomers who drifted in and out. Beyond the window Dublin floated past, leaving me no longer astonished by the changes but feeling cheated. Nobody had ever hinted that things might change like this if I had stayed. I recalled Brian Lenihan laughing at the notion of full employment in an interview with *Newsweek*: 'Sure how could we all live on this one little island?'

By my fourth cup of coffee I felt sick but I stayed online, checking for mail every ten minutes and trying to talk myself out of risking the visit to Ebun but in truth I was just counting down the minutes until seven.

Pete Clancy might have simply deleted my message, dis-missing me as a crank. The café filled up as offices closed, with newcomers impatient at my hogging a terminal. At six o'clock I sent him another copy of my e-mail, this time to his official address in case he was only checking mail from there. But when his reply came at six-forty, it was from the private address he had given.

Shyroyal,
Whoever you are you're fond of games. I can vaguely place Maguire's hill field, which is more than I can do for you. I work hard for anyone who genuinely needs my help, but have no time for jokers. I'm attending a party meeting in Kingscourt tonight and it's feasible that I could pass that way en route home around one thirty. But only if you could give me one good reason why I should meet you or anyone else in the middle of nowhere.
Yours
P. Clancy

I savoured the sense of power his irked tone gave me. Trying to puzzle out who I was had him rattled. A girl behind me rose, thinking that I was finished. I hit the reply button and typed in the two emptied account numbers on my father's list, followed by the words '*be there*'. The speed of my reply would panic him further into definitely turning up. I just still didn't know if I had the balls to confront him.

It was a twenty-minute walk to Ebun's flat, where I waited behind a parked van to watch Lekan and Niyi leave. The bottleneck of rush-hour traffic was starting to ease as I scanned the row of bells at the front door, few of which had names attached. The door opened and the two Romanians from last night appeared. One muttered something before gesturing with a flick of his head that I could enter. The stairway was deserted, with a hubbub of noise behind doors on each landing. I had to knock three times at Ebun's flat before a chain was put on and the door opened slightly. The side of Ebun's face appeared, frowning slightly.

'Yes?'

'You said I could call.'

'That was before.'

'I can explain,' I said.

'Men with guns always can.'

'Do I look like a criminal?'

Ebun turned slightly so I could see her hair. I wondered was she addressing somebody else in the flat. 'This life turns us all into criminals.'

'I'm dealing with dangerous people,' I said.

She turned her head again so I could see her eyes scrutinizing me. 'You don't know danger. Danger is being sealed in a truck by men with guns who say "trust me". Danger is not knowing if you will be shot or suffocate as you're driven across the Mali bush before the doors are unlocked again. Danger is being on a rusty boat at night from Morocco to Spain, not knowing if you're going to be thrown overboard.'

Her almost patronizing tone hurt.

'I'm not a bad man, just out of my depth,' I said. 'I took a risk coming back here. Now you want me to go away again, is that it?'

A man began shouting on a lower landing. His footsteps ascended as Ebun closed the door fully. He had reached the landing below me when I heard the chain being taken off and the handle turn. Ebun beckoned me in and closed the door.

'I don't want you to go away,' she said. 'I want you to hold me. It's been so long, Brendan, since someone just held me.'

She pressed her body against me, her arms around my back. Yet our hug wasn't sexual, at least not at first. The voice shouted on the landing below us, with somebody else shouting back. I couldn't understand a word of the quarrel but didn't need to. People crammed together, feeling violated if the least of their few possessions were touched. People stranded at a crossroads with no signposts, tortured by doubts over whether they should have stayed at home, by thoughts of faces beyond reach and memories nobody else could understand.

Ebun felt so warm, the succour of her skin through her dress, the way her leg pressed between mine. We stood, wrapped together and yet apart, each seeking solace for a grief the other could not grasp. Gradually our trembling stopped. There was a brief plateau of calm as we drew breath, looked at each other and almost laughed. '*Mo féé*,' she murmured. '*Mo féé.*' Then a different trembling began, hands no longer restrained, seeking a more physical and immediate healing balm.

I had never seen a black woman naked before. I wanted to undress her and slowly take my time. Ebun insisted on matching me, button for button. The weight of her breasts was in my hands as we kissed and her fingers stroked my nipples. Shouts from a block of flats beyond the gardens, girls' voices calling, a dog's incessant bark. The wonder of her skin, softness like no other. The down of pubic hair that she shielded with her hand, not allowing me to look. Ebun's weight on top of me as she seized command. A sensation of being pummelled as her buttocks heaved up and down. Her flesh was mesmeric and different, illicit to the small-town boy inside me who had never changed. My eyes closed. It almost felt like being back in that outhouse with Cormac, the newness of his hand and tongue opening me up. Then the image changed from Cormac to Conor and how he must have looked with Charles in my old bedroom.

I opened my eyes, disturbed. Ebun looked down, her hands leaving the pillow to grip my shoulders. She held me there, saying nothing but making me focus on her and the present tense. On my head thrashing on the pillow, my body suddenly

arched and buckling. On the cry drowned in my throat by
her tongue and how her body kept moving, prolonging her
silent pleasure long after I had come.

It was eight-thirty by her cheap watch on the dresser when
I woke. Ebun lay beside me with the blanket tight around
her. I had the impression she had been watching me while I
slept.

'*E káalé,*' she said, almost teasingly.

'Are you OK?' I asked.

'Why would I not be?' she replied. 'I feel good, clean. You
must leave before they come back.'

'Tomorrow . . .'

'Yes?'

It felt awkward, with different lives colliding. I had always
lacked Cormac's gift of moving chameleon-like between different sets of circumstances.

'I do not know if I will still be around.'

Ebun pulled the blankets tighter. 'What do you think I am
after? Marriage, a passport?'

'Don't take me up wrong.'

'I might not be around either,' Ebun retorted. 'I do not
know when a knock on the door will come to deport me.
Either way I will never be owned by any man or family
again.'

'This business that I came back for . . . I don't know where
it will lead. But if I can I want to see you again.' I gazed
around. 'This room is the only place in Dublin where I still
feel at home.'

'What did you expect?' Ebun replied. 'Once you leave
there is no way back.'

'It's different for me.'

'Everyone housed in this building says that. It's only different because you ran away. You didn't see your family

butchered, your son dragged off to be a soldier or your daughter whimper to death. You suited yourself.'

'I needed to find myself.'

Ebun's laugh hurt for being incredulous, as if at a child. 'I do not understand "find yourself"? I understand about finding food and water. Finding money to bribe a criminal to stick you in another truck from Spain to Ireland where you almost choke on your own vomit from the fumes. Lekan had to come home to find his wife raped, his child dead. All you had to find was yourself and now you think you have the right to come home.'

'I've more right to be here than . . .' I stopped myself.

'Than me?' She stroked my face. 'Perhaps so. But I have more need.'

I left the bed and splashed water on my face. People shouted again in a foreign language downstairs.

'We both have needs,' I said. 'I need my son.'

'Then go to him. Because I would give my life to see my daughter for one moment.'

I turned. 'You left a daughter behind?'

'In a hole in the ground where her aunts could not hurt her again,' she said. 'Do you think I would leave her if she was alive?'

'What happened?'

Ebun lay back. Her voice didn't sound like her own. It was distant, factual, as though there was no emotion left to be wrung. 'What can happen to girls at a certain age, what my father insisted would not happen to me and I swore would never happen to her. It is illegal but Ede, where my husband brought me to live, is remote. The head of police in that part of town is from my husband's family. Almost everyone important is. My husband's mother and her sisters, they made sure I was out of the compound. I knew they had played a trick once I got off a truck in the square. You could hear my daughter's screams even at that distance. Maybe they rushed the job for fear I would come back. My mother-in-law hated that I answered back and spoke for my husband at their family gatherings because he would not speak for himself. I did not know my place. They said that only a widow had the right to speak like I did. My daughter was too like me. It was their way to brand her as one of them.'

Cold water dripped down my face. 'I'm sorry,' was all I could think to say.

'It is easier for Jewish boys. They get presents, they do not bleed to death.'

The room felt cold. I put my shirt on, desperate for a cigarette. The sense of healing was gone.

'What did you do?' I asked.

'The deed was done and covered up. His family did not approve of what his mother did, but they protected her. I left with Lekan who came for me.'

'And Niyi?'

'I do not talk about Niyi.'

'Why not?'

'My husband's cousin had money. He was well named – Niyi means Wealth has Value. But always he was the black sheep. He did not approve of what they did, but even he did not go to the police in Lagos. Instead he paid for all three of us to leave.'

'So you owe Niyi.'

'I owe nobody nothing. But I will never go back, even if your people deport me. My home died with her last cry. Death would be better than back there.' She looked across. 'Please leave now. They will return soon. Go to your hotel, go anywhere.'

'I'm going to a bar,' I said, making my mind up.

'How will getting drunk help you?'

'Last night I spied on my son and heard him mention he might be there.' I put on my jacket. 'What does Ebun mean?' I asked.

'Gift of God.'

I took out the envelope containing the account numbers and Shyroyal documents, wrote Pete Clancy's name and office number on the front and placed it beside her on the bed.

'Keep this safe,' I said. 'I have no one else to trust. Later tonight I must meet someone. If I do not call again and they try to deport you, phone this man, read out the first number inside and tell him he can have the rest when your permit for asylum arrives.'

I did not kiss her and she did not smile. I undid the chain and opened the door. Niyi stood on the landing outside. He looked scared and watchful. I had no idea how much he had heard. Neither of us spoke as I brushed past and headed down the stairs.

———————◼︎———————

If Sarah-Jane's christening was the talk of Navan, then her first birthday was to be celebrated more quietly seven months after we fled to Cremore. It happened so quickly that I never even knew the house was being sold until the day Phyllis began packing. But things started to lurch in that direction on the night, two weeks after the christening, when I attended Navan dog track for the second time in my life. There was a party function on in Cork that night with my father glad to escape overnight from this new nocturnal world of night feeds and sleep deprivation. Normally Cormac would never risk visiting the outhouse before midnight, but at 9 p.m. I heard his knock on the wood. Fully dressed, he almost danced on the path.

'She's zonked out with the light off. She won't wake till the baby wakes at twelve. We've been talking all evening with Cranky Eamonn out of the way. I finally got her to tell about my real father, a man she met in Scotland. He sounds lovely. She fell in love with him, even though she didn't know his name. I want to do something crazy, let's go to the dog track.'

How did Cormac know that I loved spying through the corrugated iron fence at the greyhound track? He always seemed to guess people's weak spots. If we were caught I knew that I would be beaten and he would not. But I let myself be persuaded, as both of us ran with half-tied laces through back lanes with the stench of alcohol and cigarettes blown out through pub extractor fans.

Stopping at the public toilets he beckoned me in. The floor was flooded, the lights broken. He guided me into a cubicle like an archaeologist exploring an Egyptian tomb and struck a match to reveal the graffiti there. Crude drawings of oversized breasts and penises, slogans for the IRA and against the EEC and dangerous messages scrawled in biro: *Be here at six-thirty, Tuesday, I have nine inches for you.* Underneath in a different hand: *I was here. Where were you? Friday lunchtime, I'll kneel and suck you dry.* Under it again, in black marker: *Fucking queers, you should be burnt alive.*

'Come on, Cormac, it's disgusting. Let's go before someone finds us.' He ignored me and lit another match, his mesmerized look disturbing me.

'Who is this man, do you think? Where would you find him?' He pointed to a name mentioned in three different messages on the wall — Bartley Dunne's.

'I don't know. Come on before someone comes!'

Eventually my anxiety spurred him into leaving. There were two races left when we reached the dog track. The gates were open, with punters already departing. Nobody challenged us. I found a programme on the ground and studied the names and strange codes of times and form.

'Let's bet.' Cormac took a ten-pound note from his pocket.

'Where did you get that?'

'I just did. I was saving it.'

I remembered my father ransacking the outhouse but telling nobody what he was searching for. Before I could challenge him Cormac was walking along the line of bookies with their leather bags. Each refused his bet until the last one glanced around, then took the tenner and gave him a ticket and three pounds change.

His dog limped home second last. Cormac seemed unperturbed, more interested in observing Pete Clancy and his overweight mother among the crowd. 'I'll get him back for you one day,' he said, 'just like I got all the others. I'm no good at betting, you try your hand. I'm going to the toilets.'

I knew he didn't need to, he just wanted to study any graffiti on the walls. But I didn't care what trouble he got himself into. Here I actually was at last on these steps, holding a programme between my shaking fingers and with money to burn. What was the smallest bet I could put on? Fifty pence maybe. What would Cormac say if I lost it? The printed times meant nothing to me, nor the condensed shorthand notes that outlined each dog's form. A small crowd gathered around the parade ring. I liked the look of number five, how he strained at his lead and something about his eyes. Pete Clancy glared over, knowing I had no right to be among decent people. Tomorrow I would get a kicking after school. But I didn't even care if they dragged me off to his makeshift wigwam by the river like he always threatened to do. I was going to finally place a bet and not just for fifty pence. It was everything or bust. The bookie didn't want to take it. 'What the hell age are you, sonny?' he snapped. 'Do you want me to lose my licence?'

'My da sent me down,' I pleaded. 'He's in the bar. He'll beat me if I don't get a ticket.'

Greed and not pity made him take the bet. Three pounds on a no-hope outsider. Number five didn't deserve to win, but the leaders collided. Even then they were catching him all the way. I didn't shout or scream like others in the crowd. I was totally still, transfixed for twenty-nine point eight two seconds. No other life existed. No Pete Clancy, no outhouse. Just me and that dog racing as one. Cormac returned as people started to disperse. He glanced at my face.

'You lost, eh?'

'No,' I replied. 'I won. What does nine to one mean?'

Nine to one plus the stake back meant thirty pounds. The bookie demanded to see my father. Alone I would have fled, frightened that the row would be reported back. But Cormac stood up to him, exacting every penny. We walked home, shell-shocked by our fortune.

'You're a genius,' he said. 'A sheer fecking genius. What will you do with the money?'

'There's a hole in that tree in the lane. We'll keep it there.' My euphoria was gone. Thirty pounds would not change my life. Even with three hundred I would lack the courage to run away. I yearned to be back in the outhouse where I could relive the sensation of placing that bet again and again.

A week later I woke to hear the outhouse door being thrust open. It couldn't be Cormac who always had to knock four times as I had the hidden key. I pulled the blanket tight around me, convinced that my father had been told about the dog track and I was due a midnight beating. Phyllis stood behind him in a nightdress. This had to be really bad. I started shaking, too scared to cry.

'Where is he? Where the hell do you have him?'

The light blinded me. I put my hand up to cover my eyes and when I took it away my father was shifting the filing cabinets, looking behind his old desk, snatching at my blankets. If he had a knife he would have slashed the mattress open.

'Where is he, Brendan? Tell me.' Phyllis spoke pleadingly, her use of my name disturbing me. Normally I was just 'you' or 'him'. They looked haggard. Sarah-Jane had croup and neither had known a proper night's sleep all week.

My father stopped searching, finally convinced that Cormac wasn't hiding in the outhouse. Phyllis started crying. 'Have you seen him, Brendan?' she beseeched. 'He can't swim. What if he goes near the river? You know him. Surely you know where he is?'

She was wrong on both counts. It wasn't possible to know Cormac. At most you could hope to share the same space as him. I had no idea where he was, beyond suspecting that our thirty pounds was gone too. They treated me as their only hope. My father didn't want the police involved. We drove for half the night, along every back lane in Navan where I scrambled onto the back of parked container trucks and peered into disused warehouses, calling his name. Then out along the Boyne as far as Bective, as I searched one riverbank while my father took the other and Phyllis shivered up on each bridge, jigging the whimpering baby wrapped in a white blanket.

I almost drowned, wading into reeds with a stick, and lost a shoe in thick mud. Phyllis didn't scream about the waste of money. Instead she called me a great boy and asked would I keep on searching barefoot. A heron fished at a weir where the reflection of trees turned the water green in the dawn light. I didn't want to find Cormac, I wanted to search on, basking in their gratitude as I tore my face and clothes. This was what it must feel like to be him, I thought, the focus of attention.

I climbed into the ruined abbey at Bective, scouring the nave and oratory, heedless of stones cutting into my soles. A tractor started nearby, with cattle being herded for milking. Phyllis, who had driven on towards Trim, returned and beeped the car horn. I knew they didn't want to be seen. All the way home she convinced herself that Cormac would be waiting there and warned my father not to strike him. His bedroom was empty. It was years since I had stood in the doorway. I was afraid the dried blood from the cuts on my feet would stain the carpet.

'I have to go to school,' I said.

'Skip school for once,' Phyllis replied. 'You deserve it. Wash your feet, take some food and go to bed.'

She looked puzzled before I realized that I was smiling at her. Tentatively she smiled back and I almost swelled with pride. No longer tired, I felt like a dog with two tails. My euphoria lasted to the foot of the stairs where I overheard her tell my father: 'Keep him home for as long as Cormac's away. We don't want lies spread around the town.'

Two nights later four knocks on the outhouse door announced Cormac's return. He looked different, like an inflated version of himself.

'Where the hell were you?' I asked. 'They have the guards trawling the river for you.'

'Why?' He looked incredulous. 'I hate water. Bartley Dunne's isn't a man, it's a pub. I hitched to Dublin and had the most wonderful time.'

'Where did you stay?'

'A man's flat. I met him outside the pub. It was wonderful. He thought I was a fifteen-year-old Protestant escaped from the Freemasons' boarding school.' Cormac affected an upper-class accent that made him sound older. 'We tried everything together. Everything.'

'What do you mean?' I glanced through the chicken wire, terrified of lights appearing in the house.

'I'm not alone. There are dozens in Ireland like me, hundreds even, maybe.'

'Like what?'

'I don't like girls the way you do, Brendan. I have to describe girls to get you excited, but I get excited just seeing you.'

I was confused, scared for him and myself. He looked so animated I was afraid he would climb onto the outhouse roof and tell all of Navan about his adventures. He jigged around describing the man's house in Sutton with views of the sea and a special machine he had to make real apple juice.

'I had to seduce him,' Cormac said. 'He kept saying I was too young, so I told him all about you.'

'You told him what?' I was truly petrified now.

'That you were twenty-six with a job in the bank and we'd been lovers for two years.'

'Jesus, Cormac. You didn't tell him my name?'

'Don't be silly.' Cormac smiled. 'Brendan is too common for a Protestant name. I made one up. That's all you need do if you want to be someone else. You don't always have to be you, you know.'

'I don't want us to do those things again,' I said. 'They're not right.'

'That's true.' He took out a packet of cigarettes and offered me one. 'With you they're not right. You're not one of us. I can tell the difference now.'

Sarah-Jane started crying in the house, an angry scream, demanding attention. The bedroom light came on. We watched Phyllis's silhouette pacing the floor, trying to soothe her.

'Your mother's been crying for days,' I said. 'Don't you care for her?'

'Yes.' Cormac's voice sounded sombre. 'But it was better when there was only the two of us in a flat and your father came and went. I remember her waiting at the window and it always felt like Christmas when he came. Navan was never the same. What I did in Dublin wasn't wrong, but what they've done to you is. I knew it from the day they put you in here. I just never found a way to make her understand.' He looked at me and laughed. 'Let's live in Dublin. It's the place to be. There's an open market called the Dandelion and proper record shops. We'll make them move.'

'How?'

A second silhouette appeared at the curtain, my father jadedly taking his turn. Cormac touched me. I stepped back wincing but he calmed me, rolling up my vest to examine my bruised back.

'It was Pete Clancy, wasn't it? I saw him give you a hiding in the lane on Monday with boys looking on. I want to make him suffer.'

'Don't be crazy. Nobody can touch a Clancy.'

He stubbed out his cigarette and walked outside to toss the butt into Casey's garden. 'Lock the door,' he whispered, 'or they'll know you have a key.'

'What are you going to say to them?'

Cormac didn't reply, just picked up a pebble and aimed it at their window. I locked the door, hid the key and watched through the chicken wire as his second pebble caused the curtain to twitch. Phyllis was the first to make it down. The baby cried away ignored upstairs while Phyllis wept and hugged her son. Finally she let him go and looked back towards my father in the kitchen doorway.

'I want an explanation,' he said. 'It's been three nights.'

'I was afraid.' Cormac broke down in tears.

'Afraid of who?'

'Pete Clancy.'

Phyllis looked back at my father, silencing him. 'Why are you afraid of him?' she asked.

'He did things to me. Things I didn't want to do.'

'What things?'

'Dirty things. After school on Monday in the wigwam they've built by the river. He said he'd drown me if I didn't let him.' He leaned forward and whispered something. Phyllis stepped back as if she'd just been slapped and turned to my father.

'Do something,' she screamed, causing lights to come on in back bedrooms along the street. 'You have got to do something!'

My father looked rattled, unsure of what to believe. 'How the hell can I?' he snapped. 'What proof do I have?'

'This.' Cormac spoke clearly enough for the listening neighbours to hear. He slipped his shirt off and turned so they could see his bare shoulders in the light from the kitchen doorway. Phyllis ran her fingers lightly along his neck and turned away.

'You can see the nail marks,' she wailed. 'That Clancy bastard almost clawed the skin off his back. What are you going to do, Eamonn? Are you a coward or what?'

Even if my father did nothing, I knew that by teatime tomorrow adult whispers about Pete Clancy would have insidiously reached every corner of Navan. Rumours more damaging than even the most savage beating I had fantasized about. Watching my father I should have felt a thrill of revenge. Instead I felt such anger that I found myself shaking. Four years ago I had cried, telling him the truth about Pete Clancy beating Cormac up. The man had refused to allow

himself to believe what he knew was true. His face told me
that he was sceptical of Cormac, yet I knew he would allow
himself to believe this lie.

Over the next few days my father did what any official in
his position would do. He talked of going to the parish priest,
the school principal and the police. He swore to have it out
with Barney Clancy and bring that man to his knees because
of his son. Then he went silent, knowing that his bluff was
being called by the rumours about Cormac and Pete Clancy
which had been exaggerated as they spread throughout the
town. To my father power was about the control of perception
and this time he was powerless. He sat up drinking for two
nights, unable to bear being in the same room as Cormac. A
week later he came home with a determined look, summoned
me from the outhouse to sit with Cormac and drove off with
Phyllis and the baby.

That afternoon he showed Phyllis the solution to the problem, keeping his back turned as he stared out of the bay
window and talked about the move being in everyone's inter-
ests. He would have been too embarrassed to watch her breast-
feed Sarah-Jane in the empty living-room of the house he had
hastily purchased in Cremore.

———◄|►———

Half an hour after leaving Ebun's flat I slipped down a lane
beyond George's Street and discovered that I knew the Oliver
Twist pub and yet I didn't. I had drunk there during a different
incarnation, when it was Boyle's Bar. The long marble counter
was all that remained from the days when a white-aproned
Mr Boyle patrolled its length, refusing to serve pints to women
and deciding, with his own perverse logic, who to bar on
sight and who to eventually initiate as an accepted regular by

plonking a '*Baader Meinhof*' before them – a cocktail concocted and christened by himself 'because it would blow the head off you, boy'.

Golfers qualified for the US Masters easier than most drinkers qualified for a '*Meinhof*'. This was why a ripple of awe passed through the bar when Cormac earned us both one on our first visit, due to Mr Boyle's child-like amazement at Cormac's disappearing ten-pound note trick.

Like all of Cormac's scams it was simplicity itself. He asked Mr Boyle to take ten pounds from the till, write his initials in one corner, place it inside the white handkerchief in Cormac's hand and stare intently at the raised handkerchief for forty seconds. This was long enough for me to discreetly pick the banknote off the floor (where Cormac had dropped it when raising the handkerchief), use it to get change for the cigarette machine off the dozy barman at the far end of the counter and disappear into the toilets before Cormac opened the handkerchief with a flourish to reveal a note inside announcing, 'It's in the far till behind you'.

Mr Boyle had been enthralled (plus unwittingly ten pounds poorer) and – aged twenty-one and twenty-two – we became his youngest accepted regulars by around twenty years. Cormac might have felt more at home in the Oliver Twist now, but the barman would have given him the same 'here comes another cradle-snatcher' look as I received when I sat at the counter to order a drink.

The funny thing was that it was here, watching ranks of openly gay men converge around crowded tables and cram onto the small dance floor in this utterly changed pub, that I felt in danger of being recognized. Not that I knew many faces, but several old acquaintances of Cormac's stood out. Men with whom he had brief and casual affairs, with Cormac allowing them just close enough to realize afterwards that they had only the vaguest sense of who he was. Nobody ever penetrated the vague friendliness behind which he kept the world at bay, until Alex Lever arrived from Scotland to work in the newly opened Blackrock Private Clinic.

If few people present might remember Cormac, his relationship with Alex Lever would still be talked about by many gays who came out in the 1980s. One man glanced across to scrutinize me and looked puzzled, confronted by a hybrid of memories. With my dyed hair I looked enough like Cormac to fool customs officials who glanced quickly at his passport, yet still sufficiently like an older beardless version of myself to confuse the drinker who turned away. He had been a volunteer doorman in the Hirshfield Centre, Dublin's first gay club in Fownes Street among the cobbled rundown lanes in what became Temple Bar, on the night I brought Miriam there after the pubs closed on our first proper date.

She was incredulous at first, refusing to believe we were actually going in even when I explained that – unlike Zhivago's or McGonegal's or other straight night-clubs – there was no hassle from bouncers or barmen ripping you off. Girls from the Dunnes Stores meat counter often arrived en masse to enjoy the company of stylish male dancers without the hassle of being drunkenly pawed.

I had made it sound like an adventure she could laugh about with friends, but in reality I wanted to show her off to Cormac. A girlfriend was probably the only thing that Cormac would not borrow and forget to give back. This was before Alex Lever, when Cormac was still the carefree centre of attention among a group of young men in the TV room upstairs. Immediately he charmed Miriam, feeding her the most outrageous lies about me. I remembered how natural everything seemed that night with Cormac's friends making

Miriam welcome, teasing him and being teased back as they conveyed the image of a perfect Peter Pan world.

So why did the world inside the Oliver Twist seem sinister now as I scanned the tables for any sign of Conor? AIDS had occurred in the meantime, but it was more than that risk or Conor's age which made me uncomfortable. It was hypocritical to feel that what had been all right for a brother was not okay for a son. Still I hated the notion of Conor belonging among this pumping music and the mêlée of hands touching shoulders as men passed. It reinforced just how much of his growing up I had missed. I spotted Charles who danced with another young man in the ruck of bodies, with Charles whispering in his ear. I must have stared so hard that eventually his companion noticed and said something. Charles looked across, giving me a cheeky dismissive wink, then continued dancing.

I turned to order another drink, with the barman mustering a sympathetic 'I-told-you-so' look. Younger voices suddenly besieged my shoulder, calling him by name, clamouring for attention. Immediately I knew that Conor was among them. I recognized his laugh and heard within it not only a disconcerting echo of Cormac but of my own father's voice too.

Conor stood directly at my shoulder, pressing against me in his anxiety to be served. The child wasn't old enough to be in any pub, let alone here. I wanted to turn and look up into his face but couldn't bring myself to. Yet I could almost feel his breath and sense his aura of youth, so eager for experience and open to hurt. His hand came down onto the counter next to mine, lifting the first drinks and passing them back. Such long fingers he always had, made to play the piano. Chatting about the march they had been on, he handed the money over, hovered for his change and was gone.

Eventually I found the strength to turn and watch him

laugh among a large group which Charles had also joined. His hair was the same colour as mine had been once, yet he looked more like Cormac. Charles drifted away, pausing to joke with somebody before following the youth he had danced with into the gents. I had simply wanted to feel close to Conor for a while, but found myself following Charles.

The music was even louder in the toilets, the walls dominated by an archly ironic mural, a pastiche of *The Bathers* by Seurat. I half expected to find them in some cubicle together, but the other youth was washing his hands at the gold-topped taps, while Charles urinated with his back to me. As the youth left, Charles looked up, taking in my presence in the mirror above the urinals.

'You got a problem?' he asked, starting to do his buttons up. I didn't reply. He turned and brushed past me to reach the washbasins.

'How old are you?' I asked.

'What's it to you?'

'I'm asking.'

'Old enough to know better.' He flicked water towards me. 'But still young enough to enjoy it.'

He dried his hands and walked towards the door, deliberately barging against my shoulder.

'You hurt Conor in any way and I'll come looking for you, pal.'

He looked back, perturbed and less cocksure, unable to decide if I was an admirer of Conor's or a family member dragging in the dangers of the outside world. His uncertainty made him look younger.

'Who the hell are you?'

'Still young enough to burst your balls, Charlie boy.'

He didn't reply, just stared one last time and left. I found myself trembling, knowing that I had said too much and should leave now. But I felt like a fly trapped on insect paper. The thought of Conor being so tantalizingly close was killing me. I closed over a cubicle door, staring at the graffiti and the small hole punched in the wall into the next cubicle. What was Charles telling Conor now? Suppose he came in, demanding to know who I was? I couldn't bear the thought of meeting him in a toilet. Unlocking the cubicle, I splashed water on my face and went back outside.

Every seat along the counter was taken. The pub was packed, with more punters spilling in. Screens on the walls displayed videos while music blasted from the speakers. The former door-man from the Hirshfield Centre appeared at my shoulder.

'I just can't put a name on you,' he said. 'But I know your face from years back. Was it on holidays somewhere?'

I shook my head, afraid to let him hear my voice. My collar was stained with red hair-dye in the heat. Charles must have said something because Conor glanced over, half-threateningly and half-scared. Who did he see? Yesterday I had not recognized him and he was only seven when I disappeared, but surely some memory of me remained with him? Not that I wanted us to speak because I wouldn't know where to begin.

Men jostled me as I blocked the crowded floor, but I refused to budge, watching Conor intently and not caring how others at his table had started jeering at him over having an admirer. My son was just so beautiful and I was so proud of him and ashamed of myself. He checked his watch, with Charles obviously offering to accompany him. But Conor shook his head, grabbed his jacket and headed for the door. His friends looked over as though defying me to follow. I half-thought they were going to block my path, but I would have fought my way past them because my resolution was gone. I couldn't bear to be parted from the sight of my son.

It was cold outside in the dark lane. Conor had almost

reached George's Street. He glanced back to register my
presence and ducked into a smaller alley, confusing me. Could
he be waiting there? The thought was horrifying – maybe he
liked older men. Then I remembered that a shortcut there led
out into Dame Street. I prayed that he was trying to lose the
person he presumed to be an admirer, but I followed just the
same.

His footsteps quickened as he heard me enter the alley.
They almost broke into a run, then stopped like he was waiting
for me or trying to hide. I was afraid to call, not wanting to
frighten him. I turned the last corner. Dame Street lay ahead,
through an archway fifteen yards on. Conor had stepped back
against the steel door of a restaurant kitchen, with the sound
of pots being banged inside and an extractor fan billowing out
the stench of cooking oil. He confronted me, trying to act like
a practised hardman, but unable to disguise his vulnerability.

'What do you want?' he demanded. 'Why are you following me?'

Under the glaring pub lights he had seemed older, a stranger
with a blonde streak. But the light here made his face young.
I could see the child I had chased on the beach at Donabate,
both of us tumbling down between sand dunes in a tangle of
excited limbs.

'I don't want anything,' I said.

'Yeah, sure.' In another year his sneer would be perfect. I
searched his eyes for any recognition of my voice but they
were distant and watchful.

'Except maybe to talk,' I added.

'About what?'

'Listen . . .' I had to stop myself from using the word, son.
'Could we not go somewhere?'

'I don't go down alleys.'

'I'm not . . . I didn't mean . . .' I had no right to feel upset at being misunderstood. In fact I had no rights at all. I didn't even know what I wanted to say. I had fucked up his life once already, so why risk doing so again? 'I'm not looking for sex.'

'Men your age always say that when they come on to you.'

'What men?'

My concern perturbed him. He looked down the alley for reassurance at people passing on Dame Street.

'You're a funny old buzzard, aren't you? Charles said you were.'

'Come for a coffee, just you and me, please.'

'You listen . . .' For a moment I thought he was going to touch my arm in sympathy. 'Go back inside. You'll meet someone else. There are lots of lads in there up for it. Younger than me even.'

'It's only you I want to talk to.'

'I'm sorry but I have to get home,' he said, 'my mother's expecting me.'

I couldn't tell if this was genuine or a tactic to emphasize our age difference.

'Does she know . . . about you?'

He tossed his head back and laughed, his voice natural this time with all the defensiveness gone.

'A bishop wouldn't ask me that.'

'Let me walk you to your bus stop, please, Conor.'

'How do you know my name?' He was cagey, on guard.

'I overheard it in the pub.'

He scrutinized me carefully, as if trying to place me. Perhaps he sensed something familiar – though maybe this was wishfulness on my part.

'Come on then.' He smiled. 'Lucky old me with my personal chaperone.'

We left the alley and joined the throng in Dame Street.

Now that he had allowed me to be with him I could think of nothing to say. But I couldn't stop gazing at him, even though I knew this attention in public was making him uneasy.

We crossed the street where a cluster of girls sang, deliberately out of key, drinking from cans beside the world's ugliest fountain on the Bank of Ireland plaza. Several of them eyed Conor with obvious interest. The pavement narrowed as we turned into Westmoreland Street so that we had to fight our way through the crush under the porticoes of the old bank. Another new hotel was being built behind the façade of an old building across the road. Buses were pulling out where crowds queued at the line of stops. Conor glanced at me suspiciously when I chose the correct queue for Cremore.

'You don't say much, do you?' he remarked.

'I like walking with you.'

'Why?'

The queue dissolved into a scrum as a bus swung around the corner. A young couple pushed between us, the girl leading the way, her eyes fixed on any gap in the crowd ahead. Conor mounted the step then looked back at me and waved. But I couldn't let him go. The bus was packed, with the driver shouting that he could take no more. I elbowed my way ahead of two youths who cursed at me. If I didn't get on board I knew I would have to fight them. Maybe the driver sensed this too, because after he had told me again that the bus was full and I still refused to step back, he shrugged and closed the door. He sat encased by security glass, telling me to insert coins in the steel slot. I did so, then fought my way through the people standing in the aisle.

There was no sign of Conor downstairs. The bus had circled Parnell Square and reached the Black Church before the crush began to ease as several passengers descended the stairs. I climbed up to look around. The absence of smoke was what

I noticed first. When I was Conor's age, travelling upstairs meant sitting inside a tobacco cloud. Often at night you didn't even pay the full fare, but 'tipped the rent' to bribe some conductor on the fiddle who never bothered to issue tickets. The tradition of couples virtually mounting each other in the back seats remained the same however, with the last bus still acting as a fast-track method through the early stages of fore-play. Other passengers climbed up behind me, anxious to find seats. There was a space beside Conor at the very front. I occupied it, not looking at him. He glanced across defensively, betraying his sudden fear.

'What the fuck are you doing here?' he hissed.

'I didn't get to say good-bye.'

'Jesus!' He raised his eyes, then peered discreetly around. 'Some people on this bus know me from my new school. Don't try following me home, you old queen. I'll fucking kill you if you do.'

Conor's voice was so low I could barely hear it. He clenched his hands anxiously on his knee, making me want to touch them in reassurance. I glanced back, but nobody paid us any attention. We could be total strangers or just an ordinary father and son. But nobody had seemed to be paying Cormac any attention either on the night he was suddenly jumped upon at nineteen on this same bus route. There were no security cameras back then. The bus conductor was in on the attack or at least had not risked a trip upstairs until the youths stomped noisily off, leaving Cormac with his face bleeding, a rib broken and the word 'QUEER' scrawled with his blood on the window. I wanted to tell Conor about his uncle, I wanted to tell him a hundred different things. But I knew that I couldn't. Not here and possibly not ever.

'Give me a nod,' I whispered. 'Three stops before your stop. I'll get off and promise not to bother you again.'

He looked across. 'Use your sleeve,' he urged quietly, then saw I was baffled. 'You're crying.'

I raised my sleeve awkwardly, then peered through the misted-up window at streets so familiar they were heart-aching. A thousand bus journeys here alone or with Cormac. I didn't feel like a ghost any longer. This ache was so real it was unbearable. Up close Conor looked more like me, but nowhere in his glance was there any hint of recognition. We reached Hart's Corner, the tiny lane up to the gravediggers' pub, then the Botanic Gardens. He should be warning me to get off before coming too close to his home. I wanted him to so that I could be alone now, to walk down steps to the Tolka river beside the Pyramid Church and end it all with Joey Kerwin's old revolver. Those bank accounts didn't matter any more, nor revenge upon Pete Clancy or passports. I just knew that Conor had built his own life and there was no way back into it for me.

He touched my knee gently at Washerwoman's Hill, indicating that I was to rise. Maybe he meant to stay on past his own stop and double back when I was gone. But as I descended the stairs I found him following me. I stood on the kerb as the bus moved off, aware of Conor behind me.

'You're a bloody nuisance,' he said, softly now, with almost bemused affection.

'I'll wait here and get a bus back into town,' I replied without turning.

'If you've come this far you can chaperone me for the last bit. But there's no coming in, mind you, nothing like that.'

We crossed the road and walked past a line of nineteenth-century houses, with long gardens and high walls casting the footpath into shadow. Had other men walked here with him, stopping to kiss him in the shaded gateway where I once kissed a Holy Faith girl who dated me as a substitute for Cormac?

'You're one of life's great talkers,' he teased.

'Does your mother know?' I asked again.

'She knows what she wants to know, I don't think she's ready to face the rest.'

'That must be lonely for you.'

'It is since my gran went into hospital. She was great.'

He looked back at where I had stopped, though he couldn't see my expression in the shadows.

'Your gran?' I asked.

'Yeah. I've always been able to confide in her. You see, years ago she had a son who . . .'

'She told you about Cormac?'

Conor froze. His defensiveness and suspicion returned. 'There's been something bugging me ever since I saw you. How do you know about my uncle?'

He took a step forward, then backed away and looked around. This stretch of road was always lonely, with few passers-by.

'Don't be scared,' I said.

'I'm not scared. It's just you give me the creeps. How long have you been stalking me? Now fuck off with yourself.'

'Conor?' I put a hand out.

'No.' He backed further away.

'I knew Cormac,' I said. 'I was . . . we were . . .' I left the sentence unfinished, knowing he would substitute the word lovers for brothers. 'At times you look very like him at your age.'

'Do I?' Despite his unease he was curious. 'I've never met anybody who knew him, or at least knew him when he was out. Not that I've asked around, I mean you don't want to give too much of your identity away. Was he nice?'

'He was special,' I replied, 'more than nice.'

I leaned against a high wall, feeling pebbledash dig into my back.

'You look like you could use a smoke.' Conor held out a packet of cigarettes. 'Have one of mine.'

'You shouldn't smoke,' I cautioned and he laughed.

'Jaysus, you sound like a parent. I mean, your preachy tone.'

'What do your parents sound like?'

'Mam's a social worker, so you can imagine. Normally she doesn't like me out this late but it's my midterm break. Dad died years ago.' He lit his cigarette, then held the match out. I stooped to take a light, aware of how the match lit up my face. Cormac dropped it suddenly as the flame almost scorched his fingers.

'Do you miss him?' I wondered were there still photographs of me at home or had Miriam put them away.

'If he was anything like his own dad he might not have been too understanding.'

'Never judge a son by his father. What was your granddad like?'

Conor's tone hardened. 'You ask too many questions, pal. I know your face if I could place it. Maybe off the telly. That's what this is about, isn't it? The bloody tribunal he was supposed to give evidence to. He's barely cold in his grave and you're digging for dirt to use him as a scapegoat. I've read about how the dead can't sue. Well, he never had a penny and any peace he had was destroyed by solicitors and anonymous bloody phone calls before that scumbag broke in.'

'What phone calls?'

'You're the bloody reporter. You figure it out.'

Conor stalked off. When I followed he began to run, then slowed to a walk as if determined to show that he refused to be intimidated.

'Please . . . *please*.'

He turned to confront me at the corner of Cremore. 'What?'

'I swear to God I'm not a reporter.'

'Then who the hell are you? You've never even said your name.'

'I knew you when you were small. You loved the Wombles. You had a cuddly toy of one, Uncle Bulgaria, with a plastic bead for a nose. You loved the noise it made when you banged its nose against the window.'

'How do you know that?'

I could see that he barely remembered himself. 'You lived opposite St Anne's Park in Raheny.'

'We moved in to mind the house after Granddad died. It didn't stop sickos breaking in during his funeral though, grabbing anything they could find, even my passport from my room. We still get late-night calls, heavy breathing like an asthmatic with a poker up his arse. You're not the first guy to hang around watching me. Who can blame me being paranoid when these last months have been hell.'

'Tell me about being assaulted.'

'How do you know about that?' Conor asked, suspicious.

'I read it in the paper. After your grandfather's funeral.'

'I left the pub one night,' he said. 'A car pulled up, I thought it was a hackney. The driver was huge. He drove down a lane and clattered me a few times. "That's a warning for someone close to you," he said, pushing me out. A policeman found me bleeding. I had to pretend it was random young fellows, I didn't want to admit to being in the bar and all – I mean I'm under-age. Gays get attacked the whole time but normally we're beaten up worse than that.'

'Who do you think it was?' I asked.

'A relation of somebody in the pub trying to teach them a lesson through me. Maybe I'd danced with their son. Or maybe a parent from school because next morning graffiti was sprayed on the wall there. Phone threats started then. Mam's renting our house out until I finish the Leaving Cert. I'm in a new school where nobody knows me and there's no hassle so far at least. That's why I have to be home on time. I promised Mam . . .' He looked at me. 'Would she know you?'

'We're talking about a long time ago.'

'But you were obviously in our house . . . maybe with Uncle Cormac. I've never seen you around the pubs or the . . .'

Conor left the sentence unfinished and me racking my imagination. Cormac had always maintained that the gay saunas in Dublin were among the most promiscuous he'd ever known. Where did Conor spend his weekends and taking what risks? There were so many questions that I knew I couldn't ask.

'I've been away.' I hesitated, then asked. 'Does your mother miss your father?'

'That's her business,' Conor said brusquely. 'What's it to you?'

'I knew them both . . . through Cormac.'

Conor gazed up the road towards where a light burned in what was once my father's house. 'There was a long limbo when they tried to establish how many were killed. They found nothing of him, but he was caught on security camera buying a ticket.'

'But she did get compensation?' I obviously sounded panic-stricken, because Conor stared at me.

'Eventually,' he said flatly. 'She never talked about it much.'

Loud footsteps approached, a courting couple in the midst of a petty squabble. We fell silent, standing further apart as we waited for them to pass. They crossed the junction and stopped at the far corner, the youth leaning back against the wall to put his arms around the girl. Both glanced proprietorially over, letting us know we were on their patch.

'How's your gran?' I hated using that word for her.

'Chemotherapy never worked. They'd sent her home before the break-in because there was nothing else they could do. She's very ill, gets confused, even over what she heard that night.'

'What do you mean?'

'She told the cops that Granddad cried out "quick". Afterwards she thought it was "Mick" or "sick", but didn't want to look foolish by changing her mind. What's wrong?'

My fingers gripped the revolver in my pocket as I remembered a boy's leering face.

'Nothing,' I lied.

The couple stared across, their presence disturbing Conor. He wanted to go in, yet I couldn't part from him under their gaze. Conor sensed it too and walked up the incline towards my father's house. I followed in silence. The gardens were raised up from the road, filled with mature shrubs. Trees grew on the grass verge, creating a mosaic of shadows. Conor stopped under a tree, our view of the couple blocked by a parked van.

'I don't want you coming any closer if you don't mind.'

'I understand,' I said.

'You're still not my type . . . just in case you were thinking . . .'

'I wasn't.'

'Maybe I'll see you around.'

'I have to meet someone later,' I said. 'Business to sort out. I don't know if I'll be around. I just want to say –'

'Don't,' he interrupted gently. 'Things people want to say at this time of night they generally regret in the morning.'

He glanced down the path, then leaned his face forward. I drew back, surprised, and he smiled, in control now like I was the child.

'I'm not going to bite,' he teased and kissed me once on the lips. He drew back, unable to read my expression. 'That was for Cormac,' he said.

He turned to walk off quickly, but I knew he was moving in a deliberate way. Not flaunting himself, but conscious of his youth and allowing me to enjoy the sight. I walked to the corner and looked back up towards the house. Conor never glanced around, even when he opened the door. A shadow appeared briefly at the landing window. My wife concerned for her son. Refuting the rumours about him, but uprooting herself from her home to give him another chance elsewhere.

The courting couple had made up their quarrel. The youth raised his eyes from where he was dug into his girlfriend, trying to intimidate me into moving away. But I knelt down to search the pavement for the cigarette butt I had stubbed out. A present from my son. I held it in my palm as I walked all the way to Finglas Bridge, gripping it so tight that by the time I hailed a taxi it had crumbled away into a hundred flakes. But still I wouldn't let it go as the driver drove in silence along the motorway to Navan. Ebun would understand because she would never know such treasure. Sitting in the dark cab I alternated between tears and elation, hardly able to focus on my forthcoming confrontation with Pete Clancy. Nothing mattered except that I had met my son who was being threatened by something that I was sure he knew nothing about and that I swore I would sort out for him.

IV

———·—·———

TUESDAY, A.M.

The new extended licensing hours meant that the pubs in Navan were still only emptying as the taxi manoeuvred its way through the narrow streets around Market Square. The town seemed to stretch out forever now, with estate after estate of mock period houses built in the style of Late Irish Grotesque. I let the driver drop me off at the pillared entrance to one such development on the Slane Road. There was no sign of life through the ornate gold-tipped railings, as though a curfew came into existence at eleven o'clock.

The driver was watching so I strolled up towards the first house and waited until he had done a U-turn back towards Dublin before slipping out again to walk along the Slane Road. A straggle of old labourer's cottages were interspersed with modern bungalows. Earthmovers had ploughed up the uneven gravel verge, entering fields marked out with crosses for new houses. Beyond a deserted garage forecourt two last streetlights watched over a junction where a night-bird alighted from a five-barred gate as I passed.

Eventually I reached an unchanged stretch of roadway where I could recognize every bend, the stream which sometimes flooded two low-lying fields in winter and the whin bushes by Jennings' low wall where fattened cattle liked to shelter. The stars were not as bright as I remembered them, but the halo of orange light cast by Navan had quadrupled since I had last walked here.

Being dropped off in Navan allowed me to arrive by stealth

at Maguire's field and try to ascertain whether Clancy came alone. My right hand kept fingering the loaded gun in my pocket. It was a new experience for me and I was terrified of it suddenly going off. Several times headlights warned of an oncoming car, allowing me time to shelter in a ditch. But one car surprised me from behind, its headlights blinding me. I anticipated it swerving across the road. A glancing blow with no witnesses and a quick respray would solve Clancy's problem of unwelcome e-mail, but not gain him the account numbers he so obviously needed. The car sped past and at heart I knew he would never risk such an accident until he discovered who I was.

I left the road where it bent past a crooked rowan tree and took the small potholed lane leading to Maguire's farmhouse over the hill. Halfway up I backtracked through a sloping field of wheat to the hill field under pasture where I had told Clancy to be. A car was already parked there, its lights off. I crouched beside the stone wall, watching. But there was no sign of anyone keeping guard at the edge of the field, in the bushes bordering the road or by the closed gate. The car itself could be empty for all I knew.

I lay on my back to stare up. From here the stars looked as bright as I remembered them. Memories flooded back of a night spent lying here, having hitched from Cremore at fifteen, knowing that no search parties would be sent out. Logically I should have enjoyed Dublin. My own bedroom with no 'Hen Boy' jeering in my new school and even Phyllis making an effort to pretend we were one happily unhappy family. Instead I had found the house suffocating at night, missing the noise of rain on the corrugated roof. Navan used to feel safe because everyone there knew that I was nobody. But cast adrift in adolescence in Cremore I couldn't cope with neighbours who treated me like Cormac's equal.

Several times I had absconded to Meath, breaking into the outhouse. Once I was discovered crouching there by the new owners and fled out into these fields. Lying here I had imagined imponderable rendezvous with my unknown future. First love, first kiss, first sex with a girl, first win at a racecourse, first everything to be savoured.

The future lay behind me now, but it lay ahead of Conor. I could ensure he needn't skimp like me. He wouldn't have to search for a factory job on the day secondary school ended, while Cormac spent the summer on an exchange holiday in Paris to increase his chances of getting the points for university. If I played my cards right Conor could have money to study wherever he wished, open a business or simply travel. He need never know where the money came from but I would have left him with more than just bad memories of his father in a betting shop.

A car door slammed. I peered into Maguire's field at a solitary figure in an overcoat, waiting to see would he speak or signal to anyone. After a few moments Pete Clancy turned to open the car door again, as though having put the whole episode down to a hoax. Before I could change my mind I chanced my weight upon a thin strand of barbed wire and clambered through the gap. I stumbled, then regained my footing but remained crouched. The noise halted him. Clancy closed the car door and walked slowly towards where he figured I had to be. But he didn't call out or betray any sign of nerves. His stride was almost nonchalant, as if vaguely amused to be here. I suspected it was not the strangest place he had ever met people.

I rose to my full height, fingering the gun in my pocket. He stopped fifteen feet away, but still didn't speak. He had become his father, the same stocky build, same unruly hair tamed by Brylcreem. I watched him try to place my face in the moonlight.

'I haven't got all night,' he said at last, disgruntled that his silence hadn't lured me into speaking first.

'It's not the first time you've been in this field?'

He sounded baffled. 'I'm a politician, there isn't an inch of Meath I haven't been in.'

'Not the first time you were in this field at night.'

My voice was familiar to him, even with the Navan accent almost gone. I could sense his mind like a computer, searching back-up files but still unable to place it in any way that made sense.

'What are you saying?' He didn't sound defensive, just baffled. I knew he didn't remember the incident.

'A summer's night years ago. You gave a girl a lift home from a dance in Trim.'

'That wouldn't have been unusual.'

'You joked about your father never getting a first preference vote off her family.'

'Who the hell are you?' His memory banks were working furiously, his tone aggressive. 'And what are you insinuating?'

'Lisa Hanlon. A slight girl, not especially pretty.'

'I remember the family. The grandfather was a Blueshirt in the thirties. The mother died recently.'

'I'm not discussing her family. You didn't try to rape her family. I'm discussing her.'

'I remember her, all right!' Pete Clancy muttered irritably. 'A scrawny sparrow you couldn't get two words out of. Who says I tried to rape her? Do you think I'm going to be frightened by some trumped-up blackmail threat?'

'"You're not getting out of this car until you give me something," you told her.'

On that night I had been with Cormac and his university pals at an illegal bar set up by the students' union in the Junior

Common Room in Trinity. There was a riot when porters tried to close it. Police stood outside on College Green, harmless country lads just unleashed from training in Templemore. Cormac blew them kisses, passing me a joint under their noses. 'Young Men in Uniform,' he'd shouted in a Polish accent, hands raised in a Papal blessing, 'I love you!'

'There was no penetration,' Clancy said testily, jangling his car keys irritably.

'Your father always said there were more ways than one to skin a cat.'

'I remember nothing untoward,' he said. 'Nothing that wasn't common practice back then.'

Cormac's friends were back at our flat on the North Circular Road, playing poker at dawn, when the police arrived. Dope was being hidden, windows opened, hard-drinking Maoist students reverting to scared South Dublin boys who hoped their daddies had sufficient connections to squash any possible conviction, when the police asked for my help in identifying a girl pulled from the canal.

'Lisa thought she was going to choke,' I said. 'The way you wouldn't release her head.'

'There was no penetration and no complaint,' Clancy snapped. 'That was twenty years ago. Now what the hell business is it of yours, Hen Boy?'

'What did you call me?'

'Nothing.' He stopped, shaken. 'Your voice . . . for a moment it reminded me . . .' He stepped forward, an edge of menace entering his tone. 'Say something!'

I remained mute, watching him examine my face more fully. The moonlight nullified the red dye in my hair, while Clancy – unlike Miriam or anyone else who first met me after the age of seventeen – knew my face when it was beardless. He had held it close to his, taunting, spitting, threatening. His eyes were wide now, scared. His hand was half-raised as if about to tear my glasses off.

'You're dead,' he whispered finally. 'I was at your memorial mass, along with fifty bookies and loan sharks looking for what you owed them.'

I gripped the gun in my pocket so hard that it hurt my fingers, holding his gaze and aware that my silence was unnerving him.

'Say something, fucking Hen Boy, with your stink reeking the schoolyard.' He was trying to provoke a response, unnerved by a situation slipping beyond his control. 'Shyroyal, my arse. Slypeasant more like. What's one spluttery blow-job off a buck-toothed Blueshirt bitch when all of Navan knows that you rode the arse off her, then disappeared back into the arms of your red-arsed queer bastard brother.'

The jibe about Lisa struck home. I remembered how small she had looked in the hospital ward and shame at how my initial feelings were of relief that she had tried to commit suicide because of him and not me. I was the one who had failed her, yet it was I who held her hand and persuaded her to tell the doctors her name, lying that everything would be all right. She knew it wouldn't be, that the taste would never leave her mouth. Yet there seemed no point in going to the police about a Clancy back then. This was six months after I met Miriam. A fortnight later I heard that Lisa had emigrated, having never told her parents why she was going.

Pete Clancy's face came close to mine. 'Speak, you fucking fraud! You're meant to be dead! What the fuck are you doing here?'

'I've come to haunt you.'

'Really?' Clancy blew air into my face and stepped back. 'Is that meant as a threat?'

'My father died of a heart attack when somebody tied him up.'

'I know,' Clancy replied. 'Unlike you I attended his funeral.'

'Maybe I was saving myself for the inquest.'

'Dead by misadventure. He would never have had to leave Navan only for that shirt-lifting brother of yours. Do you know how many years his lies haunted me? That's why your father wound up in Dublin, at the mercy of some Dublin junkie.'

'A methodical junkie,' I replied. 'He ransacked every drawer and cupboard.'

'Money for drugs, anything for a fix.' He managed to sound sympathetic, his manner still not composed but regaining a measure of watchful cunning.

'He made a poor job of the attic though.'

He opened his mouth, then glanced quickly towards the bushes. 'He was probably trying to grab what he could and run,' he reasoned.

'He seemed in no hurry.' I advanced on him. 'Until Da's heart attack scuppered his plans.'

Clancy stepped back, uneasily taking in how my hand clenched something in my pocket. 'Your father was a good friend to my father.'

'Maybe not such a good friend to you.'

'You're talking riddles,' he said.

'I'm talking digits,' I corrected him. 'Sorting codes, numbered accounts to mask identities, bogus names, watertight serials your father thought untraceable once.'

'Leave Daddy out of this.'

'We wouldn't be here, Clancy, if it wasn't for our fathers. Did they fall out?'

'How would I know?' he snapped. 'I was never that interested in your bloody father.'

'I doubt if they did. Lap dogs are never unfaithful, no matter how often their master kicks them. The problem is that they're only ever faithful to one master.'

'You're still talking in fucking riddles, Hen Boy.' Clancy was finding it harder to control his unease. Froth coated his lips. A car passed on the road. We both turned, startled by the intrusion, and watched tail-lights disappear from sight.

'Say what you came to say,' Clancy snapped. 'I haven't got all night!'

'Temper,' I mocked. 'You always had a worse temper than even Slick McGuirk.'

The name perturbed him. He lowered his voice to a whisper. 'Do yourself a favour, Brendan, piss off back to under whatever rock you're after crawling out from under.'

'Why should I?'

'We're different people living in different times now. Even if we regret certain things we can't change them.' I found it disturbing how different Clancy now looked as he spoke – weary and concerned. 'The past is finished, kaput, over and done with.'

'What if it's still gaining interest in the Channel Islands?'

'You're an arsehole, Brogan.' His voice was so low I could barely hear it. 'If you have something of mine then post it to me. Now for your own sake turn around and walk away. You've been away so long you understand nothing.'

I stepped back, deliberately raising my voice. 'I understand that you don't mind stitching up Slick McGuirk. Phyllis overheard his name only she was too frightened to tell anybody. She could be persuaded to change her mind.'

The movement in the ditch seemed to startle Clancy more than me. I wondered was it perhaps the first act Slick McGuirk had ever done that wasn't at his command. I had enough time to shoot him, whole seconds that stretched forever. But cowardice or greed or puzzlement at Clancy's unexpected tone stopped me. Once I fired a shot my last hope of a passport was gone.

By the time Clancy reacted I had already reached the gap in the ditch through which I had entered. The barbed wire almost broke beneath my foot. I threw myself towards the wheat, crouching under cover of it before rising to run. One set of boots pounded through the gap to trample the wheat behind me. Then I heard Clancy shout as the barbed wire gave way and he fell heavily. Cursing loudly another man clambered past him. This had to be P. J. Egan. It was twenty years since I'd last seen him, but Clancy would only trust people who went back so far and were as enmeshed as himself.

Both men ran blindly behind me, but closing all the time. I heard an engine start – Pete Clancy must have hobbled back to his car. The road lay to my left with the lane directly before me, but neither would provide cover. Until my words provoked McGuirk into emerging I was still bluffing, without enough proof to be convinced that he had killed my father. If Clancy had come alone I could have struck a bargain with him – Clancy would do a deal with the devil. But McGuirk and Egan were different. I could almost smell their animal fear and hatred behind me. I needed to escape and consider my next move.

I veered right, crouching down in the moonlit wheat. The field narrowed here as the lane swung around. Beyond it lay a small enclosure with no cover, used for grazing in the old days. Maguire's farmhouse lay over the hill if I could get that far. McGuirk and Egan still seemed to think that I was heading for the lane, until they were alerted by a stone clattering off the wall as I clambered into the enclosure. I heard Egan shout and knew they had changed direction to follow me.

The going was heavier in the enclosure, slowing me as I ploughed through cowpats and long tufts of grass. Both men scaled the wall, panting heavily. Without turning, I could visualize their beer bellies and sweat under the armpits of their Terylene shirts. I heard a car speed up the lane, lights off as its windscreen buffeted the overgrown hedgerows. But if I reached the farmyard before Clancy I knew that he would never dare to drive in after me and waken the Maguire household.

McGuirk and Egan knew I had reached safety too. I heard them slow up as I crested the steep hill to climb the gate into the farmyard. Maguire's farmhouse lay in darkness, its outhouses silent. I jumped down, hearing Clancy's car bump over rough stones where the tarmac ran out. Headlights came on suddenly, blinding me. I turned my eyes away and saw the farmhouse properly now, with slates gone from the roof and windows boarded up. Far below on the other side of the hill light glowed from a new bungalow built beside the ribbon of the Slane Road. McGuirk and Egan climbed over the gate, too breathless to curse. The cobbles were strewn with straw and spilt feed, the sheds padlocked. I ran past the huddle of old outhouses, knowing that a narrow gate in the far corner led into another field where the car couldn't go.

But I never reached there. Clancy's headlights were right behind me, making my huge shadow shake against the white-washed walls. Something snapped inside me. *All right, you fucking bully*, I thought, *the pair of us will go to hell together.* Drawing out the gun, I turned, feeling a surge of adrenaline as I pointed it blindly at the car, a gush of power so strong it was almost sexual. My finger squeezed the trigger for one second, then two. Long enough to realize it was jammed and remember Barney Clancy's mocking laugh upon seeing it years ago, long enough to curse Joey Kerwin and endure the oncoming realization of my own stupidity. The chicken-shit Hen Boy outfoxed again.

I crashed onto the cobbles, trying to avoid the car. But Clancy must have swerved violently as he hit the brakes, because he managed to halt the car with its back wheels skidding around to finish inches from my face. Had McGuirk been driving I would be dead. Clancy's henchmen were upon me within seconds, shapes indistinct as they dragged me forward into the headlights. One of them picked up the gun from the cobbles. I heard a car door open.

'Why did you brake for?' McGuirk complained. 'It would be simpler to just run over the cunt, for Christ's sake.'

'No.'

'If you're too chicken I'll do it for you.' McGuirk's tone was wrong, lacking the servility of a lieutenant who knew his place.

'I said no, Slick.'

McGuirk sounded mutinous. 'He knows about me and his da.'

'Who knows?' Clancy's legs broke the beam of light as he walked around to stand in front of the car. 'The Hen Boy died in Scotland years ago. His widow copped such a packet in compensation that my dad had to dissuade Eamonn Brogan from soliciting a contribution. There was a time when the dead might occasionally vote but they sure as hell never could talk. I remember canvassing here as a boy and watching old man Maguire kill a pig in this yard. Buckets of blood for black pudding and the screams when his throat was cut. The difference of course was that the pig existed. This fucker doesn't.'

I rose to face them, trying to prevent my legs from trembling. My forehead ached and my knee was heavily bruised. My mouth tasted of blood. P. J. Egan was examining the gun he'd picked up.

'The little bollix has no respect for culture either,' he said. 'He's after robbing the National Museum.'

'You need me.' I addressed Clancy and ignored the others. 'I know too much.'

Clancy laughed. 'When I was Junior Minister for Culture,' he said, 'this Polish conductor at the National Concert Hall rowed with the orchestra. "You think I know fuck nothing about Mozart," he shouted, "but I know fuck all." You've been away too long, Brogan, you know fuck all too.'

'I know the location of your father's outstanding account numbers, which my father managed for him. I know where the instruction mandates to activate them are.'

'Really? Where?'

'In Dublin. With someone you'd never find.'

'Your queer fuck of a son? What happened? Did Cormac get confused one night because of your wife's boyish arse?'

McGuirk and Egan had already primed themselves to antici-pate my rage. Egan caught my fist before it reached Clancy's face, twisting it violently behind my back while McGuirk caught me in a headlock. I could smell sweat under his armpit and knew how he longed to break my neck. Clancy had adapted to my resurrection with the stoicism of a man who had lost the ability to be surprised. If the Blessed Virgin had appeared naked to P. J. Egan on the bog beyond Nobber he would merely have called out 'Hardy morning, ma'am' and walked on. But there was a primitive superstition in McGuirk's headlock, as though I was the walking dead come to avenge my father.

'Leave my son out of this,' I warned, 'he knows nothing whatsoever.'

'I'll fecking kill you,' McGuirk muttered. 'I'll bury you where not even the worms will find you.'

'Easy, Slick!' Egan cautioned. P. J. had always been a per-petually cautious boy, as though his father had instilled in him the grave consequences that can arise from even one momentary lapse, citing his son's conception as an example. Mossy Egan's misfortune had enlivened many an after-hours pub conversation, with jokes about him enjoying the shortest courtship in the history of Navan – approximately seven and a half seconds. Previously he had seemed destined for life-long, contented bachelorhood until he forgot his trademark caution with a girl two decades his junior in the back of a Hillman Hunter, fired up by the excitement of a Sean Lamass address to a party meeting in Trim.

'Did they ever wipe the rest of you up off that car seat, P. J.?' I mocked, knowing the old Navan jibe would incense him.

'Fuck you, Hen Boy,' he spat. 'At least my da didn't cross the street when he saw me.'

'Woooh, boys.' Clancy sounded like he was calming horses. 'Hen Boy doesn't give a shit about his father. The feeling was mutual. I knew men who gave three-legged greyhounds they'd lost their shirt on a better life than Eamonn gave the Hen Boy. Maybe it was on account of his big fat head.' He switched to an Italian accent. 'I loved-a your Moma's tight pussy until you came along-a and split it with-a your big-a fat-a head.'

The others laughed, in a bizarre grown-up echo of a sound I had never forgotten. I wanted to make them suffer slowly, to do to them what they now had the power to do to me all over again.

'You never fucking changed, Clancy,' I spat. 'Still needing bully-boys to do your dirty work for you.'

'Let him go.'

Egan released me at once, but Clancy had to repeat the command before McGuirk uneasily relinquished his headlock. He stepped back, watching intently, like I was a ghoul liable to disappear. Clancy lit a cigarette and leaned against the bonnet of his car.

'Hand me his gun,' he told Egan, 'and open up the boot.'

Everyone knew the gun was useless. Clancy stared at it, as incredulous as his father had been years before, then pocketed it. I could have tried to run, but my leg was stiff and McGuirk hovered, like a bloodhound heart-broken at not being able to tear his prey apart. Egan whistled at the open car boot.

'Talk about come prepared, what?' he said. 'You were obviously in the Boy Scouts, Boss. Don't bother giving me that shotgun back if you use it though. You might lose it for me and I'll say it was stolen.'

He reappeared. I cupped my palm over my eyes to see Egan hand Clancy a double-barrelled shotgun and lean a gleaming spade against the car. He had a ball of twine in his hands.

'Jaysus,' he said. 'God be with the days of halfway houses.'

'I'll do what is necessary, no more and no less,' Clancy replied evenly, his eyes fixed on McGuirk who hovered beside me.

Egan shrugged. 'It looks like a spot of digging you might be planning so.'

'A spot of filling in if need be,' Clancy replied. 'If this bastard doesn't play ball. Aldershot Manor.'

Egan laughed. 'You mean what used to be Mickey Reed's field out the Trim road? All-The-Cows-Shat Manor more like?' He looked at McGuirk. 'Where do you get these fecking English names from at all, Slick?'

'From overpaid shites of market researchers,' Slick replied, sourly. 'It beats Egan Heights that still floods every time somebody takes a piss in the Boyne.'

'Leave it out, lads,' Clancy said. 'I passed Aldershot this evening, Slick, and told your security guard that I'd heard a bunch of travellers were planning to move onto your site beyond Kells. I said you'd be happier if he kept an eye out there. He's in Kells now, blabbing to the locals. It will put the skids under their planning objections if nothing else.'

'Hang on, Boss,' McGuirk argued, 'I want no messing around in Aldershot.'

'You want this sorted, don't you, Slick? Now should it come to it, who's going to dig back up the foundations of the apartment blocks there? They're already half-filled in, so if Hen Boy doesn't play ball won't it save your men work if they're slightly more filled in by tomorrow?'

'I don't know,' McGuirk cautioned. 'I mean they're Gold Shield homes and all.'

'Fuck your Gold Shield homes,' Egan rounded on him. 'If you hadn't gone crazy tying Brogan up he'd still be alive and we wouldn't be in this fucking mess. Where in the name of Jesus did you learn knots like that – those Japanese bondage videos you're always watching?'

'I'm sick of being cheated,' Slick muttered, 'and my father before me. Now if I could bring Brogan back to life I would. We'd not be in this shite with ghosts appearing from no-where.'

He glanced at me with something I never thought to see in his eyes – fear. I knew he wanted to touch me again, just to make sure I was real.

'Neither of your big mouths are helping,' Clancy said quietly.

McGuirk turned to him. 'OK, but not near the showhouse. I want no fucking around with my showhouse. I love it.'

'Is that why you spend every second night sitting up in it drinking yourself stupid?' Egan asked.

McGuirk ignored him. 'I'll show you a good spot,' he said. 'If the worst comes to the worst you'll need a hand mixing cement.'

'I'll manage just fine.'

'I haven't made cement myself in years.' Slick sounded like a child refused a bucket and spade.

'That's what your missus keeps saying,' Egan needled. 'Not even three and a half inches.'

'Leave it out, P. J.' Clancy aimed the shotgun at me. 'I don't need no one to do my work for me, Hen Boy.' He indicated for Egan to toss the ball of twine to McGuirk. 'Tie the fucker's hands as you're so practised.'

'If I'm not back by tomorrow,' I said, 'I have a friend going to a journalist with the documents.'

The lie was enough to frighten McGuirk who pulled the twine so tight that it cut into my wrists as he twisted them behind my back. Ebun would not go to the newspapers, but if she phoned Clancy's number what fate might await her? Slick forced me onto my knees.

'Give me five minutes with the cunt,' he pleaded, 'I'll make him sing like a skylark.'

'Leave this to me,' Clancy replied.

'How do I know you won't fuck up?' McGuirk was mutinous and suspicious.

'Because unlike you, I don't rush in. I use my head.' His voice could have been Barney Clancy icily dressing down a subordinate twenty years ago, except that no subordinate back then would have risked the look that McGuirk shot back. 'If you want this business sorted out for once and for all then go home, Slick,' Clancy added. 'That's where you were the night Eamonn Brogan passed away. P. J. was with you and your niece. You spent long enough searching Brogan's attic. If Brogan's grandson had turned up tonight, then maybe I'd still believe that he had them. But Eamonn wouldn't trust this cowboy with the steam off his piss. I knew men who played poker with the Hen Boy. Every hand he tried to bluff and lost. There's nothing more pathetic than the compulsive gambler always backing the wrong horse.' Clancy stepped towards me, the shotgun barrel pressed against my cheek. '"*I have a friend going to a journalist . . .*"' He sneered. 'You never had a friend in your fucking life, Hen Boy, and you're still bluffing, aren't you? What do you know about Shyroyal? Tell the truth, don't fuck with me!'

Something in his eyes that I could not decode seemed to say *Trust me.* It reminded me of Phyllis luring me into unlocking the bedroom door years ago, knowing that she was lying yet still wanting to believe her.

'It's just a name I heard years ago,' I lied, trying to second-guess what Clancy wanted the others to hear. 'I read about the break-in and felt it was suspicious. There's no friend, nobody even knows I exist. I don't care about my father. Just give me a few bob and I'd disappear again.'

'When did you last speak to your son?'

'When he was seven,' I lied. 'What has Conor got to do with anything?'

Clancy's eyes never changed as he looked back at McGuirk. 'This cunt is as much use as a spoiled vote,' he said grimly, reaching into his pocket to toss McGuirk the old pistol. 'Have a souvenir, Slick. You always liked antiques.'

'Leave his missus out of this.' Egan's drawl was sly, as if in cahoots with Clancy, deflecting McGuirk's anger onto himself. I knew he didn't trust a word I had said.

'Fuck off, you,' McGuirk told him.

'Only joking, Slick,' Egan said. 'She still has a fine pair of child-bearing thighs in need of firm handling by a strong man.'

'I'm twice the man you are.'

'Don't I know? Isn't she killed telling me so in bed.'

'Least I was conceived in a fucking bed,' McGuirk retorted.

'You were hatched out off the bog,' I hissed, with sudden

anger overriding everything else as I imagined my father tied up, eyes frozen open by death.

Egan caught his fist as McGuirk went to swing it. 'Leave him to Pete and the job will be oxo. Come on. He won't be joking in half an hour's time.'

McGuirk hesitated, then allowed himself to be cajoled. He aimed the old pistol at me and pretended to pull the trigger.

'Stick him in the byre,' Clancy told him. 'This could be a long night.'

McGuirk used an iron bar to break the thin lock on the byre door and pushed me into the corner. I stumbled and landed on some filthy straw. He used another length of twine to attach my wrists to an iron ring on the wall, then knelt beside me.

'Aldershot Manor,' he whispered. 'You're coming up in the world. I remember a time you weren't allowed near a house at all.'

Egan called him from the doorway. As I strained to hear Clancy's persuasive voice address them both through the half-open door I wondered why he wanted the others to think that I didn't have those mandates. I should have known fear but was too consumed by regret. A few hours before I had walked with Conor, talked to him and even felt his kiss. Yet I had never uttered a word of what I longed to say. The prospect of dying didn't horrify me now, it was the fact that Conor would never know. I could face my fate if I had seen some acknowledgement – even if only anger – of my identity in Conor's eyes. It was too late now to warn him about these men.

Clancy's voice was raised slightly before the door clanged shut and darkness embraced me like an old friend. I turned my head, half-expecting a pair of unblinking cat's eyes to watch from the corner, a patient ghost having waited years for this vengeful rendezvous.

———◼———

Everything would have been perfect on the night that Miriam and I moved into our own house in Raheny, had I not been startled by the cat's eyes at midnight in the shed. Because she was an outdoors stray who adopted the Crosbies, we'd never noticed her when initially viewing the house or on later trips – after the sale was agreed – to buy odds and ends of furniture off the Crosbies, an elderly couple moving to a new bungalow in Clontarf. For the previous eighteen months we had lived together in the top half of a house in Phibsborough – half-tenants and half-caretakers for a doctor working in Kuwait who intended coming home if the economy picked up to open a practice below. A neighbour was paid to cut the lawn and the doctor's brother materialized once a month to collect the rent and vanish quickly in case we asked him questions about maintenance.

It was a fool's paradise where we had the responsibility for nothing. A perfect limbo in which we grew to love each other. Sex after work on the doctor's white sofa we were always afraid of staining. Walking down to Broadstone three nights a week to take Miriam's mother drinking. She never pushed us towards marriage – her own experience being bitter enough – and, in truth, I was afraid of any change. Here was an equilibrium I had never thought possible, a new country called happiness in which I was terrified that my citizenship might be revoked at any moment.

Yet it was me who kept pushing the relationship forward – breaking down in tears one evening on the cliffwalk between Greystones and Bray as I suggested that we buy a house and get married, always feeling a desperate compulsion to prove myself to her. Life with her was just so different from the old days of waiting outside O'Neill's pub (as I was too self-conscious to drink alone inside) for Cormac to show up with his Trinity pals who patronized me.

Frankie Goes to Hollywood had a hit with 'Relax, Don't Do It' that summer. Cormac would sing it to tease me every time I called over, full of my intentions, to see him in the flat we had shared from the time we both left Cremore until the advent of Miriam. Not that Cormac was so relaxed himself that summer. There was something different about him, as he fussed over his appearance. He'd peer anxiously before the mirror when going out, reminding me of his mother on the morning of Sarah-Jane's christening. Yet his clothes had taken on a more respectable, almost young-fogey, look.

I discovered the reason when letting myself in with my old key to watch the 1.15 from Doncaster one Saturday without Miriam knowing. Alex Lever was shockingly old for Cormac, forty if a day, with severely cut hair starting to grey. Cormac's lovers were normally fey and giggly. This one looked like a Bulgarian trade diplomat, as he pulled the blankets up and regarded me caustically.

'My big brother,' Cormac explained, moving his hand under the sheet. 'He's minding a doctor's practice while I'm undermining one.'

The North Circular Road was not to Alex Lever's liking, nor the manners or humour of Irish people. I dragged Miriam along to the Hirshfield Centre one night to find Cormac among his usual scrum of admirers, who swapped bluer and bluer jokes. 'Wait, wait, wait,' Cormac waved his hands to get some hush. 'Alex has one that will kill you.' Reluctantly Dr Lever spoke, his clipped upper-class Scottish accent generating not only silence but such an edge of tension among the listeners that he might have been delivering a life-threatening diagnosis: 'A deer encountered a distressed-looking antelope on the range. "What's wrong?" enquired the deer. The antelope sniffled and replied, "I've just heard a discouraging word."'

Cormac roared with laughter, oblivious to the baffled silence of his companions. Finally it was Miriam who started to laugh, not at the weak pun on 'Home on the Range', but the expression of Alex Lever's face.

'At least the lady has some conception of popular musical culture,' the doctor remarked curtly, overcoming the prejudice he shared with my father about social workers. 'Home, Cormac. It is time we moved on.'

Moving on was something the doctor was most particular about. Moving Cormac on from the North Circular Road to share his expensive Ballsbridge flat overlooking the Dodder. Moving on Cormac's dress-sense, his book tastes, developing his interest in opera ('The biggest queens you ever saw, Brendan, and they were only the straight ones'). Suddenly Cormac found himself moving through strata of Dublin life he had never previously been aware of. Parties with liberal politicians and dandruffed artists; Bloomsday mock funeral jaunts with members of the bar in mourning dress; boxes at the horseshow next to girls with long legs and hyphens in their surnames. If – as politicians kept lecturing us – Ireland was living beyond its means, then Alex Lever's friends seemed determined to lead by example.

'Alex was quite cross with me,' Cormac remarked in one of many long calls from Alex's apartment to the payphone in the hall below our flat. 'He claims his boy let him down, but I think it was because people at the party seemed to enjoy my company more than his.' The remark reminded me of Phyllis after my father first brought her to official functions in the Ard Boyne Hotel. 'Alex can be a bit of a jealous dear really. Says he'd like to meet my folks. Can you imagine?'

We giggled like schoolboys at the thought. In the past Cormac had often mimicked a fantasy where, on Sarah-Jane's eighteenth birthday, Phyllis interrupted a performance at the Gate Theatre by running onto the stage to scream, 'Is there a doctor in the house?' Cormac would pretend I was the doctor, hugging me around the knees and catching Phyllis's accent perfectly as he begged; 'It's my daughter, you must marry her.'

Alex Lever was the sort of man my father would instinctively look up to, the son-in-law Phyllis had always longed for. The problem was that Sarah-Jane was still only a smoulderingly rebellious pre-teen and Alex wanted the hand of her darling son. Phyllis was incapable of accepting Cormac's sexuality, no matter how many hints he tried to drop when he moved out at eighteen following the late-night attack on the bus to Cremore. Always it was somebody else's fault – especially mine for stealing him away from her influence by agreeing to move out too and share a flat (or, in other words, pay almost all the rent). She would rail about Trinity College types leading him astray and that no girl would date him anyway with me hanging around. But if really pushed she retreated to her mantra that 'what that bastard Pete Clancy did to him made him shy around girls'.

Ironically my father was the most understanding – or at least implicitly and silently understood the most. Not that himself or Cormac spoke much on the rare occasions they met (as a man capable of removing an exact sum from his wallet in shops without the wallet ever leaving his pocket, my father had turned circumspection into an art form). But his unspoken animosity left no doubt that he felt he finally had Cormac's measure. If this made him regret the apartheid he had previously practised with his own son, then I never allowed him to get close enough to say so.

While it surprised my father that Cormac and I set up flat

together, it was a source of consternation to Phyllis who had never called at the North Circular Road for fear of encountering me. Even after Cormac shifted to Ballsbridge and I moved in with Miriam, she still believed we lived there, unaware of Alex Lever. Cormac would laugh after meeting her for coffee in Bewleys as he recounted her concern that we might share clothes or bed linen in case mine were lice-infected.

I didn't find this funny. In my new world I wanted no reminder of the past. Our landlord doctor was coming home, with his money made and war stirring in the Middle East. Miriam and I would have to move out. Another flat would have done us but I cycled around Dublin for weeks, searching for the perfect house to buy. I sat for hours on a bench in Saint Anne's Park, looking at one house for sale opposite it, almost afraid to imagine the perfection of a life there with Miriam.

Miriam loved the house when I showed it to her but argued that we could not afford the Crosbies' asking price of thirty-one thousand pounds. She had already pooled her savings of eleven hundred pounds in a joint account with six hundred pounds I had managed to hold onto. The Cheltenham festival was on. I phoned in sick, withdrew twelve hundred pounds without her knowledge and placed three separate bets in different bookies – all on the same double, a 5/2 favourite and a 3/1 horse who loved heavy ground. It was the ultimate bet that I had always dreamt of. I sat out the first race in Dominick Street Church – not to pray, just to be alone. It was a photo finish, still undecided when I reached the nearest bookie's. The result flashed up for the favourite. Both my bet and life with Miriam were still on. There were two more races before the second half of the double. Time felt different, as if all previous bets had only been dummy runs before the life-and-death reality of this gamble.

Everything hinged in the balance, with nine thousand pounds plus my stake back if I won – giving us the dream deposit for a house. And if I lost? Part of me wanted to lose, to be exposed to Miriam as who I really was by failing her. She would walk away then, returning me to the darkness where I belonged. My horse seemed out of it, running in fourth with two furlongs left. People shouted at the screen but I said nothing, numbly watching the leaders tire on the heavy ground, seeing my jockey use his whip and knowing that he was going to catch them from a hundred yards out. My legs trembled, my chest hurt but I still didn't make a sound, even when he raised his whip in triumph after crossing the line, winning by a short head.

That was the night I promised Miriam never to bet again, that night when she took off the engagement ring I had purchased that afternoon and almost threw it into the canal after discovering where the money came from. I believed I would stop too. The win was so monumental and complete that surely it had purged my compulsion. For the first time in my life I was ahead and with her support I could stay there.

Miriam insisted on us asking my father and Phyllis to the wedding. I never felt more nervous and sick about any occasion, like I expected Slick McGuirk and P. J. Egan to be lurking in a back pew, ready to throw straw among the confetti as they cackled and shouted 'Hen Boy!' Phyllis wore a hat, which she refused to take off before Miriam's mother removed hers. She played the role of the groom's mother to perfection without ever managing to look into my eyes. Alex Lever sat among the guests, like he had arrived to carry out a VAT inspection on the hotel. He watched Cormac and the bridesmaid dance with strained forbearance.

Barney Clancy's arrival at the 'afters' caused a stir – mainly of derision among younger guests. Miriam and I hadn't asked him, but my father looked puffed with pride like he had pulled off a coup on our behalf. Perhaps the only person impressed was Alex Lever. He touched my shoulder. 'I'd like to meet him,' he announced, 'I know people who greatly admire that man.'

Clancy stood at the bar like a deity awaiting supplicants. He shook my hand warmly and winked. 'I should have warned you,' he joked, 'beware of slow Meath horses and fast Dublin women.' I introduced Alex and got caught in the crossfire of their small talk while my father hovered like an unwalked dog. They muttered about mutual acquaintances and the state of the country while I watched Cormac dance with Phyllis. Both looked so suddenly alike, with so much in common – having reinvented themselves for the love of far older and duller men. Barney Clancy raised an invisible wing to draw my father into the conversation, their voices lower now as they praised some banker named Des Traynor and mentioned the name of a builder I'd vaguely heard of. Miriam waved from across the room. I moved off and my father followed me for a few paces, putting his hand on my sleeve.

'Is he from Miriam's side?' he whispered.

'No. Ours.'

'Really? *You* know him?'

I hated the sudden respect in his eyes. I wanted to say, *He's fucking Cormac, Da. He's one of those funny bunnies you always say should be put up against a wall and shot.* But I said nothing, just walked towards my new wife who held her arms out.

We honeymooned at a small exclusive guesthouse over-looking a lake in Mayo. It was the type of place I knew we could probably never again afford. Indeed we couldn't have afforded it then, except that, swearing it was a one-off, I broke my vow to put thirty pounds from a wedding whip-around in work on a Jim Bolger horse at ten-to-one. I re-sealed the envelope afterwards for Miriam to open and affected amazement at the amount collected for us. We were the only guests but they set the dining-room fully for us with a log fire and complimentary champagne after discovering we were newly-weds. Their daughter played the piano in the small foyer for our benefit. At fourteen she had the most beautiful hair and blushed whenever we praised her playing. It rained for two days but we didn't care, walking in the wood and even trying our hands at fishing.

Dublin was always going to be a comedown, yet – despite a hike in mortgage rates while we were away – it seemed an adventure as well. Four days after our honeymoon we moved into the house the Crosbies had vacated in Raheny. It looked different in their absence. Rooms had gained an echo with the furniture gone, the pipes were suddenly loud in the attic. We were both shaken by the sudden reality of what we had taken on. Nervously we laughed as we laid a mattress down in the back bedroom with a blanket being used temporarily as a curtain.

Miriam undressed listening to the radio, but I had to walk my property one last time. My own home, my own back door, my own pebbledash wall. I kept touching things, like a dazed explorer. I had opened the shed to check that the Crosbies had cleared it out when something stirred, then a pair of eyes held my gaze. I found the light switch and stepped back. The black cat was grossly overweight with one tooth protruding like a fang. Although the ugliest creature I'd ever seen, I might probably have stopped on the street to pat her. But finding her here late at night was the first tainting of paradise. I hated her on sight because she was simply too much like me. I chased her out and blocked up the old cat-flap.

Shortly after dawn Miriam woke and went to fetch an extra blanket downstairs. Her scream brought me running down.

It wasn't just how the black cat scratched with one paw on the kitchen window or the sight of her single fang which looked so unearthly. It was the look in her eyes, like we were intruders invading her home. Yet her gaze wasn't hostile, merely pleading to be allowed in. The cat meowed and slowly scraped her claw along the glass again, fixing me in her gaze as if recognizing a kindred spirit. Miriam recovered her composure but I was petrified. I knew that longing to be inside too well.

After breakfast Miriam phoned Mr Crosbie, accepting his apology that the cat had escaped from their new bungalow. He warned her against feeding it, saying he would call over. Miriam stood in the yard as we waited, allowing the cat to brush against her ankles though she gave Miriam the creeps too. Mr Crosbie was full of apologies. Their dog didn't care where he slept once there was a fire and the two white cats we'd seen on an earlier visit were adjusting well to their new home. But the black cat had grown frantic in the bungalow, racing from room to room until she found a way out.

The black cat reluctantly allowed Mr Crosbie to pick her up, but was back the next morning. She was barely collected by Mr Crosbie before she escaped again and made the two-mile trek to scratch at our window. Every time it took the man longer to come and each time his hint grew that perhaps we might adopt her. Finally he said he could do no more. Next time she appeared we would simply have to call the cats' home.

Next morning I was relieved to find the windowsill deserted. Stepping over frozen puddles, I went to get my bike from the shed. The cat had somehow found a way in there during the bitterly cold night. Her eyes watched from behind a pile of boxes. She had nothing to lie on, but kept purring, delighted to have found some niche to call home. Miriam entered the shed behind me to get the moped she had bought for her new job in a Citizens Advice Bureau in a crumbling shopping centre that was due to be totally redeveloped. 'Shag it,' she laughed, 'maybe it would be simpler to keep her.'

I couldn't explain to her why I got so uptight, shouting about Mr Crosbie trying to emotionally blackmail us. But I felt increasingly terrorized by that cat. The problem was that I knew exactly how simple her needs were, the depth of her unthinking gratitude at merely being allowed to exist at the end of the garden. I loved animals, yet couldn't bear to constantly be reminded of myself and keep seeing my own eyes staring back.

'What's wrong?' she asked, noticing me shaking. 'It's just a cat. We'll call the ISPCA, they'll find a home for her.'

We knew they wouldn't. At best she would endure four days in a cage before being put down. Feeling like Judas we left food and milk in the shed. In work I couldn't concentrate, snapping at people until I relieved the tension inside me by losing fifteen pounds in the bookie's at lunchtime. The ISPCA man arrived at teatime. There was something blackly comic about him crouching with a wooden pole trying to coax the cat into a cage. The cat kept a watchful distance, occasionally shooting me a hurt, baffled look.

After twenty minutes I had enough. Ordering the ISPCA man out I phoned Mr Crosbie to demand that he take responsibility for his cat once and for all. The old man arrived and said he would take her to the vet to be put down. He walked to his car without looking back. We never saw him or the cat again.

The funny thing was that the cat was more of a haunting presence in my life after it was gone. Taking the rubbish down to the shed last thing every night, I was almost afraid to glance at the boxes behind where she had tried to set up home. I would turn the shed light out and gaze up at the kitchen window where the woman I did not deserve was framed, then cast one last glance back into the dark. For the briefest second eyes would watch me there – not the cat's eyes but my own, aged nine and ten, crouched on the floor, begging not to be left alone and refusing to let me go.

———————

The byre door reopened. I knew without turning my head that Pete Clancy was alone, Egan having managed to lure Slick McGuirk away. A match was struck and for a second I suspected that Clancy was about to set the straw ablaze. Instead I smelt tobacco and heard the flame being blown out.

'Boys o boys,' Clancy affected a thicker Meath accent, 'you were always fond of sheds, Hen Boy.'

'Trust you to bring your bully-boys along, you bollix.'

There was a scrape of metal as he upended an old bucket to sit on. I turned to watch him in what dim light filtered through the doorway, adjusting my position painfully with the twine behind my back.

'Slick invited himself, and P. J. tagged along to keep a watching brief on him,' he replied. 'Didn't I warn you to only use my private e-mail address? Slick's niece runs my constituency office. She informed him, like she tells him everything. They were waiting for me outside the party meeting in Kingscourt. We could have been alone if you hadn't copied her in on your demand for this stupid moonlight encounter.'

He tapped his cigarette ash onto some loose straw on the floor where it began to smoulder. Idly he watched a wisp of smoke rise and then stamped it out, watching me as if he had guessed at my phobia about fire since that train crash.

'I have those account mandates and you know it,' I said. 'Lie to your stooges but you need me.'

'I need you about as much as I need Slick's niece for a secretary. It's a terrible thing to run out of relations of your own, especially as Carol has both her uncle's slyness and his arse.' He uncocked the shotgun to remove both cartridges, then blew into each barrel, polishing the gun absent-mindedly. 'Why is it, Brendan, that people think I'm a bottomless well of favours?'

In the open I could have faced anything, but this confinement contained too many echoes. I hated myself for being unable to stop shaking. Clancy reloaded the shotgun, closing it with a click.

'Eh?' he enquired. 'Did you say something?'

'You're a cunt, Clancy, always were and always will be.'

'You could be right there, Hen Boy.' His tone seemed almost friendly, until he knelt to grab my hair. 'But I could be the cunt who's about to blast both these barrels up your arse unless you start talking. Now what the fuck do you really want and where have you crawled from?'

I lashed out with my foot, heedless of his gun, and Clancy knelt on my thighs, crushing them as he gripped my hair tighter.

'Don't annoy me, Brendan,' he said. 'This last year I've grown a tad sick of surprises, bits of the past that refuse to stay in their boxes and keep trying to jump out and ambush me.'

'Is that why you had your thug kill my father?'

'My thug?' His voice became almost infused with nostalgia. 'God be with the days when he and P. J. were. Loyalty went out of fashion in your absence. Your da was the last honourable man, not simply out for himself.'

'Like your da was,' I sneered.

Clancy released my hair but kept my legs pinned down. He had fattened out so much into middle-age that in the dimness he might have been his father's ghost. I half-expected to see braces and smell Barney's aftershave which nobody else in Navan had ever worn.

'Daddy might have been a tad crooked by the standards of today's squeaky robots,' he said, 'but he was still my daddy. That's the way with daddies, eh? Look at you. Eamonn only ever gave you dog's abuse as a kid, yet you're still seeking revenge – or is it that you're just out to fill your own pockets?'

'Barney was a gangster,' I said, 'and you know it.'

'I know that Daddy did great things for Navan, visionary acts when other politicians were still wiping their arses with clumps of grass. The contradiction isn't incompatible. Daddy made sure things got built in Navan, and by locals instead of foreign businessmen who'd fuck off afterwards. When things are built money gets made and spread around as an unavoidable consequence.'

'He didn't spread his share too far, did he?' I sniped back. 'I've seen the list of off-shore bank accounts.'

'You know feck all, Brendan. Daddy could never walk the length of Navan without having to empty his pockets.' Pete Clancy mimicked a succession of women's accents: ' "My child is sick, Mr Clancy." "My husband's gone to England and left me." "You're my only hope with three weeks rent due, Barney, and sure didn't I know your father at school." "These new-fangled vibrators have my heart scalded, Minister, they eat their way through batteries." '

'Very droll.'

'Very taxing. Priests pulling their wires in the confession boxes in the cathedral could just dole out a few Hail Marys, then bugger off back to their housekeepers for a steak dinner.

Daddy sought their votes instead of their souls and people expected their dividends in pounds, shillings and pence.'

'He was still a crook.'

'He was a man of the people. Voters knew exactly who he was and they got what they voted for. Honesty is a luxury for figureheads like the president, which is why we keep sticking in high-minded Protestants and gawky long-winded women you wouldn't ride on a dark night. But it's fuck all use when helping out a constituent in a tight corner. Daddy had the biggest funeral in the history of Navan. People queuing to pay their respects, every second one dropping hints about him having promised them something. I felt surrounded by greedy mouths like chicks in a nest hungry for worms. Daddy's funeral and I wanted to vomit.'

He sat back on the upturned bucket, releasing my legs. I watched distrustfully, ready to kick out if he reached for the shotgun.

'Look at me gabbing away,' he laughed. 'But I feel like I'm talking to a ghost. The Hen Boy, of all people, eh? You sly fuck. Go on, tell us why you disappeared?'

'I had my reasons.'

'Don't we all?' He shook his head in amusement. 'The two great male fantasies, eh? Acquiring the young bombshell mistress and disappearing with your clothes left on the beach. Much good it did you and Eamonn for managing to do both between you.'

'My father was a widower,' I corrected him. 'Phyllis was no saint but hardly a mistress either. Barney had the franchise for that, with his private room up in Groom's Hotel.'

Pete Clancy laughed. 'The legendary room in Groom's, eh? My mother found out, you know. She arrived up with me in tow when I was nine. Daddy did the only decent thing possible, collapsed clutching his chest and croaking for an ambulance.

Thrashing about the floor, with my mother and the queer hawk both screaming. He sees me crying my eyes out and gives a sudden wink. Ten days in a private ward and the night he gets out he has the Bishop of Cloyne renew their marriage vows up in the house, with altar boys, incense and all. But you know the shockingest thing, Brendan? Daddy was humping an old lump of a heifer you'd pass on the street and not turn your head. A fat American with notions about herself who wrote for the papers and never shaved her legs. The type who would be better off sticking to knitting than spreading her thighs. But Phyllis, on the other hand, was worth risking a marriage for.'

'I've told you before —' I began angrily.

'You've told me nothing,' he interrupted dismissively. 'Your mother may have been cold but she certainly wasn't stiff when Eamonn landed Phyllis with Red-Arse himself as a bastard son.'

'How the hell would you know?' The twine dug into my wrists as I jerked forward.

'How would you know different, Hen Boy? You and Eamonn hardly had many cosy chats spitting into the fire. But Daddy groomed me for this job, every useable speck of dirt on every family for three generations. Who do you think Cormac's father was? This convenient mythical Scotsman that Phyllis dreamed up? She was just a kid from the cabins off Dorset Street scrubbing away in the kitchens at Groom's, when Daddy dropped the hand on her passing through the dining-room. She couldn't even take it as a joke, slapping his face. Eamonn found her crying in the yard, out among the bins. She thought she was going to lose her job. He walked her home, told her not to worry. She thought he was cultured because next day he posted her some half-arsed love poem with her name in it. I mean what the fuck rhymes with Phyllis apart from syphilis and knickerless?'

He shook his head ruefully, picking up the shotgun to aim it randomly around the byre. He settled on an imaginary target and mimed squeezing the trigger.

'Those were the times that were in it, Brendan,' he said, lowering the gun. 'Ireland was opening up, with spoils for the brave and a man's only crime was getting caught. Daddy blamed himself. It made Eamonn feel special that Phyllis took him when she could have been the minister's mistress and the fact that Daddy once wanted Phyllis made her seem special in Eamonn's eyes. But your mammy and you never suffered. Only those few in the know knew and none thought any the less of him. The problem was that Eamonn didn't understand the get-in and get-out rules of affairs. He was a romantic, and Phyllis was worse, caught in his fantasy. He started talking crazy when she got banged up with a kid. God knows what would have happened if Daddy hadn't arranged for her to disappear into a convent in Athlone. But she did a runner instead, having Cormac in some Glasgow dosshouse. How Eamonn tracked her down, two and a half years later, I don't know. Still I never believed your mother found out. That corner of Ludlow Street was always a dangerous bend where anyone could get mown down. It never stopped Phyllis from blaming herself though. Daddy told them it was wrong to keep you in that shed, like they could banish every reminder of her. But Phyllis never liked Daddy and after your brother's lies she never liked me either.'

A Swiss army knife had appeared in Clancy's hands. He knelt forward watching me drag myself back towards the wall.

'Easy now, Hen Boy,' he whispered. 'We'll have no pig-killing here, it would ruin my jacket.' Slowly he reached behind my back to cut the twine binding my bound hands to the iron ring.

'Turn around,' he ordered. Reluctantly I allowed him to

lower the knife behind my back and felt the blade brush against
my skin as it dug into the twine around my wrists before
snapping it. Blood began circulating into my stiff fingers again.
Clancy sat back. I didn't trust his snake's eyes. I'd seen him
release small boys, allowing them to get several paces away
and take their first breath of relief before his foot flailed out
to trip them again. His gesture couldn't be humanitarian; it
had to be an initial negotiating gambit. I couldn't even be
sure if McGuirk and Egan were actually gone. I watched him
put the knife away and wipe sweat off his palms with a white
handkerchief.

'Wipe all you like,' I said, 'but there's still blood on those
hands. At least Barney never killed anyone.'

Clancy folded the handkerchief and replaced it carefully in
his pocket. 'Granddaddy did enough killing for any family,'
he replied. 'Michael Collins chose his apostles well, but even
borrowing P. J.'s shotgun twice a year to fire the bloody thing
and start golf classics gives me the willies. Your father died of
a heart attack, Brendan. He was an old man, irascible, on
tablets for high blood pressure. It could have happened at any
time. I'm sorry for your troubles, but you've only made them
deeper by butting in here. Now what do you want?'

'You're the man who knows the value of everything,' I
said angrily. 'What price my silence, what price my father's
life?'

'Your silence comes cheap, seeing as you face a jail sentence
for embezzlement. As for your father, nobody can put a value
on a man's life.'

'Why have Slick tie him up and terrorize him so? And why
is my son being followed when he knows nothing about any
of this?'

'It's news to me that anyone keeps following him,' Clancy
said, then shook his head, half-amused. 'Though the fact is

that Slick is obsessed by the boy. He fancies him if he'd only admit it. How do you know this?'

'I spoke to the kid. He doesn't even know who I am. Did you honestly believe my father would testify against Barney's memory? He'd have walked into that tribunal and remembered nothing, pleading ignorance and senility. Now I have someone in Dublin with a complete list of your father's account numbers which can be posted anonymously to Dublin Castle.'

Clancy rested the shotgun under his arm as he undid his zip and urinated against the wall. 'Go ahead and this will be your reward as far as I'm concerned,' he replied. 'You can have the steam off my piss. You were never the brightest, Brendan, so why not just drop the iron bar now?'

He turned, with one hand unhurriedly doing up his zip and the other aiming the shotgun towards me. I couldn't see how he knew that I had picked up the iron bar McGuirk had forced the lock with. He released the safety catch as I dropped it.

'Maybe you missed it on your travels, Hen Boy, but some years back the Government brought in a convenient tax amnesty. It wasn't just for Dublin drug-dealers and crooked Cork dentists who think that eating prawns in pink sauce with their wives in the Irish Club in London is posh living. It was a straight fifteen per cent on all money declared, with anonymity guaranteed and no questions asked. I don't know what account numbers are on your list and how you would prove their connection to my father. What I do know, because I'd to virtually wring his neck to make him comply, is that any money in Daddy's war chest smelt of roses by the time he died. It was an expensive move, later cost me a fortune in death duties, but I always knew a day of reckoning would come. Play the sleeveen informer, Brendan, but you won't hurt my pocket, so you've picked the wrong man for a crooked little blackmailing scam.'

'Yeah? Then why burgle his house if you're so clean?'

Clancy's hands moved so fast that I was certain I was about to be shot. I crouched, flinching and only just caught the shotgun before it hit the concrete floor. Puzzled, I clutched it and stared at him as he lit another cigarette.

'Good thing you grabbed that,' he commented, 'it might have made an awful mess going off had it hit the floor. This isn't about your father, Brendan. It's personal, I see it in your eyes. I bet this is how you always dreamt of it, with you the big man this time, the bully with the gun. You like the sense of power, don't you? You've seen me load it so come on, try aiming for my heart.'

My hands shook as I raised the shotgun, suspicious yet somehow more scared now that I had the responsibility of the weapon. I'd had no time to think when aiming at his car in the yard. But here the actuality felt different from any fantasy played out in my mind. He watched impassively as I struggled with the sudden ability to splatter his brains against a wall.

'You've every right to hate me,' he said. 'I made your life hell. I had the power back then, you see, that was the difference between us. People like Slick are born bullies but like most kids I just filled whatever role was allotted to me. I was my father's son – even the teachers seemed half-afraid of me. You were one lonely snot-nosed fuck, but at times I envied you your freedom to be an insignificant nobody. Slick and P. J. stuck to me like fucking leeches, their daddies would have placed them in my cot if allowed to. Anything to keep close to the court of King Barney. I bullied them too, especially Slick, gave them tasks to be in my gang. They ate worms, rolled naked in mud. I knew their daddies would beat them black and blue if they dared fall out with me. But they were different, Slick especially, lapping it up like a rite of passage. Bullying you was almost a pure experience, the smell of your fear. You were such a perfect little victim. But victims grow up. So you have the gun now, Hen Boy, you even know where to bury me. All-The-Cows-Shat Manor. The cement will be dry by morning. It won't help your son but do you care? You tried to kill me out in the yard, so what are you waiting for now, permission?'

'Fuck you,' I snapped, rattled.

'Squeeze the trigger, Hen Boy. It will probably be like sex for you – unless you do it real slow it will be over so soon you'll hardly even remember having done it.'

The shotgun blast was louder than I could have ever imagined, deafening me and almost dislocating my shoulder. It took me a moment to make out Pete Clancy still standing in the same spot. His face was white, the cigarette had dropped from his hands and flakes of whitewash coated his hair and shoulders from a section of plaster blasted off the wall above him.

'Missed,' he noted wryly.

'When I want to I'll hit you,' I replied. 'Now shut the fuck up. You're messing with my brain.'

'I'm trying to clarify it. Like most people you don't really know what you want. I wanted to kill Daddy in disgust when I found out all the scams and rackets he was tied up in. I mean I looked up to him just like you looked up to Eamonn. But surely you knew Eamonn was into every scam.'

'I knew nothing.'

'That's what I tell people but they keep saying it was in front of our eyes. Every dog on every street knew, only none of them ever seemed to have bothered barking.'

'I'll use this other fucking barrel if you don't shut up.'

'Go on then, do so. I'm forty-four. Life is downhill from here, with my great future behind me. Maybe that's why I sent our two friends packing. Maybe you'll be doing me a favour.'

I took two steps closer, bringing the hot barrel right up against his shirt. I wanted to see fear in his eyes, I craved respect.

'Be afraid of me before I blow your brains out, you bullying cunt.'

'Sorry, but you'd simply be murdering the wrong man.' His gaze was man-to-man. 'You can't kill that school bully because he died long ago. Life killed him off slowly with a thousand little cuts, never letting him crawl out from Daddy's shadow. He wanted to change the world, but junior ministers with clouds over their families change nothing. He grew up into somebody else, like you did on your travels, and neither of us can have our pasts back. We're different people, Brendan. This "little boy-inside-you" psychology shite is just shite that shrinks peddle so they can afford foreign holidays and conservatories. Our daddies both let us down, but this is between you and me, the way we are now, grown men of the world. I swear to you I had nothing to do with your father's death or any danger your son is in.'

'It's not just between us,' I reminded him. 'Slick and P. J. know too much about me and I know too much about them.'

'What P. J. knows and says are two different things. Slick is different and difficult. He never left that schoolyard. He was born a bully and will die one and like all true bullies he's frightened of his own shadow. There was a time I could control him but not any more. He frightens me and should frighten you. Himself and your father were at war almost from the time Slab got so bad with the Alzheimer's. I'll be honest, we wanted Slick to rob the house in Cremore but when your father wasn't in. P. J. and I knew nothing about him going on a solo run until he turned up shaking and crying. He didn't mean to kill him, just went too far tying Eamonn up, like he goes too far with most things. He's the man Conor has to watch out for.'

'Why?'

'He just is. After tonight he'll want you dead and anyone else who might link him to Eamonn's death.'

Clancy stubbed out the smouldering cigarette with his toe. He knew I wasn't going to shoot him. My stomach felt cold and queasy. Holding the shotgun gave no sense of power now. It felt childish and embarrassing.

'That doesn't mean we can't get around Slick,' he added. 'I'm trusting you with my life here. But you've got to trust me in return.'

'Maybe I'd sooner trust the devil.'

'I'm as close as you get, except that I'm real and the devil's a convenient fiction to scare children. I've only bought us this time because Slick thinks I'm burying you at present or at least beating you up so badly that you'll never show your face again.'

'You could always control Slick.'

'Maybe there was a time when Daddy could throw Slab the odd bone, bend the rules, indicate the inside track. But politics has changed so much that you daren't breathe now. Europe, civil servants, newspapers dissecting your every decision and peering up your arse day and night. It's a liability for any builder to even know a politician now if he wants to get ahead. I've had to change, but Slick and P. J. simply took over where their daddies left off. Their vision never got bigger, just their greed. Apartments on every postage stamp of land they can buy up. Builders don't stand for election, they needn't give a fuck what anyone thinks of them. Making a holy show in the winners' enclosure at Navan race track trying to impress strangers with champagne when some syndicated horse they own half a leg in comes home. Slick belongs nowhere except on a building site, while P. J. is better but still a generation away from not being a peasant. Neither trusts the other as far as he could throw him. But there was always more to you than met the eye, Brendan. That's why I kept kicking you as a kid. One day this worm will turn and show us who he really is, I thought. Now, listen to me and listen close . . .'

I didn't want to listen. I had listened to Phyllis on the day I opened the locked bedroom in Navan. Afterwards I had never blamed her for beating me, I blamed myself for being stupid enough to hope that she meant what she said. I wanted to interrupt Clancy before I fell under that same spell. But his eyes never wavered, his voice was almost hypnotic. One shotgun barrel was still loaded. If he'd made a sudden movement I might have fired it. But he just stood still, talking.

'A judge would call what Slick did to your father manslaughter, but only if it wasn't his own father. Eamonn wouldn't play ball with him, you see; even when Eamonn retired he remained too much the high and mighty civil servant. The problem with official keepers of secrets is that after a time nobody is quite sure what they know or don't know, what they might or mightn't tell. After he retired he thought he would become a sort of prime-minister-in-exile up in Dublin with grateful old friends dropping in to receive advice and shower him with retainers as a consultant. Maybe Slab McGuirk promised him some sort of tin-pot role and Mossy buttered Eamonn up too. But the day Eamonn retired from Meath County Council he became yesterday's man and in the real world Slick and P. J. were never going to be bound by some vague promise made by their fathers in the back of a pub.'

'So they ditched him,' I said.

Clancy shrugged. 'He was on to me day and night in the early years, ranting about promises broken and his "position". I gave him any work I could –'

'Rent collector,' I jibed.

'At least I gave him work. P. J. and Slick ignored him until the tribunals got them scared. It wasn't his advice they needed now, but his silence on the past. They weren't going to be ungenerous either, there was a decent backhander going for him to clear his attic. It didn't have to be a suspicious fire or flooding. He hadn't even been called as a witness at that stage. Hiring a skip was all that was needed and Slick needed it most because the Slab in his heyday was as big a crook as Eamonn was a hoarder. Slab kept most of his dealings in his head until he went daft. He's in a home in Mullingar now without a snowball's clue of who Slick is and why he won't leave him alone. Meanwhile Slick is driving himself crazy not knowing what skeletons could jump out in the tribunal. Slick didn't know Phyllis had been released from hospital, honest to God, he thought the house would be empty.'

Clancy shivered as if cold. He looked tired and far older than his years.

'Half the County Council task-force files were up in your father's attic,' he continued. 'Slick already had two plastic sacks filled when your father took his heart attack. Something inside him died after you and Cormac went and even Daddy had problems retrieving documents from him. Slick had been getting more and more agitated about what papers Eamonn might be holding. Then three months ago he found out about the money.'

'What money?'

Pete Clancy watched me, suddenly alert again. 'The four off-shore accounts that are still open.'

'You said your father laundered all his money in the tax amnesty,' I reminded him.

'I did, didn't I?' Clancy replied. 'I went over every tortuous penny with Eamonn. Are you saying I shouldn't have trusted him?'

If Pete had seen everything then surely he knew that only two accounts remained open. I had often envisaged the scene when the quarterly bank statements arrived, via Des Traynor, two months after my disappearance. Phyllis, beyond tears, curled into a ball in their bedroom, clutching Cormac's photograph as though she might somehow bring him back to life. And in the attic above her, my father sitting on a sack of old papers, rocking inside his own unfathomable grief, closing his eyes and opening them again to stare at the statements as if the correct balance might somehow reappear.

'You're the one who keeps saying how honest he was,' I replied carefully.

'He was too honest for his own good,' Clancy said. 'Money was secondary to Eamonn's need to be used. Some people are like that, they crave being used, it gives them status. Normally they become treasurers on Tidy Towns Committees. They can't spend money but love counting it – even when it's not theirs. Eamonn would do anything for Daddy. Right to the end he saw Daddy as the sort of hero I imagined him to be when I was twelve. He loved him.'

I had almost forgotten the shotgun in my hands. I placed it carefully on the floor between us and hunched down against the wall. 'Give us a cigarette,' I said.

Pete lit one himself, then tossed the packet and the matches over. I struck a match and inhaled. 'You know the mad thing,' I told him. 'I believed the old cunt loved me. In his own fucked-up way that put every other thing first.'

'It was the way of fathers back then,' Pete replied. 'Business first and last, with us wheeled out for press photographs.'

'Don't even try and compare,' I said.

'I'm not. Your father was in a league of his own – 007.5 Daddy used to call him – the Walter Mitty of secret agents. I'll never forget the day I examined the accounts with him. Daddy didn't exactly keep tabs on personal expenses, he operated deliberately on a need-to-know basis. Eamonn could have robbed Daddy blind but every penny was accounted for, every quarter per cent of interest. He was like a kid with a model train set, intent on showing how each part worked. When I asked if he got the same rates on his own offshore account he looked at me like I had ten heads. "Hasn't your daddy set me up in a job for life," he said, "with a grand salary and friends to look after me when I retire. I don't need one."' Pete shook his head incredulously. 'Every second businessman in Ireland was on the make and here, at the heart of it all, was this soul of fucking integrity.'

That was the joke. There was always something within my father – a grain of integrity or even naïve patriotism – that seemed to set him apart and had made Cormac's revelations all the more shocking. Maybe at heart every son thought that about his father. The sense of childhood innocence betrayed seemed like an unspoken bond between us as Pete and I smoked in companionable reflective silence.

I needed to piss. The pressure on my bladder made me recall Ebun's weight as she straddled me just a few hours before. My body had passed beyond tiredness. A greyish hint of dawn shaded the air. Although I often fantasized about maiming Pete Clancy, on many occasions when I actually dreamt about him we were like this – reminiscing as equals, discovering sudden respect for each other. At that moment it felt good, like I was finally somebody.

'Tell me about the accounts that are still open,' I said.

'Keep your friends close but your enemies closer,' Pete replied. 'Daddy never trusted Slab McGuirk or Mossy Egan. Whenever Daddy helped himself he helped others too. He wanted to see Meath changed, building a future for itself. If he received a contribution along the way then that was just the way of things, the grease that kept the fast-track wheels moving. Certain builders understood that and landowners too. They weren't corrupt, it was just the system of doing things. Eamonn understood it. Eamonn wanted nothing for himself, but he wanted Daddy up in the big house with the state car to show how far we'd come. That was how you got people's respect. If Daddy had gone to England he could have been as big a millionaire as old Joe Murphy but he stayed at home instead. He served people queuing at our door with their hands out. You can't manage that properly on a TD's or even a minister's salary. But Slab was different, only out for himself. If he had started throwing money around at certain times there was a grave danger of boats being rocked and questions asked.'

Pete stubbed out his cigarette and rose to drag open the byre door with a low rusty squeak. He stood silhouetted against the inkling of light.

'I love Meath in the dawn light,' he remarked.

'You still haven't explained the remaining accounts,' I said and he looked back.

'You tell me.'

'What do you mean?'

'You're your father's son. What do you really know about Shyroyal holdings?'

'Nothing.'

'It started in the early seventies when Daddy got word of a British firm sniffing around Navan, attracted by the mine, looking for a site outside town to build a shopping centre.

Daddy put together a consortium to buy those old cottages behind Emma Terrace. It needed a lot of donations and quiet words across party lines on the Council to keep blocking any application by the Brits while his own proposal was being put together. It was the making of Slab and Mossy and other contractors who never looked back afterwards. The site changed hands three times before being officially re-zoned, a chain of shell companies stretching back to Shyroyal Holdings. Money was made all right – Daddy owned half the shares – but more importantly every penny stayed in Meath with the Brits kept out.'

I smiled wryly, remembering how I had blamed Phyllis's hatred of Josie, who wound up in a block of Council maisonettes.

'Once was enough for Daddy,' Pete Clancy went on. 'He never got directly involved in development again, beyond ensuring that the right schemes got the nod. Because the Brits had wanted a green-field site out the Dublin Road, part of Daddy's plan to block them involved Shyroyal buying up small strategic parcels of land to make it hard for the Brits to get their preferred site together. Profits from building the shopping centre more than covered the outlay for these sites that were simply leased out for grazing afterwards. But suddenly in the 1980s those sites quadrupled in value. It wasn't so much Navan growing out as Dublin growing to meet it. The sites were too small to develop themselves but Daddy made sure that anyone wanting to build an estate nearby had to buy them up at the right price and include them in their plans. It was easy for Eamonn to officially block every planning application on the Dublin Road as unsuitable. Then Daddy could swing a re-zoning motion once the builder agreed to play ball. There was a new generation of hungry fucks of clean-living politicians coming up and Daddy needed every penny to hold them off when fighting in his last election. Shyroyal Holdings provided the funds. From being a sleeping princess it was suddenly rich with cash. There had been one police investigation years ago and Daddy didn't want another with Slab McGuirk drawing the taxman's attention down by flashing around his cut. It wasn't Slab's fault that he was going daft, but he wasn't trustworthy any more. That's where Eamonn came in.'

'I'm not following you,' I said.

Pete Clancy strode out into the farmyard. I followed, shivering with cold. In half an hour the view would be magnificent from up here. Rooks were stirring in the old trees near the gate. Pete Clancy stopped at his car, running his finger along the roof as if searching for dirt.

'Do you like cars?' he asked.

'No.'

'I don't use this one much – people like to see the state car. Daddy always said it gave status to a town, symbols are important. In England the under-secretaries drive around in what are only bangers by comparison. Crap cars but grandiose titles and traditions. They're still only bloody subjects, not citizens. A republic is different. Daddy's generation could make up their own rules from scratch. The Brits had Barings Bank for their inbred aristocrats until Nick Leeson fucked up. We had Des Traynor, bagman to the Taoiseach, running our own private bank from his office in Cement Roadstone. No doormen or frills, straight in to see the man if you were in the know. And Eamonn was in the know. He thought Des was a saint, the way he selflessly looked after Haughey's finances – not that Haughey wasn't long shafting the poor man's memory after he died – and Daddy always ensured that whenever a stone dropped into a pond in Meath a ripple eventually reached Haughey via the same Mr Traynor. It's how the world goes round.'

Clancy opened the driver's door. 'Sit in and we'll watch the dawn,' he said. 'You'd freeze to death out here.'

My blood went cold as I walked to the far side of the car. I saw Lisa Hanlon's face in her hospital bed, her voice barely above a whisper: *Sit here, he told me, and we'll watch the dawn.* I sat in the passenger seat as Pete Clancy stared amiably ahead. Was this how he had looked on the night he turned on her, hands gripping clumps of her hair as he held her head down over his open fly? How did I come to sit here, trusting a man I had half-intended to kill? He looked over.

'Tax rates were high, people felt penalized. All the banks were happy to run scams for selected customers, but Des ran banking for his own circle at its informal best. Once you were in that circle, and had a few bob you needed kept quiet, you simply gave him a call and popped over to the Burlington Hotel any lunchtime where he was available to receive envelopes with no questions asked. You'd be amazed who you'd meet there. Sometimes old P. V. Doyle himself was loitering around the doorway of his own hotel, with his tongue out. Well obviously Daddy couldn't go in person and Mossy and Slab were too small fry to shake hands with the great Des himself. A circle only works if it's kept small. But Eamonn was so well in with Traynor that it was simple for him to act as a middleman for Shyroyal and become master of his own circle. Des was a cultured man who wouldn't have been overjoyed to know he was dealing with a clatter of Meath builders who never washed behind their foreskins. So the fact that Eamonn held no accounts of his own was a godsend. Daddy made the others agree to a moratorium on touching the money until after the election. Your father was the honest broker. Using his children's names Eamonn set up three sets of accounts via Traynor who presumed that it was all your family's money.'

'Who was I?' I asked quietly.

'Mossy Egan.'

'Sarah-Jane?'

'Joey Kerwin. He had a small stake.'

'And Cormac?'

'Why?' He watched me carefully.

'Answer the question.'

'Slab's fifteen per cent stake was held in his name. Joey Kerwin drew the money down the day after the election. He was fond of lost weekends in Soho and giving donations to the church. He died soon after. Mossy Egan thought Channel Island banking was so good that he buggered off to Guernsey himself with poor P. J. left holding the reins and still vainly waiting for him to die. But Slab never touched his share. He didn't want to know about amnesties or anything else that involved parting with a penny. Why pay fifteen per cent when you can pay nothing, when the Taoiseach's bagman runs the scam and you know that no revenue official will ever dare poke his nose in? In truth, as his illness got worse I think he just forgot about the money'

A small flock of birds crested the hill in the weak light, their wings making a faint clacking noise. I recalled the lobby of the bank in St Helier six weeks after the crash when I showed Cormac's passport, the cashier scrutinizing my glasses and freshly dyed hair, then calling a higher official. I had already gambled away Cormac's present by then and was desperate. The inner office was huge, a gold fan whirling overhead with an echo of the noise the birds' wings were now making. I had wondered if he was the same official Cormac had conned as he examined my forgery of a forgery of a signature – Cormac's name as my father would have scrawled it.

'Not many of Mr Traynor's clients withdraw money in person,' he had informed me. But I had chosen my time carefully – an Irish bank holiday which fell on an ordinary working day in the UK and meant that nobody was contactable in Dublin. I had sweated as we made idle talk, waiting for the money to be brought in. The official was young and good-looking. He kept drumming his nails on the desk and glancing at me. Maybe Cormac had flirted with him weeks before. Stepping into his shoes there was so little I'd really known about who might recognize Cormac's name, have intimate knowledge of his body, see through my dyed hair and bogus mannerisms. When the money arrived, the official had stood up. We shook hands. At the door I turned to blow him the faintest kiss.

All the way across the marble-tiled lobby and down the steps beneath the white portico, I had resisted the temptation to run. Holidaymakers cluttered the narrow streets below while Fort Elizabeth rose in the distance, encircled by the harbour. In my real life I should have been avoiding fellow workers I owed money to in the factory, after enduring gridlock traffic on two bus journeys to work. Instead I had been living out a fantasy with a suitcase of stolen money. I had never confronted my father about my childhood. I had never got angry with him, but now I had got even, freed by the knowledge that he was crooked. The gambler in me had loved the thought of it being Barney Clancy's money. In this, as in most things, I was wrong. I wondered now how many excuses my father must have invented to stall Slab McGuirk until his son made him eventually pay with his life?

'Did my father want Slab to avail of the amnesty?' I asked.

'Eamonn was insistent I didn't push him. He got quite agitated.'

'That's because half the money was missing,' I replied. 'Cormac and I stole it.'

I couldn't believe I had just told Pete Clancy. It came from an almost boyish desire to confide in and please him. Me and my new-found friend, bonding together. I don't know what reaction I expected, maybe that he'd turn on me as quickly as he once turned on Lisa Hanlon. But he just took a last drag of his cigarette, then stubbed it out.

'We're all human,' he commented, matter-of-factly. 'With money involved things always get complex.'

'When I forged Cormac's signature I signed my father's death warrant.'

'You didn't tie him up. You're not to blame. How many accounts did you close?'

'Two. Cormac closed one and I closed the other. That's all the account numbers we had.'

He whistled softly. 'There were four parcels of land, four separate accounts. I can see why your father drew up strict new mandates for the two that were left. You are certain you do have those?' His tone was less matter of fact now.

'If it's Slab's money why are you so concerned?' I asked cagily.

'This business should have been closed long ago, for everyone's sake. Jersey was just a starting point for Traynor, a dummy run before he got into his stride and shifted his major clients to the Cayman Islands. The tribunals are so busy chasing the labyrinths of money on the Caymans that they've never explored what got left behind in Jersey.' He shook his head, amused. 'Your father refused to shift accounts from Jersey. He loved bloody Jersey.'

At least Phyllis did. There was something blackly funny there. While other men made and hid fortunes, my father's obsession had been to protect the free holidays in a cheap hotel that he cadged for himself and Phyllis twice a year.

'If these last two accounts are closed down nobody need know about Jersey,' Clancy said. 'It will be dead and buried with nothing to rake over. But if a trawl of active accounts throws up these two then lawyers will start digging. Neither P. J. nor I want that. It won't matter to the media that I made Daddy accept the amnesty, all that will matter is that my father was involved.'

'And that he was on the make.'

'We're all on the make, Brendan, it's the human condition. You and Cormac were on the make when you stole that money. Your wife and son were on the make when they creamed your life assurance.'

'They knew nothing about it.'

'Do you think the newspapers will care? Why let truth get in the way of a good story? Everything is black and white for those fuckers, except their own expenses. I'm sick to death of reporters.'

'Why not just quit?'

'And do what?' he replied. 'Go where? My father gave me the seat that his father gave to him and I won't be the one who surrenders it. Every year I see the loss of respect more. People don't like me but their dirty consciences mean they're never sure they won't need me if their young son goes a bit wild, their granny starts shoplifting or an upstanding father of seven is found with the hind legs of a squealing ewe tucked into his Wellingtons. The day I lose that seat they'll stab me in the back so hard that I'll be a pariah, unable to walk through Navan.'

He turned on the radio and skimmed through the stations until he found a classical music one, then turned the sound down low.

'I've enough enemies without Jersey blowing up in my face. Slick doesn't know how much money was in those accounts anyway. Slab hated his missus with a vengeance and hated Haughey for giving equal property rights to wives. He didn't just hide money from the taxman, he hid it from his missus and told Slick nothing in case he squealed to her. It was only when Slick met Joey Kerwin's son at Cheltenham this year that he found out about his father having a share in those land sales in the 1980s and that your father had babysat the money. P. J. and I were never going to tell him. He went to your father but they had a blazing row. All Eamonn had to do was lie and say that Slab took out the money years ago, but not Mr Fucking Integrity Retired Civil Servant. Eamonn never liked Slick. He had a notion that all your bullying came from him. It was his way to re-write the past. To hear him talk you'd swear that he and Phyllis had rigged up a luxury granny flat for you as a child after you refused to sleep in the house despite his pleadings.'

A fox appeared at the gate, sniffing the air and eyeing us distrustfully. He crossed the cobbles cautiously, then bolted into the undergrowth.

'When Daddy died Eamonn became like a sort of scared keeper of Daddy's memory,' Clancy went on. 'The slightest innuendo and he would start firing letters off to the papers. He was obsessive about Daddy's achievements being lost under accusations of sleaze. But that's politics – the new stallion always has to piss in every corner of the stable to douse the scent of the old one. Eamonn said he was writing a book about Daddy. He was doting and getting dangerous. He had minutes of meetings that were dynamite. All over Ireland company accounts were being shredded, people losing bank statements and their memories and he was hoarding documents to write an apologia for an era. Slick went too far but he wasn't just desperate for Slab's money, he was terrified of being contaminated.

'The money is in limbo now,' Clancy continued. 'Only two people could activate those accounts – your father and the family member whose name he put them in.' He looked at me. 'How did you clear the second account out?'

'I've travelled on Cormac's passport ever since I disappeared.'

'You always were a man for the gamble.' Clancy paused, letting his meaning come clear. 'I'd say you're still a gambler.'

'I haven't bet for four years. I lost everything so often that I'd nothing left to lose.'

'You took a gamble coming here. If you have those last account numbers and the mandates, why didn't you just go to Jersey to clean them out and run?'

'Firstly I want my son to stop being hassled,' I replied. 'Secondly I can't get Cormac's passport renewed without checks being done on it back in Ireland.'

The barely suppressed flicker of a smile crossed his face. 'So you thought to try your local TD, did you?'

'Fuck you, Clancy.'

'That's more like it. Maybe one time a TD could swing a passport. Before computerization and officials started tightening regulations up.'

'Are you saying it can't be done?'

'When does it expire?'

'A few weeks.'

'Time enough for someone to enjoy a short break in Jersey and return home with everyone's problems solved. That is if you really have the account mandates.'

'I've told you I do.'

'With who? Your queer son?'

'Stop calling him that.'

'Slick has become an expert on gay bars. He won't let this money go. He feels that people made fun of Slab for years and used his illness to cheat him. He's convinced your family is holding out on him.'

'Conor knows nothing. I want a guarantee that Slick never goes near him again, a fresh passport and five thousand Euros to get me the hell away from here.'

'You work cheap.'

'I also want our own tax amnesty. Twenty-five per cent of all monies go into a legal, up-front account for Conor. Slick's accountant can structure it as an anonymous trust fund. The boy need never know where it came from.'

'Slick is greedy. He won't like it.'

'He'll huff and puff, but he'll do what you tell him. Only for Conor I'd cut his heart out for what he did to my father. But I need to disappear again without fuss for the boy's sake. How do you explain the missing money Cormac and I took?'

'Slick doesn't know how much there is. Don't forget he's still as thick as shite on a blanket. P. J. and I will puff up whatever he gets in his mind until he feels like a dog with two mickies, especially if he knows you've vanished. He's having nightmares since your father died, seeing his ghost in every corner.'

'Who broke in during the funeral?' I asked.

'Slick is a loose cannon.' Clancy drummed his fingers on the steering wheel. 'P. J. stuck to him like glue after the event, knowing he'd fuck up alone. We were all at the church for the funeral, but Slick vamoosed when the cortège was heading for Navan. P. J. followed him to Cremore where Slick was scouring the attic again. P. J. tried to burn the place down. With P. J. what you see is what you get – a heartless bastard.' He started the engine, then stopped. 'His shotgun,' he said, with a laugh. 'Where would I be for starting golf classics without it?'

I had left it on the byre floor. He climbed out, with the engine running, and walked back to retrieve it. A minute passed, then two, as I sat there alone. If I wished to I could simply drive off, abandoning him and his plan. Maybe he was deliberately giving me time to consider that option. All my life I had hated Pete Clancy. I'd come seeking revenge but wound up agreeing to run risks for him like a messenger boy. I told myself it was for Conor's sake. But part of me was thrilled just for once to be inside the big boys' clique.

The prickling sensation I got before placing a bet possessed me. Odds played out a terrible familiar dance inside my head, that obsessive yearning for the adrenaline rush of success; once a gambler, always a gambler. I had sat in Gamblers Anonymous meetings in different cities, forsaking greyhounds, horses, football results, boxing matches, blackjack, poker, slot machines, roulette wheels, but always some other medium turned up for the poison to seep out.

I closed my eyes to imagine that bank in Jersey, the gleaming white portico, the inner office. The risks would be higher after all these years, with every crooked banker in Europe knowing there were too many investigations for comfort in Ireland. An Irish passport would not be a welcome sight, but they might be happy to see the back of those final accounts.

If I was caught Clancy would deny all knowledge of me. But the nerve-ends of my fingers tingled, pumped up, hungry for risk.

There was still no sign of Clancy in the rear-view mirror. I opened the glove compartment, which contained a pile of party leaflets and a photo. Taken abroad under a non-Irish sky, it showed Pete Clancy with his arm around his wife, while two young girls smiled shyly beside their mother and a boy of ten stood beside him, staring almost belligerently at the camera. The boy had a Simpsons T-shirt and shorts with a Manchester United logo. His haircut was stylish, yet his eyes and mouth belonged in a schoolyard long ago. He looked more like the Pete Clancy I knew than the man I had just spoken too.

'The Clancy clan.' Pete's voice startled me through the open window. I had not heard him approach. I replaced the photo as he climbed in. 'I keep it with me. Sometimes I need to be reminded why I put up with all the shite I have to deal with, just who I'm building a future for.' He released the handbrake and eased the car slowly down the overgrown lane. 'The girls are lovely, aren't they? They take after their mother,' he added. 'I need to protect them. I had enough rumours about my father thrown at me as a kid. I don't want them to ever have to make the excuses I've had to make for him. You understand that, you're a father too.' He swung left, driving slowly so that overhanging branches wouldn't scrape his paintwork. 'Getting a passport will be risky.' He looked across. 'It's a good thing we're old friends.'

'We were never friends . . .'

'We go back a long way. There's few enough people left who understand where we came from. I've more in common with you than with those two monkeys on my back. You don't have to like someone to be their friend. Now do we have a deal?'

Steering with his left hand he spat into his right palm and held it out, the way cattlemen did in the square in Navan years ago while dumb beasts waited for slaughter. I couldn't tell if he was being ironic or genuine. I didn't go so far as to spit into my own palm, but cautiously I gripped his hand and shook it.

'Get me a plane ticket,' I said, 'and I'll go.'

We had reached the road. Clancy glanced left and right, anxious that no early motorist would spy us. 'That's the thing,' he replied, 'you won't have to.'

'What do you mean?'

'Two months after you died Eamonn told Daddy he was switching the accounts out of Cormac's name. He said it was because Cormac had passed away, but now I realize he was afraid of the rest of the money being stolen. Cormac's passport will get you nowhere in Jersey.'

'Then what the hell have we been talking about?' I asked, puzzled. 'What do you want me to do?'

'Persuade. Provide sound fatherly advice. You know how sons always look up to their fathers.'

He allowed the implication to sink in.

'No way,' I said, 'no, no, no.'

'Why do you think Slick keeps following Conor like a dog? Those accounts are in Conor's name. Since your father died he's been Slick's only hope. I've managed to hold off Slick until we discovered if Conor held the mandates or not. I don't want him hurt and neither do you. Slick would be less than subtle in any approach, especially since you've turned up. He'll feel that your whole family is working together, trying to cheat him. I can't be involved, so it makes sense than you persuade Conor. Tell him anything you want, but as little as possible, and most especially don't mention me. This is Eamonn's mess. Conor's had to leave one school because of graffiti on the wall – not that Eamonn wasn't warned in advance. CONOR BROGAN IS A QUEAR. Slick was never good at spelling. The boy seems to have settled into a new school in Glasnevin, and your wife is vulnerable enough in that house if Slick flips. I'd hate for things to come tumbling down.'

'Is that a threat?'

'I'm threatening nobody. I'm sick of the whole business. I'm telling you I can't hold Slick off forever. Your son is in danger. You haven't been much of a father so far, so here's your chance.'

'The boy doesn't even know who I am.'

'Then maybe it's time he found out and discovered just how much shite his mother will be in if you stick around much longer. Nobody else knows, do they?'

His voice was sharp. I thought of Ebun. 'Of course not. You're one bad bastard, Clancy, you always were.'

'I'm my father's son. He trained me for this job. Apply every bit of useable dirt subtly, when the time is right. Slick is a peasant, frightened of queers because he's one himself and Conor had such a pretty face at Eamonn's funeral that I'd hate to see it destroyed.'

'Fuck you,' I said. 'I'm taking no risks with my boy. I'll make a clean breast of everything to the cops.'

I stepped out of the car and started walking. After twenty yards I heard the car start to follow. Clancy slowed down and lowered his window.

'Don't stalk off on me, like you walked off on your family. Thirty per cent to your boy, six grand to you and a fresh passport. That's a lot for you both to gain, but by Christ you've far more to lose. Go to the cops and what proof do you have of anything? I have an alibi for tonight, just like Slick has an alibi for the night your father died. You'll just do six years for embezzlement, your wife may be charged as an accessory, and your son will be left holding two illegal bank accounts he can't explain. At nine a.m. on Thursday bring him to Dublin airport with the mandates. My name is not to be mentioned. A ticket will be waiting for Conor. Don't worry about his passport, Slick stole it from the house on the day of the funeral. P. J. will hand it to him before he goes into departures and will be on the plane to give him instructions. Give your old passport and a new photo to P. J.. Meet me here at midnight on Thursday with the Shyroyal documents. I'll have your fresh passport and cash. After that I never expect to see you or your family again.'

The sickness in my stomach was an echo of the sensation I had known a lifetime before lying under my bed in Navan with a pool of urine seeping into my clothes.

'You bastard!'

Clancy touched a button and the window began to wind up. 'Everything will be settled, Hen Boy,' he said. 'Just like your father would have wanted.'

I heard a truck in the distance. Clancy accelerated away before it came into sight. The truck driver glanced at me as I sat on the grass verge, then shook his head, dismissing me as another drunk taking the long way home.

V

TUESDAY, DAWN

It began to rain as I walked towards Navan, the sort of torrential downpour that rarely lasts long in Ireland. But it caused entire colonics of snails to materialize on stone walls, antennae raised, bodies straining forward on tortuous journeys. The sight made me sick as I picked my steps carefully along parts of the flooded road to avoid crushing them. I felt mugged, robbed of a treasured possession that was worthless to anyone else. The fantasy of a reconciliation with Conor had always existed in my mind, the moment when I decided to reveal who I was on my own terms and tried to make sense of my life. Now Clancy had stolen that moment from me, leaving me with an impossible choice. Any approach I made now would have to be to persuade Conor to collaborate with men who killed his grandfather. Yet by shirking that task I might leave him at the mercy of McGuirk's unpredictable violence.

Without the mandates Slick McGuirk was stymied. But destroying them and disappearing would serve no purpose. He would presume I had given them to Conor to claim the money or I was biding my time by keeping them for myself. Either way Conor could get hurt, while Slick tried to extract them from him or else as a warning to me of what might happen if I didn't return and cooperate. It was impossible to decide which lesser evil would best protect my son. For now only the last vestige of authority conjured by the Clancy name kept Slick in his box. If Pete Clancy was the devil, at least he was the devil I knew. But it wasn't my soul that I was being forced to bargain with.

I was drenched to the skin, not even bothering to try and hitch a lift from the occasional vehicle passing in the dawn light. When a truck stopped unbidden twenty yards in front of me, I cursed the driver, wanting to be alone. Yet I climbed up into the cab when he leaned over to open the passenger door.

'Did she kick you out of the bed from getting crumbs on the pillow?' he asked heartily. 'Where in the name of Jaysus would you be going on a morning like this? Is Navan any good to you?'

'It never was before.'

He studied my face, then laughed. 'Jaysus, but you're an awful man,' he said. 'It must be a woman has you this shook up. There's no smell of drink off you at all.'

Occasionally he shouted some question at me over the rattle of the engine, then shook his head, amused at my lack of response. I didn't have to ask myself what Cormac would have said to him in this situation. He would have said nothing. Cormac had remained steadfastly silent on the evening, ten years ago, when a farmer stopped to pick him up in the rain near Kinloch Rannoch in Scotland, after walking for two days. The farmer pulled in outside the police station in Aberfeldy, leaving his mute passenger in the car. Cormac made no attempt to flee and offered no resistance to the police officer who first suggested he leave the car and then physically helped him to do so. He had committed no crime. When they put him in an empty cell it was purely because it contained a bed that he would lie on until examined by a doctor.

That night was the second time in my life when the police came looking for me. Miriam had hovered at the top of the stairs, convinced I was going to be arrested for something I had not told her about. I was convinced too, the moment I saw the uniforms. I had felt a strange surge of relief that finally I was caught for some unspecified crime, out of the thousands that I felt I deserved to be charged with. Instead they were as apologetic as the policemen who had called to the North Circular Road on the night when Lisa Hanlon tried to drown herself. They came because our phone was off the hook all evening, with me blaming Conor when it was a trick I often did myself for fear of who might phone looking for money with Miriam in. I should not be alarmed, the police said. There was nothing physically wrong with Cormac. He had been found in a distressed state and gave their Scottish counterparts my name as next of kin. It was advisable that someone be with him, as a precaution in case he inflicted damage on himself.

Cormac was a Trinity graduate, I explained, knowing this would impress them. He had gone to Scotland five years ago for work. They nodded, recounting tales of distant relatives who graduated with first-class degrees, yet wound up working in petrol stations here before being forced abroad. 'Emigration's a killer,' one stated, 'especially for the man with brains.' They drove off, relieved that I had found a way to avoid discussing what might actually be wrong with Cormac. It was five years to the month since Cormac had phoned one Friday evening, bubbling with excitement, while Alex's half-exasperated voice scolded him in the background.

'We're on the move,' Cormac announced. 'Alex told me just this second. He's been offered a job in Perth. I've always wanted to see Australia.'

I could hear Alex in the background shouting: 'Can you never listen to what I'm saying to you?' Cormac had sounded like an upset child as he replied: 'He's my brother, I want to tell him first.' Their voices grew faint, as if

Cormac had dropped the phone, leaving me feeling like a voyeur as I strained to hear them. There was a silence before Cormac picked up the phone, his voice filled with disbelief. 'Cancel the champagne,' he said. 'It's Perth in bloody Scotland.'

The words Scotland and bloody co-existed in most of Cormac's sentences over the next five years, even though, despite himself, he quickly adapted to life over there. The adjective was more ironic than anything else. Bloody Perth was like Navan with fewer pubs and more Protestants. Bloody Edinburgh was as repressed as a priest in a closet. Bloody Glasgow was like Westmoreland Street on a Friday night, filmed by Cecil B. De Mille. Local mocking slang entered his speech, with Aberdeen becoming Scabadeen and Dundee Scumdee, but the more he complained in letters and phone calls, the more I knew that behind the bluster, he was having a ball.

Some evenings I came home to find that he had kept Miriam on the phone for an hour, enquiring about correct temperatures for clothes in a washing machine and recipes for brown bread. 'The day he bursts into "Such are the dreams of the everyday housewife" I'll shoot him,' Miriam would declare, exhausted from her day's work in the Citizens Advice Centre, while Conor crawled around at her feet. I doubted if Cormac's safaris into domesticity lasted long, but he loved the notion of us both being settled down, and, indeed, for most of those years he and Alex seemed a more happily married couple than Miriam and I.

Their advantages, of course, included not having a child to raise, plus exotic holidays twice a year. We only went abroad once, when we visited them – courtesy of a secret treble at Folkestone, after which I went straight to the travel agent's without giving myself time to lose the lot on the next race.

It wasn't the scale of their apartment, occupying the top two storeys of a Victorian house, which stood out, but how ornaments were casually placed on low shelves that a child could reach. Most of the holiday was spent saving them from four-year-old Conor's clutches.

A change in Cormac was evident on that trip and not just in the glasses that he had started wearing. Cormac had been wide-eyed, subservient and financially dependent on Alex when they first met. Now in his late twenties he had a good job in Perth (though not as good as his degree would have got him in a bigger city) and there was less of a boyish quality about him. Alex and himself seemed more like equals, knowledgeably discussing wines when they took us out for a meal and debating the merits of little-known resorts in Tunisia and Morocco. His impromptu magic tricks and devil-may-care impersonations had been suppressed as he slowly became a mini-version of the man he loved. But an impish version of his little-boy-lost persona resurfaced at night when Alex imperiously sat down with his *Financial Times* and Cormac made the mock plea, 'Can I read the funnies, Daddy?'

I was proud of him. When they were both at work and Miriam and Conor were soaking in the huge bath on cast-iron legs in a room to itself on the top floor, I sometimes opened his wardrobe. I would finger his suits and jackets, as scared of being caught as if I had sneaked upstairs in our old house in Navan. My kid brother who towered over me. The family success, married to a doctor.

Not that Phyllis or my father saw it that way, though it was hard to discern what my father chose to see as communication between us had virtually ceased. Miriam maintained some contact because she felt Conor should know his grandfather, though her reports of my father doting on him only caused an unspoken ire within me. Phyllis's barely concealed antipathy towards Miriam was sufficient to make such dutiful visits infrequent and Cormac was never mentioned during them.

But it was for Phyllis's sake that Cormac returned home three times a year and even lured her to Perth when Alex was safely abroad at a conference. Once he even insisted on taking us all for a family meal in the Trocarado restaurant in Dublin. It consisted of my father who spent the evening complaining about the prices though he wasn't paying; a teenage Sarah-Jane with her musician escort who, if he made up for in bed what he lacked in basic speech, could bring her entire sixth-year convent class to orgasm; Miriam who wasn't speaking to me after discovering a betting slip in my jeans and Phyllis who could have passed for Nancy Reagan from the adoring way she gazed at Cormac every time he spoke.

But mainly he met Phyllis alone, though once he insisted upon dragging me along to a coffee shop with them. Her conversation was a labyrinthine code, in which she enquired about his 'flatmate' (Alex); his health (AIDS); his job (potential promotions); how much danger existed in the world (AIDS); did he meet many new people in work (had her prayers been answered by a girlfriend); and her worries for Sarah-Jane (that she might contract AIDS even quicker than Cormac).

Cormac's conversation was more direct and increasingly one-track – his real father. Apart from being Scottish what did Phyllis recall about him? Lowering her voice, embarrassed at my presence, Phyllis had pleaded that she had nothing more to tell. It occurred when she was young and naïve, working in a Glasgow hotel. He had come in with an older self-important man who was so demeaning and suggestive that she ran from the building crying. He had followed, upset at her being upset. 'Your father was a nice man, a gentleman,' she repeated, holding Cormac's hand across the table.

The man had insisted on walking her home and she felt safe with him, so safe that things happened which neither of them had planned. He was trapped in a loveless marriage, but had not revealed this until the end of the night. He had come back to the hotel looking for her, but she ran away because she did not want to be the destroyer of any marriage.

'Surely he had a name at least,' Cormac had persisted.

'What married man gives a real name?' Phyllis replied. 'You'd never be up to married men, son, always looking for somebody young.' Her tone was unconsciously woman-to-woman as I watched their heads bend closer together over the café table.

Next came my father's entry into the fantasy which I now think she had been weaving for so long that she half believed it herself. Her own family had cut her off as she struggled to keep Cormac from the grasp of district nurses and sour-faced nuns smelling of peppermint who wanted to snatch him away into an orphanage. One evening she was put out of her digs in Glasgow because Cormac wouldn't stop crying. She repeatedly walked the long stretch from Argyle Street to Gallowgate until rain drove her to shelter on a bench in the vast concourse of Central Station.

She claimed that my father heard her Dublin accent as she tried to hush Cormac. He was in Glasgow on business, with my mother not long dead. Seeing her distress, he had bought her tea in the cramped station buffet that was about to close for the night. It was he who paid for a guesthouse for her and Cormac and brought them back to Dublin. At first she had told him she was widowed too, out of shame. When they married in Dublin they decided to maintain the pretence in Navan, so that people would not look down on Cormac. Even if some neighbours weren't fooled, they would have gone along with the deception only for 'that interfering old bitch Josie'. But my father never showed favouritism, she emphasized, refusing to glance in my direction. He had been a good father to Cormac and it would break her heart if Cormac went snooping around Scotland looking for someone else.

I remembered the dread in her voice again now as the truck entered Navan, getting snarled in early morning traffic. Commuters swarmed from new estates, fighting their way towards the Dublin Road. In the light of what Pete Clancy had said I went over Phyllis's version, filtering out the pure invention, half-truths, excuses and special pleadings. Being evicted from lodging houses was probably true, with doors slammed in her face at the sight of the child. Perhaps my father had tracked her down in the station concourse in Glasgow, two years after fleeing Barney Clancy's plans for the nuns to get their hands on her child? But my mother had still been alive when he tracked down his illegitimate son. Was their marriage loveless or was this another veiled self-justification invented by Phyllis? I would never know how much my mother had known when she stepped off the footpath at Ludlow Street.

The driver looked across as we passed that. 'Where do you want to be dropped?' he shouted.

'Here.'

'Right so.' The street was so narrow that he didn't pull in, just simply stopped. There was a loud beep and one car with a Cavan registration somehow squeezed past.

'Mean fecking Cavan cunt,' the driver said, ignoring the build-up of traffic behind us as he watched me climb down. 'You heard what the Cavanman said when he found a fly in his pint?' He squeezed his forefinger and thumb together, addressing the imaginary fly trapped between them. 'Spit it back out, you thieving bastard.'

He drove off, still laughing at his own joke. I stood on a corner of my hometown, as lost as Phyllis surely must have felt on the afternoon when we first drove into the papier-mâché world of lies and evasions that comprised her life in Navan. Maybe initially it was to protect Cormac, but she had continued lying to her adult son in order to shield my father and preserve the façade of his first marriage. Cormac's voice had sounded so plaintive in that café years ago as he asked, 'Then why can't I remember anything of Glasgow?'

'Children forget, love. You were much too young.'

Children may forget, but they vividly remember everything again in middle age. My head ached from the night's events. I needed to lie down and think, needed to get away from passers-by staring at my dishevelled condition. My legs traced a familiar route along streets soon to be thronged with school-children. I kept my head down, dodging into the back lane. The estate agent had said that the Hanlon house was empty, with Lisa not due home until the morning of the auction. The trees in the back lane were much bigger now. The pot-holed surface remained the same, although more overgrown with no through traffic now. Most entrances to the sheds where men once laboured over furniture were bricked up. But I could still discern the rates, in pounds, shillings and pence, that Lisa Hanlon's father had painted on his wooden door when he used to respray cars in the late 1960s. A battered chair had been dumped with other litter beyond it. Hanlon's shed roof had seemed so high once. It was easier to reach up to it now, yet I found it harder to climb.

Nobody stirred in the back gardens as I dropped down. I ducked under the apple trees, stumbling over windfalls in the long grass. The original iron windows were still in place. If you banged at the centre of the small middle frame its handle popped up. I climbed onto the sill and reached my hand in.

The handle of the main sitting-room windowframe was stiff after countless coats of paint, but eventually I managed to prise it open. The furniture there held no grandeur this morning. I just needed somewhere to rest before deciding what to do next.

There was an antiquated black phone in the hall. I picked it up, surprised that it was not disconnected. I had no idea what I wanted to say, but I needed to make sure that Conor was OK. The old Cremore number rang eight or nine times. Just when I was convinced nobody was at home it was picked up and a voice said 'Hello?'

It was Miriam. Sweet Jesus, I realized how much I had missed her voice. I listened to my wife say 'Hello?' several times before she put the receiver down. I kept waiting for her to say, 'Brendan, I know it's you out there.' They were the words I'd wanted every time I had phoned after my disappearance until the number was disconnected. Surely just once she must have guessed it was me.

I sat back on the floor, resisting the temptation to dial the number again. Her voice had made her shockingly real. The woman I had once imagined would always be there, putting up with me, ready to forgive and start afresh. The peculiar curve of her breasts that always thrilled me when they tumbled from her bra, the way she preferred to make love in the mornings kneeling up on the bed. Her pet names for me, names she only whispered when close to orgasm, her voice suddenly child-like. The love I had despoiled and thrown away. For what? The freedom to escape from obsessions that continued to haunt me. The freedom to gamble away every penny in an orgy of stupidity and not have to face her eyes afterwards. The right to play at being anyone other than myself.

I wanted to put my arms around somebody: Miriam,

Conor, Ebun, Cormac, my father as he had once comforted me in a bed two doors away. His strong arms and unshaved chin. How could I make a deal with his killers? I wanted arms from further back, arms that I strained to remember like Cormac had strained to recall Glasgow. I wanted the comfort of being a child asleep in Josie's attic, knowing that Daddy was coming home tomorrow. I wanted to lie beside Conor at the age of four when he whimpered with a temperature and I curled into him all night, not caring how wrecked I would be in work, just thrilled to find a niche where I was genuinely needed.

I don't know what I wanted, just that eventually, curled up in a ball on Hanlon's hall floor, sleep managed to catch me out.

———◼———

A sixth sense made me wake with a start, ready to lash out. I don't know what I had been dreaming. My limbs were stiff from lying on the floor, my eyes raw. Hanlon's gate opened with the same creak they had not fixed in twenty years. A shadow appeared at the hammered glass. I looked around, knowing it was too late to hide. The letterbox was pushed open and a hail of circulars and special offers tumbled noisily onto the mat. The caller retreated down the path.

I climbed the stairs with pins and needles in my leg. Through the box-room window I watched the postman stop to chat with old Mrs Kelly across the road, checking through the letters in his hand. His skin was jet-black. Laughing at some remark, he walked on.

I had no idea what time it was. Every clock in the house was stopped. There was a radio on the bedside locker in what had been Mrs Hanlon's room, beside a plastic Virgin half-filled with clouded holy water. Keeping the sound low I flicked through endless rock music and nonsensical ads until I found RTE. I walked into Lisa's old room to look carefully out through the blinds. A child of seven or eight played in my old garden. He propelled a red plastic tractor around the white stones, using two levers to scoop up a hoard of stones as he dug with intense pleasurable concentration. Behind him the door of the modern outhouse was open. A man came out with a sheaf of papers and locked the door, placing the key under one of the grey stones they had obviously robbed from a beach. He called the boy and they walked into the kitchen together.

I had forgotten the sound of the noon Angelus until bells rang on the radio in Mrs Hanlon's bedroom. The mid-day news headlines followed it. There was a second march by locals in Tramore against the attempted deportation of the refugee and her children. Further reports of evasion from the tribunals and the morning sitting of the Dail suspended in a row over a minister refusing to answer questions. Had Pete Clancy been there, I wondered, taking his place on the Government bench despite his lack of sleep? Greeting fellow ministers, briefing journalists, dealing with the incessant problems landing on his desk. A man who lacked the spark of his father, but was known as a safer pair of hands at a time when conformity and not initiative was needed. He was waiting now like a patient angler, knowing I had to resurface, no matter what rock I swam under.

Finding an extremely ancient razor I splashed some water and soap on my face and made a crude attempt to shave. I dried myself with an old towel from the hot press. There was so much stuff that Lisa would have to throw out. What had happened to my own clothes ten years ago, I wondered? Donated to some charity shop in Dorset Street probably, with

Miriam getting a lift from a friend to bring down the plastic sacks. The last trace of me, except for the betting slips and pawnbroker tickets she had probably found hidden in peculiar places for years afterwards.

A life totalled off in bags and cardboard boxes. At least Miriam did me that service which I was supposed to do for Cormac. Alex Lever must have presumably done the necessary, though he was such a fastidious man that maybe he found a team of professionals to clear out the wardrobe of his ex-lover – or ex-tenant, as he described him to the police in Aberfeldy the night before I flew to Scotland.

The Aberfeldy police officers were courteous that night when I phoned them, after their Irish counterparts had pulled away from our door in Raheny. After being cut off twice for non-payment of bills, our own phone was doctored to take only incoming calls. We had to walk to a coin-box near the shops, with Miriam and Conor waiting outside as the slot swallowed half the coins we had gathered up from around the house. They weren't holding him, the police explained. The doctor had just suggested that Cormac should rest up for a few days, and the psychiatric wing was the only ward of Nine Wells Hospital in Dundee with beds available. It had been months since I heard from Cormac, but I was too preoccupied with my own problems to take note of his silence.

'But what does Dr Lever say? Alex Lever. His . . . friend in Perth.'

'Cormac just gave your name.'

'Could you phone Dr Lever, please, then call me back.'

I had waited in the callbox while the queue outside glowered at me and Miriam mouthed a dozen questions through the glass. Finally the sergeant from Aberfeldy phoned back.

'There was no reply at that home number you provided,

but we contacted him via the hospital. He was quite brusque, I must say. He claims Mr Brogan is an ex-tenant of his under notice to leave and this would be best handled by the family. He seemed quite insistent that I pass on the message that you can well afford to fly over.' The sergeant sounded embarrassed. 'I don't think I'd fancy him much as a landlord.'

Conor was discovering the joys of chips that autumn. We bought him some as we walked home past the shops. The Italian proprietor made jokes with him as Miriam sat him up on the counter and allowed him to pour his own vinegar. We sat on a bench near the park, our concern for Cormac breaching the hard crust of slights and accusations that generally made conversation impossible. I can see us still sitting there as Conor slowly ate his chips, looking to all the world like a happy family. It was the last walk we ever took together.

That night was also the last time I ever saw my father, when I cycled over to Cremore. Phyllis was already in bed. It was the year before my father was due to retire. Several months previously I had gone to him, not for money – I knew he hadn't money – but to see if he could pull any strings with Clancy to bypass the waiting lists for a hospital bed for Miriam's mother. All I had got was a lecture on how democracy worked and that health service cutbacks were necessary if the country wasn't going to sink under the National Debt.

He had made me feel grubby for asking and so I'd hated having to go back to him again. I spied him through the window downstairs, working late on some papers by the light of a small reading lamp. I tapped on the glass and he rose, startled, then came closer, recognizing me. He put the papers carefully in his briefcase before opening the door. We were awkward with each other as he ushered me into the living-room, anxious not to wake Phyllis. His tone was almost formal as he offered me a whiskey. He seemed to avoid my eye directly, a technique he practised on pushy builders. I took the glass, noticing how he had poured himself a larger one. I never visited him, therefore he knew that either somebody was dead or he was going to be touched for money.

'It's Cormac,' I began. 'He's in some sort of trouble in Scotland.'

He lowered his voice to ask, 'Does his mother have to know?'

'Not necessarily. I can probably handle it.'

'Good man.'

I hated myself for feeling a flush of pleasure. But how often had he ever praised me?

'You can phone me in work,' he added, 'I have a direct line now, a private number.'

'Dad . . . ?'

He looked directly into my eyes now. I wondered what he saw there. His failed son, a glorified factory hand, going nowhere.

'How are you fixed?' he asked cautiously.

'It's very short notice. I only found out tonight. They think that someone should go over.'

I could see the momentary suspicion in his mind. They knew enough about my gambling for Phyllis to drop veiled barbs when Miriam visited. I think he wanted evidence, a form signed in triplicate perhaps. Yet I had never come to him for money in the past and I was only here now because there was nobody else to whom I was not already secretly in hock.

'There's a boat from Larne, isn't there?'

'I'm flying,' I hissed angrily. 'The first flight I can get.'

'But you'll have to pay top dollar at short notice,' he argued. 'Unless maybe you stay a Saturday night.'

'For fuck's sake!' My voice was louder, knowing that he

would panic if he thought Phyllis might wake. 'Just because he's not . . .'

'What?'

'Nothing,' I said bitterly. 'It would make no difference anyway if he was your fucking son.'

'Son . . .'

He sounded genuinely distressed. But I felt cheap having to ask him for something. I put the whiskey down.

'I'll get the fare somewhere else,' I said quietly.

'No. Just tell me what you need. Please.' He spoke slowly, almost like a plea. 'What do you need?'

There was something perturbing in his gaze, like he was seeing me properly for the first time in decades. He looked lost and, I suddenly noticed, far older than I remembered. I repeated what Cormac had once told me the full fare to Glasgow was, but that didn't seem to answer his question. There was a long silence during which I could think of nothing more to say, while he waited, almost expectantly. Then with a shrug he turned and walked to a small bookcase in the corner. He took down a tattered hardback with its dustjacket missing, counted a pile of banknotes out from between its pages, counted them again, hesitated and then added several more to the pile. I checked the amount when he handed it to me.

'There's too much here,' I said.

'You might need it, or maybe get the young lad something.' He poured himself another whiskey. 'Miriam hasn't brought him over since her mother died. It isn't because . . .'

'She's been busy,' I replied. 'I know there was nothing you could do about the hospital. I never told her about the time I called over.'

'That's good,' he said, relieved. 'It's always best to keep things among ourselves.'

I watched from Hanlon's window until the street was deserted, then picked up an estate agent's leaflet from the hall so as to look like someone on business and slipped out the front door. There were few enough familiar faces on the route to Market Square where a bus for Dublin had always stopped outside McAndrew's pub at one o'clock. I was starving and went into a small newsagent's on the square for some chocolate. The shop assistant was in her late teens, near tears as she tried to cope with the three shrieking Romanian women who jabbered in broken English at her with carefully controlled hysterics.

'I gave you back your huge banknote but you haven't given me all the change. Please, you've left me forty short.'

All three shouted at her again in unison, creating as much noise and confusion as possible. They did not want the magazine they had bought, it was too dear, they had their money back, she had her change back, they did not understand, they were leaving.

A door opened and a man appeared from the kitchen behind the shop, taking in the situation. 'Call the police,' he snapped, 'they've tried that same bloody trick in every small shop in town.'

The women glanced towards the door, their exit strategy coming into play. 'Look,' one said with a beatific smile. 'On the ground. Money. Is not ours. Must be yours.'

'Get out and stay out,' the man glowered, then turned to the girl as they exited. 'How long were they here, pet?'

'It seems like forever, Daddy. They wouldn't stop shouting. They had me so fazzled I was about to tell them to just go.'

He looked at me, slightly taken aback by my half-shaven

appearance. 'I wouldn't mind if they tried it out on the likes of me,' he told me. 'But they wait till they see an old woman or a child alone. Anyway, sir, what can I do you for?'

I ate the chocolate ravenously in the queue of people sheltering under the striped awning of the butcher's shop beside McAndrew's pub. Gradually I became aware of being observed. Panic-stricken, I searched for a name which came to me just as the old woman approached. It was Mrs Kennedy who lived on the corner. Barney Clancy once got her husband appointed as a Peace Commissioner. The title had fascinated me as a child, even after I discovered it was utterly meaningless.

'It couldn't be . . . ?' she began, almost against her will. 'I'm sorry, but your face just reminds me of . . . would you be related to . . . ?'

'*Desculpe ter de a enganar*,' I replied, staring blankly at her. Embarrassed, she backed away, mistaking my Portuguese for Romanian or Polish. I repeated the sentence, my accent as thick as possible – *I'm sorry I have to fool you*. People glanced at me.

'He's probably with those women who were thrown out of the shop,' one man muttered, presuming I had no English. 'Up to every scam. To think we worked our guts out for years to have this shower fleece us.'

Mrs Kennedy surprised me by glaring at him. 'Apart from lifting pints, what work have you done these past twenty years, Jimmy? I raised four children who all had to leave. I hope they got a better welcome than you're giving people here.'

'That wasn't the same,' he muttered, defensively. 'Your children actually worked in England.'

'They were given the chance to.'

The bus pulled in, breaking up their argument. Terrified to say a word of English, I paid my fare in silence by letting the driver pick what he needed from the proffered coins in my palm. I stared out of the window, aware of whispered conversations about me. This was everyday life for Ebun, perpetually judged by self-appointed juries of strangers, the stigma of looking different.

That was the funny thing about meeting Cormac in Nine Wells Hospital in Dundee on the morning that I flew into Glasgow and caught a train. From how the police had described him on the phone I'd expected Cormac to look different or share the heavily medicated look worn by many of those who wandered along the corridor there. But he looked more like a junior doctor who all the nurses would fancy. We sipped coffee in the canteen while I waited to speak to his doctor. Cormac shook his head, mildly abashed, as if his antics during the previous days had happened to someone else. Perhaps it was the light sedatives I knew he was on, but his wide-eyed look reminded me of the time he ran away to find Bartley Dunne's in Dublin and woke me in the outhouse on his return. Except that back then there had been a wonder in his gaze, the sense of a sailor straining to embark on a wondrous voyage. Now his eyes seemed filled with puzzled bemusement, as if surprised to glimpse the harbour walls of his destination rise, suddenly grey and dreary, before him.

'What the hell were you at, Cormac?' I asked.

He shrugged. 'I can't see why there's so much fuss just because I went for a walk.'

'It was one long walk. The police said you looked like you'd been walking for several days.'

'There's nothing wrong with walking.' A shadow of his old smile returned. 'Once you're not doing it in stilettos down somebody's chest.'

'Be serious, Cormac.'

'How's the little monster and the Iron Lady?'

'They're grand,' I said, determined not to have the conversation deflected.

'And you . . . still betting on two flies crawling up a wall?'

'You're the patient here, Cormac. Where's Alex? Why isn't he with you?'

'You've lost your knickers again, haven't you, brother? I've only lost my marbles. How much are you in hock for?'

'Stop changing the subject,' I insisted. 'Where's Alex?'

'Alex who?' He smiled again. ' "Don't ever call me Al," he says on our first night. Take away the Al from his name and what's left – ex. My ex.'

'It's over?'

'Not quite. He's not my ex-landlord yet. But he will be on Friday when he wants the keys back.'

'But I thought you pair were . . . ?'

'As snug as bugs in rugs? In my world, Brendan, the day you meet a man is the day you should start preparing to lose him. Go and see who's in charge here, will you, and get me the hell out. This place freaks me. Do you know there's one corridor a mile long? A patient sat down beside me this morning and said that if you walked all the corridors you'd have run a half-marathon. If I stick around much longer he'll come back with running shorts and ask me to join him.'

Cormac did seem fine despite the doctor's concerns about him needing more rest. I didn't mention his forthcoming eviction, but promised to stay around to mind him until he was back on his feet. I was due a week's holiday from work, which I had never taken as we lacked the money to go anywhere. But Cormac was in such flamboyant form that suddenly this trip felt like a holiday as we fled the hospital, as giddy as miching schoolboys.

Cormac flagged down a taxi and asked the driver to suggest a good hotel for lunch. He laughed at my attempts to insist that we head to Perth where he could get some rest. They had found nothing wrong with him beyond chronic exhaustion and he would sleep better after some fresh air. Once we hit Perth there would be packing and decisions to face. He hadn't seen me in months, so why not relax and enjoy our day.

I should have argued more strongly, but perhaps at heart I didn't feel capable of the responsibility of minding him. Certainly it felt like Cormac was minding me that afternoon, insisting on buying lunch and choosing a good wine, even though the doctor had cautioned against drink.

'A glass or two won't kill me,' Cormac said when I protested. 'Besides, I'm absolutely clear-headed now. The walk did me the world of good. I wasn't thinking straight in Perth, behaving like a hysterical schoolboy. People leave one another all the time. There's no need to climb onto the rooftops in some grand gesture.'

'You didn't?' I said, alarmed.

'Let's just say that with my fear of heights I didn't get far.' He grinned ruefully at the joke against himself. 'All I did was hug the chimney with Alex glowering from the skylight, telling me not to be ridiculous in his most doctoral voice. Some woman across the street phoned the police. Their arrival frightened me but it frightened Alex more.' He mimicked Alex's accent. 'My *position*, my *position*.' Cormac laughed. 'I thought we had left all that "the neighbours" crack behind in Navan, but poor Alex was always cursed by respectability. The day he showed me our flat I said he should stick it in *The Guinness Book of Records* as the largest closet in the world.'

'What did the police do?'

'Nothing. I'd come down by then, shivering with the cold,

trying not to snivel. They came in and looked at us like we were dirt. God knows who Alex thought he was fooling by talking about a disagreement with his "tenant". That was the night he took his things and told me I'd a week to get out.'

'Why is he leaving you?'

Cormac shrugged. 'I thought he was dependable. Broody and full of contradictions, a bit like your da, but dependable all the same. He loved boxing and spent hours watching it. If someone went down he'd shout at the television, "Stay down, take your count of eight. What are you jumping up for?" But that was me that night after the police left, up and trying to shadow-box on the count of one, determined to show him I had it in me. Never mind Friday, I was gone ten minutes after he slammed the door. Do you know the funny thing, brother?'

'What?' I asked, noticing how little food he had actually eaten.

'You never lose a habit. The first day I arrived in Scotland I peered out the taxi window all the way in from the airport convinced that at any moment I would recognize my father among the passers-by. That was why I went walking. I kept praying, "Father, if you're here, then now is the time to find me. I'll keep walking until we meet on some bend of the road".' Cormac looked at me. 'I always thought I had come to Scotland just to be with Alex. But then I thought maybe there was a reason for this pain, that my destiny, the reason for this journey, was to meet my real father. Funny isn't it, how you fool yourself, when he's sitting somewhere, doting on his grandchildren, oblivious to my existence.'

Cormac allowed me to harangue him into eating a proper dessert and reluctantly accepted my decision that he could not order another bottle of wine.

'You'd make a great mother hen,' he remarked as we left

the hotel, 'not that of course I've ever actually been laid by you.'

Outside another argument ensued about his refusal to return to Perth. He claimed that he felt at ease for the first time in months. He needed to be out in the fresh air and so did I, by the look of me. We required an afternoon without thoughts of Alex and Miriam or other problems. My resistance was weak enough for him to overcome any objections to purchasing two more bottles of wine in an off-licence. I felt lighthearted suddenly. Cormac was the only person I ever felt truly myself with. At my most wretched in Navan he had seen something to cherish in me. He seemed closer than any real brother I could have had, the saviour who had brought me in from that shed.

Even if my married life was a mess and Cormac had nothing to look forward to in Perth, we made each other forget our cares that afternoon. We were so close that it felt like those secret nights in the outhouse with the world blocked out. Not that there was any physical contact now, but an almost spiritual togetherness. I was his guest and he was intent on showing me Dundee or at least the quickest way out of it.

Again we travelled by taxi, past a sprawl of housing that only ended when we reached the golf courses at Carnoustie. We stopped once so he could show me a sweet-factory laid out as a 1940s museum, with boiled sweets I had last seen in the windows of tiny shops in Navan. He insisted on buying a brown bag of them and on us downing several malt whiskies in the theme pub beside it while the taxi waited.

The clouds that had buffeted my plane that morning had disappeared and the autumn afternoon was warm. We were getting further from Perth, but Cormac seemed to know where he was going, directing our taxi driver. The road grew smaller and just when it seemed to peter out we reached a quiet pub carpark overlooking a beach reached by steep steps. The tiered tee of a golf hole protruded through the dunes bordering the strand where the tide seemed to be miles out.

We paid off the taxi with Cormac assuring me that we could call another one from the pub after we had finished our picnic. This seemed a grandiose term for bullseyes and wine, but – after asking me to wait at a bench outside – he emerged from the pub with two sandwiches in his hands and two stolen wineglasses under his coat.

'The old "It's behind you in the till" ten-pound note trick still works,' he observed, with a grin. We laughed about old Mr Boyle in his apron and swapped a hundred other memories as Cormac led us across the sand to a small but steep headland which split the beach into two and was crested by the remains of a small tower. He had also managed to smuggle a corkscrew from the pub. The first bottle of wine was white. It tasted good outdoors, even though I felt it go to my head. I knew Miriam was waiting for a phone call about Cormac's condition, and my father too in his County Council office, hogging his special phone line like Commissioner Gordon in *Batman*. But I was engaged in minding my brother and just now Cormac seemed like a reincarnation of the free spirit with whom I had once shared a flat in Dublin.

The beach was deserted, with just a few cars parked outside the pub as golfers conducted friendly post-mortems on their rounds. Cormac opened the second bottle – a Rioja – even though the white wasn't finished. I had relaxed my concern about him. We were simply two brothers taking time away from the massive problems in our lives to savour a few snatched hours of freedom together. The red wine tasted cloudy, with Cormac blaming himself for having broken the cork inside the bottle. But I drained my glass anyway as I lay back to watch the evening sky deepen.

'There's a beach like this in Jersey,' Cormac said, 'Portelet Bay. Visit it if you ever go there.'

'What in God's name would I be doing in Jersey?'

'Stranger things have happened, take my word for it.' Cormac leaned across for my glass and replaced it a moment later, refilled. 'We should have had more days like this, just the two of us, eh? Two little boys with two little toys.' He looked down. 'You do forgive me?'

'For what?'

'Everything. Your life.'

'There's nothing wrong with my life.'

'Did I say there was, brother?' He looked serious, then grinned. 'Still I bet you even money there is.'

'I could stop gambling if I wanted to.'

'I believe you. The only thing is that I don't believe you do. You've no clue about how special you are.'

'That wine is going to your head,' I said, half-embarrassed. 'There's nothing special about me.'

'Miriam could see it one time, that's why she married you. The promise you never delivered on because you're afraid.'

'Afraid of what?'

'To let go of the past you're carrying around on your back, to simply float free.'

'That's bullshit,' I said.

'What would you do if I gave you fifteen thousand pounds?'

'You know well that I'd blow it on a horse.'

'That's what you'd do with fifteen pounds or even maybe fifteen hundred.' Cormac poured himself more white wine, draining what seemed to have become his personal bottle. 'But maybe you just think you'd blow it because you've never felt the power of fifteen thousand pounds in cash in your hands.'

'Nor am I likely to,' I laughed, 'unless some crazy accumulator comes up.'

'Or your kid brother gives it to you. You might be surprised about what I have in the bank. What you have too.'

I sat up to look at him and then at the tide which had come a good way in. 'Maybe we should head back,' I suggested, though I felt too lethargic to move. 'The drink is getting to you.'

'I was never more sober. Possibly it comes from being a tight-arsed Irish cunt, as Alex so succinctly phrased it.'

'Look at who was talking? No disrespect to him, Cormac, but Alex turns off his windscreen wipers going under bridges to save energy.'

'That made it all the harder for him to discover that I had been sponging off him in Ireland, feigning poverty while in college. He saw our bank statements, you see.'

'What bank statements?'

'The ones in the possession of someone called Des Traynor.'

Utterly confused now, I took a long sip of red wine, trying to place where I had previously heard the name.

'Alex was in Dublin two months ago to withdraw some money he has stashed away. I think he never paid tax on it, but he has it somewhere with this Traynor geezer that people are not supposed to know about. He was visiting Traynor in an office but not an actual bank when Traynor started complaining of stomach pains and wanted a medical opinion as a sort of *quid pro quo*. Alex sent him off to provide a specimen. It's an old doctor's trick when they want a good root around. Traynor seems to be a fairy godmother to half of Ireland and Alex, spotting a computer printout being put away in a drawer on his arrival, wanted to know which half.' Cormac brushed some grains of sand off his trousers. 'It turns out that I was among those on that printout, with several accounts listed in my name. You're there too, and Sarah-Jane.'

'Stop taking the piss.'

'That's what I told Alex, when he arrived home with a face on him like a wet Sunday in Stirling. The bigger fish didn't have names at all, just anonymous account codes in the Bahamas and Cayman Islands. But we were using our own names on Jersey. Alex managed to copy down two account numbers before Traynor returned with his specimen. Alex was furious with me, claiming that I'd deceived him. Things haven't been the best between us lately. Even in Dublin he used to see people.'

'Boys?'

'Younger ones. Fleeting adventures. He'd a nose to sniff out sex and I could always tell afterwards by the way all his tension was released. He'd be so guilty, so kind, finding a hundred unspoken ways to try and make it up to me. The funny thing was that the times when he was being horrible to me were the times he was being most faithful. Then I'd see his tension build again, bickering, finding fault, claiming that I was squandering money. One week before I finished college he started leaving me a flask of hot water to make tea with during the day and took the flex of the electric kettle to work. He unscrewed the radiator tops so I couldn't turn them on.'

'Why did you stick with him?'

Cormac refilled my glass with the dregs of the bottle. 'That was a good week. I came home late from college at the end of the week, walking to save the bus fare, and he had every light on, the apartment warm, a fabulous meal waiting and a new coat for me as a present. I locked myself into the bathroom, bawling. I knew that some young fucker had just sucked him off.'

Aware that I was supposed to mind Cormac I tried to say

something soothing, but he ignored my words. An anguish, concealed earlier behind his apparent stoicism, came to the fore.

'Isn't the fact that you love someone enough reason to put up with them? But since he found out about these bank accounts Alex has been so mean to me, refusing to believe that I know nothing about them. He doesn't care about the truth. I know in his heart he's been searching for a way out. He'll never take me back because he's found someone younger to bully and then make up to in his special way. Jesus, Brendan, in bed he could be so . . .' Cormac let the sentence trail. 'Some little pink-pricked cunt,' he muttered, almost to himself.

'You'll get over him, people do, Cormie.' It was years since I had used his pet name.

'I will be free of him, I promise you.' He looked across. 'We're loaded, brother, money to burn.'

'Maybe Alex was making it up?'

'Not Alex. He has great hands but a lousy imagination. The accounts are real, I know.'

'How?'

'Simple. I flew to Jersey last week, walked in and flashed my new passport. The old one got stolen with our luggage in Tangiers in the summer. The bank was surprised by my presence, because normally all transactions go through your father. They said that he's the other signatory who normally makes withdrawals. I told them he was sick in Dublin. The cashier was cute, with lovely hands. I was just amazed the poor boy didn't get wanker's cramp having to count out fifteen thousand in cash. That's how I know Alex won't take me back. The night of our final quarrel I tried to give him every penny of it, but it only made things worse.'

Suddenly I remembered where I heard Traynor's name

before. At my own wedding, when Alex was talking to Barney Clancy.

'Traynor has something to do with Clancy,' I said.

'You bet your life he has. "Kneel up on the bed," Alex used to joke. "Let's see if you're as good a dog as your daddy."'

'That's not funny.'

'Nothing's funny about your father. Maybe he beat the crap out of you, but he ignored me. I was an illegitimate charity case put up with as part of the baggage of the woman he wanted. So how come he's opening accounts for me, when he allegedly never had two pennies to rub together?' Cormac looked at me. 'Maybe you know the answer? I mean he is your father?'

I drained the stolen wineglass and flung it onto the rocks below us where the waves were crashing. 'Come off it, Cormac,' I said angrily. 'You know I know nothing.'

'Yeah.' Cormac was apologetic. 'I shouldn't have said that. I've just grown paranoid this last while. Don't you get cross as well.'

I couldn't stop my fury – not at Cormac but at my father. I remembered how cheap he made me feel when I had wanted him to try to improve Miriam's mother's chances of a hospital bed. Funds were being openly raised in business circles that month so the Tanaiste, Brian Lenihan, could fly to America's most exclusive clinic for a liver transplant. But Lenihan was different, my father had snapped when I raised it. He had served his country whereas Mrs Darcy was part of the minutiae of ordinary citizens forced to pay the price of having lived beyond our means. If my father was putting money aside for me then surely that had been the time to give it.

Instead I had blown a week's wages on crazy bets after he turned me down, hoping against hope to win enough money to buy her a few weeks somewhere as a private patient. We'd endured months of trying to nurse her, calling twice daily at her rented house in Broadstone because she refused to move in with us where Conor would have to witness her suffering. There had been short stays in hospital when her relapses were sufficiently bad to briefly merit a bed, before her eventual death, almost unnoticed, waiting on a trolley in the corridor. Money would not have saved her life, but she might have died with some dignity in one of the gleaming new private hospitals around Dublin, which nobody was quite sure how people could afford.

'The bastard,' I snapped. 'I could have gone to university like you if there was money. I might have done things and been someone. For my twenty-first birthday he gave me ten pounds, for my wedding a wall clock made in Taiwan. He knows we're crucified by mortgage rates. If he has money earmarked for us then what's he waiting for?'

'What makes you think it's his money?' Cormac asked. 'Or will ever be ours? Clancy is behind it. It's an open secret in the circles Alex moved in that Clancy fixes planning permission in Meath with your da as his poodle.'

'That's rubbish,' I snapped angrily. 'I know he gives up almost all his free time to be at Clancy's beck and call, but at work he's a good public servant. I've read reports in the *Meath Chronicle* of him fighting his corner at Council meetings to block re-zonings. Clancy isn't even on the bloody County Council!'

'Easy, Brendan, easy.' Cormac gently put a hand on my shoulder. 'That's why I never told you about it before. I know how you still look up to your father. But he's just a stooge. All his huffing and puffing is used to block developments until the builders are willing to grease a few palms that Clancy controls. Alex has the inside track. But he doesn't want to understand that your father would have no scruples about letting Clancy use our names, as a front to pay for his shirts and cigars and mistresses with no money trail pointing back to him.'

'You stole Clancy's money then?' I felt a mixture of fear and a boyish thrill of revenge.

'Let them prove it. Do you think Clancy will run to the cops about his slush fund of bribes and backhanders? I didn't want his money, I wanted Alex back. For weeks now he's kept totting up, totting up. Every penny for every year before I started work. Every holiday, every bus fare, every fucking tube of KY jelly. He made me feel like a little tart and even cheaper still when I returned from Jersey with money like I was trying to buy him back. He couldn't leave me with any self-respect. He had to justify it in his own mind by cheapening every moment of our past until all I was ever was a cheap slut with my mouth open for his cock and my hands open for his cash.'

'Stop it.' I put a hand on his shoulder. 'Stop thinking of yourself like that.'

He put his fingers up to touch mine and held them for a moment, warm in the dusk. 'I was never cheap, was I?'

'No.'

'Still, I seduced you, years ago. I shouldn't have done that.'

'It's long forgotten,' I said, embarrassed. 'I don't really remember . . .'

'You remember everything,' he insisted. 'You were the first person I ever fell in love with. It would have been wrong if we were real brothers, wrong to even think that way. What would you do with fifteen thousand pounds?'

'I told you, I don't have fifteen thousand pounds.'

'You do now. Make something of yourself. Ask yourself who you want to be.'

I didn't reply, staring at him in the gloom. All my life I

realized that I had wanted to be him. To be inside Cormac's skin, know the thoughts he knew, experience life in a way that was different from the second-rate staleness of everything I experienced. Even his pain seemed more valid than mine.

'I'm glad it's over,' Cormac said. 'I won't want to be Alex's new lover with a heart full of hope and a back scarred by the clawmarks of Alex's nails. I've seen them together. He's twenty-one with a cute bum and no idea of what's in store for him. Kiss me.'

'What?'

'Old time's sake. One kiss. I won't bite you, I promise.'

His face was close to mine. I could barely make out the beach behind us now, the darkness broken by the lights of the pub back up the cliff steps. Nobody could see us, we were as alone as in the outhouse. Our early experiences had led me to tortuously question my sexuality in adolescence before quickly realizing that I loved women. I had never wanted to kiss any man since, yet I opened my mouth to taste his tongue again after all these years. It felt wrong, yet it felt right. Just for a few seconds, then he withdrew his tongue.

'I lied to you,' he said, 'this is no headland, it's an island cut off at high tide. You tell Phyllis I loved her and I was serene making my own choices again, the way I did before Alex. The time I ran away to Bartley Dunne's she got so upset I might have drowned that she taught me to swim. I bet she'll regret she didn't bring you along. I love you, brother. Honestly, I'm not worth drowning for.'

I put my hand on his shoulder. His fingers gripped mine and intertwined, then next moment he had slipped free and was scrambling over the rocks. Sluggishly I tried to follow, but Cormac was getting further ahead all the time. Dark waves covered the sand behind us. I called his name but he never looked back, just poised for a moment before diving off a rock to swim towards the shore.

I picked up a small container he had dropped, recognizing it as one the doctor had given me with sleeping capsules for him. That Rioja was not contaminated by cork. Sleight of hand was always his speciality. The dose wasn't enough to put me asleep, just to leave me groggy and off-guard.

Cormac must have heard me call across the deserted sands, but he walked calmly on up the steps towards the pub. I realized why he had asked me to wait outside there. He could laugh with the barman now about getting caught by the tide when out walking alone, as he ordered a hot whisky to keep warm and waited for a taxi to arrive.

Several times over the next few hours I tried to wade out but the water was too deep. I called for help but nobody heard. It was almost dawn before the tide retreated sufficiently for me to wade across. The pub was shuttered up, the roads a winding maze until I hit a main road where I could hitch. Even then no one stopped until a taxi came along, the driver suspicious at the state of my clothes. I had to pay in advance before he would take me to Perth and even then we argued as I persistently urged him to hurry on.

I knew I was too late anyway. Cormac had left the key in the front door, with a note for Phyllis on the table. Beside it, an envelope with my name contained two account numbers and the address of a Jersey bank, along with fifteen thousand pounds in cash.

I picked up the chair he had kicked over, standing on it to cradle his body and try to undo the knot around his neck. But single-handedly I was unable to release his hanging body. I phoned the police and waited for them to come, throwing the wad of bank notes in a wastepaper basket. With my hands around his waist, I talked incessantly, telling Cormac secrets that I had told nobody, begging his ghost to haunt me, pleading that I couldn't cope without him in the world.

I couldn't tell if the police took ten minutes or ten hours. But when the knock finally came I stood up and lightly kissed his hand.

Make something of yourself. His voice inside my head kept repeating the words. Retrieving the money from the bin I stuffed it into my pocket before letting the two policemen come in.

It was two o'clock by the time I climbed the steps to Ebun's front door. My first priority was to retrieve the bank mandates. Sixteen hours earlier I had walked down onto this street, loins saturated with the after-glow of lovemaking, unsure of whether I might see her again. Now my body felt cold as I repeatedly rang what I hoped was her bell, peering through the letterbox in the hope of seeing feet descend the stairs.

A man walked up from Dorset Street, taking out a key. He looked Romanian or Polish and shrugged when I asked whether I might check if Ebun was in. I climbed the stairs in front of him and knocked on her door but there was no reply.

Twenty years had passed since I last entered Gardner Street church, opposite Ebun's flat. But with time to kill I went in to marvel at its curiously ornate ceilings and the side altars, I was often reminded of inside churches in Portugal. One shrine to St Euphemia near my flat in Oporto had always been festooned with beeswax replicas of heads and limbs, left as *promessa* – payment for successful intercessions or tokens by those seeking cures. A tiny yellow arm to represent an arthritic one or a wax model of a neck left at the shrine to St Braz by a mother with throat cancer.

The Irish were more coy about revealing the intentions behind their prayers. Three old women prayed separately at a side altar before a statue of Mary, lips moving almost imperceptibly with the faintest murmur of prayer barely audible as I passed. An office girl prayed in silence, light from a stained-glass window catching her hair. She looked beautiful, kneeling several pews behind a black woman who rocked back and forth, oblivious to the reserve usually pertaining there.

Here seemed a good sanctuary to wait until Ebun returned. An old man lit a candle at the shrine to St Joseph the Worker as I knelt out of some childhood instinct and tried to pray. But it was so long since I had prayed that the words turned to muck in my mouth. I used to love Navan cathedral as a child, especially the side aisle when suffused with light. It had been a refuge from Phyllis if she was forced to bring me down town with her and called in, as was her habit, to light a candle for some silent intention. I had discovered that by bowing my head in silent prayer I could make her feel guilty about disturbing me and therefore postpone my return to the outhouse while savouring the cavernous solemnity there.

I could not remember what I prayed for back then. But once an old woman slipped ten pence into my hand and, while Phyllis was trundling through the Stations of the Cross, I lit a candle for my mother like a secret act of subversion. Cormac's subversion had been more public during our final week in Navan, even if nobody could directly confirm the suspicion that he was responsible. But a bush-fire whisper spread around Navan that every candle on St Anthony's shrine had been lit and arranged to form the burning outline of two testicles and a bulbous rampant penis.

The funny thing was that Cormac did believe in God in a way I never could. Often in Dublin he had dragged me into churches (in the same way as he often talked me into attending bizarre parties) to watch him light a single candle and pray. Once he told me that his first erection had occurred at eleven, kneeling before the alabaster limbs of a crucified Christ in the cathedral. Subsequently his private vision of Christ seemed to have become a figure of infinite forgiveness and eroticism.

This had made the Scottish policeman's question about Cormac's religion seem blackly comic on the morning they cut his body down in Perth. I had sat in a corner being questioned by one officer, while his colleague liaised with the paramedics who appeared from nowhere in Cormac's flat. Queries about age, nationality and occupation I could cope with, but the religious enquiry started me off into uncontrollable laughter. The paramedics paused, as if about to descend upon me with needles to administer a sedative. But how could I pigeonhole Cormac in a way that would satisfy the officer going through his standard routine? The policeman watched me, still not fully convinced that I hadn't been involved.

'I can put him down as an atheist,' he suggested, then – upon deciding that my hysterics had grown into incoherent tears – simply wrote down 'unknown'.

They did give me a mild sedative while en route to the hospital in the ambulance. It held me together long enough to phone Miriam and then my father's private office number. I dreaded having to phone Cremore if he wasn't there, but the phone was picked up after one ring. My father the crook. It felt like phoning a stranger. His silence was so prolonged after I told him that I wondered whether he had hung up. I kept waiting for him to ask, 'Why couldn't you have minded him?' Cormac had been released from the hospital into my charge and I was too incompetent to have kept him safe for even one night. Yet when my father spoke it was in the whisper of an old man as he thanked me for phoning him before Phyllis, as though I had done him a service. I felt the thick envelope in my pocket and almost told him about the money, torn between accusing him of using us and warning him about its disappearance. But then he was gone.

From their tone I sensed the police had figured out that Cormac was gay. They seemed disconcerted to discover that the flat belonged to a specialist in the hospital to which we had taken Cormac's body. They suggested that I break the news to Alex before they called later to take a statement. I had met Alex's secretary once before. She recognized my face as I entered his suite of rooms.

'He has patients all morning,' she said stiffly, then lowered her voice. 'He's told me not to let Cormac near him. That probably means you too. It's terrible, we all love Cormac here.'

I felt more sorry for her, having to break the news, than for Alex. I waited until his first patient left and she came back out in tears.

'He said nothing when I told him,' she whispered, 'just turned his face away like the blood was drained from it. To see him hunched there you wouldn't know if he was alive or dead.'

If I had confronted Alex myself I would have flung the fifteen thousand pounds on his desk before stalking out. But I hadn't got the heart to drag his secretary into the quarrel by handing her the money.

The police were waiting for me with more questions. After contacting the hospital in Dundee and their colleagues in Aberfeldy they had now absolved me of suspicion. I sat on in the canteen after they told me that I was free to go, almost paralysed by the responsibilities ahead. Finally I returned to the apartment. A policeman on duty asked me to touch nothing in the living-room where he had died. Cormac's bedroom was cluttered, with bundles of clothes taken out as if he had made a half-hearted attempt to pack.

I opened a drawer which contained a hardback book of 1950s art photographs – young men naked except for the remnants of cowboy outfits or Roman gladiator garb. There was nothing pornographic about them. The men were obvious amateurs, enjoying the novelty of play-acting out fantasies as they waited for their real lives to begin. I closed the book and picked up Cormac's passport beside it. His photograph, taken just a few months before, had the same quality of barely suspended disbelief, as if Cormac was struggling to keep a straight face in the role he found himself in. The policeman opened the door, keeping a discreet eye on me. I pocketed the passport and closed the drawer.

My memories now were shattered by a noise behind me in Gardner Street church. A young Garda officer stood there, as if having materialized from nowhere. I fought against the irrational conviction that he was pursuing me – an echo of the panic which often swamped me upon seeing police officers during my early days in Europe. But he seemed to be routinely checking the church as he ascended the centre aisle, making as little noise as possible, and then retreated, happy that nobody untoward lurked there. My perception about his presence changed. Possibly it was lack of sleep, but I became convinced that he was a sign, sent by Christ or Cormac or whoever might extract me from this mess.

The nearest police station was beside Mountjoy Prison on the North Circular Road. Maybe just for once I could break with every instinct bred into me. It wasn't that people didn't tell the truth in Ireland when I was growing up, it was just that we told invented truths so vehemently that we wound up believing them ourselves. If I went to the police I would probably end up in jail, but Miriam might not have to return the insurance money. Everything seemed secondary now to keeping Conor safe from Slick McGuirk's clutches. I desperately needed advice as I left the church and returned to Ebun's front door.

I had no more success than before and no idea of where an asylum-seeker with almost no money would spend her days in Dublin. I walked the length of Dorset Street, then onto Dominick Street and doubled back along Parnell Street. Dozens of small shops had sprung up, with black faces in the windows and children peering from doorways. I looked into each one, hoping to glimpse her. Foreign faces gazed back, cautious or belligerent, then indifferent as they sensed I was not a threat.

I arrived back at her flat to ring her bell and then every other bell in the hope of someone opening the front door. Nobody did, though a window opened high up and a head peered down in silence before withdrawing again, ignoring my shout. I needed rest and knew I should return to my hotel. Yet despite my exhaustion I couldn't stop walking.

The North Circular Road was choked with lorries. Traffic-calming ramps and tiny roundabouts in garish brickwork lent a Noddyland feel to the adjoining narrow streets where Phyllis had been born. The grocer's shop beside the police station had become an accountant's practice. My mind was decided, I was giving myself up. Fuck Clancy and Slick and fuck my father's reputation too. I might go down but I would bring them with me for burglary, manslaughter and tax evasion.

The public office looked the same as I remembered it, the old clock on the wall, huge ledgers waiting to be filled out. A sergeant looked up from the phone, indicating that he would be with me shortly. An old man sat on a chair, dazed, his hand bandaged. I tried to rehearse my statement about how a Meath builder was threatening my son. Except that Conor knew nothing about it, not even that I was alive. The only proof was my word – as a man who had spent the past decade living a lie – against that of a respected junior Government minister.

I had no documentation to link the bank accounts in Conor's name to anyone, while a maze of offshore companies protected Clancy and McGuirk from any connection to the sale of the land the money had come from. No doubt an investigation might eventually yield some damaging evidence, but the tribunals had only been grudgingly set up by the politicians because of their own reluctance to tell the truth. For decades the police and revenue commissioners had known better than to dare investigate such matters. Any statement I gave might take years to be acted upon and in the meantime Slick would still hover dangerously in the background, in dread of being implicated with his other accounts and dealings under scrutiny. It might further panic him into violence with the police refusing to act until Conor was seriously hurt.

The only person who could back up my accusations was Phyllis. She must know that my father had recognized Slick when he bent over to ungag him. Yet, through fear or loyalty, she had deliberately altered my father's dying word. Her silence would remain steadfast because my father would not want a Clancy in trouble, even to avenge his own death. Phyllis would disown me and Clancy deny having seen me in ten years. His e-mails were proof of nothing except having politely answered an anonymous crank. There wasn't even a message to confirm that he would show up.

The sergeant put down the phone and walked over to the counter. 'How can I help you?' he enquired.

I started trembling, not even thinking about Conor now.

Clancy always had my measure and knew that I was too cowardly to face being confined to a cell. I had done my time as a child. The thought of bars and doors was terrifying. I felt claustrophobic just standing in this police station. The sergeant leaned forward, watching me closely.

'You have forms for a driver's licence,' I stammered.

'Maybe we do.' He produced one, holding it slightly away from me. 'Will that be all?'

'Yes. Thank you.'

He didn't bring the form any closer so I had to reach for it with my hand shaking. I walked out, aware of him observing me quizzically. I didn't look back, cutting along Berkeley Street towards the Mater Hospital. Turning down Eccles Street I wanted to run. Pete Clancy had me by the balls. Nobody would believe my word. All I could achieve by blabbing would be to screw up Conor's world. His life with Miriam would collapse in a welter of suspicions. P. J. Egan might be less impulsive than Slick but he would be more clinically lethal if he felt in danger of being drawn into any investigation. I had no option but to persuade Conor to travel to Jersey and trust Pete Clancy to clear up this mess before McGuirk panicked at my reappearance and got to Conor before me.

I knew that Clancy would make sure that Conor received his share of the money, because he only felt safe doing business with those who were implicated too. But I would insist on also travelling to Jersey to watch over him in the way that I had failed with Cormac. After that I would vanish from his life forever.

The man in the black leather jacket was discreetly begging outside the Mater Hospital again. I gazed up at the windows behind which Phyllis lay dying. If my father hadn't persuaded me to meet her in Glasgow airport after Cormac died I might never have disappeared. I had always done everything possible to avoid being alone with her, because she had become not just a hate figure but a repository of blame for my every failing.

Yet I felt so alone now that it took all my will power not to enter the smoked-glass hospital doors. Even if Phyllis and I had only hatred in common, surely if I stood beside her bed she would have looked into my eyes and recognized our common rank in the fellowship of the truly guilty.

———|■|———

Two hours sleep left me drained and sickened in myself when the alarm clock woke me in my hotel. But eight o'clock found me back outside Ebun's front door, ringing any bell that might gain me admission to the house. Eventually I heard footsteps and a woman's voice shouted something in a language I could not understand. I knocked insistently and, after what seemed a moment's hesitation, she opened the door.

'Ebun,' I said. 'I want to see Ebun.'

She stared blankly at me and tried to close the door again, then stepped back, scared of being attacked, when I forced it ajar with my foot. Repeating the same phrase, she looked over her shoulder into the empty hall for support. Her lack of English made me angry, her apparition in this city where people should understand me and the way she brought home how lost I was.

'Ebun!' I pointed upward and she shook her head, cowering against the wall when I brushed past. Without those bank statements I could do nothing. I just wanted them back in my possession now and to get on with what had to be done. The house had never seemed so empty, my footsteps loud as I climbed the stairs, knowing in my heart that Ebun or Lekan or Niyi weren't in. I knocked repeatedly, aware of the scared woman in the hallway. If men arrived who spoke her language I could be in trouble. I pounded Ebun's door a final time, filled by an irrational foreboding of things slipping beyond my control, then ran down past the woman and back out onto Gardner Street.

Eight-fifteen. At what time would Conor leave for the Oliver Twist? Surely Miriam didn't let him go drinking every night of his mid-term break? I was aware of my hypocrisy in questioning her parenting skills, but tonight I didn't want him going there. Not that Slick McGuirk would set foot inside a gay bar – being too terrified of what he might see or find reflected about himself. But I could imagine him parked out-side watching.

I walked up the long straight length of Whitworth Road, hearing a train pass along the tracks far below the wall that bordered the road. The pool-hall that Cormac once loved was still down a lane beside the canal at Cross Guns Bridge. Clusters of new apartments were crammed behind the railings of the old orphanage. Two buses passed while I tried to scan the faces in the upstairs windows.

The off-licence on the corner at the end of Botanic Road had a new name. Around the corner, even the Botanic Gardens had changed, with raised paving stones outside the entrance where cars used to park. This was as close to Cremore as I dared to go. I boarded the first bus into town, and scanned the seats upstairs before disembarking at the next stop. I did the same with the next two buses in search of Conor. There was a twenty-minute wait before a fourth bus arrived, as I shivered with the cold, not even sure if I had already missed him.

But he was upstairs when the bus came, at a quarter-past-ten. I saw him look down from an upstairs window, surprised and suspicious to see me. Nobody else sat at the front of the bus. He glanced across as I sat beside him.

'I was hoping to catch you,' I said.

'I'd never have guessed.' His tone was sarcastic, but not overtly hostile.

'Don't go into town tonight, Conor. Let's have a drink around here.'

He shook his head, amused. 'I've told you before, you're not my type.'

'I really need to talk to you properly.'

He glanced at a couple in the rear of the bus oblivious to anyone but themselves. 'You're a bloody nuisance,' he grumbled, but was still flattered enough by my attention to ring the bell. We got off at Hart's Corner.

'Where to now?' he asked.

As a parent I should not be encouraging him to drink at his age, but we could hardly walk around the streets all night. Besides, I needed a whiskey for my nerves.

'Is Kavanagh's – the gravediggers' pub – still there?'

He nodded. We walked in almost companionable silence down the narrow lane into D'Corcy Square. At first the small Victorian houses seemed unchanged since the time when it was one of Cormac's favourite haunts, but up close I could see that many had been modernized as old inhabitants died off and young professionals moved in. A disused gate into the oldest part of Glasnevin cemetery dominated the square. Kavanagh's itself backed onto the graveyard, although the hatch where gravediggers once knocked for porter was long since closed off.

Music came from the lounge, but the bar looked unchanged since the 1980s when cemetery workers, hardchaws and students shared its counter with a hard-drinking Abbey actor whose much scribbled copy of the *Racing Post* bore testimony to our shared obsession.

Conor grew uneasy as we entered. I understood why. His

chances of getting served on his own were small, but I
beckoned him over to two stools in a dark corner and ordered
for us both. The barman glanced down.

'Is he over eighteen?'

'We're celebrating his birthday. Don't worry.'

He hesitated, then reluctantly decided to trust me. The
pints he pulled seemed to take forever to settle and be refilled,
while I stood at the bar, downing the brandy I had ordered
for myself as well. I glanced over at Conor. A son's first pint
with his father was a landmark moment in the Irish psyche.
My father had brought me for such a drink on my eighteenth
birthday in Dublin, going through an old Navan ritual with
neither of us knowing what to say to the other. I carried the
pints down, aware that Conor was oblivious to their sig-
nificance.

'Cheers,' he said, taking a sup, then looked up, aware of
me intently watching him. 'What is it?'

'Cheers.' I took a long sup of my pint as well.

'You look like you were in a fight,' Conor said. 'What is
it you want to talk about?'

'Your grandfather.'

'Why?'

'Did he get upset when graffiti about you appeared outside
your old school?'

'We never told him. Why upset the old lad?'

'Because maybe that's what the graffiti was meant to do.
Maybe it had nothing to do with you.'

'It was just lads acting the bollix.'

'Lads today can spell "queer".'

Conor set down his pint with a bang that caused the barman
to look across.

'You give me the creeps,' he said, openly suspicious now.
'Something about you. I'm going into town.'

'Listen to me . . .'

'You listen. I never told you that "queer" was misspelt on the wall. How could you know, unless you wrote it yourself? Is that what you're telling me? You were trying to get at Granddad?'

'No.'

'Then why do I mistrust every word from your mouth?'

'You're caught up in something you know nothing about, Conor. Men have been following you.'

'I'm looking at one of them,' he interjected.

'I'm trying to sort out a mess your grandfather should have settled years ago.'

'Why?'

'Because I care about you.'

Our voices had attracted the manager who appeared at the counter, looking down at us and obviously reprimanding the barman. Conor finished off his pint in one gulp, aware of their scrutiny.

'I want to leave now,' he said.

Draining my glass, I followed him out. A cat watched us from beneath a parked car, then ran out to squeeze through the cemetery gate.

'I'm getting a bus into town,' Conor said, 'and I want you to leave me alone.'

'Let me walk you home instead.'

'I'm not going bloody home.'

'It's late.'

'Maybe it is for you.' He turned away as three women left the pub and walked towards a car, talking loudly.

'I wasn't even in Ireland when that graffiti was written,' I said, when they had passed. 'Now please, don't go near the Oliver Twist tonight.'

The women drove off, leaving us alone.

'All right,' he shrugged. 'You've ruined my night anyway. But walk me to the main road and nowhere else.'

A narrow lane led onto Botanic Road. The last time I had walked down it was with Cormac and a straggle of drinkers invited to some impromptu party on Marguerite Road. There was a fall of snow that night and we slid about, laughing when people slipped to the ground. I wanted to share a hundred such memories with Conor, who kept his distance, seemingly eager to escape. Yet he lingered at the corner when we reached the main road.

'Why do you keep trying to scare me?' he asked.

'I'm trying to protect you.'

'From what?'

'Do you miss your grandfather?'

'Yes,' Conor replied. 'Maybe it was how he died, but I still find myself in tears.'

'Did you know him well?'

Conor shrugged. 'He was my grandfather, wasn't he?'

'That's not the same thing.'

Conor watched a bus pull out from the stop across the road. 'I think I knew him,' he said at length, 'though we never had a proper grown-up conversation. I always stayed aged eight in his mind. When I'd help him do his garden as a kid he'd have a bag of chocolate buttons buried for me to find with my plastic fork. He'd laugh and say the fairies left them there. All he did out in the garden was play games and tricks with me. Mam says that after my own father died everything changed for him. Other people were always in a hurry, but Granddad found time to play, no matter what. I think he was gutted by Dad's death. I don't remember him much before that, I'm not sure he took much notice of me. But for a time afterwards we were so close it was almost scary. He'd never mentioned Dad, but sometimes when handing me a rake he'd say "Hold this, Brendan", and not even be aware he was saying it.' Conor looked at me. 'What's wrong?'

'Nothing.'

Several youths emerged from a pub up the road and spilled out into the traffic. One shouted towards us.

'Don't worry,' Conor said, 'they're not coming this way. Besides, we don't look suspicious. When I first came out I thought the whole world was watching, ready to pounce on me.'

'Did you ever tell your grandfather?'

'I never wanted to disappoint him. That sounds bad, like being gay is something to be ashamed of. But Granddad made me feel special, and I knew that, years ago, he and Uncle Cormac had a falling out. I think that Gran knew about me before I did, but she was different. I suppose maybe because Cormac wasn't his own flesh and blood –'

'That's more lies they fed you.' My anger was partly directed at myself for being too stupid to have figured the truth out years ago.

'What are you saying?' Conor was disturbed by my tone. 'And what's it to you anyway?'

'Cormac was his son,' I replied, 'your half-uncle. But Phyllis is nothing to you. She was his mistress in Dublin while your real gran in Navan was being cheated on.'

A gang of teenagers emerged across the road and waited to cross at the pedestrian lights, drinking from cans of beer. Conor glanced at them.

'Leave my gran alone,' he hissed, 'and leave me alone too.'

He walked off, making it obvious I was not to follow. The lights changed and the teenagers crossed over, following Conor down the path. There was something effeminate about his stooped shoulders. He had the same walk as Cormac when upset and vulnerable. One girl's muttered comment was met by a laugh containing an edge of menace.

Talking loudly they began to close on him, girls shouting, lads trying to outdo each other in bravado. Conor glanced behind, making himself more noticeable, then hurried slightly. A taxi stopped across the road, with two girls getting out and drawing a wolf-whistle from a youth in the pack. Conor glanced back again, drawing their attention even more.

One girl looked around to notice me and said something. I couldn't shake the image from my head of Conor and my father finding chocolate buttons in his garden and playing like we had never done. Cars streamed past the traffic lights at the off-licence, forcing Conor to halt. The gang was on top of him now. Grabbing a beer bottle discarded on the pavement, I rushed forward, ready to smash it for use as a jagged weapon if necessary. But the gang simply passed him and headed up Mobhi Road towards Ballymun.

Conor crossed the road. He was shaking, though I couldn't tell if it was because of the gang or what I had said. He glanced back, taking in my presence and the bottle clenched in my hand, then walked quickly on past the Addison Lodge pub. Dropping the bottle I dodged across the road, hearing brakes slam. My flesh and blood was as afraid of me as I had once been of my own father. I had almost caught up with him when he started running.

A car turning right at the Pyramid church slowed him down as he tried to cross Botanic Avenue. He reached the far pavement and looked back as if defying me to follow. The road was clear but I waited, trying not to make him afraid. Then I walked very slowly towards him. I could hear the river behind the church, loud after rain.

'What the hell do you really want?'

'To talk.'

'Why? Just who are you?'

The lay-by at the Tolka House pub beyond the bridge was

busy as motorists pulled in for a late drink. 'Not here,' I said. 'Let's go down to the river.'

'You must be kidding, pal.'

His tone annoyed me. 'You know I don't mean for that.'

'How do I know what you mean? You give me the creeps and you wouldn't be the first old lad to try and wheedle a sympathy hand-job out of me.'

Conor's deliberate attempt at crudeness infuriated me. He tried to back away as I grabbed his jacket.

'Let me go or I'll scream.'

'You listen to me good,' I hissed, pulling him close. 'I don't want anything like that and I'm sick of hearing you say it. We're going for a walk by the river and you'll listen to what I need to say.'

I released my grip. Conor nodded slowly. 'But not together,' he insisted. 'Not with people around. You go first, I'll follow.'

He turned to re-trace his steps without waiting for my reply. I walked on, past the church with its grotto and across the bridge before turning onto Mobhi Drive. When I looked back Conor had disappeared from sight. The long steps were steep as they descended to a narrow path secluded by a bank of shrubs. From above nobody could see who was down here and nobody down here could expect help if the wrong people were waiting. But tonight the riverbank was empty of cider parties.

My hands still shook from holding Conor in an angry grip when I had longed to embrace him instead. Beneath the bridge I could glimpse the flash of a weir in the Botanic Gardens on the far side. I waited, listening to traffic pass above me and convinced that he wasn't going to come until I looked up to see him watching from the bottom step. He glanced furtively along the path before approaching. Had he no memory of how his father had looked? I knew my appearance was different now, but we had been so close once. The more estranged I grew from Miriam, the more meals we ate in brittle silence, the more often I saw her remove her wedding ring when peeling potatoes and leave it on the draining board for hours almost as if hoping to lose it, the more important Conor had become to me. As a child, he had sensed the unspoken tension, clinging to me and not wanting me to leave his bed when I cuddled him at night.

I longed to put my arms around him now. But I knew the slightest movement would frighten him away. Moonlight made his face so young. He stopped at what he judged was a safe distance if he had to flee.

'I love you so much.' The words came unbidden, but he didn't turn away.

'You don't know me,' he replied softly. 'Even if you did, there's nothing I can do.'

He was trying to be gentle and not hurt me as he played at being wiser and older.

'You don't understand,' I said. 'I don't know how to tell you. I'm frightened of losing whatever love you have left for me.'

'What the hell are you talking about? For the last time, I don't know you.' His unease was palpable.

'Think. Please. Look at me.' I removed my glasses and put them away. 'You do know me. You just never thought to meet me again.'

This time he didn't reply. His gaze was quizzical and suddenly scared.

'Your father and grandfather were never close. At least not after he re-married. Your grandfather had a new life then, he didn't care; or, if he did, he didn't know how to show it. He was caught in all kinds of contradictions, in the greed of that grab-all-you-can-and-bury-the-evidence world where he was Barney Clancy's lap-dog. I hated him and yet I loved him. I wanted his respect, yet I wanted to kill him. Is it any wonder I was such a poxy father to you when I had only him for a role model?'

Conor still didn't speak. I sensed him desperately trying to comprehend what I was saying.

'Surely to God you recognize your own father?'

'Why?' He spoke the word so softly that I almost didn't hear it. I bit my lip, wanting to step towards him but not knowing if he would flee.

'Why?' His voice rose slightly above a whisper. 'You bastard.'

'I never stopped loving you.'

'Why are you making up these lies?'

'Look at me. I had a beard and my hair wasn't red. But you have my eyes and my forehead. Can you not even see something of yourself here?'

Conor took a step forward so that I was backed up against the wall, his face inches from mine as he stared with a mixture of fear and disbelief. I couldn't tell whether he meant to kiss me or spit.

'I don't know you,' he whispered.

'You had a red blanket, Joe the Blank you called it. You took it everywhere. We had to wash and dry it when you were sleeping. The corner of the garden beside Boylan's was your garage where you kept your plastic tools in a box, spending hours pretending to fix the yellow car we bought you. On your sixth birthday you fell outside the betting shop in Artane when I was putting a bet on. I made you promise to tell your mother it happened in the playground in Stephen's Green. You have three tiny stitches above your temple, though the scar will be long gone by the time you grow bald like your grandfather.'

'Dad?' Barely even a whisper, it was the most beautiful word I had ever heard.

'I've come home, son.'

'Who says you can?' Conor stepped back, struggling to control his emotions. 'On my fourteenth birthday I looked up the newspaper accounts of the crash in the National Library. Until then part of me never accepted he was dead. I always had a secret hope he would turn up, having survived the crash but lost his memory, lost everything. But when I read the papers I finally accepted he was dead because no one could survive the fire on that train. You're not him.'

'You know I am. I boarded the train but got off again. I can't explain, but I think Cormac was guiding me that day.'

'You bastard.' He was in tears now. 'You fucking fuck of a bastard. You . . .'

Footsteps pounded the steps above our heads. They stopped and we listened to a man urinate in the bushes. A voice called and the feet clambered up again. Conor seemed to be in shock, our conversation possessing the surrealism of a nightmare that he felt trapped within.

'I knew from the moment it happened that what I did was wrong,' I said. 'But I had set a lie in motion and suddenly it was too late to stop.'

'Why?'

'Because your mother and I . . . we were broke . . . in every sense. I'd wanted to give you both so much, yet all I gave was debts and grief. I made a mess by trying too hard to be a good father . . .'

'You weren't around to try at all.' His bitterness was the more intense for being so quietly spoken.

'When I was around you saw places you should never have seen,' I said. 'Bookie shops, money-lenders chasing me. You were bribed with crisps to sit outside pawnbrokers and never tell your mother afterwards.'

'I fell in the playground in Stephen's Green on my birthday.' Conor was insistent. 'I remember jumping off the slide and hitting the concrete.'

'It was outside a bookie's in Artane. You wouldn't stop crying for your mother. I brought you into the Mater Hospital, asked the nurse in Casualty to keep an eye on you for a second. She thought I went to the toilet. I was racing to the bookie's to see if my horse had come in. Afterwards I brought you to Stephen's Green, gave you sweets and ice-cream, showed you the slide. We acted the accident out, making up the story between us.'

'I'd have never lied to my mother.'

'You lied because you loved me. We were men together.'

Conor sat on the low wall, leaned against the exposed roots of a tree, and took out his cigarettes.

'Can I have one?' I asked as he lit up.

'Buy your fucking own.'

'I'm trying to tell you how it was and was always going to be. They would have repossessed our house if I'd stayed. I did the one thing I could do for you. By dying I could give you more money than I'd ever earn alive.'

'Is that all you can talk about?' he asked. 'Has your whole life simply been about money?'

'No.' I sat down, at a careful distance. 'It's been about status, self-respect, proving that I was more than some fucking Hen Boy in a shed. I bet Phyllis never told you about my pain, eh, how I was treated? Suddenly the chance came when just for once in my life I could prove that I could get ahead. It was a scam and the world I grew up in valued scams above anything. Da's friends talked of little else. Cheat the County Council, the taxman, the VAT-man, your wife, your friends, your neighbours, yourself. That was how you won respect, the slyer the better, the more devious the bigger a man you were. People thought I was a nobody in Navan, but I pulled off a bigger scam than they ever dreamt of. It was like a dream accumulator, an adrenaline rush so strong that I was finally free.'

'Free from me and Mam,' Conor said. 'Free to fuck off while I cried for you at night.'

'No,' I replied. 'Free from the curse of being myself. All my life I've wanted to go somewhere.'

'Where?'

'Valparaiso.'

Conor screwed up his eyes. '*Where?*'

'It's in Chile, I think, but it's not a real place. I mean it is but it isn't. It was an Irish poem we did in school about a man who sees a boat and longs to escape from the world he's trapped in to a different life where he can start again as a different man.'

Conor took a contemplative drag of his cigarette. 'You abandoned us because of some poem?'

'By the time I started thinking rationally again it was too late. Contacting your mother would have made her an accessory to a fraud.'

Conor rose, tossing the half-finished cigarette into the water. 'Then why couldn't you stay dead where at least I might respect you?'

'Conor . . .' I stood up as well.

'Don't come any closer or I'll throw you in that fucking river.'

'I never stopped loving you.'

'I don't give a shit, pal.' His shoulders were hunched like he'd been struck. 'Things are bad enough just now without you turning up.'

'I've come to sort those things out.'

'What are you talking about?'

'It wasn't a thug who burgled your grandfather's house. You're caught in something that should have been settled years ago. That's why I didn't want you going near town tonight. They know you drink in the Oliver Twist.'

'Who the hell are *they*? Why do you keep trying to scare me?'

'Former associates of your grandfather. The less you know about them the better. One of them thinks that he cheated him.'

'And did he?'

'I did . . . and Cormac . . . without knowing . . . we left my father to take the blame.'

'Why?'

'Jesus, Conor, when you get older you'll realize there doesn't always have to be a why. Now with your help I can do a deal.'

'You mean you've only turned up because you hope to pull off another scam?'

The half-truth in his accusation hurt.

'I never found Valparaiso,' I said, 'just a succession of jobs and flats in cities that never felt like home. I was in hiding, always looking over my shoulder. But you could travel to real destinations, places you always wanted to see. I want you to have enough money to go anywhere you want.'

'And you're going to give it to me?'

'Think of it as a gift from your grandfather who earned it in his own way.'

'How?'

'All you need know is that there's money sitting in a bank in Jersey in your name.'

'You mean it's mine?' Conor asked.

'Thirty percent of it will be.'

'Then why is it all in my name?'

'Trust me,' I said.

'That's rich from a gambler. And you get the rest, is that it?'

'I get a passport so I can get the hell out of your life and leave you in peace.'

'Then do exactly that,' Conor said angrily. 'Fuck you. And fuck whoever's money it is too.'

'Son . . .'

'Don't call me that. You lost the right years ago.'

'I'm trying to earn it back.'

'A bit fucking late,' Conor snapped. 'Where were you when I had no idea what was happening to my body? When I spent years tiptoeing around Mam's grief, having to take your place? You'll not earn it by robbing Phyllis. Any money Granddad left belongs to her first and to you and Aunt Sarah afterwards.'

'I don't want it.'

'What makes you think I do? "Earned it in his own way." It's crooked you mean and every whisper about him was right You've only come back to try and bring me and Mam down to your level.'

'Leave my wife out of this.'

For a moment I thought Conor was about to strike me. 'She's not your wife, damn you, she's your widow.' He lowered his voice, aware of footsteps on the bridge. 'It's true what they say,' he hissed.

'What?'

'Like father like son. Money was the real God for both of you.'

'We're totally different,' I retorted. 'You've no idea how he treated me. At least I want you to have what you're entitled to.'

Conor's laughter was deliberately snide. 'I'm entitled to

nothing. You're saying it's hot money. Bribes or God knows what.'

'He never took a penny for himself. A whole chain of people used him. Nobody was innocent back then, the whole nation was on the fiddle. He was a man of his generation.'

'And you're one of yours,' Conor sneered. 'I want no part of your scam, so piss off and stay dead!'

'I'm your father.'

'I have a mother and a gran, nobody else.'

'She's not your gran,' I said.

'She feels more like a gran than you'll ever feel like a father.'

'Get rid of me so. Do this for my sake if not your own. I never wanted to ask you for anything, but without a fresh passport I'll be found out. It was your grandfather who put your name on those accounts, not me. The man who owns that money is a savage. He was the bastard who broke into Cremore the night your granddad died, the one who tried to lure you into that car. You're the only person who can unlock those accounts and he won't leave you alone until you do. I'm trying to protect you and your mother. If you do this then I promise to vanish and make sure you've enough money to be whatever you want.'

'I don't need to buy a life,' Conor snapped. 'I already have one you know nothing about!'

'Maybe I know more than you think,' I snapped back. 'I saw you sucking Charles's cock up in your room.'

'When?' Conor was suddenly scared again.

'It was me who disturbed you on Sunday night.'

'You were spying on us?'

'I didn't know you lived there. I was looking for the bank codes that they couldn't find.'

'So you're in league with them after what they did to Granddad?'

'I hate them more than you'll ever do.'

'Then go to the police.'

'How can I? I don't exist.'

'I do.' Conor's voice was quiet but hard-edged. 'Let me nail the bastards.'

'It's not so simple.'

'Maybe not for you. On the day I came out I swore that I'd face down every bastard and bully.'

'Your grandfather was part and parcel of them. Things would come out in court that he'd never want uncovered. Now I can't bring him back and I don't want you in more danger.'

'What do you want for Mam?'

'What I always wanted. To make her happy.'

'Is that some kind of joke?'

'We were happy at first. She was special and made me feel special. I'd never felt special before.'

'She deserved better than to be cheated.'

'It was a different country, Conor, with no hope. I loved you so much that I wanted you never to be part of my cheating again. Never to be forced to tell lies. I loved you more than I loved her and she resented it. I knew she'd leave me when she found out how much we were in debt. I'd be on the outside, cap in hand, fighting to be allowed to take you out for a few hours at weekends. I couldn't have borne living with you so close and yet out of reach, so I stood aside and let her keep everything.'

I don't know what response I expected. I had lived out this moment on numerous occasions, imagining us meeting in hotel lounges or by chance on trains. Father and son recognizing each other, instinctively drawn together. A hand reaching across a table. But now I felt dirty, standing before Conor like the accused in a dock.

'I don't believe you.' His voice was matter-of-fact. 'You did a runner for yourself and at heart you're only back for your precious passport. Everything else is horse-shit to fool yourself. All you're offering me is blood money when maybe I still want a bloody father. We would have faced down those men together. Maybe I'd have hated your guts and you'd have hated mine. But we might have found out if you'd offered yourself, pure and simple, instead of some cheap fucking hustle.'

'I've nothing to offer anybody,' I said. 'At heart I've always just been a coward and a nobody.'

'You're my father. The only one I have. Does Mam know you're back?'

'I didn't want to implicate her.'

'Just us men together, eh? Nothing has changed except that the bribe of crisps outside the bookie's just got bigger.'

'It's not like that.'

'No. This time you want me to go in and place the bet for you. Where did the money come from?'

'It's the oil that greased this country for twenty years.'

'Then give it back.'

'To who?' I said. 'Everyone was involved, like a cancer riddling the whole land.'

'Why pass it to me so?'

'So we can bury it and move on. So you can make a fresh start.'

'And you can keep running.'

'You know nothing about me.' I was near tears.

'I know that I lay awake for years missing you. I suffered nightmares about how you died. I mourned you and so did she. Maybe Mam didn't talk about it. But she brought me up to respect you and I know her grief was real and her guilt too for maybe not having loved you enough. But I suppose you squared that off on your balance sheet, eh, with so many thousand for Mam's grief and so many thousand for my fucked-up childhood?'

'It wasn't like that.'

'I grew up on crooked money and now you ask me to help myself to more of it. Go back to wherever you've been hiding because there's nobody who wants you here.'

He strode towards the steps. I knew he couldn't wait to get away and find Charles in the Oliver Twist. The pair of them in bed with Charles stroking away his tears.

'Don't tell your mother I'm still alive,' I begged.

Conor stopped on the bottom step. 'She's been through enough already.'

'I'll sort this out. But you need to mind yourself. There are men out there –'

'Real ones,' he said. 'Men who wouldn't let their father's killers walk free.'

'It's not that simple,' I said again.

'That's the difference between us. I think it is.'

He climbed up the steps without looking back. This time there wasn't even a cigarette butt left behind that I could hold on to.

———————

For half an hour after Conor left I sat on the low wall beside the river, wishing that I had explained to him the full truth about that crash. But how could I when the truth made no sense?

On the morning of the crash I had sat alone in a first-class carriage in Perth waiting for the Glasgow train to start. Something about my appearance must have suggested trouble, because passengers who passed my window looked in and then moved on to other carriages. Rumours of an election were sweeping Britain, but I could focus on nothing in the paper I had purchased, not even the runners at Kempton.

The fifteen thousand pounds cash in my breast pocket felt uncomfortable. It would solve all my immediate problems in Dublin if I managed to get it home intact. But the debts would quickly start to build up again.

The previous evening, after the police eventually finished their examination and left, the phone rang twice in Cormac's flat. The first caller was Alex's secretary offering to make the arrangements to fly Cormac's body home after the autopsy. The woman seemed heart-broken and embarrassed at the implication behind the offer – that Alex wanted Cormac's body out of Scotland as soon as possible.

The second caller had been my father in Cremore. I knew Phyllis was in the room with him, relaying questions. She was flying into Glasgow next morning. My father wanted me to meet her at the airport and bring her to Perth. Confronting Phyllis seemed a worse ordeal than finding Cormac's body. I knew we would have nothing to say to each other. Her eyes would just stare, silently asking God why I could not have died instead. Before he rang off he asked me how the money was. I froze, then realized that he meant the cash he had given me for my plane ticket. I fingered the fifteen thousand pounds on the bedside locker which I had counted and recounted. Cormac and Alex would probably still have broken up if the older man hadn't found our names in Des Traynor's office, but maybe not just yet and not like this. I was filled with that irrational outrage which boils up inside adolescents when they realize their fathers are human. I wanted to shout down the phone and blame him for everything but I didn't. I just told him I was fine for money and would meet Phyllis at the airport. Then he said goodnight, the last time I ever heard his voice.

That night I cleaned every corner of Cormac's room, folding and refolding his clothes, fingering his shirts, lying on the bed to hug a blue jumper that I knew he loved. My mood kept alternating. One minute I wanted the room perfect for Phyllis, to show that I had been a trustworthy guardian. The next moment I wanted to peel the wallpaper off the walls and violate it like she had violated the room I once called mine.

Before leaving for the station I had left the room spotless, yet in the carriage as I waited for the train to start I grew edgy, convinced there was some last thing I hadn't done. I opened the door to gaze down the platform which was empty at that moment. My irrational unease would not let me go. There was some vital thing I had overlooked. I could not bring Phyllis back to the flat as it was. A goods entrance was directly opposite me, with a mail handcart resting there after men had loaded parcels on board. I told myself that I could take the later train in an hour's time and still make the airport. But perhaps in my heart I knew I lacked the courage to face Phyllis. I hesitated, then jumped down, vaulted over the barrier and walked out through the goods entrance. The goods yard was empty, with a gateway to the left where a sloping path led down to the street.

I tried to shake off my fear and not run, but I couldn't get back to his flat quickly enough. My fingers shook so badly I could hardly turn the key. I don't know what I expected to find but at first everything seemed normal, the living-room tidy, the kitchen shining, even the legs of the bath gleaming after I got up to polish them in the middle of the night.

Nothing seemed touched in his bedroom. But every drawer and the doors of his wardrobe and bedside locker were wide open, despite the fact that I had carefully closed them all. Autumn sunlight filled the room, almost dazzling my eyes. I was scared, unsure of what was happening. Something told me to open the window. The air was still outside with not a breath of wind. I know that nothing blew in past me. But when I turned five autumn leaves lay on the carpet, haphazardly blown together, yet from that angle they resembled a boat. I knelt to touch their crinkled surface and I could feel Cormac beside me as a child. I knew I had just to reach out behind me and he would have handed me back the yellow and burnt orange leaves I had placed in his care on the afternoon when Phyllis condemned me to the outhouse.

Footsteps sounded along the riverbank, with some girl's voice answering a youth. I felt for the spectacles with plain glass lenses in my pocket and flung them into the Tolka, sick of disguises, before climbing up the steps onto Mobhi Drive. It was a twenty-minute walk to Ebun's flat. I was ready to kick down the door this time if necessary.

Yet the front door of Ebun's house was wide-open. I didn't bother with the bell, just climbed the stairs to bang on her door. It was opened on my first knock by Lekan who registered my presence with barely concealed disappointment and an element of caution on his face.

'I need to see Ebun,' I said.

He glanced behind. 'This is not a good time. Maybe just now she does not want to see you.'

'E jòó.' I raised my voice, calling past him, using one of the few phrases of Yoruba I had picked up from her. 'Ebun, it's important.'

A low voice said something behind him and, with a shrug, Lekan undid the chain. Ebun sat on the bed, knees pulled up to her chin.

'Your papers,' she said quietly, 'they are gone.'

I glanced around the room. Some possessions were missing, not many but there had been so few to begin with that their absence was notable.

'Niyi?'

'Gone with them.'

'I don't understand,' I said, but I did. All day the memory of Niyi standing outside this door as I left the flat had perturbed me. How long had he been there and what had he overheard?

'He did not know what was in the envelope,' Ebun replied. 'But he knew it was important, something to bargain with.' She searched for the correct word. '*Owo.* Currency. We have no currency here.'

'Where has he gone?'

'We do not know.' Lekan spoke behind me. 'We do not even know his name for sure.'

I sat down on the single armchair, feeling sick. Niyi would have called the phone number on the envelope. Maybe Clancy was meeting him right now, with Slick and Egan lurking in the background.

'He was your cousin-in-law,' I argued.

'Niyi was,' Lekan agreed. 'Niyi found us the money to come here after Ebun's daughter died. Fifteen of us trafficked across Spain first in one van, then in two sealed vans with almost no air. Niyi was never strong. The heat of the earlier journey across Mali had been hard on him and the boat was rough that smuggled us into Spain. In France in the van he was the first to complain that he could not breathe. Soon all of us could hardly breathe with fumes. We banged on the sides, begging the driver stop. But he could not – or did not want to – hear. Niyi told us to stop banging, he would be all right, we could not risk discovery. But one man kept shouting that Niyi would die. He had helped us to mind him on the boat, giving Niyi his coat for a pillow, trying to nurse him. He and Ebun kept banging until the driver finally stopped. But Niyi died vomiting. It was the side of some motorway. I do not know where. The driver said that we must leave Niyi's body with no identification. This man helped me to carry him into a field. They had told us to burn our papers but I saw him slip some document into Niyi's pocket.'

'Who was he?' I asked.

'When people die others may need their clothes or shoes. The man who helped us needed a new name. He told us a story but we do not know if it is true. We like him and three seemed better than two.'

'People thrown together, knowing no one else, they grow to need each other,' Ebun said from the bed. 'In Ireland we did not think he would stay with us, but he was strong and good at finding and sharing things. But I do not like the way he looked at me. Lekan and I talked of ways to make him leave.' She looked at me. 'He did not like you. I was scared last night when you left. I thought he would rape me. He had that look a man has when he thinks he owns you. But I am nothing to him except in his head. He was angry but also scared. I do not know why.'

'He came with me on the march,' Lekan interjected. 'He liked always say his opinion. People were there last night we had not seen before. Two began to shout at him, call him a name we never heard, Seyi. He very scared and he run away. They chase him. I do not know who they were or who he was – maybe good, maybe bad. Life is not simple. But they disappear in the crowd and never come back.'

'How do you know he has my papers?' I asked.

'This morning he was gone along with them,' Ebun said. 'I thought I had hid them but he is clever. All day I am looking for him. What was in them?'

I did not reply. Slick's niece would have answered the phone in Clancy's office. A quick call to her uncle and a meeting could have been arranged without Clancy knowing a thing. Somewhere isolated where the Nigerian could be surprised. All that had held Slick back from confronting Conor was the missing account mandates. With them Slick could bypass Clancy to muscle in on Conor, delivering a good hiding if the boy refused to cooperate. Slick would enjoy that, like he'd enjoy attacking the man I had known as Niyi, somebody from outside his ambit who threatened his horizons. Ebun seemed to read my thoughts.

'He is in danger?'

'I don't know,' I said.

'You do.' She was angry. 'You know much but say little. We are at enough risk in our lives without you making things worse.'

'I have to go,' I told her.

'Where?'

'A pub. I must check if my son is there.'

'I will come with you.'

'No.'

'Yes.' Her hiss was fierce. 'What would you have me do? Sit here? Last night you seemed to care, today you just want your papers and to go.'

'I care,' I said, 'but I don't want you in danger.'

'I care also. But you do not let me help.'

'Then help me,' I said. 'Put your arms around me.'

———————————◼———————————

They had stopped serving in the Oliver Twist by the time we got there. Most punters had left, and the barmen were trying to nudge the remnants off the premises. There was no sign of Conor and only on my second sweep around the room did I spot Charles talking with two youths at a high table.

'Has Conor been in?' I asked him.

He scrutinized me, having to revise his opinion of my intentions when he spotted Ebun.

'What's it to you?'

'It's important that I know.'

'Is that your missus or a faghag?'

'Answer the fucking question, right?'

The other youths leaned slightly back on their stools, increasing the distance between themselves and him. Charles ran his tongue over his lips, reminding me of a nervous dog.

'Why can't you people just fucking leave him alone?'

'What people?'

'Men your age buzzing around like flies. One was here an hour ago, annoying him over something. I wouldn't mind only he was in bad enough form when he arrived, impossible to get a word out of. One minute he was drinking with us, the next he was gone.'

'Gone where?'

'I'm not his minder.'

'What did the man look like?'

'Not my type. Like a pin-up from a 1979 Mr Muscle Man calendar after going to seed.'

'Did Conor leave with him?' I snapped.

'I told you, I'm not his minder.'

'You're supposed to be his fucking lover.'

Charles shifted. 'And just who are you?' he asked.

Ignoring him I led Ebun to a public phone in an alcove near the gents' toilets, handed her the receiver, put in money and dialled the number for Cremore.

'What do I say?' she asked.

'Just ask if Conor is in.'

'And if he's not?'

The phone was answered before I could reply.

'Conor?' Miriam's voice said anxiously. 'Is that you, Conor?'

I took the receiver from Ebun's hand and replaced it. Charles stood behind me, more aggressive now.

'I asked who the hell you are?'

'Have you a car?' I asked.

'Yes,' he replied, slightly thrown. 'Actually, my mother's . . . I'm a named driver.'

'Do you love Conor?'

'What sort of question is that?'

'Answer it.'

He looked back at the other youths leaving and lowered his voice. 'Yes.'

'Show me where the car is parked. Trust me.'

Charles led us outside where two men pressed themselves into the shadows. He took out his keys and there was an electronic bleep as the Ford Fiesta was unlocked.

'Where do you want me to drive you?' he asked. 'I mean I don't know what's happening here.'

I took his hand in mine squeezing the wrist until his fingers reluctantly opened.

'You're walking home tonight,' I said, taking the keys. 'You'll get it back.'

'You must be joking.' He started to struggle. 'What will I tell my mother?'

Ebun already had the passenger door open. I pushed Charles back so that he stumbled over a row of bins.

'Mothers understand true love,' I said.

Ebun locked the doors as I started the engine, swerving to avoid Charles who tried to clamber onto the bonnet, then thought better of it. He chased after us screaming until I lost him in the rear-view mirror as I swung into George's Street. Ebun looked back.

'Where are we going?'

'It's time you met my tribe,' I said.

VI

—■—·—■—

WEDNESDAY, 2 A.M.

A small wooden police hut still stood inside the electronic main gates, a relic from Barney Clancy's heady days as Minister for Justice when he had required twenty-four-hour armed protection. Ivy from the high boundary wall had spread across its roof to make the hut resemble a decorative folly. I didn't know if junior ministers merited police protection, but a video camera was angled to monitor anyone approaching the gates of Rosnaree House – or Fort Clancy, as locals had christened it.

It was 2 a.m. as I sat in the parked car well beyond the camera's range. Inside the gates coloured lamps among the bushes along the curving driveway cultivated a discreet landscape of shadows. I drove past with my headlights off and turned left down an overgrown sideroad that bordered the property. The ornate wall, erected gratis by Council workmen in the year that my father started work there, now blended seamlessly into the original stonework in the undergrowth. Further down the lane a camera probably guarded the back entrance too. I parked the car close to where I knew that a narrow turnstile in the wall was used to access a stretch of river on which the Clancys owned fishing rights.

Pete Clancy was obviously no fisherman because the turnstile was padlocked with a chain and looked unused for years. But the lock was rust-eaten and several blows with a car-jack were enough to sever it. I squeezed through with Ebun behind me, the rusty turnstile groaning as it turned. This stretch of the grounds seemed to have been deliberately let grow wild as a contrast to the ordered lawns and walled garden to the right which Pete Clancy or his wife had painstakingly restored. The orchard on my left held no hint of bees now. The curved wing added by Barney Clancy made nonsense of the house's original Palladian order, but light from a basement room looked beautiful as it spilled onto the grassy slope which formed a dry moat around the building.

Another light burned on the top floor, but the remainder of the house lay in darkness. I am not sure what I expected to see as we crept forward – Seyi and Conor tied up, Egan and Slick arguing or Clancy naked with some maid. The house's size lent itself to such speculation. I knew that Ebun felt so too by the way she hung back as if fearful of being entrapped.

However, when we got close enough to peer down Clancy sat alone in a room so functional it could have been a cell, signing letter after letter piled before him. Trays of correspondence besieged his desk, handwritten, typed or scribbled on postcards. The minutiae of a local politician's life. Ebun shifted beside me, wondering why I had stopped. But I kept spying, trying to decipher who Clancy actually was by his unguarded expression. He could have passed for a medieval monk though, from the slow scrutiny with which he examined each letter.

Finally I flicked a small pebble against the glass. Clancy looked up but could see nothing. I flicked a second one. This time he rose and opened a drawer. I expected him to take out a gun, but instead he put away a small Dictaphone. Opening the French doors he remained on his side of the glass as if ready to slam them again.

'Who's there?'

I walked down the slope. He peered past me at Ebun hanging back in the shadows.

'Who is she?' His voice was too low to carry up the slope.
'A friend.'

'Get rid of her.'

'This concerns her.'

'This does not concern her.' His hiss was sharp. 'This concerns nobody. This does not exist so far as outsiders are concerned and neither do you. You have no right to come here. How did you get in?'

'The old turnstile.'

'Did anyone see you?'

'No.'

'Does she know who you really are?'

I nodded.

'You disappoint me, Brendan, like you did your father. Secrets are for families.'

'You're not family.'

'This party was closer than any family at one time and your father was at its core. Now get rid of her.'

'Tell me where her friend is so.'

'What friend?' He sounded genuinely puzzled.

'Don't mess with me. My son is missing. You know that a Nigerian man phoned you today.'

'What are you talking about?' Clancy looked perturbed. 'Why did he phone me?'

'I left the mandates and your constituency office number with her last night. He stole them. Now stop playing games.'

Clancy looked back into the room. 'Half my letters were not ready for me to collect and sign this evening.' He turned, his voice loud enough for Ebun to hear. 'Why did you bring fucking outsiders in? I could have sorted this. No fuss, nobody hurt, a quiet word and a blind eye. Does she know who I am?'

'*She* has a name,' Ebun interrupted, caustically. 'What have you done with my friend?'

'I don't need to know your name and I know nothing of your friend,' Clancy said curtly, starting up the slope towards Ebun who stood her ground. He walked up to take her by the arm, steering her away. 'Let's move away from the house. You should not have brought her, Brendan.'

'I don't take my orders from you,' I replied, following them as he led her towards the orchard. 'Now where is my son?'

Clancy opened a wooden gate into the small enclosure of mature apple trees that were bereft of leaves. 'I know nothing about your son except that you only had to mind him for twenty-four hours in the last decade and still managed to lose him.' He stopped beneath a tree, obviously judging it a sufficient distance from the house.

'The last entry in the telephone log in my constituency office was for half-two this afternoon. I found the lights on, a letter half typed and no sign of Carol. She always wanted to see the world if only her miserly uncle would give her the money. I suspect Slick may be quite happy to see her travel for a long time.' He looked up at Ebun. 'What age was your friend?'

'In his thirties . . . I don't know.'

'Height?'

'Five nine, five ten.'

Clancy shook his head.

'What is it?' I asked.

'My wife said there was a phone call before I came in. The *Meath Chronicle* looking for a quote. I don't know the details . . . I . . .' Suddenly he gripped me by the jacket. 'You never changed, did you? Still a fucking Hen Boy with chicken-shit for brains. Did you learn nothing from your father? He kept things tight, never made mistakes except for having you and your bastard brother.'

'Fuck you, Clancy,' I replied, shaking off his grip.

He glanced at Ebun. 'I think you've more exotic creatures to do that with.'

This time it was me who grabbed him, shoving him against the treetrunk. I might have punched him if Ebun hadn't stepped between us.

'Stop it!' She pushed me back, then faced up to Clancy. 'What do you know? What are you not saying?'

'I'm not saying nothing. You were never here, do you understand me?'

'Why was the paper phoning you?'

'Looking for a quote.' He stepped away from Ebun and leaned against the side of the tree. 'I'm sorry but I can't afford to be involved. A black man was found beaten up tonight by the river below the town. They think he stumbled into a cider party. Whatever way he banged his head . . . I don't know the details . . . he's in the morgue at Our Lady's Hospital.' He looked at Ebun. 'I don't know who . . . or if he is . . . I'm sorry. But nothing can be served by dragging me into this.'

I should have felt grief for the Nigerian. Instead I could only feel terror for Conor. Ebun hunched down on the grass, crying silently.

'I tried talking to Conor,' I told Clancy quietly. 'He wants nothing to do with this business. The kid is scared but stubborn. What if he won't cooperate with Slick?'

'That could be a good thing. It would buy us time. It's a catastrophe if Slick gets on that plane.'

'I thought you wanted the accounts closed? I mean it is Slab's money.'

'Fuck the money,' Clancy said, almost to himself.

'What do you mean, fuck the money? What else is there?'

Clancy looked at me coldly. 'Give me the number of your hotel and wait there until I phone. Bring her with you. That man the police found may not be her friend at all. Do not contact them or your wife or anyone. Do you hear?'

'I said what else is there apart from the money?'

'You're not listening.'

'My son is missing and you're not talking.'

'You're out of your depth, Brendan, so leave the thinking to me if you want him unharmed.' Clancy knelt beside Ebun. 'You want to stay in this country, don't you, miss?'

His soft tone could not belie the inherent threat. Ebun looked up, not replying. Clancy reached into the long grass to produce a fallen apple.

'You people are like windfalls, never knowing when you're going to get stood on. Now I'm not saying good decisions can necessarily be arranged. But bad decisions may be indefinitely postponed until you've been left lying in the grass so long that you become part of the landscape. There again if you draw attention to yourself someone might just pluck you up and feed you to the pigs. You understand?' Clancy spoke like a man quietening animals. 'I've been to your country,' he continued. 'An EC fact-finding troika. I know how difficult things would be if you're sent back. On your journey here there must have been things you were told to forget. Tonight is one of them. No matter what he says to you, trust me on this.'

The spit was loud in the night air, as if Ebun had been storing up saliva in her throat. Clancy didn't flinch, just dropped the apple and slowly rose, taking out a handkerchief to wipe his face.

'I've never seen you in these last ten years, Hen Boy,' he said quietly. 'There was a lock on that turnstile. I know nothing about either of you except that you are breaking and entering. Now get this bitch out of here before I set the police on her. Let her friend be a lesson. Things can happen, items can be planted, raids take place. The Women's Prison in Mountjoy is no bastion of enlightened racial harmony and a criminal conviction would be her quickest ticket home.'

'Where is my son?' I asked. 'I'm going nowhere until you tell me where Slick has taken him.'

'Do I know Slick's mind?' he replied. 'The "L" in his name slipped out years ago. Now he's just Sick, paranoid, thinking the world is perpetually cheating him. Your appearance freaked him out last night and if you turn up again you'll freak him into doing something stupid. Leave this to me. I was taking care of it before you screwed up and I'll take care of it now. Get a passport photo taken in the morning and stay in your hotel room. Don't try to contact me until I call you. I'll sort out the kid and by Friday morning I want you on a plane.'

'What else is there except for the money?' I asked for a final time.

But Clancy was moving away from us through the dark, discarding his handkerchief on the grass.

'You ask too many questions, Brendan, and never the right ones. Your passport will be ready tomorrow night and the boy safely back with his mother. It will be like nothing ever happened. The incident by the river tonight was an attack by kids, someone in the wrong place at the wrong time. Make sure your friend keeps her mouth shut or she'll be another bloody person I can't protect. She's already seen what happens to people who try blackmail. Now leave the same way that you came in.'

———◼———

St Mary's Hospital in Navan was larger than I remembered it, with a new carpark occupying the space where a line of

old trees once stood. It was 2.50 a.m. as I parked the stolen
Ford Fiesta in the further corner from the squad car positioned
outside the Casualty department.

Inside the nurse summoned a young Garda when Ebun
asked to see the body that had been brought in. Her cousin-in-
law was missing, she explained. She had heard reports on the
radio in Dublin and driven up in the hope that she could
check if it was him. The Garda seemed unsure of the exact
procedures, complying out of human sympathy and because
of the late hour.

We walked around by the side of the building to reach the
mortuary discreetly tucked behind a small grotto. Inside it was
cold and the fluorescent light seemed unnaturally bright. The
policeman roused an attendant who disappeared through a
doorway, leaving us waiting in silence. A few moments later
he returned to beckon us forward.

A drawer had been opened, the bodybag unzipped so that
the face of the man I once knew as Niyi was uncovered. But
it was hard to recognize him. He had been beaten around the
face with something heavy. The skin was puffed up, his eyes
open like a sailor scanning an unfamiliar horizon. Ebun leaned
across, her fingers about to touch his skin lightly, when the
Garda held her wrist.

'Sorry, miss, but don't touch . . . the State Pathologist hasn't
examined him yet. Is he . . . ?'

Ebun studied the face again. 'No,' she replied. 'This is not
my cousin-in-law.'

'Are you sure?'

Ebun looked up. 'He has gone to England, I would say,
he never liked Dublin. I do not know this man's identity.'

The attendant zipped the bag up as the Garda led us away.
We shook hands in the carpark.

'I'm sorry you had to come all this way,' he said. 'No man

deserves such a fate. We know the culprits too, kids drinking, bloody messers. That riverbank isn't safe to walk along at night. They scarpered but we'll have them in a day or two. What baffles me though is that I know their antics. They're not above laying a few digs on someone wandering about there, but not like that, not the way his face is. It's like he was beaten up already and they applied the finishing touches.' He touched Ebun's arm gently. 'It's a worry for you, even if you don't know him. Ireland's changing, things are coming out that we never wanted to admit were there. Are you both OK for a ride back to Dublin?'

'Thank you,' Ebun said, 'we'll manage.'

We waited until he went back inside the building before seeking out the car. We sat inside it in darkness, my arm around her as Ebun cried.

'Why did you lie?' I asked.

'I am not used to policemen not sneering or looking for bribes. He is no more than a boy. I told the truth. The body is not my cousin-in-law. If I were sure of his full name I would give it back to him. But he's like the real Niyi now, an unknown corpse in a foreign land. No name will help to catch the young thugs who killed him. And if the men who beat Seyi up have your son then it is you who must deal with them.'

'What does Seyi mean?' I asked.

'It translates as "God Has Done This".'

'It wasn't God's fault. I set him up.'

'He set himself up. He was always going to. Nothing here would ever be enough for him. He would always need more.'

'That's why he never liked me,' I replied. 'He didn't just see me as a rival, he saw too much of himself.'

'I was not to be won by rivals. I chose for myself.'

'Then why me?'

'I picked you because I thought you would not stay around long enough to really hurt me. All your life you will keep running from shadows.'

The Garda emerged onto the hospital steps as if scanning the carpark, then got into the squad car and drove off.

'Maybe I don't feel like running any more,' I muttered.

'Then do not trust that snake in the big house. I know his type in my country, only they are fatter and their armpits stink. How could you trust such a man with your son?'

'He asked me to,' I replied lamely.

'That is no answer.'

'He treated me like an equal, made me feel that we two were on the inside track and the others were gobshites. He made it feel that this was how it was between our fathers. Men who trusted each other. I might have been his confidant had life worked out different.'

'Would you have wanted that?'

'I don't know. People despised the Clancys but you knew they were clever. They never fucked up for themselves and if you tucked into their slipstream they'd never fuck up for you. Since I was a child I've felt that if I earned his respect I'd finally be someone.'

'If he had threatened my daughter I'd have stabbed out his eyes.'

'I'm caught in a web. Whatever way I turn I'm in trouble.'

'I would not mind if he spun the web,' Ebun said. 'But you have spun it around yourself.'

I leaned forward so that my head rested on the steering-wheel. 'I'm a fool and I'm scared,' I said. 'He sees right through me.'

'I just see you.'

'Then who am I?'

'Yourself. Not perfect but not damned either. We are

allowed flaws, to make mistakes and screw up, if we don't lose sight of ourselves. But when you look in the mirror you seem to see just an empty space.'

I started the car engine.

'Where are we going?' Ebun asked.

'The fanciest address in Meath.' I released the handbrake. 'All-The-Cows-Shat-Manor.'

———————|■|———————

Tar barrels were placed across the entrance to what soon would become Aldershot Manor at the bend of a pot-holed sideroad. The billboard contained an artist's impression of idyllic townhouses encircling two apartment blocks. Only the show townhouse was completed, with silhouettes of half-finished walls arrayed around it like tombstones in the moonlight.

Ebun and I pulled in a few feet from the entrance and watched for any sign of a security guard, before leaving the car there obscured by bushes at the entrance to a field. The tar barrels were surprisingly easy to move, with just a few rocks inside to keep them upright. We manoeuvred our way carefully across the haphazard building site. A light shone in the kitchen window of the showhouse. Gripping a car-jack, I stumbled towards it.

Ebun's eyesight seemed better than mine. Twice she prevented me from slipping into uncovered trenches before we finally reached the window. Conor sat on a kitchen chair pushed back from the table as though trying to maintain a distance from Slick McGuirk who sat up on the table, flicking a set of oversized darts at a wooden plank beside the door. A bottle of whiskey and two glasses were beside him. McGuirk leaned over to top up Conor's glass, which looked like it had hardly been touched. I noticed that he did not refill his own.

'It's better that I go in alone,' I whispered to Ebun. 'Take the car and ditch it when you get near Dorset Street.'

'What if I don't want to leave you?'

'This is not your concern.'

'You mean it's your real life that I have no part of.'

'It's not like that,' I hissed. 'Slick is one dangerous bastard. If he sees you he'll feel it's getting outside his control. Just leave this to me, please.'

McGuirk leaned forward, gesturing to Conor and obviously laughing at some joke of his own. His eyes never left the boy's face.

'How will you get to Dublin?' Ebun asked.

'I don't know. Start the car and wait five minutes. If I don't come out then bugger off.'

'Don't talk to me like that.'

McGuirk gripped the wooden back of Conor's chair. The boy shifted uneasily while trying to look tough.

'For Christ's sake,' I snapped, rattled by the scene inside the room. 'I've only known you three days. Now I'm sorry about your friend but will you just go!'

Slick glanced towards the window as if he had heard something. I ducked down and when I looked up to apologize Ebun was already backing away.

'I'm sorry,' I whispered. 'I didn't mean it like –'

'Keep practising,' Ebun interrupted. 'One day you will sound exactly like your friend in the big house.'

I went to speak but she slipped silently away into the dark. McGuirk had risen to retrieve the darts. He threw one which landed in the wooden armrest at Conor's elbow, then laughed and flicked the remaining two simultaneously back at the loose plank by the door. I couldn't wait any longer.

There was no proper front door yet, just a steel one left open with the bolt and padlock off. The hallway was dark, with a blade of light beneath the kitchen door. I was about to walk towards it when a set of headlights distracted me at the bend on the road. They swung in towards the entrance and were switched off. Somebody got out of the passenger door to roll back more barrels and allow the car through. The driver drove carefully across the mud, halting to let his passenger get back in. The brake-lights briefly illuminated a crouched figure flitting between the barrels as Ebun slipped away.

From behind the kitchen door came the scrape of a chair being pushed back along the concrete floor.

'Just don't you even think about it!' Conor's raised voice was scared yet defiant.

'Take it easy, lad. That's just Slick being Slick. Sure your daddy and me are old school buddies. He'd tell you there's no harm in old Slick.'

McGuirk's seemingly slurred voice was deliberate, a safety mechanism to allow him to explain away anything that might happen as just clowning around under the influence of alcohol that he could not remember afterwards. Pete Clancy cursed outside as he tripped over something nearby. There was no door in the front-room which I slipped into, but I could not be seen unless Clancy turned on the hall light. He strode in and pushed open the kitchen door with P. J. Egan close behind. Egan blocked the doorway but beyond his shoulder I saw McGuirk glare belligerently at both intruders. Conor seemed to have retreated into a corner.

'Boys-o-boys,' Clancy said. 'This is a cosy tête-à-tête, eh?'

'What the fuck do you want?' McGuirk was rattled, the slur gone from his voice.

'To save you from your worst excesses, Slick, like always.'

'Who says I need your help? This time I'm looking after things quite nicely by myself.'

'Like you looked after the African?' P. J. needled.

'What African?' McGuirk's tone was insolent. 'I know nothing about any nignog.'

'I hope the police believe you,' Clancy said, swinging a chair around the wrong way so that he sat on it with his elbows leaning on the backrest.

'There won't be cops.'

'There will,' Clancy replied. 'And newspaper columnists and lentil-munching Civil Liberties types with bad haircuts elbowing each other in the scrum to get their indignant mugs on television. His body is up in the mortuary at St Mary's.'

'You don't scare me,' McGuirk sneered. 'Even if I met some jungle bunny all he got was a few digs for himself.'

'Where did you leave him?'

'Moaning in his bare feet by the river.' McGuirk laughed. 'Thought he looked more natural . . . authentic . . . without the shoes. I'd have left the sponging bastard back in Africa if I could. I did you a favour, Pete, he was trying to blackmail you in your own country – not that he'd a clue what the account numbers were. The gobshite actually thought I was going to lash out money for them. He won't go near any cops. There's feck all wrong with him beyond a few cuts and bruises he'd get in any honest day's work on a plantation. He limped off with a flea in his ear.'

'He limped off into the clutches of a cider party,' P. J. said. 'The Forensic boys will be lifting specks of thread and dandruff off him. I'd burn those clothes if I were you, Slick, because you're in deep shit.'

McGuirk looked at Clancy helplessly. 'I did nothing beyond give him a few digs.'

Clancy ignored him, rising to move out of my line of vision. 'Are you OK, son?' I heard him ask.

'Just tell this ape to keep his hands to himself.' Conor's voice came from somewhere in the room.

'Your father was worried about you.' Clancy moved back in vision, while McGuirk fretted at the table and Egan invasively watched proceedings, never leaving the doorway.

'Worried about his passport more like,' Conor retorted.

'That's a bit harsh. He's a sensible man who doesn't cause trouble. I hope you take after him.'

'I know your face from the funeral and off the telly. You're that TD.'

'You could forget my face,' Clancy replied gently. 'Like I can forget what I know. The name of your school principal. The name of the first-year UCD arts student who's fucking you despite knowing you're under-age. The fact that your mother conned an insurance company and compensation board.'

'Mam knew nothing about that.'

'A court might see it different if I testified that she did know. That your grandfather came to me for advice on the matter. Both these men here will testify that she boasted about getting away with it.'

'That's fucking lies,' Conor replied angrily, picking up enough confidence – now the others were present – to venture closer to McGuirk where I could see him.

'Your granddad wasn't above telling a few porkies either.' Clancy sat down. 'To be honest, Conor, I want nothing to do with this business and neither do you. You're an innocent party but so is Slick here. Your granddad used you. He was paranoid about putting his own name to anything. He died before he had time to return certain things to their rightful owners. Your father explained this. Take a flight to Jersey with my friend in the doorway and by teatime tomorrow this will be all over, with you handsomely rewarded.'

'What do you mean with P. J.?' McGuirk snapped indignantly. 'It's my money. I'll travel with the kid. We might even make a night of it. He's already agreed and for none of this percentage shite you apparently offered him.'

'I want nothing that doesn't belong to me,' Conor said. 'But I won't say a word, don't worry. Give my share to my father along with his passport. I'll do this for him. It's what he came back for.'

'There it is from the horse's mouth.' McGuirk sounded triumphant. 'Me and the kid will see this through ourselves.'

'That's not going to happen,' Clancy said curtly.

'Who says so?' McGuirk retorted.

'I do,' I interrupted, appearing at Egan's shoulder. 'Do you think I'd let my son board a plane with you?'

Startled, P. J. turned with his fists raised. McGuirk rose from the table as if about to attack me. Only Clancy seemed unperturbed by my appearance.

'The prodigal,' he said. 'Take it easy, lads, let the Hen Boy in.'

Conor backed away towards the sink by the window, looking discommoded by my appearance.

'What are you doing here?' he demanded.

'Trying to mind you.'

'That's a laugh.'

I looked around at Clancy. 'He's getting on no plane with Slick or with any of yous. Fuck your passport. I'll take my chances back in Portugal without it. The boy walks out of here.'

'Stay the fuck out of this, Hen Boy,' McGuirk threatened.

'Leave my son alone or I'll have you up on more charges than you ever dreamt of. I don't know how long I'll serve, Slick, but you'll be there on manslaughter charges to keep me company.'

'Fuck off back to your nignog friends,' McGuirk sneered.

'Who is this African?' Conor demanded. 'You told me my father gave you the account numbers.'

'He was the unfortunate legacy of a romantic attachment that your father has hopefully sorted out,' Clancy said. 'Brendan appears to have hidden charms.'

'Maybe it's because officially he's been stiff for the past decade.' Egan alone laughed at his own joke.

'It's hardly sexual attraction,' McGuirk sneered luridly. 'Maybe she liked him because he kept the flies off her.' He made a sudden chucking noise and darted towards me. 'Get up the yard, eh! There's still a smell of hen-shite off you!'

'Leave him alone!' Conor raised his voice as he attempted to shrug off Egan, who held him back.

'Leave it out, Slick,' Clancy cautioned patiently.

'I won't leave it out. It's me who has the numbers not just for my own accounts, but every fucking account your father ever had.'

'Is that why you really left?' Conor asked quietly as if we were alone. 'Were you screwing around even when you still lived with us?'

'This isn't the place, son.'

'Don't call me son. You won't be calling me that once you get your precious passport.' He glanced at Clancy. 'If I do this you'll get him one, won't you?'

'Wheels are turning as we speak,' Clancy assured him.

Conor turned back to me. 'So don't come the concerned father. Fuck off to Valparaiso for real this time. Fly Chilean Airlines, first class. You'll find it's just another fucking city to get lost in.'

There was a hatred in his eyes I had never thought to see. He looked close to hysteria.

'Is that what you really want?' I asked.

'Yeah. Stay out of our lives, you hear me?' He addressed

Clancy. 'I don't care who the fuck I go with, just get me on a plane.'

'You heard him,' McGuirk said. 'He'll go with me. First flight in the morning. This is my fucking show. Barney cheated my father, I know he did. And others too, taking advantage of his illness before we understood it. Slab gave things away, paid for goods twice, three times, he didn't remember. Barney was like a sponge sucking up every penny. But you'll not fucking divvy up my father's money between yous all now with nothing left for me.'

'No one's going to cheat you,' P. J. said evenly.

'So how come there's only two accounts open on this list when there were three sites? Someone's already rifled one account.'

'Pete told me there were four parcels of land,' I said.

McGuirk turned on me. 'There were three sets of fields, two Mickey Mouse ones and one a good size. I walked them with my daddy often enough, never knowing who owned them. But he couldn't pass the road without looking in at them. So what else did Pete tell you?'

'Nothing,' I said, aware of Clancy's glaring at me behind Slick's back. Something didn't add up, but this wasn't the time to say it.

'Well you needn't listen to him,' Slick said. 'Because every time he says something he twists it some way so your head gets fucked up. Me and the kid are going to Jersey alone.'

'No,' I replied firmly.

McGuirk brought his face close to mine. 'Why not? What exactly are you fucking insinuating, Hen Boy?'

'Don't you call my father that,' Conor said sharply.

'Brendan is right,' Clancy interjected soothingly. 'It's not wise for you to rush off abroad after what happened this afternoon. I know it had nothing to do with you and when they find the thugs I'll do everything in my power to see that no other questions are asked. But you shouldn't do anything out of character that might be suspicious. Go and play golf.'

'I hate fecking golf,' McGuirk snarled.

'Why join the bloody club then?' Egan asked.

'My father helped found that club.'

'Well play golf badly in the morning then,' Clancy urged. 'Look relaxed. You were with P. J. when the African met his little accident.'

'My missus made tea for us, with pinhead scones and all,' P. J. added. 'Remember, Slick.'

'Give me the account mandates and the kid's passport,' Clancy said. 'Go beat the shite out of a few golf balls and P. J. will join you in the clubhouse, straight from the three o'clock flight. He can say he was visiting his father. You'll have cash in your hand and everything settled, with Brendan on a flight out of here that evening.'

'Why would the police be watching me at the airport?' McGuirk sounded bewildered.

'They watch everyone these days.' The hint of a threat entered Clancy's voice. 'Remember that poor chap in Dublin arrested at the airport with bags of cash from the Isle of Man? Besides, Slick, what if the missus heard you were getting on a plane with a young lad?'

'What harm would there be?'

'Did Pete say there'd be any?' P. J. piped up. 'It's just that it wouldn't be the first time and she was upset at that misunderstanding.'

'Just shut the fuck up and go then,' Slick muttered uneasily. 'The envelope is in my jacket pocket. But if yous cheat me I'll kill you.'

'Ask him the real reason he doesn't want you to go,' Conor said quietly from the corner.

'Eh?' Slick turned, puzzled by the interruption.

'Ask him what he doesn't want you to find out.'

'Shut the fuck up, kid,' Clancy said. 'It's all settled now and doesn't concern you.'

'Just who the fuck are you to tell me to shut up?'

'Take it easy, Conor,' I cautioned.

'I'll take it any way I want,' the boy replied. 'When I think of poor Granddad in thrall to these Clancys. From the way he talked you'd swear Barney Clancy shot streamers of gold dust from his dick when he came.'

'That will do about my father,' Pete Clancy warned tetchily.

'It won't do.' Conor glanced at Slick. 'Was he nice, this boy you went off with?'

'For the last time I went off with no boy,' Slick bellowed. 'Can't a man pay a young neighbour's bloody airfare without people jumping to conclusions? I gave money to Carol to go off with herself this evening. That doesn't mean I'm bloody well trying to jump her.'

'It's a brave man who would, with that arse on her,' P. J. muttered.

'I bet it was nice,' Conor said, ignoring P. J. 'I bet you came so hard with him you had to wipe it off the ceiling.'

'Shut the fuck up, you twisted queer!' If I hadn't blocked McGuirk's path he would have struck Conor. He glanced at me and backed off. 'Why wouldn't he be twisted anyway, the offspring of a man who was half fucking 'hen?'

'At least I have offspring,' I replied quietly.

McGuirk sat back on the table, motioning warningly to Clancy who seemed about to say something. 'Keep talking, kid, and none of yous interrupt him.'

'Granddad had his share of secrets too,' Conor said. 'I don't know them all and I'm not sure I want to. But I know that one haunted him. The day the tribunal summons was served on him I called over to Cremore to see my gran.' Conor glanced up, defying me to contradict her title. 'A moron had sprayed graffiti at my school. A moron who couldn't spell.'

'Don't rub it in, kid,' Slick growled, embarrassed.

'I wanted to tell Gran,' Conor continued, 'but she was more concerned for Granddad. He was digging in the garden, weeding out weeds that weren't there, putting off the moment when he'd have to go indoors and face the shame of that summons again. That's how he felt, humiliated before the world no matter what he said at the tribunal. I don't know what he'd done in his life, but he was just an old man in a garden with his world collapsing around him.'

'All he had to do was keep his gob shut,' P. J. interjected. 'Plenty of people did it before him.'

'I knew that after his name was in the paper he and Gran would be like prisoners in that house. I went out to the garden to help him. No chocolate buttons in the ground now, just worms and loose stones being turned over. I didn't know what to say. He kept saying how barristers make people look stupid. Phyllis was watching at the window, so I says, "Just tell the truth. You've nothing to be ashamed of, Granddad." He said – and I remember his voice like something was broken inside – he was only ashamed of two things. That he hadn't loved his son more and had helped to cheat a sick man.'

'What sick man?' Slick demanded.

'I wanted him to talk about my father,' Conor said, 'but he started this story with no names about a builder gone crazy in the head who'd bought up scattered plots of land years before. The sort of guy who didn't let his left hand know what his right hand was doing, hiding things from the taxman. He had a shareholding in some secret company with three other men. Granddad was in the background somehow. These men persuaded him that he had been only minding these plots of land for them, filling his head with rubbish and getting him to transfer ownership from his own company to their one. Granddad tried to stop them, but the main shareholder – someone Granddad never respected again – turned on him savagely, telling him to keep his mouth shut.' Conor looked around. 'Is this making sense?'

'Eamonn Brogan was a bitter old fart,' Pete Clancy said sourly. 'Only a fool would believe a word from his mouth.'

'Let the kid keep talking,' Slick commanded. 'It's making sense to me.'

'That's because he's a fucking little liar,' P. J. interjected, 'tailoring lies to suit you. You know well that Brogan would never open his gob about any of us.'

'None of yous were in the fucking dock,' I told him. 'It was my da being summoned to court.'

'It isn't a dock,' Clancy explained. 'It's just a tribunal set up to keep the lid on things. Its terms of reference are so broad that we'll eventually collapse it after it flounders around for long enough because few enough people who really count will help it. Joe Public always gets sick of their fetish for the truth once details of the legal fees get leaked. Few of us voting for it in the Dail expected anybody beyond a few sheep to be stupid enough to tell the truth, for God's sake.'

'Granddad might have,' Conor said. 'Everything else was squared off in his mind. But it rankled his conscience to see a daft man diddled by his friends. Nobody ever called to see him after he retired, nothing to do but collect rents once a week for a fucking pittance. That day in the garden he said he wanted his conscience clear. For years he'd lied to the man's son, hanging on to what wasn't his. But he had documentation about the land transfers, company records in a safe deposit account in Jersey that nobody would ever find.'

'He kept phoning me after he got that summons,' Slick said

to Clancy. 'You said not to take his calls, that his phone was tapped. If I heard his voice I was to put the receiver down.'

'This kid is conning you, Slick,' P. J. said, advancing on Conor. I stepped in front of him.

'Leave my son alone.' I turned to Slick. 'How many land deals did Joey Kerwin's son tell you about?'

'Three. I told you, I know the bloody sites well.'

'Cormac and I cleaned out an account each years ago. If two accounts are left in Jersey then only one has money from those lands in it.'

'That's enough,' Pete Clancy announced firmly. 'Anything that happened happened between our fathers.'

'Are you saying it's true?' Slick demanded.

'I'm saying that whatever money is in Jersey is all the money that's left. The past is like a jumper, try picking out one stitch and the whole yoke falls apart. How many crooked deals was Slab involved in? Would you have wanted them all dragged out by Brogan so you could get revenge over a few lousy fields? Slab was no saint. Maybe he got a dose of his own medicine at the end, but the land bank he'd built up has left you a millionaire many times over. My father and Mossy should never have played a lousy trick on him in his condition, but compared to today's land prices it was just chicken feed. Now I respect Brogan for not liking it because I didn't always like what Daddy did either. But how would it help Slab to let Brogan do his "old-man-making-peace-with-God" spiel in Dublin Castle? We'd all be fucked and under the spotlight.'

'You pair sent me to Cremore to tie him up, never telling me he'd a weak heart,' McGuirk said.

'We never told you to tie him that tight.'

'You wanted him dead and for me to get you those account mandates so P. J. could bugger off to Jersey with the kid and destroy the evidence of how my father was cheated. You used me. All my life you've used me.'

'Easy, Slick,' P. J. said. 'We're all friends here.'

'I don't have friends,' McGuirk said, 'I have you two and a wife who can't bear to be in the same room as me. I've neighbours who call me a thick cunt and they're right. I'm so thick I never saw through yous.'

'It was just a few fields,' P. J. wheedled. 'Your father didn't even know he was losing them. Think of what you'd have lost if Brogan blabbed up in the Castle.'

'I don't care about the money,' Slick replied. 'I've money oozing out my armpits, money I can't even count any more. I've Jackeen gobshites queuing to buy these shoeboxes I'm throwing up here when my father used to build stronger cowsheds.'

'Sure you're on the pig's back,' P. J. said. 'Slab would be proud of how you've built up the company if he knew who you were and haven't I advised you every step of the way. And Pete too – many's the tight corner he got you out of. It wasn't just airline tickets you were buying one time. Remember when your car was stopped by cops in the Phoenix Park? Those fucking rent-boys would have done you, only Pete had a quiet word at the station. Your wife was going to finally walk that time too, only Pete brokered a deal with her. Sure she has your house only classic now, with gold-tapped bidets to wash your arse and all. Brogan was always a sneaky fuck, a public servant insisting on this and that by-law, then grasping for handouts when he retired. God knows what else he has in that safe deposit account, papers that would hang us all. But now that you know we can go to Jersey together, make a bonfire of the whole shebang and let that be the end to it.' P. J. glared at Conor, whom I still shielded. 'We'll reward the boy well, despite his big gob. Wave a few grand before these kids' faces and they become less high-minded and principled. It wouldn't be the first time he's taken money off a man with pleasure, I'd say.'

'I don't care about the money,' Slick repeated, picking up his jacket. 'I don't even mind being used. I'm just sick of finding out that everybody except me knew how my daddy was cheated.'

He reached into his pocket but it wasn't the envelope he took out. It was Joey Kerwin's old pistol.

'Holy for fuck,' P. J. laughed, 'put that antique away before you do yourself damage.'

'There's feck all wrong with it,' Slick explained. 'It just needed a good cleaning. Look.'

He aimed almost casually at Egan and squeezed the trigger. The blast was deafening in the tiny kitchen. I flinched, instinctively turning my head and so it wasn't P. J.'s face that I saw but blood and bits of brain on the half-finished tiling behind Conor.

Nobody moved or screamed. Even P. J. died silently, his feet beside mine and his shattered head close to where Conor crouched. Smoke and a stench of gunpowder filled the kitchen. My ears rang. Time felt different.

'Slick.' Clancy softly uttered the same last word as my father. His eyes watching the gun barrel looked different from when I aimed P. J.'s shotgun at him in Maguire's byre. He seemed scared and deeply human, a Pete Clancy I had never known.

Only it wasn't his last word. Fingers trembling, McGuirk crouched so low that his nose almost touched the hot barrel, eyes squinting as he aimed carefully at Clancy's heart. The gun went off, louder and with more smoke. A screaming brought back the sound of greyhounds having their tails docked during my childhood. Clancy stood utterly still and Slick was also still for a second. At least his legs and chest were. What was left of his mouth kept screaming and bits of jagged bone stuck out where his elbow should have been. The remains of the gun lay on the floor beside fragments of his fingers. Particles of the exploding metal had shot upwards, burying themselves deep into his eyes and face. He staggered forward, reminding me of a chicken my father once killed which got up to stagger around the table with no head. Slick's scream continued as he slid onto the floor.

Conor had fallen forward onto his knees. At first I thought he had been hit by a piece of shrapnel, then I realized he was being sick. I knelt beside him, trying to shield him from the sight of P. J.'s head just a few feet away.

'Are you all right, son?'

'Just fuck off, you!'

He was sobbing uncontrollably. I glanced up at Pete Clancy who stared at me, man to man.

'What do we do now?' he asked.

I knew what he was thinking because I was thinking the same. If Conor were not there we would be walking out that door. Slick made a different sound, too weak to be a scream and then went silent except for faint rasping breaths.

'Phone an ambulance, for God's sake.' I tried to sound like a father. 'Slick's still alive.'

'You're right.' Clancy glanced at Conor too, but made no move to produce a phone. 'This is terrible . . . terrible . . . if that little cunt of Kerwin's son had kept his mouth shut . . . if you and your brother hadn't been fucking thieving . . . if your father had just played ball and destroyed his documentation like everyone else . . . I could have sorted this.'

Conor looked up. He was shaking, his face white with a streak of someone's blood across his forehead. 'Why are you not phoning an ambulance?'

'You're right, sonny, we should.' Clancy seemed distracted,

staring at McGuirk. 'Half his head is missing though. He'll never make it.'

'You've got to give him a chance,' I argued, afraid to touch Conor who had started to retch again.

'Maybe we've got to give ourselves one.'

'What are you saying?' I tried to relieve the ringing in my ears.

'A way out. Do you want this to blow up in our faces? They're both as good as dead. There's no need for us to be involved. Slick shot P. J., then killed himself by mistake. They were always arguing anyway.'

Conor looked up, eyes moving slowly between both our faces. 'He's dying, you pair of bastards,' he hissed. 'Now get your fucking phone out.'

'Your da is ten years dead too, remember?' Clancy said. 'Try explaining that to the cops. Slick's finished, I tell you. He killed your grandfather. What's it to you if he breathes his last here or in an ambulance. Take a cloth and wipe everything you've touched. It's half-three now. Let his workmen find them in four hours time.'

'Fuck you,' I said. 'You're not going to let him die.'

'I'm not going to interfere in what I can't prevent. I'm offering you both a chance. There's a lot of money in Jersey. Split it between us. The other account number is for a safe deposit box. Burn every document in it. None of them concern you. Now do either of you really want the other involved in this fucking mess?'

I could no longer hear the rasp of Slick's breath. It was hard to tell if he was alive or dead. Conor looked at me, confused and in shock. I knew he wanted this to be a dream he could wake from.

'What do we do, Dad?'

'Hand me your fucking mobile,' I ordered Clancy.

The man shook his head wearily. 'You're both right,' he said after a moment. 'I don't know what came over me. I panicked. I mean I was never involved in anything like this in my life. The phone's in the front seat of the car.' Clancy took out his keys. 'Here, kid, get it for us, will you?' He watched Conor who tried to rise but didn't seem to have enough strength. 'It's OK, I'll get it myself.'

Clancy trooped out disconsolately, leaving us hunched in silence. Conor looked up after a while. 'Mam will be out of her mind with worry about me.'

'I know,' I said. 'Miriam was always a worrier.'

'She never goes to sleep until I come in.'

Clancy returned so quietly that I never heard his footsteps, just the sudden shotgun blast from the doorway. I threw myself forward to shield Conor, not knowing if he had already been hit. I looked up at his face but he was still alive, staring over my shoulder towards the table. Following his gaze I saw blood and innards ooze from a fresh hole in Slick's stomach. Clancy uncocked P. J.'s shotgun to replace the cartridge.

'That's fairly conclusive now,' he remarked. 'Slick can be officially struck off the voters' register.'

'What the fuck are you doing, Pete?'

Clancy closed the shotgun, aiming it towards us. 'I don't know,' he said. 'I'm not a violent man. You may laugh but it's true. I've tried to live my life cleanly, bursting my balls for people who don't care. But the past always catches up with you, doesn't it?'

'Put the gun down, for fuck's sake.'

'Michael Collins says to my grandfather, "Take a seat in Meath and hold it safe for us. We need someone strong we can depend on." For eighty years we've held the fucking thing until our fingers bled. I look at my son – he has no interest, doesn't have the balls of iron and backbone of steel that it takes. I keep fooling myself that maybe one of my daughters will want the seat when they put away their dolls – a woman would be good, add a fresh twist. Even at two years of age I was staring into their eyes, trying to see myself there. None of them have the stomach for the rubber chicken and hand-shaking and shite-swallowing that comprises my glorified life. They want to sit down for Christmas dinner and not have passers-by thinking they can arrive with forms for signing. Eighty years on I'm still holding this fucking seat by my fingertips with no one to pass it on to. So why can't I let it go?'

'Pete,' I pleaded, 'be sensible.'

'I can't be the Clancy who fucked up. You understand guilt or you wouldn't have come home. If you two leave here you'll talk. It's human nature, secrets always come out. There was never a snowball's chance of a passport, Brendan. I can't swing such things any more. I was just buying time, stalling you like I stalled Slick all year.'

'You knew Slick would kill my father, didn't you?'

'I knew your father had a weak heart. But it was Slick who tied the knots.'

'Let Conor go at least,' I pleaded. 'All this was before his time.'

'It wasn't me who made him part of it. But I'm not worried about Conor, he's not a problem.'

'I'm not leaving without my dad,' Conor said defiantly.

'Who says you're leaving?' Clancy replied. 'I mean that killing you is no problem. Slick always had the hots for faggots. You're a useful bit of sex to throw them off the scent. A lover's tiff that P. J. tumbled on.'

'You can't close those Jersey accounts without me,' the boy said defiantly.

'Fuck them. Banks will happily sit on dormant accounts

forever. With Eamonn dead and Slick no longer causing hassle it's unlikely any tribunal will trawl through your family's names anyway. Your father is the problem. DNA testing, dental records. The Hen Boy makes everything more suspicious than a bout of sexual hijinks gone wrong. I can kill you here, Conor, but the Hen Boy's body has to disappear.'

Some instinct made Clancy turn or else he heard something. Ebun had stood in the doorway long enough to remove both darts from the plank of wood there. She aimed at Clancy's face. The first shotgun blast shattered the window behind me. One dart had stuck in him above his eye, while the other protruded from his cheek. He fired again wildly as I lunged forward. The second cartridge ripped a hole in the ceiling. A dart fell out as we toppled over Slick's body, but the one in his eyebrow swayed back and forth with blood pouring from the tip.

'Run for Christ's sake,' I screamed at Ebun. 'Take Conor with you.'

Conor knelt behind me, trying to hold Clancy down, but Pete lashed out, knocking us both away. He searched his pocket for more cartridges as he slithered under the table to buy time to reload.

'Come on,' Ebun screamed, 'run, run!'

'You run. Get the boy out of here.' I didn't care if I was killed as I aimed kicks in at Clancy. It felt like this was the moment I had come home for, to finally settle old scores between us.

I don't know how Ebun dragged Conor away; just then the first shotgun blast came from under the table. It scorched my left shoulder before tearing a hole in the wall above the deserted doorway. I dodged into the hall, hearing his footsteps follow. A car engine had started. The car came towards me, with somebody throwing the side door open. But Clancy was out by now, dazzled in the headlights. The dart was plucked from his eyebrow, but blood streamed down, blurring his vision.

He aimed blindly into the glaring lights. The Ford Fiesta sped forward as though Ebun was trying to ram him, then swerved violently just before he shot. The side window shattered as it bumped its way towards the gap in the tar barrels, crashing into one before swinging left to career into the dark.

Clancy ducked back into the house to reload. My shoulder bled from where his shot had left a flesh wound with a burning sensation like somebody had placed a hot iron against my skin. I looked around for somewhere to hide. A trench lay to my left, beside a cement mixer. I tumbled down into it, cutting my knee on rocks at the bottom. My courage was gone. I was alone now with Pete Clancy and the old familiar certainty that the bully would find me.

Clancy came out, having wiped the blood from his eyes, but both facial wounds still bled deeply. He looked around, bewildered, like he could not believe the events of the previous half-hour.

'Brendan?' he cajoled. 'It's time to talk. This has gone too far.'

He scanned the moonlight for any movement. I gripped a rock and tossed it towards some stacked rafters. It struck the wood with a soft clunk and Clancy turned instinctively, firing in the direction of the sound.

'Don't startle me like that, Brendan. Call first, then come out slowly. Your black bitch has probably got the cops by now, so what would be the point of my killing you? We're both fucked. This has blown up in our faces. We need to coordinate our stories for damage limitation. So don't hide any more because my nerves are in tatters. I'm afraid you're going to jump me. Come out and I'll put this gun down.'

He was only feet away re-loading by feel, blinded again by

blood seeping from his eyebrow. He could see nothing but I swear that he could smell the cold sweat I had known as a child every time he approached me. My heart was so loud he had to be drawn towards it. Yet the doubt gnawed that maybe he meant what he said. He could no longer control events, so why did he not put the shotgun down instead of walking blindly on holding it?

He fell forward into the trench with an almost graceful motion, hands releasing the gun as they reached out to break his fall. He landed on the shotgun and there was a blast before he fell sideways on top of me. I thought he was dead for a second. Then his hands reached out to grip my hair, clinging to me like a drowning man as he pulled himself up, his voice hoarse and rasping.

'Fuck you, Hen Boy, for ever coming back.'

There was such strength in those arms that I struggled to break their grip circling my neck.

'Don't leave me in this fucking ditch,' he ordered. 'My leg is busted from how I landed and I'm shot in the belly or you are . . . there's blood there but no pain. Get me into my car.'

'You're going nowhere.' I pushed him down and scrambled out, looking for something to finish him off with. The site was bare, Slick's meanness ensuring that nothing worth stealing was left out.

I heard a noise behind me. Clancy had somehow managed to pull himself up. He tried to rise but found that he couldn't, then began to crawl towards his car, leaving a trail of blood from his stomach. He winced from the pain from his left foot which sprawled awkwardly behind him, yet he never cried out, even when his ankle knocked against a stone. He just kept inching his way towards his car. I waited until he was only feet away before blocking his path, my shoes inches from his outstretched fingers.

'How will you drive?'

He looked up, with no fear in his eyes or even a plea for mercy. 'I never needed help from the likes of you,' he wheezed.

'You did,' I spat. 'My father and thousands like him built your family up, scurrying like worker ants desperate for your approval.'

'Eamonn would have stayed a nobody if Daddy hadn't taken him up. Like you still are, with the stench of chicken-shite off you, Hen Boy.'

His voice was weaker, fighting for breath, yet the matter-of-factness of his tone infuriated me.

'Say my proper name! Who am I? Say it, you bastard!'

'The same person you'll always be. Brogan, the Hen Boy.'

The violence with which I trod on his fingers surprised me. He rolled over, momentarily shielding himself. 'Who does that make you?' I said. 'Who the fuck are you, you bastard? Who gave you the right to be you? Swaggering around the schoolyard with a superior smirk of your arse. Mr Fucking Untouchable, eh? Well I was as good as you once, I was fucking better.'

Clancy half sat up, still without a trace of fear in his eyes. Blood poured from the wound in his stomach. Yet I could have searched his pocket for more cartridges to finish him off without his expression changing. 'You were always one jealous wee cunt, Hen Boy.'

'I was the eldest son like you. So where was my respect? Why did I count for nothing?'

'Out of my way, you little prick, because I'm sick of the sight of you and all the others like you.' He found strength to reach into his pocket for his keys. 'There's a doctor in Kells who owes me a favour. Now just open the bloody car door, boy.'

'You're going nowhere,' I taunted, and stepped back so that my shoe clipped a rock. I raised it high and towered over him, the rock poised to shatter his skull. But Clancy just stared up with a half-mocking gaze, so certain he had the measure of my seed and breed that he knew I'd never have the balls to kill him. I lowered the rock wearily, tossing it away into the dark and when I looked back his eyes were still defiantly wide open, having cheated me again, almost like he had choreographed his own death.

I didn't dare to close his eyes, but eventually I walked back into the house. P. J. had never really aged. Even in death his look was cautious, as if suspicious about what he might have to declare in the next world. I wiped the shotgun and pressed it into his cold hands. Slick had tumbled over when Clancy kicked him so that I could not see his ripped face. I reached into his pocket for the envelope which had cost Niyi his life and retrieved Conor's passport too. I pocketed the darts which had Ebun's fingerprints, then went out to where Clancy's car keys lay on the mud beside his body. I left them there and walked past the tar barrels, too numb to think or even feel the burn of the flesh wound in my shoulder.

━━━━━━┥■┝━━━━━━

Navan came upon me suddenly at a bend in the road. The first of a chaotic maze of housing estates jockeying for access to a ribbon of road. Stepping into a driveway I watched two squad cars speed past with sirens off but revolving lights illuminating the shadows. I walked on, getting briefly caught by the lights of an oncoming ambulance. Even the town centre seemed deserted apart from the odd truck getting a head start on the commuter traffic.

Flower Hill seemed impossibly steep. The pain was growing

steadily worse in my shoulder. I was losing blood but somehow I felt stronger now, closing in on home with pure instinct taking over. It was hard to conceive of myself as the age I was. There was something hallucinogenic, yet unearthly real about the familiar streets I lurched through. I knew that I was going home. I could have been six or eight or any unspecified age, walking inside a memory that had never actually happened.

Finally I staggered into the entrance of the laneway. The ridge of grass down its centre looked like the spine of some reptilian creature. I put a hand out, feeling my way by the walls. O'Brien's garage still stood there, then there was something new, then Brady's doorway bricked up. Ryan's shed was demolished, yielding a glimpse into their garden where sawdust had once always been strewn about, and here at last was Hanlon's.

Twice I tried to clamber onto the roof and failed, the second time falling back and almost twisting my ankle. I searched for the battered chair I had seen yesterday. It rocked dangerously when I stood on it, but I managed to get a grip on the roof and scramble over, tumbling down onto the unkempt grass. I had only to open the sitting-room window now like yesterday morning to be safely inside where I could lick my wounds and feel warm again.

But a dim light in the sitting-room window disturbed me as it drew me close. Breathing heavily, I crouched beneath apple tree branches. Lisa sat in the same armchair as when a child. In truth she seemed little more than a child now. Her hair had not changed, still straight and mousy-brown. She might have been a ghost had she not brought me fully back to the present. The auction was tomorrow. Why not come home a day early to spend one last night alone here?

A television was on with the sound off. But from her expression I knew she was not taking in the images on the screen. Perhaps she was recalling childhood nights with her face lit by the glow of a coal fire as her mother brought her in milk and they sat together, unaware of being observed.

Few people had ever loved me. I had done little to merit her love, fleeing from the responsibility of her pain, yet I knew that I had only to knock on the window and she would let me in. Lisa Hanlon would forgive me anything, even my reappearance. I stood up, no longer bothering to hide and had reached the window with my fist clenched to tap on the glass when the sitting-room door opened.

I stepped back, half-expecting her mother's ghost to appear, but it was a man holding two hot whiskeys. He was English – I knew from his clothes and the unNavanlike way he gestured with his hands after he put the glasses down. Lisa turned so that I could see how her face had aged. A small child in pyjamas ran excitedly in behind the man to jump into her mother's arms. Lisa stroked her daughter's hair, kissing the crown of her forehead. The child looked towards the window, as if after seeing something move there.

She spoke and both parents looked out at the darkness where I crouched again. Lisa laughed and hugged the child to reassure her. This was the way people grew up and moved on. I should have felt happiness for Lisa that her life had worked out and found its correct pattern. But I just felt a terrible sense of waste, knowing it could have been me behind such a window, instead of still being outside, still hurting, unable to let go. I backed away, aware of blood on the grass which the child would spot in the morning.

I needed to lie down before I collapsed. Hanlon's shed was padlocked. I didn't have the strength to climb back over it into the lane. The wall was low into what had once been Casey's garden. I knew where I was going now to stem this bleeding and take stock.

I dropped down into my old garden. Nothing was the same, yet it still smelt of home. The spare key lay where I had seen the man leave it yesterday under the stone. I opened the outhouse door, not knowing what I expected to find. Perhaps the ghost of myself, having waited all these years for someone to unlock the door. The polished floorboards felt strange as I crossed to the computer on the tidy desk surrounded by smart Scandinavian office furniture which radiated order and control. Someone else's kingdom where someone else's son had done their homework the previous night, judging by the copybook left open on the desk, emblazoned with stars.

Without turning on a light, I managed to clean the flesh wound at the small sink in the corner. A shirt hung on the back of the office chair. I tore a strip of cloth from it, binding it tight against the wound. The pain was savage now. A press contained a small horde of drink and a wallet of holiday snaps. Brandy burned my throat, then warmed my stomach as I sat on the floor to examine photograph after photograph. Holiday snaps taken somewhere hot. A man and woman alternated in almost every shot, taking turns to pose with the young boy who was ever-present. Laughing, chasing geese, playing with a dog. The last two snaps were taken back at home to finish off the roll. The child knelt on his bed beside a wall festooned with Disney characters. Teddy bears were piled at his feet. There was no reason why I should recognize my old room with even the window frame replaced, but I knew they were taken there. I touched the walls and ceiling as if to make them real, but only the brandy was real and the tearing pain in my shoulder.

I have no idea how I managed to fall asleep, just that I woke to find the boy from the photographs watching me. It still felt dark in the shed but the open doorway was flooded with light where he stood. He eyed his copybook on the desk.

'This is my father's office,' he said. 'What are you doing here?'

'Resting.'

'You tore his shirt.'

'My arm was bleeding.'

'Does he know you?'

'No.'

'This is our house.'

I wanted to tell him how it had been mine once, but I didn't. Not just because I heard his mother calling from the kitchen and I knew that time was running out. But because it would have made no sense to someone for whom the past did not exist.

'Eric?' His mother's voice came closer, her footsteps crossing the gravel. Rising, I undid the bolts of the new metal door that opened into the lane and stepped out as the woman entered the outhouse. I did not look back as she called after me, but could imagine her in the doorway with her arms protectively around her son.

I knew that I was starting to lose it now because a mirage stood at the entrance to the laneway, watching me approach. I felt my legs buckle but when I fell I didn't hit the ground. Conor was real as he caught me.

'How did you know where . . . ?' I tried to rise.

'We passed here one time and Phyllis said it was always where you ran back to.'

'That was when I was fifteen.'

'You never stopped being fifteen.' Ebun spoke as she opened the back door of Charles's mother's car, where glass had been cleared from the seat.

'Clancy's dead,' I said.

'I know,' Ebun climbed into the driver's seat. 'We phoned the police and gave no names, just the location. We drove back to find police everywhere. I asked if an African had been found there, pretending to be looking for Niyi. A policeman at the barrels said that three bodies were found, all well-known local men.'

Conor hesitated, unsure of where he wanted to sit, then climbed in beside me as Ebun drove off.

'Did you kill him?' he asked.

'No. I couldn't even do that.'

'You told me they were Granddad's friends.' Conor shivered. 'Christ, I'd hate to meet his enemies.'

I looked back at the woman who had ventured down the laneway, her son holding her hand as he solemnly watched us exit from his world.

VII

WEDNESDAY, 9 A.M.

Traffic was chronic leaving Navan, with a three-mile tail-back of reluctant commuters coping with temporary lights as workmen tore up the road. It was freezing in the car with two windows shattered. Ebun silently gripped the wheel with more force than necessary. Beside me Conor was still shaking.

'Are you OK?' I asked.

'I'm not OK,' he snapped. 'How the fuck would I be OK? I've seen two men get their heads burst open. Every time I close my eyes I see them again. What do we do now?'

'I don't know,' I replied

'That's bloody great.' He took a deep breath, trying to pull himself together. 'Coming from the guy who wanted me to do business with those bastards.'

'Not all of them,' I said, 'just Clancy.'

'Oh good,' Conor sniped. 'Not the psychopath with the pistol, just the one with the shotgun.'

'Stop bickering,' Ebun ordered from the front. 'Let's get out of here while we can.'

I looked at the streaks of blood on Conor's face and the congealed blood around the crude ligature on my shoulder. My face was still bruised from the fight off Dorset Street on Saturday night and the black roots on my hair had started to show through the red dye. The stubble on my face was black. Drivers stared across at us through the smashed windows as they passed in the opposite direction.

'At least we're not conspicuous,' I joked grimly.

'No,' Ebun replied. 'They see me and just think it's another attack on a black person.'

Conor was quieter beside me. He looked to be in delayed shock.

'Are you OK?' I asked again.

'The mid-term break is over. I should be in school now. I'm missing double maths.'

'How are you doing at school?'

He stared at me incredulously. 'Just fuck off, Dad, right?'

At least he had called me 'Dad' I thought as the car crawled forward while we sat in tense silence. I wondered were we passing the lands that Mossy Egan and Barney Clancy had cajoled Slab into unknowingly signing away; a scam jokingly proposed in the back of some pub. Which one initially suggested it and at what stage did their eyes meet, checking the other understood how the idea had strayed beyond being a joke? The point of no return when the instinct of greed took over. A gamble entered into because it could be taken on, with no comprehension of how the ripples would seep out to form the wave that eventually swept all their sons away.

Three men lay dead on the outskirts of Navan, yet just now I could only feel a sort of nervous euphoria because I wasn't one of them and my own son had survived. It was like the relief I remembered from school after escaping the savage brutality of the yard at someone else's expense.

'Why did you come back?' I asked Ebun.

She shrugged. 'I was seven or eight miles gone before I turned around. I parked outside. When I heard shots I hid. Maybe I felt I owed you from Saturday night. When I saw that man fetch his gun I had to check you were still alive.' Momentarily she took her eyes off the road to glance back. 'We're even.'

'It's not like that.'

She looked at the road. 'I cannot be involved, you understand? Decide what you must do but leave me out of it.'

'It may not be so simple.'

'It has to be. When one of you does wrong we are told they are an exception. When one of us does something we are tarred together. After Niyi we will all be blackmailers, after me all murderers.'

'You killed nobody. You saved both our lives.'

'A powerful man lies dead. That won't be forgotten. He was right, we are like fallen fruit. We need to hide in the grass, not stand out. Do you not think they will want rid of Lekan and me? They will not say it is because of this. But they will fast-track me out of here and think themselves well rid of trouble.'

'How long . . . are you two . . . ?' Conor began.

'Are we what?' Ebun said.

'Does Mam know . . . ?' He paused. 'That's a stupid question, I know. I suppose there were others.'

'Ten years is a long time, Conor.'

'It wasn't for Mam.'

'Has she ever . . . ?'

'What's it to you?' he asked belligerently, then flicked some shards of glass out of the open window. 'Charles's mam will go crazy, she loves this car.'

The long snake of vehicles moved forward again.

'If she had men friends she kept them well hidden from me,' Conor said quietly. 'I would have been hurt, I was very fixated about your memory. Ironic, isn't it, seeing as you were shacking-up with everything.'

Ebun slammed the brakes, causing the truck behind us to beep as she pulled over onto the lay-by.

'Nobody "shacks-up" with me,' she retorted angrily.

'What do they do then?' Conor demanded. 'He's only back here a few days and you're hanging out of him. What are you after?'

'Stop it, Conor.'

'No,' Ebun said. 'Let him say it.'

'I mean what do you want? A white baby or for him to divorce Mam and get you a passport?'

'I don't need no white baby,' Ebun hissed, 'not that it would be white. Any baby born here automatically becomes a citizen. Is that what you think, boy, that I'm trying to fuck my way into staying? Why waste time waiting to trap your father? I could have got a head start by screwing everybody on the container truck we came over on.'

'I'm sorry,' Conor tried to backtrack. 'I'm just confused . . . twenty-four hours ago I thought this bastard was dead.'

'He's no bastard. He loves you.'

'How would you know?'

'Because I loved a child once.' Ebun restarted the car, nudging her way back out into the traffic. 'How come you people can only ever see us now and never the lives we lived before.' Ebun sought my eyes in the rear-view mirror. 'What will you do?' she asked.

'There's nothing to link us to that building site,' I said cautiously. 'I'm sure Forensics will find a hundred things but they won't know who to look for.'

'Unless you turn up,' Ebun said. 'That would be one link too many.'

'There's five weeks left on Cormac's passport,' I replied. 'I could return to Oporto, get back my old job in the bar and simply accept that I'm trapped there, never able to leave Portugal again.'

'Is that what you want?' Conor asked.

I gazed at him. 'Is it what you want?'

Conor looked away, burdened by the question. 'I'm just a schoolkid, Dad.'

———◆———

We parked the Ford Fiesta down a sidestreet off the North Circular Road and walked back to Dorset Street. It was half-ten. Conor phoned his mother's mobile from the callbox outside the post office where old people queued for their pensions.

'I'm OK,' I heard him say. 'I can't explain on the phone . . . I know you'll kill me . . . no, you were right to go into work, I know you're in court . . . no, I'm not at school . . . don't come home, I'll come out to you . . . soon as I get a bus . . . I'm sorry . . . real sorry . . . no, don't collect me, I'm on my way.'

He replaced the phone. 'Some things never change,' he said. 'You still have me lying to her. She's in Kilmainham Courthouse, going character witness for two of her car-thieving lads. They're always slagging her clapped-out banger, offering to steal her a better one.' He rooted in his pocket for change. 'Throw us a few bob, will you? I'd better put Charles out of his misery.'

Conor gave him the car's location, telling him to have his mother explain to the police that it had been a misunderstanding. I could hear Charles's agitated voice: 'It had better not be scratched. You know how precious she is about her car.'

'It's untouched,' Conor told him, 'not a mark on it. But come for it soon, because you know what your father always says about the Northside.' He put a hand over the mouthpiece to wink at me. 'Charles's family are paranoid about Northsiders. They'll just be thrilled there's still four wheels on it.'

The pain in my shoulder was becoming unbearable. When we reached her flat Ebun removed the ligature and tried to clean it, but shook her head. 'It will turn septic,' she said. 'You must visit a hospital.'

'I can't.'

Footsteps descended the stairs and Lekan opened the door. He took in the scene and shook his head, anticipating bad news. Ebun went over to him, speaking in her own tongue. I didn't need a translator as I saw his face pass from shock to grief. Now that Ebun was here she felt able to cry again with the anguish of someone a long way from home. Lekan held her close as Conor and I watched awkwardly, knowing we were intruders. Finally she wiped her eyes and stepped out onto the landing.

'I will go to Navan and identify him,' Lekan said. 'Better to be buried under the name he chose than no name.' He observed me gravely. 'We had enough troubles before you came, without needing you to add to them. But I will say nothing about why he went to Navan. I will leave you out of this for Ebun's sake. Now say goodbye to my sister. This morning I wish we had never come here.'

The landing was empty, with the house quiet for once. Ebun's eyes were still red.

'It's better for all our sakes if we pretend this never happened,' I said. 'If I just go away again.'

'That's why I chose you.' Ebun looked up. 'I knew you would not stay around to break my heart even more.'

'I have no choice.'

'We all face journeys we don't want to take.'

'What will you do?'

'Wait endlessly for my appeal until one day they deport me.'

'They mightn't, you know.'

'Every factory keeps screaming for workers, offering bribes for people to come from every corner of the earth, yet still

they won't let us work. You want rid of us, maybe because
we remind you too much of how you were.'

'If I can find a way to stay in touch,' I said.

Ebun didn't reply, just nodded. Conor stood behind me.
I touched her hand but we did not kiss. I descended a few
steps and looked back. Conor had stopped beside her.

'I'm sorry for what I said in the car,' he said awkwardly.

'Make sure your father goes to a hospital. *Ó dàbò.*'

Ebun put her arms around him, hugging him like I think
she would have hugged her own child, then stood with Lekan
to watch us descend the long stairs.

———— ◦|◦ ————

The queue in the Casualty Department was slow moving. We
took a ticket and found a quiet corner to sit in. Conor brought
us over two paper cups of coffee.

'You should get a bus out to your mother's office,' I said.
'She'll be back from court going frantic.'

'I know.'

'Then why don't you go?'

'Because once I walk out the door you're going to slip
away and not get your shoulder seen to.'

'The pain isn't bad now,' I lied. 'I could get it seen to in
Portugal. I'm more worried about you.'

'I'm OK, I tell you.'

'You saw things tonight I never wanted you to see, things
your granddad could never have expected.'

'If I kept your secrets before, I can do so again,' Conor
said. 'I can phone Mam, stall her for a few hours. Find me
the fare to Jersey and I'll go for you on the next plane. You
can have every penny of what's there. Buy yourself a dozen
crooked passports if you like.'

'I don't want a passport.'

'What do you want?'

'To watch you grow up,' I replied.

'I am grown up.'

'You're not. But you know I can't stay.'

'Too scared?'

'Not for myself,' I said. 'Not of jail any more. I'm scared to see you and your mother lose everything. They'll want every red cent back, everything collapsing around your ears.'

'Maybe they won't,' Conor said. He sipped his scalding coffee as I watched a trainee nurse surreptitiously eye him up. 'Either way Gran hasn't long to live. I want her to live forever but people don't. We'll be due half the proceeds of the Cremore house. If Mam got anything illegally I know that she'd want to pay it back. And maybe I'd gain something. Do you put no value on yourself?'

'Faking my death was the only worthwhile thing I ever did.'

'You helped conceive me or was that worthless too?'

'You're worth a thousand of me, son.'

'You don't know me,' Conor replied.

'I do. I spent entire nights checking your cot every five minutes to make sure I could still hear you breathing. I saw you stand for the first time and wanted to bring in strangers off the street to show you off. I was so proud and still am.'

'Then make me proud of you,' Conor said. 'I don't really remember you. I only know you through other people's stories. You might be the biggest bastard in the world but maybe you're not. If you disappear I'll never know.'

'You wouldn't want to know me,' I replied quietly.

'Let me decide.' Conor was angry. 'You don't know me now. I've a life of my own with thoughts and failings and fuck-ups all of my own. I'm confused and weak and half the time I don't know where the fuck I'm going. Maybe I need someone to look up to or look down on or just simply talk to and ask if you ever felt this way. Did you never think of that?'

'I did.'

'Then why didn't you come back? Don't mention money, I'm sick of hearing about money after tonight.'

'I was scared that you'd hate me or maybe scared you might need me and I'd fail you again. I felt that I wouldn't know what to say once you grew beyond the age where a bar of chocolate cured everything. I see Cormac in you every time we meet. I loved your uncle more than anyone before you. I was his sidekick, a dog happy to lie under any table he sat at. I couldn't live without him so I tried and failed to become him.'

A nurse came out to call the number before mine. Conor put his coffee down. 'Cormac wasn't at all like you. He was gay for a start.'

'One night in a bar in Belgium I said my name – Cormac's name – in company,' I replied. 'A man glanced up, looked at me different from how you look at people. A look I didn't understand until I realized he had known Cormac. People drifted away and I knew I should have gone too. My cover was in danger of being blown, but I couldn't leave and he sat there like we were waiting for the bar to clear, with something pre-ordained arranged between us. "Don't say you don't know me," he said, and I replied, "I know you, it's just been how long . . . ?" "Too long," he told me, "you look different but the same." I had never touched a man's body before nor ever wished to. But I stayed because it felt like Cormac had sent him to test me and if I slept with him just once and fooled him into thinking I was Cormac then maybe I would finally feel what it was like to be him.'

'What did Cormac feel like?'

'Pure as crystal. I saw him once in a window in Navan, framed by light, and I knew I could never be so pure. I knew I'd always be outside in the dark and from that moment I loved him.'

'Did you sleep with the man?' Conor asked.

'Have I asked how many men you've slept with?'

He blushed slightly and looked away. 'That isn't a question one asks.'

'What do you ask men then?'

'When I wake in the morning will you be gone?'

'Do they answer truthfully?'

'You never know until the morning.' He looked at me, embarrassed. 'So Charles tells me. With me there haven't been many men.'

'It's dangerous, you know, it's . . .' I stopped, unable to prevent myself smiling.

'What?' Conor asked.

'Nothing. Just that I sound like Phyllis.' I looked at him solemnly. 'I slept with the man in Belgium.'

'And how was it?'

'It wasn't me. I knew I had only been trying to fool myself.'

'Do something for me,' Conor said.

'What?'

'Go to jail. Maybe you'll only get a suspended sentence. But either way I'll get to know you.'

A crew-cut young man emerged from between the screens with his arm bandaged. He had the stunted Dublin look of someone raised on deep-fried carbohydrates and cunning. I tried to imagine sharing a cell with three men like him.

'You mightn't like what you find,' I said.

'Neither might you.'

The nurse returned to call my number. I rose without

replying and walked away from my son, aware of his eyes
following me. The African doctor was suspicious of my story
about having burnt myself with an iron. He asked me to wait
while a nurse cleaned and dressed the wound, then adminis-
tered an injection. I had no idea if he was calling the police
or checking the bogus name and address I had given him.
Through the screens I could see Conor in the public area. I
didn't know which terrified me the most – the prospect
of jail or of starting afresh with Conor, being expected to
live up to the term 'father'. Behind me I could see a door
marked 'Exit' through which I could slip out and run. There
was enough money in my hotel for an airline ticket. I
vacillated, too scared to move either way, until the doctor
returned.

'Take these every six hours and come back in two days,'
he said.

I thanked the doctor and rose. Conor had his back to me,
examining some magazine on the table. I thought of Ebun,
her grief, her body, the way she made me feel special. Maybe
we had no chance, both of us on the precipice of undetermined
futures. But maybe, even for a brief while, we could share
that uncertainty here together. With a last glance back at the
exit I took a deep breath and pushed open the screens to call
my son. He looked up and smiled as he nodded.

━━━━■■■━━━━

It was a semi-private room, but the other bed was currently
empty. A screen was half-drawn around Phyllis's bed. An
almost untouched dinner tray waited to be collected. Conor
went first, moving almost on tiptoes across the floor. I hung
back, waiting for him to speak but he remained silent, then
beckoned me. I would have sooner faced anything than con-

front this woman. Nurses talked out in the corridor. Conor beckoned again for me to move forward and stare down at Phyllis.

She was asleep, with her glossy woman's magazine having slipped to the floor. I picked it up, staring at page after page of colour photographs of the home of some minor inbred relative of the British royal family. It would have annoyed me once, but now I felt sorry for her need to peer in at other people's worlds. Her life had never been easy. An unmarried mother when it was a badge of shame; the reluctant blow-in to a tight-knit town; the babydoll unable to stay within her role; the wife of an ageing, cranky man whose devotion to Barney Clancy surely grew to rankle more than any liaison with a mistress ever could; the mother of a dead son with whom she could never be fully honest and who was never fully open with her; the bearer of an estranged daughter who had never wished to understand her.

Her life might have been so different if Barney Clancy had not crudely tried to bed her. If she had met somebody her own age that night behind the kitchens at Groom's Hotel instead of being comforted by my father. A youth with a motor scooter who laughed and fed her chips after dances at Red Island in Skerries instead of showing her off in middle-aged restaurants and writing bad Georgian verse in her honour. Somebody who would simply have let her get on with growing up into the person she might have become.

Her hospital bed might now be surrounded by hordes of Dublin grandchildren, street-wise and yet respectful to her, a husband reminiscing about all the fun they had despite their hard times and a steady flow of neighbours popping in from the nearby streets to see her. I doubted if visitors had come in from Cremore where she always stood out by trying too hard to blend in.

She stirred slightly, fingers plucking at the blankets. Conor sat on the edge of her bed. He had surprising gentleness for a boy as he kissed her forehead. Her eyes opened and took him in, a smile registering even though I could see she was in pain.

'How are you, Gran?'

'The better for seeing you.' Her voice was barely above a whisper.

'You mustn't get alarmed or upset, Gran, but there's somebody here you never thought you would see again.'

Phyllis turned her head slowly. Her expression didn't change, just her eyes. She thinks I'm Cormac, I thought as I recognized the awful hope in her look. Then I realized that she didn't think this, merely wished it with all her heart. Conor beckoned me closer, then when I didn't come he physically drew me over, taking my hand and placing it in hers. Her fingers felt knotted and cold.

'My baby,' she whispered, 'my poor boy.' Her eyes were piercing, the only strength left in her. 'You saw him last. He's not gone, you know. Friends of his I didn't know . . . three of them . . . wrote or called to see me. The same dream . . . Cormac in a garden tending water lilies. They said he was happy, you know the smile he had . . . never in my dreams but theirs. Cormac knew they would tell me.'

I knew the painkilling drugs were having an effect, but this was pure Phyllis. No interest in where I had been for ten years or any wonder at my reappearance from the dead. She could only ever focus on what was important to her. *Why didn't you mind him?* The question wasn't spoken, just framed in her eyes as she moved her hand away. My anger returned. I wanted an apology from her, I wanted her to break down in tears at my presence or at least show some emotion beyond a flat disappointment that I was not somebody else. I needed her to take this chance to make amends, yet deep down I knew it was impossible for her.

'You were always sneaky,' she whispered. 'Even as a child you had to be as good as Cormac . . . had to steal the limelight at his death. You were never on that bloody train at all.'

'No.'

'Now you've come back to gloat.'

'No.'

'Gran.' Conor looked near tears. 'Aren't you happy he's alive?'

Phyllis gazed at him anxiously. 'He wants to steal you from me . . . poison you about me.' She looked back. 'Your father's dead.'

'I know.'

'They wanted to drag him through the courts. He said it would be like Nuremberg, questions, questions. What would your father know? He knew nothing.' She looked at Conor. 'Are you OK? I worry for you.'

'Why?'

'There are bad men.'

'The man who tied you up in Cremore is dead,' I said. 'The men who threatened Conor are dead.'

'What do you know about it?'

'My father knew more than his prayers.'

'He was a good man,' she whispered. 'All the neighbours . . . nurses in here . . . even since his name was in the paper . . . they think your father was a gangster . . . I see how they look at me . . .'

'It's OK.' I put my hand cautiously on her shoulder. 'I'm here now.'

I could feel the bones through her skin, her arm wasted away that had often lashed out at me.

'What the hell ever use were you?' She was in tears now, silent ones that got caught up in the lines on her face.

'Please, Gran,' Conor said.

'I'm sorry.' It was hard to tell who she was addressing. 'So many things I'm sorry for.'

'Did Granddad tell you things, Gran?'

'What things?'

'About money in my name in a Jersey account.'

'Who told you that?'

'Pete Clancy.'

She snorted. 'What would he know, the little pip-squeak? Any money was long spent.'

'What do you mean?' I asked.

'It didn't belong to your father or Barney Clancy either . . . but he made your father spend it . . . badgering and cajoling him to release it in drips and drabs and never tell Pete about it. Pete wanted to be Mr Sheen leaving everything clean, but Barney had expenses he never wanted his son to know about. Some old pluckered crow he hung out with. Barney claimed the man who owned the money would never come looking for it but his son did.' She turned to Conor. 'Your granddad was a good man, he just lived too long.'

'But the account is still open,' Conor said. 'There's two accounts in my name.'

'I wanted to tell you but it's hard to break the habits he bred into me. There's no money in either.'

'What was in them then?'

'The one I'm supposed to know of has stuff about Clancy,' Phyllis said, breathing heavier now with the effort to speak. 'Papers about land deals your granddad didn't want to fall into the wrong hands.'

'And the other?'

'Things he didn't want me to know he had kept. I was

very jealous when I was young, I couldn't help it. They are things he wanted you to have, belonging to your grand-mother. Letters and poems he wrote for her when they were courting in Navan, photos, a lock of hair in an envelope. He used to keep them in the garden shed at first in a filing cabinet. He thought I never knew or maybe he just liked to pretend I didn't.' She looked at me. 'Does Miriam know you're . . . ?'

'No.'

Her left hand hovered, afraid to touch mine, reminding me of that night decades ago when I cried out and we first confronted each other.

'She's been good to us . . . better than we deserved.' Phyllis took a long breath, eyeing the drip beside her bed. 'Why have you really come?'

I looked out at the Dublin skyline. 'Because yous are the only family I have.'

Her hand lightly brushed my fingers, then this time held them. As two guilty people we recognized each other.

———▪■▪———

Lunch-hour traffic was choking Phibsborough, the narrow crossroads blocked with cars and buses. A light rain had started falling. Pete Clancy's face stared out from the early edition of the evening paper in a newsagent's window, along with a picture of Egan and McGuirk taken at a racecourse. *Mystery Deaths*, the headline read. *Rumours of business quarrel gone wrong*.

Conor turned away from the window, holding his stomach. 'I keep seeing that man when the gun blew up in his face,' he said. 'He was a lonely geezer. You see lots like him in the saunas.'

'What saunas?' I demanded.

'Christ.' He straightened up. 'I'm going to have to start remembering you're a parent.'

I hailed a taxi on the North Circular Road. 'Is your mother still working in that same Advice Bureau?' I asked. 'She'll be going out of her mind.'

We sat together in the back, watching streets flash past. I reached into my pocket to take out his passport, examining the photograph before returning it to him.

'Have you fresh clothes?' Conor asked.

'In a hotel down town.'

'I wouldn't book out just yet if I were you.'

'I think the fatted calf's neck is safer than my own one just now.'

The taxi sped on, taking the new motorway and then turning at a massive roundabout. I was utterly lost, relying on Conor to direct the driver. We stopped in the carpark of a huge shopping centre, with central fountains and long aisles of British High Street shops. It felt like being inside a spaceship that had docked at the motorway interchange.

'Times have changed,' I remarked. 'I knew they had plans to develop the scabby shopping centre where Miriam worked, but I never thought it would become this.'

'It didn't,' Conor replied. 'This isn't it. But the motorway blocks the old road into it and it takes forever to get there by taxi. It's simpler to come here and walk.'

We strode through the shoppers pushing trolleys back to their cars and came out the far side into a loading bay where lorries queued up. A security guard eyed us, speaking into his walkie-talkie.

'Mam stopped shopping here,' Conor said. 'They don't really encourage locals and used to spot us coming in this way. Twice I was put out of the centre for loitering when I waited for her outside a clothes shop. She went ballistic the way Mam does and word went around that she wasn't a local at all, she was a troublemaker.'

Boulders had been placed at the back of the loading bay to prevent any car entering from the small path which Conor led me down. There were few shoppers here, with locals put off by the prices. It took us ten minutes to reach a huge bank of dumped earth which had never been properly seeded so that it was a mass of weeds and nettles. Beyond it the path led down into a valley. There was a footbridge over a small stream and above it, beyond a wasteground where horses grazed, the rows of grey estates of cheap houses caused me to catch my breath. I knew this sight, yet I had been away so long that it was foreign to me, like the walls of an unfamiliar exotic port suddenly rising up out of the sea. A row of shabby shops bordered the wasteground, half of them closed down.

'That was where the new shopping centre was meant to be,' I said. 'It was planned for years.'

'There was a massive re-zoning around eight years ago,' Conor said. 'A Council vote that came out of the blue. Mam is always talking about the fortunes made. Even the banks pulled out of here then.'

We walked down the hill together and crossed the tiny bridge. I felt for the two darts in my pocket and fired them into the water. Horses tethered to long ropes watched us with patient eyes.

'Let's go to Jersey together,' Conor said. 'Before you give yourself up. Get those documents and post them anonymously to the tribunal. I don't want them sitting in my name. I want . . . what's the word . . . ?'

'Closure.'

'Yeah.' Conor nodded. 'And wouldn't Mam just love for people who voted for some of the re-zonings around here to sleep that little bit more uneasily in their beds at night.'

We reached the shabby row of shops, both of us apprehensive now as we stopped outside the rundown Citizens Advice Bureau.

'She'll kill me,' Conor said.

'No. I'll explain.'

'You?' Conor raised his eyes. 'Jesus, she'll really kill you.' He paused. 'You and her, you don't ever think . . . ?'

'What's past is past,' I said. 'Maybe we'll be friends . . . eventually.'

We peered in the window at Miriam working at her desk.

'Do you think you'll go to jail?' Conor asked.

'Probably. Why?'

'It just might be safer than going in here.'

Conor walked forward to knock on the glass. He looked back as the glass door opened. At first Miriam only had eyes for him as she hugged Conor, drawing him to her in relief, unable to decide if she should scold him or cry. It took her a few moments to look up. When she did I could not translate the look that entered her eyes nor really comprehend what I felt myself.

Somehow it didn't matter what she said or did, what the authorities did or what fate awaited me. I had no way of knowing if she would ever forgive me for the grief that I had caused her and for my deception and lies. I just knew there was nowhere else I wished to stand except exposed before her. I held her gaze.

'Hello, Miriam,' I began. 'It's a long story.'

Dermot Bolger

Temptation

'Addictive . . . a will-they-won't-they adultery tale, told fast
and furiously.' *Sunday Express*

'Alison Gill stands on the cusp of middle age, assailed by
doubts about her marriage and insecurities about her changing body. Her expectations of life have dwindled until they
are all contained in the five-day break the family spends each
year at Fitzgerald's Hotel in Wexford. When her husband is
recalled suddenly to Dublin, Alison's longed-for holiday
seems doomed, but the reappearance of old flame Chris
Conway appears to offer possibilities. Whether Alison can or
will offer Conway the succour he needs is revealed in a beautifully understated novel whose portrait of a self-doubting
woman is handled with rare and sensitive perspicacity.'
Daily Mail

'It is rare that a man should be so adept and insightful at
identifying the preoccupations of a mature woman and
mother-of-three, but Bolger does just that in this tender,
thoughtful novel.' *Harpers & Queen*

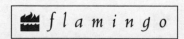

Dermot Bolger

Father's Music

'Lies, manipulation and suspicion are at the heart of *Father's Music* from the very start. In the opening scene of this, Dermot Bolger's sixth novel, Tracey Evans, a promiscuous young Londoner haunted by her Irish roots, makes love in a seedy hotel with Luke Duggan, a member of a notorious Dublin criminal family now leading what is on the surface a respectable business and married life in exile . . . After this dramatic prelude, the novel pulses to the rhythm of a taut romantic thriller. It is the work of a master craftsman, with intricate plotting and the interweaving of characters' lives casting a hypnotic spell.'　JACK HANNA, *Irish Times*

'*Father's Music* is the real McCoy, a gripping adventure story in which the characters' struggles to confront their own demons are every bit as important as the mechanics of the plot. It is a consummate piece of work. The Irish novel is really flying at the moment and, in the galaxy of young talent, Dermot Bolger shines as brightly as anyone.'

DAVID ROBSON, *Sunday Telegraph*

'Everything of the alienated urban underbelly is here, sloshing around in a potent brew . . . Dermot Bolger creates a Dublin, a particular world, like no one else writing can . . . It is the urban landscape of the thriller that Bolger has made exclusively his own.'　ANNE HAVERTY, *Sunday Independent*

'Bolger has written a cracking, compelling and entertaining novel . . . *Father's Music* has a verve that is all but irresistible."

ALLAN MASSIE, *Scotsman*

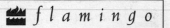 *flamingo*

Maeve Brennan

The Springs of Affection

'Superb. Maeve Brennan could sing with words.'   *Irish Times*

'These are remarkable stories. The nexus of the action is a little suburban terrace in Dublin which becomes, by the end, as familiar and significant as one's own hand: the spare, neat rooms, the three steps down to the kitchen, the doors that seem always to be softly closing against husband and wife. The stories give a striking sense of largeness. Read together, they overlap, illuminate and undercut each other so richly that the effect is as disturbingly profound as if Brennan had written a major novel.'   *TLS*

'Why was this woman not celebrated while living? Her eye for detail, her documentary style, her passion made her far more worthy of attention than she received. So much is laid bare and so much is left unsaid – but all is understood.'

Tatler

'Whatever the impulse that drove Brennan to walk the Sandford Road instead of Broadway, we are the richer for her finely strung sensibility. If you only buy one book this year . . .'

RTE Guide

'Among my favourites of all time . . . pure and strong.'

ALICE MUNRO

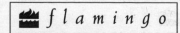

Gretta Mulrooney

Araby

'Tenderly funny and genuinely moving. I loved it.'
FIONA MORROW, *Time Out*

'On hearing of Kitty Keenan's admittance to hospital, her
grown-up son Rory returns to Ireland to comfort his father
and await the diagnosis . . . Rory's narrative, charting the
steady decline of her health, is interspersed with a series of
flashbacks through which Kitty emerges larger than life. For
Rory, these snapshots of the past are part of a process of
unpicking the odd tangle of love and petty grievances that
characterise familial relationships. Mulrooney's ability to
make sense of the contradictions in clear, precise prose is the
most remarkable achievement of the novel. A beautifully
observed study of reconciliation, *Araby* makes astute points
about conflict and shifting values between generations.'
JAMES EVE, *The Times*

'Kitty is a magnificent diva of discontent: contradictory, ludi-
crous, sharp-witted, thick-skinned, the sort of character best
enjoyed from a distance . . . The narrative of her decline and
death is worked with frequent flashbacks to Kitty's heyday,
and her enthusiasm for Catholicism, medicament, hobbies
and quarrelling . . . What is admirable about Mulrooney's
writing is the way she manages to keep the tone buoyant,
while alluding to many heartbreaking strands of family
history. For both Kitty and Rory, this is a story of gallant
survival.'
RUTH PAVEY, *Independent*

Gretta Mulrooney

Marble Heart

Nina is a sophisticated professional, crisp and clever but
stricken by illness; Joan, her care worker, is a simpler soul –
thoughtful, generous, and thrilled that, at last, she is to be
married. Nina has specifically asked for Joan to tend her, but
the latter does not know why. She never suspects that the
little she has had in life Nina is about to destroy . . .

'Mulrooney has taken as her subject not the indigenous
people of Belfast who have grown up with the Troubles,
but outsiders who have gatecrashed it. There is the absurd
spectacle of Nina, a middle-class girl from Maidstone, and the
"comrades" plotting the revolution over wine and French
cheeses in a huge, inherited house. All this is wickedly,
sharply amusing. But when they really join the party with an
act of meaningless terror, Mulrooney shows how contagious
and destructive that situation was. And as Nina slowly takes
the sweet-natured Joan as her final victim, *Marble Heart*
proves itself to be an excellent lesson between cleverness and
wisdom.'   *The Times*

'Mulrooney slows the pace leading to the shock denouement
by deftly layering each chapter with different characters'
voices. She shows herself to be an acute observer of all the
intricacies that comprise female friendship. By making her
readers wait, she not only heightens the gripping tension
of her story but positions us with Joan and Nina, who are
also waiting – Joan patiently [so she] may be married; Nina
fearfully, for her secret crime to be brought into the open.'
                                                   Time Out

🏭 *f l a m i n g o*

Kate O'Riordan

Involved

'O'Riordan's powerful storytelling icily conveys the horrible ordinariness of evil.'   PENNY PERRICK, *The Times*

When Kitty Fitzgerald falls for Danny O'Neill it seems nothing could spoil their perfect relationship. But the carefree Danny Kitty knows in Dublin is not the person she finds when they both travel North to meet his family.

The O'Neills – Ma, the formidable matriarch, her daughter Monica, and the disturbed and menacing eldest son Eamon – are bound by blood and history to a past they can never forget. As time goes on, long-kept secrets rise to the surface, and Kitty finds herself locked into a bitter struggle for the possession of Danny's soul . . .

'Kate O'Riordan is a very skilled writer whose vivid prose has an elegant subtlety. Her narrative rarely slackens. Both Danny and Kitty are impressively rounded characters and their struggle to keep their faltering relationship alive is delineated with a rare, and almost painfully stark, honesty. An acutely interesting writer.'

EAMONN SWEENEY, *Irish Times*

'In the spirit of a thriller, *Involved* gathers quite a pace; though not overly political, it can hardly escape its own bigger ripples. In the vein of Bernard MacLaverty's *Cal*, though with a strong female voice, here are those years of violence de-nationalised, made personal.'   TIM TEEMAN, *Independent on Sunday*

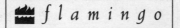 *flamingo*